To D

Thanks for the proof read here's to many more Bell St nights.

North of Los Angeles Late Autumn 1991

Train 21637-91 left the switching yard in a heavy rain. It moved down the spur line at less than 10 miles an hour through a hot, humid morning with the daylight delayed by the rain. The engineer had 27 years experience, the first twenty of which had been on long runs, crossing the continent with freight several thousand times.

The siding ran through a no-man's land of broken limestone chunks and twisted scrub brush. Down to one side was a sluggish river that had been re-channelled to let miners get at the lucrative limestone that had been formed there eons ago. The other side was a line of hastily made berms that were created when the overburden was scraped back to allow quarrying to get underway back in the mid 1800's. The mine's creators were grateful for the cover of scrub poplar, white pine and brambles that Mother Nature had provided to hide the chaos they had brought to the landscape. No one came there.

The train was comprised of two old, but well-serviced locomotives, and 89 empty auto carriers. Not a hard haul for the locos. Between mile six and seven on the siding, the engineer felt a 'softness' as the loco passed over a rail junction. Someone less experienced would probably not have noticed it, but he knew what he had just felt and he called it in.

"Yard, this is 637."

"Yard, go ahead."

"637. There's a partial washout between miles six and seven on the northeast spur line. We're bound out with empties. Nothing loaded should move down there until a crew has had a look."

"Yard. Understood. Crew being dispatched now."

And that's how it began. Or ended.

The rail maintenance crew drove out to the site in their heavy vehicles that were modified to use the rails. They found the washout quickly and dismounted from their trucks to set about fixing it. They had everything they needed with them and the job would have been done in two hours had not one of the men been a birdwatcher. He spotted a ring-necked pheasant and stepped nine or ten paces into the scrub for a better look at it.

The pheasant flew off, leaving the man staring at the body of a nude woman lying serenely on a Hudson Bay Company blanket that had been carefully arranged to provide her with a comfortable resting place among the sumac bushes. A camouflage pattern tarp had been strung from some of the larger sumacs to provide overhead cover. She was slim, and beautiful, and only recently dead. The birdwatcher turned and called out to the rest of his crew. "Don't knock yourselves out boys. This line is gonna be closed for a few days."

Chapter One

Los Angeles 1991. It felt like death by PowerPoint. The consultant had been working on the project for eleven weeks. There was no question about his knowledge of the subject at hand. Robert groaned silently when the consultant brought up his ninth slide. They were still working through the executive summary.

Robert had felt his pager vibrate three times and, as per the rules of meetings in his company, had ignored it. Everyone in the room was startled when an administrative assistant entered and timidly handed Robert a small slip of paper. He looked at the handwritten note, which simply said, "call wife now." Robert arose from his chair and was aware of the envious looks from his colleagues as he exited the boardroom.

He closed the door to his office before dialing Jenna's work number. She picked up on the first ring and said "Aunt Gerta is dead. The police just called me. We need to get home." Robert had had three years to get to know his wife. The only time he had heard her speak so tersely had been when she had called him from a phone booth at a roadside two years before to tell him that a drunk had run a stop light and totalled her car.

"I'll pick you up out front in ten minutes," he said.

The early afternoon rush hour had started so it took him nearly 15 minutes to get to Jenna's building. She was opening the car door before he had come to a full stop and Robert, taking his cue from her, used the driving skills that he prided himself on to get them through the traffic as rapidly as possible. He kept glancing at his watch as Jenna told him what had happened. Jenna realized that he was timing himself to see if could exceed his best time from her office to their home. When there was no one else available, Robert was quite happy to compete with himself.

"The police called me half an hour ago. They said that they received a 911 call about a possible fatality and the responding officers established that the person is most likely Gerta Ten Haan, and that they have called in the homicide branch. The cop on the phone wanted to know if I was Aunt Gerta's closest next of kin and whether I was the owner of our property. When I said yes to both, he basically told me to get my ass home instantly."

Robert was silent for three minutes as he finessed the car through the last of the core traffic and accelerated onto the ramp to the freeway. Once he had merged with the traffic, he glanced at Jenna. "Homicide branch. What the fuck?" was all he said. Robert drove well over the speed limit all of the time they were on the freeway but slowed to the limit as he took the exit ramp into their town. It was several blocks from the noise and congestion of the freeway to the quiet of their neighbourhood. As always, he was struck by the atmosphere of the part of town they were entering.

The streets were lined with mature maple, oak and chestnut trees and were wide enough to allow parking along both sides. The lots accommodating the eighty-year-old houses were very generous according to current-day real estate lingo, and all of the houses were built of locally made red or buff brick.

Just after World War I, a local land owner had decided that returning veterans would be in need of housing since, he thought, young men who had seen Europe wouldn't be keen to return to the family farm. He divided up about 500 acres that he owned. He estimated that his potential buyers would need a house big enough for four or five kids, land enough for a good sized kitchen garden, and he set aside two lots on the corner of every third block to be a parkette. His first priority after laying out the streets and putting in the underground sewer and waterlines was to plant trees. He called his development Forest Estate. Sixty years later the kitchen gardens had been replaced by swimming pools, nobody seemed to have more than two kids, and the locals referred to their neighbourhood as "the Woods". It was some of the most desirable real estate in the greater Metro area.

About a block from their house, Jenna and Robert were both startled by the scene on their usually peaceful street. At least a dozen police vehicles - cruisers, vans, and motorcycles, were parked all askew their lights flashing, fully blocking the street. Yellow tape blocked the road in two places, restricting access to their home and the two houses on either side of it. They parked at the curb and they began to walk to the line of tape that was guarded by a female police officer. "The coroner's truck is still here," said Jenna.

Before she could ask, Robert told the police officer that they were owners of the home where the victim had been found and explained that they had been told by police to attend there as soon as possible. The police woman spoke briefly on her portable radio and then lifted the tape and pointed out a burly man in a badly rumpled black suit who was talking to a group of uniformed officers on their front lawn.

"That's detective Arnon."

They approached the group of people on their lawn and stood by as the man identified as detective Arnon briefed the group of about ten officers on how he wanted the area searched. He told them he wanted "every last cigarette butt and bit of paper picked up and bagged". He ended his briefing with the words "Don't any of you dare screw up my evidence".

He turned to Jenna and Robert. "You two the owners?"

When they nodded he said, "Let's talk inside."

Without waiting for assent, he turned and headed for the front door of the house. Robert walked ahead of him to unlock the door. They entered and Jenna pointed to the living room. The detective took a chair and began by saying, "For now your backyard and the granny flat are off limits. There will be police out there in droves and I will likely post a guard on the scene for the next 24 hours. I have a lot of questions for you folks."

Jenna said, "We have a lot of questions too. Like what the hell has happened? Why are homicide cops here?"

"Where have both of you been today? With timings please."

Robert said, "We work downtown. Left here at 7 this morning. Came straight here as soon as Jenna heard."

"That's about what I figured," said Arnon. "Either of you have any people who don't like you? And I don't mean people who think you're bores, or rude, or a bit pushy. I mean people who would like to see you in pain from a really nasty disease."

Jenna felt a coldness starting in her stomach. Both she and Robert shook their heads.

"Did your Aunt have anyone with a hate on for her?" asked Arnon.

"Not that I am aware of," said Jenna.

"How long has she been living in your granny flat?"

"About three months," said Jenna. "She came here at the end of February."

"Came from where?" asked the detective.

"Holland. But she spent most of her adult life in South Africa."

"Well," said Arnon. "I knew it was going to be an interesting day when I got called to an obvious homicide up here in the Woods. Usually the only calls we get from this area are about noisy dogs and littering."

He stood up and moved toward the door. "I've got about a million things that I need to do with the guys outside. What I want you to do is get some paper and write down everything you know about your Aunt. Do it chronologically, starting as far back as you can and bring it right up to now. Be thorough. I'll be back in a while to see what you've got. And remember, stay out of the back yard."

"Should we be frightened?" asked Jenna. "Was this a home invasion?"

"I don't know what this is yet. You're going help me find out."

Robert and Jenna were left staring at the front door when he left.

After a few moments of silence, Jenna glanced at her watch. "This is insane! Who would kill Aunt Gerta?" She sat silently for a few minutes and then glanced at her watch. She realized her hands were shaking. "It's nearly four. I'm going to have a glass of wine."

"You get us wine, I'll get a pen and paper," he said.

Robert had been doing a lot of business travel lately. Jenna was at the point where she had been wondering if it was all so necessary or if he was escaping from their comfortably regulated life. She was glad he seemed to be supporting her this day. He was sitting in the dining room when she set a glass of wine on the table.

"I counted eight cops in the yard when I was in the kitchen. There are two Coroner people sitting in the shade under the trees. Obviously they haven't finished with Aunt Gerta's body yet. What the hell can be going on?"

"No clue," said Robert. They each sipped some wine then he said, "When was Gerta born?"

He was surprised when Jenna answered without hesitation. "January 1, 1930. There was a joke in the family about her being five hours late. Had she been born five hours sooner she would have been the first baby of the year born in Utrecht and her parents would have gotten all sorts of free stuff."

"So she was born in Utrecht?"

"Yes, my Dad was two years younger than her. Then there were twin girls two years younger than my Dad. Their parents were pretty well off. Opa was a doctor. Oma was a good Calvinist Dutch girl who married a Jew. She converted before they were married."

"In the summer of 1939, I know that Gerta was sent to Johannesburg to visit her mother's sister and her husband. He was a big wheel with Royal Dutch Shell. Gerta was to stay with them until the end of September, see South Africa, improve her English and then return to Holland. As my Dad used to say, Hitler rearranged that schedule."

Jenna took another sip of wine.

"When it was time for Gerta to return to Holland the war was about to start. At first this was viewed as a tragedy by her parents but they decided things were such a mess in Europe that she should stay in South Africa longer. By 1940, when Holland had been overrun by the Nazis, her parents regarded her absence from home as a blessing."

"According to my Dad, Opa had good connections with other doctors all over Europe. He had a pretty good idea of what the Nazis had in mind for any Jews they could get their hands on. He arranged for my Dad to become a protestant Dutch boy living with a family who had lost their biological son to diphtheria. It was much harder to hide two little, identical twin girls. Opa was still trying to get them to safety when the Nazis rounded up most of the Jews in Utrecht."

"It took a lot of doing, but eventually my Dad and Gerta learned that Oma and the twins died in 1943 in Bergen-Belsen. Nobody knows how or when. They just were obliterated like so many other people at that time. Opa died at Bergen-Belsen too, but probably not until near the end of the war."

"Gerta and her Aunt from South Africa were finally able to travel back to Holland in 1947. She was 17 when she learned that her parents and little sisters had been swallowed up by the Holocaust. She was able to find my Dad via one of the agencies that the Dutch government had set up. Gerta stayed in Holland until 1953. She got a Masters of Science from the University of Utrecht in '53 and then went out to South Africa to visit her uncle and Aunt. My Dad had decided to stay with the family that had adopted him during the war, and moved with them to Canada when they immigrated in 1956. He and Gerta kept in touch by letters faithfully for years".

"What did she do in South Africa?"

"Research. Health-care related research. I've no idea what it was about. I know that she lived in Johannesburg for a time, then in the early '60's - I'd have look at my Dad's papers to be sure of the year - she was living in Cape Town because my Dad went to visit her there. You probably know more about her time in Africa than I do. Didn't she talk to you about that when she was helping with the gardening?"

"Not very much. When did she go to Holland?" asked Robert.

"I think I was about 18 when I started getting birthday and Christmas cards with Dutch postmarks. I can find that out from Dad's stuff because he kept all of her letters and she wrote to him a lot."

"Do you still have the cards she sent you?"

Jenna shook her head. "I opened the cards, cashed the cheques that were in them, and tossed them. As you have pointed out many times, the sentimental bone in my body seems to have been surgically removed."

"But I've also said that is one of your endearing traits. No soulful, searching, circular discussions with Jenna. Let's talk facts!"

"Yes. When we first met you made it clear that women should be lustful and sensual and sexual, not sentimental."

"And I was the lucky guy who found such a woman."

Jenna finished her wine and stood up. "I'm going to get the box of Dad's papers. I want to check some dates so that the cop doesn't give me a bad mark on my homework. Do think they are leaving a cop here overnight to protect the crime scene or to protect us?"

Robert shrugged, took his empty wine glass into the kitchen and was watching the activity in his backyard when detective Arnon approached the back door. When he saw Robert he beckoned him to come outside.

"Do you take care of the yard yourself?" asked Arnon.

When Robert nodded the detective seemed pleased. "Good, let's take a walk."

Arnon led Robert over to the wooden gardening shed, the double doors of which were wide open.

"I don't see a padlock on these doors. Are they usually locked?"

"Never," said Robert. "We don't have a lot of trouble with theft in this neighbourhood."

"I want you to take a long hard look in here. Don't go in. Don't touch anything. Is there anything missing? Anything moved? Take your time."

One of the traits that Robert and Jenna shared was a near obsession (their friends were sure that it was a full-blown obsession) with neatness. Robert scanned the contents of the shed. "From what I can see, nothing has been moved."

Arnon led Robert to the back door of the double garage that was attached to the house. He pulled the door and said, "I guess you don't lock this door in this Eden-like community either?"

"No," said Robert as he reached to flip on the garage lights. The detective grabbed his wrist and pulled his hand away from the light switch. "I'll take care of the light," he said. Robert realized that the detective was wearing a latex glove on one hand.

Arnon said, "Same thing here, have a look. Anything out of place?"

The interior of the garage was as neatly organized as the gardening shed. Robert started to methodically scan the place but stopped and quickly walked across the empty car bays to the west wall.

"No touching," said Arnon.

Robert stopped in front of an aluminum stepladder that was hanging on the garage wall. "That's been moved."

Arnon looked at the ladder and realized that it was hanging just slightly off dead true. Give me an OCD homeowner at a murder scene every time, God, he thought to himself. "Anything else?" he asked Robert, who took several minutes more to look at the rest of the garage.

"The ladder is the only thing that is out of place," said Robert.

"Okay, good," said Arnon. "You can go back inside and I'll be in in a while."

When they stepped out of the garage Arnon called to two technicians and told them to carefully process the ladder. Robert was about to step back into the kitchen when Arnon called out to him. "Do you have any rope here?"

Robert thought a moment. "No."

Jenna was seated at the table with piles of file folders spread out in front of her.

"What was that about?" she said without looking up from the paper she was scanning.

"Somebody moved the step ladder. And that Arnon guy wanted to know if I kept any rope around."

She thought about what Robert had just said. "Oh Christ," she muttered. "Aunt Gerta must have been tied up. Why would someone robbing her need to tie her up? Wouldn't taking what they wanted and then murdering her have been enough?"

Robert shrugged his shoulders and remained silent. Jenna took a long sip from her wine glass and forced herself to return to her task.

"Dad went to South Africa to visit Gerta in 1960. It wasn't a successful visit," said Jenna, eyes still on the document she was holding.

"Why wasn't it?" asked Robert.

"Dad didn't like Apartheid. Or to put it in his words from a letter to Aunt Gerta, "Your fucking government is a bunch of racist rednecks one step removed from the Nazis. There are several letters here, going back and forth on the political stuff that was going on in South Africa then. Angry letters. Makes me wonder why those birthday and Christmas cheques kept coming."

"Have you figured out when she went to Holland?"

"Not yet, but if you'd like to pitch in here I think we can get close," Jenna tossed an envelope across the table to Robert. "Dad kept all the stamps from the cards that Gerta sent me. If you sort out the Dutch ones from the South African ones, maybe some of them will have dated postmarks."

***

Detective Arnon was being briefed by the cop who led the outside search group when the lead CSI approached him. "We've finished up in the room where the body was. Coroner's people want to know if they can transport the body now."

Arnon shook his head no, finished his talk with the cop and then walked toward the granny flat. "Give me a few more minutes," he said to the CSI. "And make sure that none of our guys are smoking or talking or laughing too loudly. This neighbourhood files more complaints about cops per capita than anywhere in Metro. Remind them that the people who live here are so anal that when they fart only dogs can hear them."

Arnon had been working homicide for just about 15 years. It had taken him two years to realize that he worked best if he took a quick look at the victim and then got to work on the physical evidence at the scene. He felt that too much time spent around the victim in the early stage of the investigation could cloud his thought processes. Or, as he put it to himself," I don't want to be pissed off when I'm trying to catch a killer." He was especially careful to distance himself from the victim when the death had been a bad one.

Arnon had taken his first look at Gerta Ten Haan's body four hours before. He had then remained outside the granny flat taking care of a hundred details regarding the investigation. He entered the place now and stood about four feet from the body. He looked at her intently, eventually moving around her in a full circle taking in every detail. Finally he called out the head CSI.

"Charlie, tell the coroner guys they can transport now. I want her at the top of the list and if there is a problem with that tell them that she was killed in the Woods and I'll only have to make one call to the Deputy Chief to get top priority for her."

"Once they've got her out of here, get your team back in to work the spot where she was lying. Your guys are still working the bedroom and the bathroom, right?" Charlie nodded.

"Tell 'em to make sure that the curling iron goes to the lab."

Arnon stood looking around the flat. It was essentially one big room with a small but adequate kitchen area of in one corner. It was an A-frame structure with a bedroom and bath housed in a lean-to like addition. The great room that Arnon was standing in was about 35 by 25. It was open to the ceiling with beams running across the structure about ten feet above the floor. Arnon stood looking at the beams for a moment.

"Charlie. Did your guys have a look at the top of the beams?"

"Yep," answered the tech. "Full set of photos each of the beams."

"Good," grunted Arnon. He went outside and had a uniformed cop take him to the neighbour who had called in to police.

The neighbour was probably in his late fifties and Arnon guessed that he was very comfortably retired. He was sitting on his porch and was clearly eager to talk about what had transpired in his neighbour's back yard. Arnon guessed that he had taken a damned long look at the crime scene before dialing 911.

"I'm detective Arnon. I understand that you discovered the body of your neighbour and called 911."

"I called 911, but it was the old man who visits Miss Ten Haan who found her. He saw me in my yard and told me to call 911."

Arnon betrayed nothing but started a slow burn. The cop who had interviewed this witness had jumped to a very bad conclusion.

"And where is this guy now?"

"I have no idea," said the neighbour. "I went into the house to call 911 and when I came back outside he was gone. I called out to him as I walked over to Robert and Jenna's yard but there was no sign of him. Which I did think was strange."

"Okay, you're in your yard and this man from next door tells you to call 911. What exactly did he say?"

"He said, 'You must call the emergency number. Gerta has been hurt.'"

"The emergency number?" asked Arnon.

"Walter's English isn't very good".

"English isn't his first language?"

"Definitely not. His accent was so strong that I had trouble understanding him."

"So, you go in the house and call 911. That takes you a couple of minutes. You come back out and go over to the granny flat, right?"

The neighbour nodded.

"You look in the door of the flat and see the woman lying on the floor. Did you go into the room?"

"No. I took one look and went back to my place and called 911 again. Told them that they were gonna need police here because whatever had happened was not an accident."

"And then what did you do?" asked Arnon.

"Well, I thought I should go back over to the flat, keep an eye on things until someone got here to take control of things."

"Just a couple more questions for now," said Arnon. "This old man you call Walter, I take it that you've seen him at the flat back there a few times?"

"It was a rare weekday that he didn't visit Miss Ten Haan for at least a couple of hours," answered the neighbour.

"Do you know where Walter lives?"

"No. Downtown somewhere, I expect," was the answer.

"What makes you think he lives downtown?" asked Arnon.

"Well, I'm pretty sure that he doesn't live here in the Woods. He was pretty old and didn't walk very fast. And he always got here about noon. The first train from the city gets here at 11:30. I figured he trained it out every day on the first run and then it took him half an hour to walk here from the station."

"Thanks for your time," said Arnon. "I'll likely be back to talk with you again soon. I take it that the officer who talked with you earlier got your contact information?"

The neighbour nodded yes. At least the cop didn't screw that part up thought Arnon as he walked back to the granny flat.

Arnon had seen the ambulance from the Coroner's office leave while he was speaking with the neighbour. The lead CSI was standing at the door of flat. "Find anything?" asked Arnon.

"Damn little," the CSI replied. "Considering all the mayhem that went on in there, we've got practically nothing. The marks that we photographed on the beams are interesting. I can't wait to get them magnified. Other than that we have a very clean scene."

"Professionally clean?" asked Arnon.

"Absolutely," said the CSI.

"Think you'll get anything off the body?"

"Probably not. I had a good look the body. Couldn't see a trace of any hair or fibre."

"Semen?"

"Not obvious. But we have one perfect hand print, full hand and all the fingerprints, which we lifted from the floor right beside the body. Twenty bucks says it's from the neighbour who says he didn't come inside but who did take a good close look."

"I'll take that bet," said Arnon. "I'll see you back at the lab."

Chapter Two

Arnon nodded to the two cops who were securing the scene and walked to the front of the main house and rang the bell. Robert let him in and showed him into the dining room where Jenna was still sorting through papers.

"What can you tell me about your Aunt's boyfriend?" asked Arnon.

"What?" said Jenna.

"Your neighbour tells me that an elderly man named Walter visits your Aunt for hours pretty much every day during the week."

Jenna and Robert were staring at each other blankly.

"I take it that you haven't met this gentleman," said Arnon.

"No, we have not," said Robert.

"That's too bad," said Arnon. "He was the first person on the scene today. I think he would be a useful guy to speak with. Probably be able to provide us with some good insights into your Aunt's life, given that he spent several hours talking with her five days a week. Did your Aunt mention her gentleman caller to either of you?"

"I had no idea that anyone was visiting her. She said she spent most of her time in the library," said Jenna. "She often would just be getting back from there when we got home from work at six."

"What have you got for me?" asked Arnon, gesturing at the papers on the table.

Jenna quickly covered off the family history up to 1953. Robert smiled to himself as she talked. You gotta love that MBA training, he thought to himself.

"So in 1953 she goes back to South Africa. Your Dad goes to Canada. They stayed in touch by writing letters. Did they ever visit?"

"My Dad went to visit her in 1960. She was living in Cape Town and my Dad stayed at her apartment for two weeks. From the letters here that they exchanged after the visit it obviously didn't go well at all."

"What happened?" asked Arnon.

"My Dad was not a fan of the South African government and their apartheid policies. Apparently Aunt Gerta was. There are letters where my father calls the government a bunch of Nazis. Gerta writes back that she is disgusted that my Dad had met with someone named Sailor Malan. The letters are heated."

Arnon leaned forward as Jenna spoke. "Sailor Malan was a mover and shaker in the anti-apartheid movement. A key guy in the Torch Commando and the Springbok Legion. Big opponent of the Afrikaans led government."

"You know your South African history," observed Robert.

"I know Sailor Malan's history," replied Arnon. "So your Dad and Aunt have a falling out in 1960, but continue to write letters. How often?"

"Before Dad's visit to Capetown they wrote at least once a month. After the visit it was three or four times a year."

"Do you know what your Aunt did for a living?"

"Research. Health-related research. In the letters she talks about being at various hospitals and universities. Epidemiology was her special field."

"No husband, no children?"

"No."

"Any other relatives?"

"Just the uncle that died in 1973, my Dad and me. The Nazis were pretty thorough."

"Were you surprised when your long lost Aunt contacted you to come live in your granny flat?"

"I was surprised when she suddenly wrote to me in 1990. I had let her know in '83 that my Dad had died and she sent a note saying that it was sad news and asked me if she could be of any assistance. I had letters from her about twice a year after that. In 1989 she mentioned that she had decided to retire. That was when we were looking to move out here from the city. I told her that we looking at a house with a granny flat and she wrote back quickly saying that she wanted to rent it. There was a check enclosed. I wrote her back and said that she was welcome to the flat but that she certainly didn't have to pay until she moved in. I also pointed out to her that amount she proposed to pay per month was far too generous."

Jenna had arisen and was walking around the room. "She insisted that she pay to hold the flat, so from the time we bought this place in '89 the checks came monthly. In late January she called from Holland to say that she'd be moving into the flat on February 2. And she did."

"Did she spend a lot of time with you two?"

"Not much," said Robert. "She made it clear that she was renting the flat from us and that did not entail us having to share our lives with her. I think what she meant is that she wouldn't be sharing her life with us."

"So did you ever do dinner with her or have conversations?" asked Arnon.

"Oh sure," replied Robert. "About every two weeks she'd join us for a meal. On some weekends when we were all here she'd work with me in the garden. She was a walking encyclopedia when it came to the natural history of South Africa. She obviously spent a lot of time travelling around when she was there."

"Did she talk much about her career?"

Jenna and Robert both thought about that for a moment. Then Jenna said, "I can't recall her ever talking about her work."

"I had a chat with her about epidemiology once," said Robert. "I work in pharmaceuticals and the topic came up one day while she was helping me in the garden. She was very knowledgeable, but after a few minutes she went back to talking about a safari she had been on to look at lions."

"Did she talk about colleagues or friends?"

"Not much," said Jenna. "She had a friend, a woman she had worked with, who lived downtown. She spent several weekends in town with her."

"I'd like her name and address," said Arnon.

"Her name is Anna," said Jenna slowly. "I expect her particulars are in Aunt Gerta's address book."

"What else can you tell me about her day-to-day life?"

Robert spoke up, "She's... she was a bit of a fitness freak. A runner. I tagged along with her once and she set a pace over five kilometres that was impressive. She usually headed out for a run about the time we were getting home from work."

"Aunt Gerta took care of herself. I don't know how you found her today, but she kept her hair and nails done nicely, used a salon around here. She maintained a very healthy diet. Politely declined a steak the first time we barbecued after she got here. Explained to us that she doesn't... didn't eat red meat."

"Anything else spring to mind?" asked Arnon.

He gave them a few seconds and when neither one of them spoke, he arose from his chair.

"What I can tell you, at this point in this investigation, is that more than one person murdered your Aunt this morning. And that is all I can tell you right now. It is unlikely that her murder is a random act. Somebody targeted her. Any further information you can think of will likely be helpful. I need to go see some people now. Do you have a recent photo of your Aunt that I can take with me?"

Jenna picked up a framed picture from a side table nearby and handed it to Arnon. It was of the woman and Robert kneeling in a flower garden with small spades in hand. Arnon was struck by the beauty of Gerta Ten Haan, who he knew was in her sixties. He said he'd let himself out.

Chapter Three

Forest Estates Transit Station

Todd Albright was twenty years old. He considered himself to be a writer and had a two year intermediate English/creative writing diploma from a local community college to prove it. He regarded his job as the caretaker of the transit stop as a way station in what would be a brilliant career as a novelist.

When he emerged from his 1:30 stint of refreshing the women's washroom, he was surprised to see the old foreign guy approaching the platform. Todd had never seen him arrive to catch a downtown train earlier than the five o'clock. He knew there would be no train for the old man to ride for over an hour and he made a mental note to speed up his job of replenishing the vending machines in the station. His writing prof had told him to be curious and he wanted to talk with the old man who seemed so out of place in the Woods.

The old guy was nowhere to be seen when Todd was clear of his routine tasks for a moment. He was startled, an hour and ten minutes later, to see the old man emerge from the men's rest room just as the 2:15 train was pulling into the station. He was close enough to the old fellow to see that he was pale and his breathing seemed ragged. He must be ill, thought Todd, as the train pulled out for the run downtown.

***

Jenna and Robert were silent after Arnon's departure. Robert idly shuffled around the stamps that he had been sorting and Jenna gazed out of the window toward the granny flat. Finally she commented that dinner didn't seem very appealing. Robert made a noise that she took as agreement.

She went into the kitchen and returned a few minutes later with some cheese and crackers and an open bottle of wine. She set the food down, filled her wine glass and pushed the bottle across the table to Robert. Jenna sipped her wine and ignored the food. After some time she said, "Why the fuck would somebody murder Aunt Gerta? The cop said she was targeted for Christ's sake," Robert rose to come around to her side of the table, then sat back down in his chair and reached across to pat her hand.

Then he said he was going to lock the garage. When he returned to the dining room Jenna could see that he was nervous. She would have liked to have talked about how shit scared she was, but she and Robert didn't do conversations about feelings very well.

***

Charlie Larkin was the lead CSI on what he thought of as the 'Woods case'. He got back to his lab about seven p.m., happy to be out of the field and in his familiar environment surrounded by evidence bags collected at the scene. For a few minutes he contentedly survived the array of tidily bagged items that nearly covered one of his large lab tables.

Larkin walked around the table, reading his list. From time to time he picked up a bag, testing its weight, but he didn't open any. Finally he went back to his desk where photocopied notes of the interview that the junior detective had conducted with the neighbour at the outset of the investigation were neatly clipped together.

He noted the full name of the neighbour and went to a microfiche machine in the corner of the room. He found the slide that listed all the fingerprints that were held for people whose surname began with the letter "J". And a smile lit up his face. He quickly went to another drawer, located a new slide and dropped it into the microfiche reader. He stared intently at the full set of fingerprints on file from the neighbour. Then he fetched the transparent slide of the handprint lifted at the scene. Larkin's contented feeling disappeared like vapour and he realized that he owed Arnon twenty bucks.

***

The old man that Jenna and Robert's neighbour had identified as Walter was close to the end of his strength. He sat motionless in the train trying to gain control of his breathing. Fortunately, he had the car to himself so there was no one to witness his distress.

The old man was experiencing a rush of emotions. There was the horror of what he had discovered when he pushed open the unlatched door of Gerta's flat that morning. There was the fear of what Gerta's death meant to his personal safety. And underlying the other emotions was the gut-wrenching feeling of being hunted. It had been many years since he'd last had that feeling. But it was back, and the old man struggled to not let his mind be filled with memories of those horrible years in the 1940's.

***

After sitting silently for some time, Robert drank off the last of his wine and arose from his chair. "I'm going for a run," he said. "Want to come with me?" Jenna didn't have to think about the offer. She shook her head and reached for the wine bottle to refill her glass. She was gazing at the granny flat, or maybe at the cop standing outside it, when Robert cut through the dining room in his running gear to leave through the front door. A pull-down staircase set in the ceiling of the upstairs hallway led to the attic, a room seldom visited. Jenna got the staircase open and unfolded with a bit of difficulty. She immediately went to a stack of two suitcases just a few feet from the staircase. The bags were her Aunt's and Jenna had remembered the conversation that she had with Gerta the day they had placed them there.

Aunt Gerta had arrived on a Friday. She arrived in an airport limo, and had only three bags with her. When Jenna asked if there were more bags to come, Gerta had made some comment on being experienced at travelling light. She had declined Jenna's offer to help her unpack and get settled.

The next day, Robert had gone off to a company trade show. Not long after he left, Gerta tapped on the backdoor. She had her suitcases with her and asked if there was somewhere that she could store them in the house. Jenna indicated that the attic was virtually unused and suggested they put them there.

Jenna had pulled down the staircase and was about to take the bags to the attic. Gerta however, stopped her and opened one of the cases and took out a smaller, very sturdy aluminum case. It was the type of case that a serious photographer would use for cameras and lenses.

"I want to tell you about this case, Jenna," Gerta had said, "and I will be very grateful if you keep this conversation between us."

Gerta then gave her two keys. She explained that one key would open the aluminum case, which she put back inside one of the larger suitcase. The other key would open that larger case. "I've put a note in this bag," said Gerta, indicated the aluminum case. "Please promise me that should I be hit with a train or drop dead of a heart attack, you will open up this case and do as the note tells you." Gerta spoke very matter-of-factly, clearly conveying that she felt there was nothing unusual about her request.

The keys opened the bags easily. A quick glance inside the aluminum case showed that it was packed solid with notebooks, some small boxes and envelopes. Jenna quickly relocked that case and set it near the staircase. She gave the bigger suitcase a quick but thorough search and assured herself that it was empty. The other big case, which wasn't locked, proved to be empty as well. She set the two big cases back the way she had found them and descended the stairs with the aluminum case in hand.

She took the case downstairs with her and went into the kitchen to look at the calendar. Robert was to be out of town on business for most of the week. Without hesitation, Jenna put the case with two others that looked exactly like it in her photo darkroom and returned the keys to their spot in her medicine chest. Then she stripped off her work clothes, put on a baggy tee shirt and shorts, and spent the next forty-five minutes on her treadmill.

Jenna found herself sobbing as she set a fast pace on the treadmill. She scolded herself, telling herself that she was crying over a woman that she hardly knew. She was getting control of herself when the truth struck her and she realized what going through the old letters had opened up. She was crying for her father.

She had stripped and was adjusting the water temperature of her shower when Robert stepped into the bathroom. His shirt was soaked with perspiration from his run and as he peeled it off he asked if she needed someone to wash her back.

"That would be great, Robert. Having my Aunt murdered in my backyard really gets me horny."

"Sorry. Just thought you could use a distraction."

***

Robert shook her awake at 3 a.m. "You're dreaming, Jenna," he said and then rolled over to lay facing away from her.

Jenna lay in the darkness, trying to erase the terror that she had been feeling just before Robert awakened her. She realized with disgust that the T-shirt she had worn to bed was soaked in sweat. She carefully slid out of bed, peeled off the shirt, grabbed a robe, and went downstairs.

She poured herself a glass of juice and wandered around the darkened living room for several minutes. Usually it gave her pleasure to walk around the room looking at the antiques that she and Robert had collected to furnish it. Tonight the dimly lit shapes seemed sinister. She was having trouble shaking off the nightmare. Throughout her life, Jenna had taken refuge in poetry. She could recite hundreds of lines from memory. On this night Emily Dickenson, Robert Frost and Longfellow had deserted her. "Stopping by woods on a snowy evening" was not going to be a comfort.

The box of her father's letters was still on the dining room table. She turned on the main light and sorted through them. She picked out a few that were written before her father had visited her Aunt in 1960 and spent the next three hours reading. By the time Robert had shaved and showered and come downstairs she felt that she knew her Aunt a bit better.

***

Arnon was telling himself that neither the CSI department nor the coroner would have anything for him until the next day and that he should go home when his phone rang. He picked it up and said, "Arnon".

"It's Detective Crane," said the voice on the telephone, "I wanted to let you know that we've received a report of a burned-out Cadillac DeVille in a field about six miles from the airport."

"And I would want to know that why?" said Arnon.

"The neighbour across the street from the victim's place in the Woods said that there was a brand new DeVille parked in the laneway of the scene for several hours this morning. Black, heavily tinted windows. He said that he would have gone over to have a closer look except that it was raining so hard."

"Why did he want a closer look?"

"He said that the homeowner of the crime scene had been making noises about buying one. He thought that maybe he had."

"Are you the one who interviewed the guy named Jenkins who called 911?" asked Arnon.

"Yes, sir".

"Okay. Three things," said Arnon. "First, I have a photo of the victim that I want you to come and get. Have a load of copies made and keep the best one for yourself. I need you to canvass the area, show the photo, and find out where the victim went during the day. Start at the library and visit all the beauty parlours in the area. Got that?"

"Yes sir"

"Second. Follow up on this car. You've done a good piece of police work there, detective."

"Thank you, sir," was the reply.

"And finally detective, learn not to make assumptions."

"I beg your pardon sir?"

"The neighbour, Jenkins, who called 911. When you interviewed him did you ask him why he was snooping around the Granny flat in his neighbour's backyard?"

There was a long pause and then detective Crane said "No sir, I did not."

"Some old fart who visited the victim every day rattled Jenkins' chain to call 911. And when Jenkins came outside after making the call, the old guy was gone. That's pretty important, detective. Could be fucking vital. Assume nothing at a crime scene."

"I'm sorry, sir," said Crane,."I was a bit rattled after I saw what they'd done to that lady."

"Here's a bit of unsolicited advice, Crane. When you get to a crime scene, establish that there is a body and that the person who caused the body to be dead is not lurking around to put you in the same state. Then get to work gathering witness and collateral evidence. Let the CSIs and the Coroner do their jobs with the victim. You don't gain anything by communing with the dead when you are first on the scene."

"That's good advice, sir."

"Okay, Crane. I'll leave the picture on my desk. Tell lab to crop out the guy and just make copies of the woman."

"Yes sir."

Los Angeles Airport

It only took a session like the one he and his two henchmen had had with Gerta Ten Haan to remind Nils Witt how much he enjoyed sexual sadism. However, the wanton brutality of the two men who had been with him in Ten Hann's little garden house had blunted his pleasure. He was glad to put the two men on a plane to Europe

Nils knew that the time difference to Germany put the time there in the wee hours of the morning. But despite having had no sleep for thirty hours, he was wide awake. He felt that his boss should be as well. He found a phone booth outside of the terminal, put a large pile of coins on the ledge, and dialled the number from memory.

It took time and a whole pile of quarters but eventually he established a very scratchy connection to Germany. The man on the other end of the phone sounded quite alert for someone who had just been dragged from REM sleep. "Johann, how nice to hear from you," he said in German.

"It's good to speak with you as well," said Nils. "I wanted to let you know that the vacation is going well."

"Have you been getting lots of sun?" asked the German speaker on the line.

"Actually," said Nils, "it's very cloudy. Hardly a hint of sun."

"That's disappointing, I hope your friends aren't upset by the weather."

"Quite the contrary," said Nils. "They had a most enjoyable day today. Despite the weather, they got to do all the indoor things they like to do. Made a real party of it, I must say."

The man in Germany involuntarily smiled, thinking of Nils watching his two colleagues at work.

"Enthusiasm is infectious, I hear," he said. "I hope you were able to share some of their enjoyment."

Prick, thought Nils. "Well the aesthetics of the day were surprisingly pleasant at first. At any rate, the cold front that concerned us today is gone. Hopefully tomorrow will be clearer."

"Weather can be very capricious," said the man in Germany. "Will you cut short your vacation?"

"No, no," said Nils. "As you know, I like to follow the sun and there is supposed to be some very hot weather in this area in the next few days. I'll stay on and try to find the perfect summer's day."

"Best of luck with that," said the man on the phone.

***

Walter had, after a lot of deliberation, made a quick visit to his second apartment, showered and changed into an expensive suit. He had shaved carefully, had taken some of the pain killer/muscle relaxants that had been given him, and he was moving much better. He called a number and spoke hurriedly for some time. The man he spoke with gave him some instructions and urged him to get to the airport as quickly as possible.

When the clerk at the airline desk expressed surprise that he was flying halfway around the world with only a small carry-on, he explained that he was going to see a dying relative. The airline, strapped for passengers, asked if he'd give them a written testimonial, which he agreed to do. He flew alone in first class to his destination. He slept a lot during the flight, and when he was awake he reflected that it was a far cry from the cattle cars he'd been subjected to when he was younger.

***

Detective Rob Crane, recently promoted from uniform, made a name for himself the night of the Woods murder. The DeVille that had been burned out was stolen. A car dealer had been reported missing. His dealership reported that he had set up to meet with a prospective buyer of the high-end vehicle early in the morning. Late in the day neither had come back. Crane identified the car and the police quickly found the body of the salesman. He had been shot once, at extremely close range, in the head. And then had been tossed into a dumpster near the place where the meeting with the prospective buyer had been arranged.

Detective Crane was on the job early the day after the murder. He had persuaded the lab to put a rush on copying the photo of Gerta Ten Haan and had left a stack of the prints on Arnon's desk. He had kept two for himself and by 8 a.m. was walking the streets of the small commercial area of the Woods. He learned that beauty salons and libraries aren't open at eight in the morning so he bought a coffee and sat sipping it in a parkette far enough away from the coffee shop that he could barely hear "Shiny Happy People" emitting from its outdoor speakers. Crane hated that song.

His pager went off. The only phone booth he could see was next to the coffee shop, so he reluctantly went back in range of the despised song.

Arnon picked up on the second ring and when Crane identified himself, Arnon said "So we've got a double murder now."

"Yeah. Somebody wanted that car pretty bad."

"Do your canvass of the business section and the library and then call me at noon. Since you're already out there, I'll want you to visit the homeowners. I'll have a list of questions for them when you call in. That clear?"

"Got it," said Crane.

With time to kill, Crane walked across the street to where an elderly man was seated on a bench. Crane gave him his best respectful smile and asked him if he was a regular visitor to the area. The old fellow assured him that he was "on guard here on the bench every day that it didn't rain".

The young cop held out the photo of Gerta Ten Haan for the man to look at. "Ever see this lady walk by?" he asked.

"She comes by every Monday and Thursday morning sharp at ten. Goes into the library for an hour or so. Every third Thursday she comes out of the library and goes to that hair dressing parlour right there."

he said, pointing at salon directly across the street. "And then on the Thursdays after she has her hair done she has lunch at that restaurant." The restaurant was two doors down from the salon.

"You say you only see her on Mondays and Thursdays," asked Crane.

"Yep. And I'd notice her because what your picture there doesn't show is that she is a real looker. I might be old, young man, but I can still look. The lady is very fit. She wears a skirt and has fine legs." Crane smiled at the old man's comment and thanked him for the information.

"Aren't you a bit young for her?" the old man asked.

"I'm a cop," said Crane.

The old man sat up a little straighter.

"The woman that was murdered yesterday. Over there on Canterbury Street. Was that this woman?"

"I'm afraid so," said Crane.

The old fellow seemed to crumple up on the bench. He sat shaking his head and had nothing more to say.

Crane visited the beauty salon first. All of the staff knew the woman when he showed them the picture. They confirmed that she was a regular customer. Always had the same style. Always got the same colouring. Was pleasant. Didn't talk much. Left a fifteen percent tip.

Crane got the same sort of information from the restaurant staff. Pleasant. Always had lunch alone. Usually had the soup of the day. Always left a fifteen percent tip.

The library would be opening in ten minutes, so Crane slipped a few feet down an alley and had his first cigarette of the day. He stood watching the action in the commercial area, or rather lack thereof. 'The Woods' was a very quiet suburb.

He was the first person to enter the library. A woman was at the information desk studied the photo of Ten Haan carefully when Crane showed it to her. After a good long look she shook her head and said that she had never seen the woman around the library. Crane was taken aback.

He retraced his steps to the front doors of the building and then walked slowly back toward the information desk. There were two doors along the route. One was marked storage, the other bore a sign that said private. He went back to the woman behind the desk and asked her what was behind the door marked private. She indicated that it was the library's information technology department.

Crane knocked on the door, which was opened by young woman. "How can I help you?" she asked. Crane handed her the picture of Ten Haan and the young woman immediately said, "Oh, that's Gerta!"

"You know her, then," said Crane.

"Of course. She's amazing! Comes in every Monday and Thursday and tutors our advanced programming class. The students love her. She has such a deep knowledge of most of the key languages in use. Really amazing that someone of that generation is so tech savvy."

"Does she get paid to do this?" asked Crane.

"No. She volunteers. The only thing that she asks for is time to use the ARPNET for a few minutes each day that she's here."

"And what would the ARPNET be?"

"It's a way of sending electronic mail, messages, through the computer. You can send a message to anywhere in the world, assuming the person you want to reach is on-line."

"And who was she writing to on this ARPNET thing?" asked Crane.

"A friend of hers in Europe. I really don't know all that much about it. I'm into the programming area. Our director can give you way better information than me."

"Where would I find him?"

"Somewhere near the top of Mount McKinley, I expect. He'll be back from vacation a week from Monday."

Crane took down the name of the director, thanked the girl and went back to his parkette to wait until it was time to call Arnon. He was relieved that she had not asked him why he was asking questions about Gerta.

Robert didn't comment when he saw Jenna sitting at the dining room table. He busied himself with the coffee press, taking longer than usual to press a cup of his favourite Columbian dark blend. He's trying to think of something to say, thought Jenna. He was saved by the ringing of the telephone.

It was Jenna's boss calling to say that she had gotten Jenna's voice note telling her that she was leaving work due to a family issue. She'd heard that a woman had been murdered on Jenna's street. She'd seen news coverage with video of Jenna's house. The papers were full of the story although they didn't provide much information. Finally she said, "How are you?"

Jenna assured her that she was okay, told her that the papers knew as much about what was going on as she did. Robert, who was dressed for work, caught her attention, pointed at his watch and then made an "I'll call you" hand gesture and went into the garage. Her boss kept nattering on the phone. When she could finally break into the flow of verbage, Jenna thanked her boss for her call and said that she had to go to meet with police. Her boss ended the call reluctantly. I have three days of compassionate leave available to me, Jenna thought.

She went to the kitchen to make coffee. There were two uniformed cops in her backyard, drinking coffee from paper cups. A thought struck her and she opened the back door and called out, "Would either of you like access to a washroom?" Both cops called back that they didn't. Robert is going to be pissed off about dead spots in the grass, she said to herself with a slight smile. Jenna was sipping at her second cup of coffee, thinking about her father, when the phone rang. It was detective Arnon.

"Mrs. Grieve, this is detective Arnon. I have one of my officers coming over to see you at about one o'clock. He will have a few more questions for you. Can you be available?"

Jenna was annoyed at the interruption in her thoughts. And, she thought, given that she seemed to know nothing about her Aunt she couldn't imagine what she would have to contribute to the investigation.

"My name is Jenna Van Velt, detective. I didn't take my husband's surname."

Arnon silently cursed. He hated errors about names.

"I'm sorry for the mistake. Can you be available this afternoon?"

"I'll be here, detective. How much longer will I have a police presence in my backyard?" Arnon hadn't wanted that question. He knew he was dealing with killers who had thought nothing of blowing away a guy just to get a car. There was something to this murder.

"Too soon to say. We'll stop inconveniencing you as soon as possible."

Jenna hung up the phone and finished her coffee. "Stop inconveniencing me?" Life had been somewhat inconveniencing for some time. She went upstairs to shower.

It was a morning of working the phones for Arnon. He called an old buddy who had gone to work for Immigration and asked him to check out records of the arrival of a Gerta Ten Haan in February. Then he spoke with the team that had retrieved the burned-out Caddy. They assured him that it would produce nothing of use. He called the Van Velt woman. And then he called an old Army buddy.

The chief CSI came into his office and laid a twenty dollar bill on his desk.

"Keep your money," said Arnon. "One of my guys fucked up and missed a witness. I knew about it when you offered the bet."

"Prick," said Charlie.

Arnon leaned back in his chair, which the CSI took as a signal to proceed.

"What we have here is a paperless crime scene. There was no mail in that place. No shopping lists. No sticky note phone numbers. We did not find a bill or a business card or a flyer. We have her purse. Nothing of note: a small bottle of regular strength Advil, a small pack of regular strength Robaxacet, no banking documents at all, a hundred and twelve dollars in cash. She liked Estee Lauder products."

"It would mean a lot to me," said Arnon, "if you told me that you have an address book and her passport."

"Me too," said the CSI. "Not a damn thing of that nature in the flat. We have to assume that the bad guys took them. She only entered the country recently, so she must have had a passport."

"What other good news do you have for me?" said Arnon.

"We had Jenkins' fingerprints on file because he worked in the defence industry. No match to the print we took off the floor by the body."

"How long does it take to get INTERPOL to run prints?"

The CSI scowled. "Often it takes months. Do you know anybody who has any sway with them?"

"Maybe," said Arnon, "Get me a copy of the print."

"Why INTERPOL?"

"Jenkins, the neighbour, said that an old guy with a heavy accent visited the Ten Haan woman practically every day. If he's European maybe he's in a file over there. He found his female buddy naked and bloody and dead on the floor, and skedaddled as soon as he told the neighbour to call 911. So it's likely that he has had some life experience that makes him want to avoid conversations with police."

"I hear ya," said Charlie. "We did the preliminary work on the curling iron first thing this morning. Just the usual residue you'd find on the thing. No sign that it had been cleaned recently." He leaned over to Arnon's desk and tossed a small stack of photos on it. "Those are shots, from every angle, of the beams. Four attachment points. There's a diagram of the beams and where the attachment points were. Two on each beam. Each precisely four feet apart."

"The bad guys had thought things through, hadn't they?"

"Man, I really don't like to think about what went on in that place yesterday morning."

"So I guess you don't want to join me for my chat with the coroner," said Arnon.

"I'll pass. Got to get back to work."

Arnon picked up his phone and, consulting a notebook that he had taken out of his desk, dialed a local number. A recording informed him that he had reached Tibbet's Memorial Field and started rhyming off a list of extensions. He hit six and after several rings someone picked up and said, "Restoration".

"It's Nick Arnon. Is Randy there?"

"Hey Nick, this is Tom Kay. It's been awhile. We gonna see you out here anytime soon?"

"If people would stop getting themselves murdered I'd be out there tonight. How's work going on the birds?"

"The Mustang is back from the paint shop and she looks beautiful. The canopy goes back on tomorrow and we'll soon see her in the air. The Fortress has a long way to go. Oh, and here's Randy walking by, pretending he's working. Hope to see you soon, Nick."

"This is Randy. What the hell do you want?" said a new voice.

"Hi, Randy, willing to do a hardworking cop a favour?"

"Sure, tell him to come on over. Friend of yours, is he?"

"You told me once that one of the guys you source parts from for the German planes had something to do with INTERPOL in Belgium, right?"

"Yeah, hell of a nice guy. He and his old man had the presence of mind to drag every wreck and derelict that they could into their barns when the war ended. Guy has a treasure trove of Messer Schmidt and Focke Wulf parts."

"I need a fingerprint run through their system. If I do it through channels, it could take months. Can you give me an introduction to this guy?"

"Don't see why not," said Randy. "I'll take a break and try him now. Must be about six o'clock over there. Can I tell him you're a homicide cop?"

"Yeah. Does this guy speak English?"

"Better than you and me. I'll try to persuade him to take a call from you and you crime fighters can sort out what you need to do."

"Many thanks, Randy."

"Don't thank me. Get your ass out here and help us with the wings of the Fort."

Chapter Four

It was eight in the evening when Walter knocked on the door of the building at the address he'd been given a few hours ago during the phone call he had made. He was greeted by a tall silver-haired man and a younger woman. The man extended his hand, pulling Walter inside. "Erich! It has been a long, long, time. Welcome home from all of us."

"Thank you," said Erich, relieved to be rid of his pseudonym. "I am very tired. Is there somewhere we can sit?"

They led him into a beautiful room. It was exactly the sort of room that he had played and grown up in before the war. A fire was burning on the grate, a coal fire, not the wood conflagrations that he'd grown used to in South Africa and North America. There were tapestries and carvings and the furniture was old and dark. He sank into a chair that he was sure was stuffed with horsehair. He was overwhelmed with the aroma of a pre-war German home.

"I hope your trip was not too difficult," said Franz.

"It was hard. Most of the last years have been hard. I saw Cologne Cathedral from the train. It is magnificent and it still stands. The last time I saw it was 1944. It still stands."

"It does indeed," said his host.

"My cousin," said Erich, "only 16, was an aircraft spotter. He helped the Flak knock down the Terror flyers. He was in the tower of the Cathedral when a bomb destroyed the staircase 200 feet from the ground. He was trapped up there with two others for three days until they could shore up the tower and rig ladders to bring them down."

"That must have been terrible for him." said the tall man.

"It was hard," said the old man.

And Walter/Erich, at age eighty-nine, sank back into the comfortable old chair in the comfortable German apartment, and died. At first, the man who had greeted him as Erich thought he had gone to sleep. After a time he arose, crossed over to the old man and rested his fingers lightly on the side of his neck. There was no pulse.

"Awkward," was all he said.

The man picked up the telephone and quickly dialed a number in the United States.

"Sam Allen."

"It's Franz. We have a problem with our guest."

"Has he been delayed?"

"No, he's here."

"What state is the old fellow in?"

"As of just a minute or so ago, a state of decay."

There was a long silence on the other end of the phone. Finally the man on the phone spoke. "Remove anything that would make it easy to identify him. Have your people put him in a park somewhere where he's sure to be found. Perhaps, given his age, the police will think he's a homeless person and will expedite a pauper's burial."

"Not likely," said the tall, dignified man, "when they see the tattoo on his right arm."

"Right. Well then, if they identify him, perhaps they'll think the Jews got him."

"We'll leave him on a bench of the grounds of the Cathedral."

"Why there?"

"I think the old fellow would like that."

"When you spoke with him earlier, you're certain he said they had left the disks with Gerta's neice?"

"I'm certain. And fucking appalled that they would do such a thing."

"The Legacy Organization will meet at my place in Canada in two days. I've got my folks working on the arrangements for all of us now. Someone will be in touch with you."

"Muskoka is beautiful in the spring, Sam."

"Chuck Holt is out in the desert somewhere jacking around with some of his security people. His team has sent a chopper out to pick him up. I expect to hear from him soon."

"Good. He has a lot of work to do. Talk soon, Sam."

He hung up the phone and frisked the old man. He removed his wallet, watch and a ring. His passport and airline tickets and boarding pass were in his overcoat pocket. He had nothing else on his person. Then the tall man had a thought and he felt carefully along the lower seam of the old man's suit jacket. His fingers found a number of hard items, so he fetched a pair of scissors and snipped the seam at several places. He removed six coins from the old man's jacket.

The young woman had remained seated on a settee as the tall man had made his phone call and then searched Walter. He turned to her as he examined the coins.

"I'm sorry that we didn't have a chance to introduce you to your great uncle. These coins are one ounce Krugerrands. They are .9999 pure gold. At today's price, they are worth about $600 each. I guess they are your uncle's legacy to you."

***

Arnon went to a vending machine down the hall and bought a couple of granola bars and a bottle of juice. The juice bottle got caught in chute of the machine. Arnon was pounding the side of the machine with the heel of his hand when one of the younger detectives walked by. He snatched his handcuffs out of their case and went into a crouch. "Once you've subdued it, boss, I'll cuff it." The message light on his phone was flashing when he re-entered his office.

The message was from Randy. He left a number and told Arnon to call the man at one today, our time. He said that his name was Jules Forget.

Arnon listened to the message a second time, carefully writing down the number Randy had left. He glanced at his watch and realized that he had ten minutes before he made the call. The coroner will have to wait a bit longer, thought Arnon. The plastic juice bottle was cracked and leaking apple juice all over his desk. Arnon tossed it into the garbage, sopped up the juice with some tissues, then dialed the overseas number. There was a lot of buzzing and clicking and then a voice said "Allo."

"This is Detective Arnon calling from the states. Is this Mr. Forget?"

"Call me Jules."

"Great. It's Nick here on this end. Randy says great things about you, Jules. I understand that you have a treasure trove of parts for FW-190s and ME-109s."

They talked vintage aircraft for a time, bonding, and then Arnon shifted the conversation. He told Jules a bit about the murder, and the very little bit he knew about Walter. The Belgian listened intently, asked a couple of questions, and explained that his organization were always happy to add another set of fingerprints to their collection even if they didn't know who the person who owned the prints was. He told Arnon to courier the prints to him and he'd have a comparison done in under a week.

***

Jenna answered the door and showed Crane to a seat in the living room. Crane was focused on the interview he was about to conduct, but that did not prevent him from noticing how attractive Jenna Van Velt was. He reminded himself to keep his eyes directed at her shoulders and above.

"Thanks for making some time to talk with me, Ms. Van Velt. You'll probably be happy to know that before I leave, I'll be sending away the cops out back. You will have your yard back. Would you please lock the granny flat and not go in there?"

"Gladly."

"We have not been able to find any sign of forced entry to the flat. Do you think your Aunt usually kept the door locked?"

"Always. She had seen some American movies and believed that all of the L.A. area was full of gangs and criminals."

"Did anyone other than you and she have keys?"

"No."

"Did you keep a spare key outside somewhere? Hidden. In case she locked herself out."

"No."

"Has anyone been in the flat in the last, say, six months other than you, your husband and your Aunt?"

Jenna sat up a bit straighter. "We had the flat painted once we knew when Aunt Gerta was going to arrive."

"Who did the painting?" asked Crane, making a note on the pad he held.

"Two guys that Robert found. They had stuck a notice up in the local bakery. Just a simple sheet with a lot of phone number tabs to tear off. We wanted a quick job done to freshen the place up for Gerta. When we called them, they were available the next day so it worked out great. They had the job done in three days."

"Were you or your husband around when they did the painting?"

"No."

"Did you give them a key to get into the flat?"

"Oh, shit," said Jenna.

"I'm going to need to know everything you know about those painters."

"I'll need to speak with Robert about this," said Jenna.

"Great," said Crane. "One of the strange things about the crime scene is that there was no paper in the flat. No ID. No passport. No address book. There was over a hundred dollars in your Aunt's purse but that and some skin care products and cosmetics were all. Did your Aunt store anything here in your house?"

Jenna was ready for that question. She told him about the suitcases in the attic. He asked to see them. She showed him the pull-down stairs. He was clearly disappointed when he climbed back down.

Next, he gave her what he had gotten by way of information that morning. The woman was stunned to learn that her Aunt only went to the library two days a week and the reason for the visits was to teach a class about computers. She remarked that all the correspondence that she or her father had received from her Aunt had been hand written and expressed surprise that the dead woman had known how to type.

"Ms. Van Velt, it's amazing what relatives can get up to. I had an uncle who we saw twice a year. At Christmas and Easter. He was a traveller for some company that sold construction machinery. No one had the remotest idea that he was married to my Aunt in Georgia and another woman in Texas for upwards of twenty years. Until a credit card statement fell out of his briefcase and my Aunt did some checking."

"How did that work out for him, detective?"

"The divorce was underway when he was found dead outside of a bar. Turns out he had a bit of a gambling problem as well. At least my Aunt got his pension benefits because they were still married."

"I love stories with happy endings."

"I guess my point was that we might not know much about our relatives. You had not met your Aunt until she moved into your backyard. Do you have any idea why she decided to move here?"

Jenna was quick to answer. "Aunt Gerta wrote me about two years ago. She talked a lot about places. For her, South Africa was home. But she didn't like the changes taking place. That had prompted her move back to Holland. But she found Holland oppressive because it was haunted with reminders of what happened to her family during the war. She said she might have to try the New World. There was a silence while Crane scribbled on his note pad, then Jenna said "That didn't work out for her so well, did it." Crane looked up to find Jenna teary eyed.

"I'm sorry for your loss, Ma'am."

"I haven't lost anything," said Jenna. "A woman who I knew not at all provided us with a lot of money over a couple of years to move into our little cottage out back. And then someone made her dead. I don't know her. I don't know her life. I don't know what she did with her life. And thanks to you closed-mouth bastards, I don't even know what was done to her in my fucking backyard. I don't have a sense of loss. I have a sense of confusion. And if you're done with your questions, please collect your guard dog out back, and be on your way."

Crane placed his business card on the coffee table and moved toward the door.

"Are we in danger here? Is whoever who did this likely to come back?"

Crane was not in a position to answer that question so he gave her the parting line. And he left feeling like he had betrayed her.

Arnon had joked with his friends that the only place he disliked more than than the coroner's lab was his ex-in-laws' house. At two p.m. he went to his second least favourite place. He was relieved to find that it didn't smell horribly, the way it did when they were working on a fire victim. When he went into the main examination room there were only two other draped bodies on tables. Neither were children. Arnon couldn't stand to see kids' bodies in that room.

The coroner was Stainer, who he had requested. He was all business. "What do you want first?" he asked.

"Cause of death," said Arnon.

The coroner gestured toward something resting on a plastic sheet on a stainless steel table.

"Looks like a pair of panties," said Arnon.

"Bingo," said the coroner. "Cause of death was suffocation with her wind pipe blocked with her own underwear. And we have confirmed it was her underwear. Willing to let me play the game a bit, Nick?"

Arnon nodded.

"Nobody's told me how old she is so I've had a look at her teeth. She's got the body of a forty-something but she has the teeth of a sixty-something. And the dental work is Europe and somewhere else other than here."

Arnon nodded again.

Stainer stepped to the table where the body rested and pulled back the sheet covering it. Arnon had of course seen the body in the apartment. It had been washed and now lay in a more dignified position. The coroner was right. The woman looked to be closer to 40 than 60 years of age.

"There are thirty deep local burns. The first two, judging by the crusting of the wounds, were on the palms of her hands. The rest are where there are the most nerve endings. Very personal areas. Burns were likely administered by any garden-variety soldering iron. There are also twenty intense compression points. K-mart pliers. Very inexpensive tools. But a lot of pain for the buck."

"Do you have a timeline on this?" asked Stainer.

"Best guess is from 7:30 a.m. to maybe 11 a.m."

"Three and a half hours. I had figured that the burns were administered over a two -three hour period. Maybe they took some time to introduce themselves. And then of course, it would have taken a bit of time for her to choke to death after they had stuffed her panties down her throat."

"Anything else?" asked Arnon.

"Strange bruising on her wrists and ankles," said the coroner.

"Got a guy coming in to look at that," said Arnon. "Any semen?"

"No," said the coroner. "But I'd bet dollars to donuts that they did her with an aluminum baseball bat. Seen it before with some of the gangs when I worked in south LA. She was sodomized as well, probably with the same object. Very serious trauma to vagina and anus. I would think that she must have lost consciousness several times during the ordeal. We swabbed the area around her nose very carefully and have sent them away to see if we can find out what they used to bring her back after she passed out. They could have used an injected stimulant and we're testing for anything in her blood. If they used an injection site in her vagina or anus, there's so much trauma there that I doubt we'll find anything."

"I expect you're right. There will be a guy named Chris Janes showing up. I called him in. He'll want to take a hard look at her wrists and ankles. Let him."

"Sure," said the coroner.

Arnon left the lab immediately.

Chapter Five

Sam Allen snatched up the phone on the first ring. "Sam here. Is that you, Chuck?"

"What's important enough to pluck me out of a detailed training exercise, Sam?"

"Erich is dead and Gerta has been murdered. Actually Gerta was tortured and murdered."

"By whom?"

"I can say with certainty that it wasn't you or me or Franz. Other than us, the field is wide open."

"I'm guessing it was the South Africans or some of the motherfuckers from Cerberus. They killed Erich too?"

"Nope. Erich found Gerta dead in her apartment and called Franz. Franz told him to get to Cologne as quick as he could. The old bastard made it to one of Franz's safe houses but died of a heart attack within minutes of getting there."

"What do we know, Sam?"

"You had your guys do surveillance on Gerta's niece and husband back when she decided to go live there. Give me the condensed version of what you found out about them."

"Good looking, boring Yuppies. Both had good jobs. The guy liked to golf. The niece volunteered in a Hispanic hospital, but only when hubby was out of town on business. Hubby liked to screw Goth hookers when he was out of town. That was the only thing the people on my team found remotely interesting about them."

"Erich told Franz that the niece is holding the disks and Gerta's diaries."

"For fuck's sake!"

"We need you to get people on the niece and her husband. Discreetly get eyes on them. The homicide cops will be all over them. We have to be sure that nothing can be linked to the Legacy Organization."

"None of us knows what's in those fucking diaries of Gerta's, Sam. For all we know she named names. If the police have them, our world is about to change for the worst."

"When Erich spoke with Franz he said the niece promised Gerta that if anything happened, she would hold the disks and diaries until she was contacted by us. Gerta gave her niece a coded phrase. Erich gave it to Franz over the phone. Thank Christ! He apparently only got out a few sentences before he died in Franz's place."

"If you think the niece has the disks, let me take a team in and snatch her and her husband and the diaries and disks. We do know what's on those fucking disks and they can never be seen by anybody but us. That fact alone makes disposing of the niece and her husband justifiable."

"We can't risk that, Chuck. Too many things could go wrong. We need you to watch them. Find out everything you can about what the cops know. And above all, keep the niece safe."

"I can do that. I think you should let me go in and get them. But I can keep the niece out of harm's way."

"We meet in Muskoka in two days, Chuck. My people are setting it up. I hope that by then Daniel and Franz will have some idea of who killed Gerta."

"We must have been the only people in the world who didn't want Erich dead. But they went after Gerta, so this is about what we were doing in Africa. My bet is on South African Intelligence, but maybe Karl Winter has gone nuts and we're going to have a war with Cerberus Corp. Sam, is Claudio still making noises about the project data on the disks and this fucking AIDS thing?"

"Claudio is joining us in Muskoka, Chuck. Don't let Gerta's niece get dead."

***

It was Wednesday morning and Robert was leaving for his business trip. The previous evening had been tense. Jenna thought Robert had been too eager to pack his bag and load it in the car. She quietly went into the yard by the garage and had seen him loading his travel golf bag into the car, furtively. She hadn't made any comment. Now it was time for him to leave for the airport and Jenna was trying to sip her coffee and not let him see how much she wanted him to go.

"You going to be okay here alone?" he asked. "Maybe you should have one of your friends come over to stay for a couple of nights."

"I'm fine," she replied. "I'm going take advantage of my bereavement days and read a book in the sunshine. Don't forget to call the cops and tell them what you know about the painters."

He left and she waited impatiently for a half hour. When she knew that he wouldn't return to grab some forgotten item, she went into her office and retrieved the aluminum case.

There were two envelopes addressed to her. One small thin one, one large fat one. She opened the thin one first and as she expected, it contained a letter to her from her Aunt.

  "Dear Jenna, I am truly sorry on a number of counts that you are reading this. This case contains what little record of my life there is in existence. The bound books are my diaries. I should have destroyed them long ago, but they were my best friends some times, and they are pretty much the only link I have with the times of my life when I was caught up with, what I thought at least, were important things. I ask you to burn them now, and that you do not try to read through them. I ask that you ensure that they are thoroughly destroyed and that you tell no one they ever existed. There is also an envelope of photos. I ask that you destroy them as well. Without looking at them. My legacy to you comes in two parts. Part one is in the second envelope addressed to you. I sincerely hope you will keep it for your exclusive use. Although you live in a different time and in a part of the world that is comparatively untroubled, my life has taught me the importance of having a means to be independent. I hope the second envelope will provide you with some options. The second part of my legacy to you may never be yours. It is in the care of some of my friends who are part of something called the Legacy Organization, and I am absolutely certain that they will move heaven and earth to provide it to you. But they will have to overcome great obstacles to do that. The other items in this case are floppy disks loaded with data that is priceless. I was entrusted to keep and protect them until a time came when this information can be used. For better or for worse, you have now become the keeper of this information. I beg that you tell no one what you have. Keep the disks safe, hidden from everyone and eventually, someone will contact you and ask for them. Jenna, you will know to whom you should give the disks to because they will, however they make contact with you, tell you that they were present when "Johanna killed a lion". Remember that. Humans are humans Jenna, and I have asked a great deal of you. I now ask one more thing. If you are human, and you find a way to read through my diaries and you look at my photos, please don't judge me. I had compelling reasons to be involved with everything I took part in and to become the person I was. And the men in my life were heroes to me. And it was a very different time in the 1960's and '70's. I do not understand what has happened to people in the last two decades. I think perhaps, people are forgetting how to freely love. My wish for you, Jenna, is that you find a few good men that you truly love. Gerta."

Jenna read the letter a second time, set it aside and opened the large envelope. It too contained a note:

"Jenna, I'll save you some time. There are 2,500 one hundred U.S. dollar bills here. They are not counterfeit. If you are intelligent and handle this money in a way to not attract attention, it will provide you with some options. Gerta"

Jenna sat silently for a time, trying to grasp how much her life had been changed by the envelope that rested in her lap. She looked at the note again, suddenly aware that her hands were shaking. She read it again, having trouble, because her eyes were blurring. She realized that her breathing had become very shallow. She forced herself to take in a couple of deep draughts of air.

A whole range of thoughts were entering her mind. She would identify one but it would be immediately shoved aside by another. All were centered on a theme of change. Jenna was fighting back a panic attack. The envelope in her lap seemed to be an unfamiliar control panel for a vehicle she had never been in.

She set it aside, and took one of the black covered books from the case. Written on the cover was 1965 – 1967. She paged to the first entry. Her Aunt's handwriting was legible and precise. And she understood why her Aunt had written "find a way to read through my diaries." The language was unfamiliar to her. Perhaps it was Dutch, but she had seen letters to her father written in Dutch and these looked different.

Jenna remembered a conversation that she had with her father when she was about fourteen. Her Dad spoke English with a very slight accent. She had asked him to teach her Dutch. He had laughed at that and had said, "No Dutch for you. Learn a useful second language. Spanish or Mandarin. Dutch is spoken by the Dutch, and only the Dutch. It is useless."

The diary she was holding, she was certain, was written in Dutch or Afrikaans. Jenna set it down on the desk with a thump and checked two more of the identical books. Same language. She looked at all of them, 1965 to 1980. And all were filled with words she could not read. She had taken her father's advice and was fluent in French. And she could get by in Spanish.

Jenna took a moment to reflect. My Aunt has been murdered in my backyard. I've just been handed a quarter million dollars. And now I may be the keeper of some sort of priceless information that people will kill for. "One hell of a Wednesday, Jenna," she said out loud.

Best find some place to put my recently acquired fortune. She went to the kitchen and got three large freezer bags. The money filled them almost to capacity. Jenna carried the bags to her bathroom. When they had first moved into the house she had noticed that the floor panel of her vanity cabinet had never been fastened in. The cabinet was fully usable as it was and she knew just how much of a production Robert would make of properly fixing the panel in place. She hadn't mentioned it to him. It took a bit of work with a nail file but eventually she was able to pry up the panel enough to get fingers under it and lift it out of the vanity. The three bags fit into the space with room to spare. "Perhaps I'll put the second part of my legacy here, too," Jenna said to herself. "Or if the house burns down I'll truly learn the meaning of easy come, easy go." She replaced the panel and then put back all of the stuff that had been stored there and went downstairs.

The envelope that contained her Aunt's photos was there, in plain sight. She took it out of the case and set in on her desk. She opened the four square plastic boxes that remained in the case. Each held ten floppy discs. Jenna knew about floppy discs. She had one sitting on her desk at work, and she felt it had been eyeing her reproachfully for the three weeks that it had been there. It apparently contained a presentation that would teach her how to use the company's new computers. Jenna despised computers.

Jenna picked up the unopened envelope of photos and went to the kitchen. She poured herself more coffee and took a seat at the table. There were hundreds of photos in the envelope held in bundles by elastic bands. Her Aunt had put small slips of paper with each bundle, each with a date on it. Jenna slipped the band off the bundle labelled 1965.

1965 had obviously not been a banner year for taking photos. It was the second smallest bundle. The first few were group shots of several men and two women. They were all dressed in what was likely the business attire of the day. Jenna looked much more closely when she realized that the blond woman in the photos was her Aunt when she would have been in her mid-thirties. She was stunning.

The group shots had apparently been taken at a railway station. There were several photos of countryside that seemed to have been shot from a car or a train. The tenth photo that Jenna looked at was very different. It was the same group of people, but this time they were dressed for the outdoors. All wore shorts and hiking boots. Of most interest to Jenna was that they were posing in front of an army tank, and there appeared to be a line of army trucks in the background.

Without thinking about it, Jenna turned the photo over to see if there was anything written on the back. And lo and behold, there in her Aunt's handwriting, in English, was the notation "With S.A. Oliphant tank near the border, Oct '65".

Jenna backtracked through the pile. All had notations on them in her Aunt's script in English. "Hallelujah" thought Jenna, and she arose from the table to fetch some Bailey's for her coffee. The rest of the photos from the 1965 stack were all shot in the countryside. The photo had the group posed by a gate set in a serious looking barbed wire fence. The notation read "Our arrival at the camp."

Jenna set aside the first bundle and went through the years 1966 to 1969 quite quickly. Her rate of going through the piles was reduced to a crawl when she opened the bundle for 1970. The photo was shot at a distance. It pictured her Aunt and the other woman who had been in many of the photos sitting on towels on a sandy riverbank. Both were smiling directly at the camera. Both were nude. Jenna hurriedly read the notation. "Christine and I on my birthday outing. New Year's Day, 1969."

There were several more shots from the 'outing'. In two more photos Gerta and the other woman were nude, but in others they wore two-piece bathing suits. "Blows away my theory that they had forgotten to pack swimwear," Jenna said quietly.

The last picture from 1970 was of a large table set for a formal dinner. Gerta and Christine were front and center in the photo, standing by two of the men who had been in previous photos. There were several other men pictured as well and all of them wore military uniforms. The notation on this one simply said "Christmas, 1970."

Jenna sat for a time sipping her coffee and Bailey's and then a thought struck her. She picked up a phone, called the general number for Robert's company and asked to speak with Ing Stoller. After a short interval of elevator music Ing answered.

"Ing, it's Jenna Van Velt. How are you?"

"Jesus Christ, Jenna, I think I should be asking you that question."

"Robert is out of town for a few days and I have tomorrow off. I wondered if you might want to come here for the evening. I have wine."

"When the old man's out of town the girls can have a right old piss-up," said Ing, turning up her South African accent. "Yeah Jenna, I'd love to have a girls sleepover. Anything you want me to bring?"

"Just yourself," said Jenna. "I'll put something together for dinner."

"Cheese and crackers," said Ing. "It's the only thing I'll eat when I'm drinking." Click.

She had met Ing at one of the torturous parties that Robert's company was fond of having. Jenna did not enjoy playing the corporate wife, and she had dreaded the event which was held at the CEO's home in the foothills. She assumed that this would be like the few other such parties she had attended.

It was a hot day and the invitation had urged the guest to be sure they brought their bathing suits. Jenna was a sun worshipper and had planned to use the pool as an escape from at least some of the inane conversations that she would be expected to engage in. She was about to break away from a group of 'the wives' who were displaying their complete lack of knowledge of the geography of the Middle East when a young woman standing behind her observed that she had a great tan.

Jenna had thanked her and they talked a bit about the best tanning products on the market. Ing introduced herself, indicated she worked for the company in marketing design. Jenna had studied graphic design and photography as a minor in university. Half an hour had gone by quickly as she and Ing talked about some of the very clever campaigns that were underway by some of the more progressive companies.

It was Ing who proposed that they take to the pool. "It's bloody hot," she observed. "Let's have a swim. Maybe if two of us go in at the same time, we'll only get half the ogling from my colleagues." Jenna fetched her bag and opened the door into the ladies change room. She was startled to find Ing inside, unbuttoning her blouse.

"I'm sorry," said Jenna, "the door wasn't locked."

"Be a dear and come in and close it," said Ing. "I get enough bird-dogging from my colleagues out there already. It would just be worse if they saw my boobs."

Nonplussed, Jenna had closed the door and locked it. Ing carried on with changing, all the while talking with Jenna about design. Jenna had felt awkward, but not knowing what else to do, had taken her suit out of her bag and began to disrobe. Ing was topless for a moment and then when the bra of her suit was in place she had removed her shorts and underwear and wiggled into her very tiny bikini bottoms. She had continued to chat with Jenna and it had been clear that she planned to exit the change room with her.

Ing had continued to prattle on about graphic design as Jenna had put the top of her suit on. When she had removed her capris and underwear, Ing observed that they were both 'shave slaves' and then she went on discussing the brilliant campaign that Smirnoff Vodka had done with Kirstie Alley as their model.

"That yellow bikini of yours is almost as revealing as mine. Let's get out there and stop some conversations for a bit."

They had grabbed air mattresses from a stand near the pool and got into the water quickly. The pool was bathtub warm, an obliging server had kept bringing drinks, and no one else came into the pool. They had floated and talked for most of the afternoon. Jenna had been sorry when dinner was announced and they had to get out and dress for dinner.

Once they had alit from their air mattresses, it became clear to both of them that the fruity drinks they had been knocking back packed a punch. Ing had made a show of wringing water out of her long dark hair, whispering to Jenna, "I'm half in the bag. Don't let me veer into someone on the way to the change room."

They made it to the room without incident and apparently without attracting too much attention. Once inside the giggles had set in, and then, the need to pee. Ing had torn off her suit and claimed the loo first, leaving Jenna doing a pee-pee dance. By the time they emerged from changing they had regained their composure.

The party had been the start of friendship, which Robert did not know about. Jenna met Ing downtown for coffee every couple of weeks, always when Robert was out of town. She knew that he would not approve of her spending time with Ing. They had had a rare fight when Robert had referred to Ing as a slut because she was sleeping with someone from the company.

***

Ing arrived at 6:15 and Jenna could feel the energy level in the house change.

"Jenna, my love," were Ing's first words on arrival. "Give this parched exile a drink. For the love of God, a drink."

Ing had given her a hug and then they sat at the kitchen table drinking wine. Ing said, "Are we going to talk about it or not?" Jenna said, "Maybe later". So Ing filled the room with tales of her dating life and after much laughter and one spilled glass of wine, Ing suddenly stood up and looked out at the chaise lounges in the back yard.

"Jenna," she said with a reproachful tone. "There is at least an hour of sun left. I have tan lines so bad that my boobs look like vanilla cupcakes. Why are you keeping me inside?"

Jenna fetched towels while Ing opened a second bottle of wine and went out to the chairs. She was completely nude when Jenna joined her and after a brief pause, Jenna stripped as well. Ing refilled their glasses, leaned back in the chair and raised her glass in a toast.

"To out-of-town husbands and boyfriends."

"I take it that Master Robert isn't aware of our little soiree tonight," observed Ing.

"Absolutely not," answered Jenna. "He disapproves of you."

"Well here's the thing," said Ing, "All the guys I know, including the priest at the parish church that I went to as a kid in Capetown, disapprove of women who turn them down. And the women they disapprove of most, are the women who have a reputation for liking sex, engaging in sex, and aren't all that uncomfortable about people knowing that they do."

"Don't mistake me, Jenna. Your Robert hasn't hit on me. I think I have way too much of an edge for his liking. But males are pack animals and if you insult one of the pack, you insult the whole pack. Robert's buddy at work, Wayne, wanted into my honey pie desperately. I made it clear to him that it wouldn't happen and then I screwed the nerdy, but really nice guy who works in the IT area. Wayne and the rest of the pack did not like that."

"I'm becoming quite disillusioned with the gender," said Jenna.

"It's all about managing your expectations, love," said Ing. "Men are like vacations. If you want to relax and work on your tan you go to St. Barts, not London. If you are clear about what you want from them, then it's simply a selection process. Pick one who can talk intelligently. Pick one who can be a supportive friend. Pick one who is good in the sack. Pick another who is stupendous in the sack but that you couldn't stand to have around on a regular basis."

The lengthening shadows eventually reached their chairs. They wrapped in towels, picked up their clothes, and went inside carrying their empty glasses. Ing opened more wine while Jenna set out some snacks. Jenna was then ready to talk about Gerta.

Jenna began by telling Ing the facts, as she knew them, right up to her Aunt leaving a case containing the diaries and computer discs.

"Christ, woman, your Aunt was tortured to death in your granny flat and you're holding on to a bunch of disks that was doubtlessly the reason that got her killed? Call the police, girl!"

"Who the hell said that Gerta was tortured?" asked Jenna.

"Oh fuck," said Ing. "I overheard Robert talking to Wayne. He told him that he had been talking with the neighbour who found her and called the police. Robert told Wayne that the guy said she was naked on the floor and that is was obvious that she had been beaten, tortured and raped." She paused and then said, "I'm so sorry, Jenna. I thought you knew this."

"Robert must think he's a fucking cop," said Jenna. "The bastard knew this and he didn't say a word to me. The asshole!"

Ing shifted in her chair and leaned toward Jenna. "As you know, Robert isn't my favourite person in the world so please don't think I'm saying he was right not to tell you what he knew. I think he was likely just trying to shield you from the nasty details."

Jenna sat mulling that one over. Ing poured them some more wine.

"Jenna," she said, "there is something very dangerous going on with your Aunt. Sixty-something-year-old ladies living in the good part of town don't get beaten and murdered without reason. It's likely what's on those disks that got her killed. Now they could get you killed. You've got to tell the cops about this."

"I can't hand them over to the cops. At least not now. Gerta asked me to keep them safe. And nobody is going to get their hands on them until I know what's on them."

"You're taking a huge bloody risk, Jenna. What happens if whoever the bad guys are come back here and give you the same treatment that Gerta got?"

"They obviously knew that Gerta had something they wanted. They don't have a clue as to whether I even know about the disks. I told you about the old guy that we learned visited her nearly every day. I expect that's who they're going to visit next."

"You hope," snorted Ing. "What if they get their hands on him and he tells them the disks are here somewhere?"

"I doubt that he would know."

"Jesus Jenna, this is crazy! He saw your Aunt every day. He would certainly have known about the disks. You can put good money on that. What can I do to get you to rethink think this?"

"Can you read Afrikaans,"? asked Jenn.

The question took Ing by surprise. "Maybe a bit. Not much. I never tried to learn it. Why?"

"You asked me what it would take to get me to go to the police with the information I have. What would it take, for starters? I need someone who can read Afrikaans, who wouldn't blab all over the place to translate my Aunt's diaries for me. And I need someone who is trustworthy, who can set me up to look at what's on the computer disks. Once I know what's in the diaries and on the disks, I can make decisions about who gets to see them."

"You're running with scissors and untied shoelaces, girl," said Ing. "I've lived in very dicey parts of the world. It's likely that your Aunt's little case of goodies could mean a very hideous death for you. I've seen hideous deaths, Jenna, in South Africa. Where your Aunt used to live."

"Do you know anyone who can read Afrikaans, Ing?"

"Probably. And my nerdy little computer guy lover could definitely do whatever it takes to give you a look at the disks. If I give him a good boff he does something to get rid of my credit card bills so your disks won't be a problem."

"When can I meet your person who reads Afrikaans?" asked Jenna.

"No answer to that one, my lovely friend. Tom isn't the sort of guy who is always available."

"Will you get in touch with him for me?"

"Well, Jenna my dear, I could leave Tom a message on his phone. But to be more effective, I will go to a bar and have a word with the bartender. He will have a word with a mate of Tom's. And then, Tom may just get in touch with me. That's how it works with my friend Tom."

"What is he? A drug dealer?" asked Jenna.

"I think Tom refers to himself as a security consultant. He's never really explained to me what that means, but I think he is really good at teaching people how not to get killed in certain situations." Ing took a long sip of wine. "Given your present situation, the security consultant side of Tom might be just as valuable to you as his ability to read Afrikaans."

"I think you're overreacting a bit," said Jenna.

"I think we should stop drinking these Californian wines and open a bottle with something to offer," said Ing.

She popped the cork of a bottle of sparkling South African wine that she had brought and then started to talk about the latest follies of some of her more colourful acquaintances. Jenna sipped the bubbles, laughed a lot, and then Ing was taking her arm and guiding her up the stairs, which had become somewhat challenging to climb.

Jenna was glad that Ing had taken command of the situation because she felt that lying down would be a very good thing. She realized that she had somehow lost her towel as Ing threw back the coverlet and sheet of her bed. Ing seemed to have lost her towel as well. Then she was lying on her bed and Ing was caressing her.

Ing's touch was light. She ran her fingers along the side of Jenna's neck and then on to her shoulders. She brushed them along her ribs and across Jenna's tummy. It was cool in the bedroom because the a/c was cranked and Jenna was aware that her nipples were becoming erect.

Ing leaned over her and began tracing the outer edge of Jenna's areola with her tongue. Jenna was at first embarrassed, thinking that Ing would mistake her erect nipples as a sign of arousal rather than a reaction to the temperature of the room. When Ing began to suck and nibble and tease her nipples with her mouth and teeth, Jenna gradually realized that the temperature in the room was irrelevant.

Ing continued to suck and nibble and used gentle pressure with her hand to get Jenna to part her legs. Her fingers traced lines all around Jenna's mons and outer labia, but never once did she touch them. Jenna was aware that she was becoming very wet.

Then, abruptly, Ing was gone from her breasts. She moved quickly on the bed and was kneeling between Jenna's legs, pushing them wider apart and having her bend her knees upward. Her mouth was hot on Jenna's labia, and her tongue probed into Jenna. Ing seemed to be drinking all the moisture that was present. Jenna thought it was extraordinary that she was about to have an orgasm with a woman.

Her vaginal muscles started to contract and then the delicious things that Ing had been doing with her mouth stopped. Jenna felt one of Ing's hands on her chest between her breasts, pinning her down on the bed. She gasped as Ing's fingers entered her, forcefully, and Ing hooked her fingers up against the front wall of her vagina. Then Ing started to use her thumb to massage Jenna's clit.

All of the light touching was gone. Ing's fingers fucked her like a short, thick cock, and her thumb was relentless on Jenna's clit, already engorged from Ing's kissing. She felt the contractions that had started resume, only much stronger.

"Come for me," Ing said.

And Jenna had screamed and bucked her groin against Ing's hand for what seemed an eternity. She awoke lying on her side, with Ing coiled against her back. Her skin was still moist with perspiration.

"What, what can I do for you?" asked Jenna.

"Oh lovely lady. You've let me take you through some changes. That's all I ask tonight," said Ing.

"It doesn't seem fair," said Jenna, sleepily.

"Nothing is," said Ing. "Go to sleep, my lovely friend."

Jenna awoke ten hours later. Ing was gone and Jenna was disappointed that the note that she had left said only, "I'll try to contact Tom ASAP. My lovely little nerd will be easier to manage."

Chapter Six

Nils placed his regular call to the usual number back in Europe. The call was answered by the man who spoke only German. "Enjoying your vacation in America?" asked the man.

"Not particularly," answered Nils. "I'm not finding much of interest here."

"I can shed some light on that," said the voice on the phone. "Get back here to see me immediately. Your American sojourn is over. You'll need to enlist a couple of your colleagues for your next task."

Nils was packed and out of his hotel in fifteen minutes flat. He got a cab from the Frankfurt airport to the railway station. He blessed Europe for its frequent trains and was bound for his destination after only an hour's delay. A car from Cerberus Corp. was waiting for him when he detrained and within a half hour he was at the office of his boss.

He didn't like face-to-face meetings with his boss. The man was intelligent and professional but there was no warmth to him. Nils didn't like to admit it to himself but it was the man's appearance that put him off.

Karl Winter, as Nils knew him, had been 15 when he was deployed to a German tank unit that was trying to stop the Allied advance across France. An Allied aircraft destroyed his tank with rocket fire. Other crew members hauled him out of the burning tank, but not before one side of his face had melted.

He had kept both of his eyes and the doctors had done their best. But the outer edge of his left eyebrow was a least an inch higher than the outer edge of his right eyebrow. And there was a large patch of shiny red skin that blazed in a fiery way when the man was upset. Nils disliked any overt displays of emotion. Karl's left cheek was radiating heat when Nils entered the room.

"Do you have people watching the old man's apartment?" Karl asked immediately.

"Yes."

"Mr. Walter Danski a.k.a. Herr Erich Krohl was found dead on a bench in the garden of Cologne Cathedral 36 hours ago. My informants in the system there tell me that he was expensively dressed, had no identification papers whatsoever on his person, and that it is extremely likely that he died of natural causes."

"Herr Erich Krohl?" asked Nils.

"In his younger days he was a thoroughly evil man. The great irony is that such a man should die, peacefully it seems, in his home town. Fate has allowed a great miscarriage of justice in this case."

Karl was then all business. He said that the fact Krohl had made it from the states to Cologne and that he was not found dressed as a poor old man, meant that he likely had an alternate residence. Probably near the apartment that Nils had been watching. That's where he would have had his good clothing, his travel documents, and his money.

"How is your American girlfriend,"? asked Karl.

"We remain on good terms. I gave her a story about having a sick relative in Europe. I can go back to see her if she can be of any use."

"You will be gracing the young lady with your presence very soon," said Karl. "I have arranged for you to work with a young man from England named James Stuart. He is an expert in computers and that sort of thing. Since the Ten Haan woman was not helpful and Krohl is now dead, we'll need to get at the computers in the library where Gerta Ten Haan taught classes. We know she was in communication with Franz Von Hesse and we know that she was not using the telephone. Stuart says she likely was staying in contact with the Legacy Organization by computer."

"When do you want me to head back?"

"There's a driver waiting to get you to Frankfurt. Pick up your tickets and instructions from my secretary on the way out. Use as many of your men as you might need and don't count on this man Stuart for anything in the way of physical help. He is a technician only. I suggest you have one of your people assigned to babysit him throughout the operation."

"And when the operation is over?"

"Have one of your more experienced travellers facilitate his safe return here. The man has valuable knowledge that we are increasingly putting to good use. My secretary will give you details as required."

Chapter Seven

It had been three days since the Ten Haan murder and Arnon was becoming impatient. Robert Grieve had called and miraculously still had the bit of paper with the phone number of the painters. Arnon had called the number, expecting it to ring unanswered. Instead, he got a voice machine telling him that he had reached A1 painting and asking him to leave a message.

His people had picked up the president and CEO, as well as his one employee in the late afternoon three days after the murder. Both were in their late 20's and neither of them appeared too bright. And when they were brought to Arnon's office they were dressed in white T-shirts and white pants that were covered in paint.

Arnon had both of them run to see if they had any sort of criminal record. They both had apparently lead crime-free lives. Or they had never been caught.

It hadn't taken too much persuading to get a court order to search their residences and the headquarters of A1 painting, which was a rented two-bay garage on the edge of the woods. Everything in the three locations pointed to the fact that they were painters. After 24 hours he had to let them go.

Arnon's buddy in immigration wasn't able to give him any details about Gerta Ten Haan's arrival at the airport. He told Arnon that nobody named Gerta Ten Haan had come through immigration at the airport in the months of January or February of that year. He was combing through logs in his spare time and told Arnon he'd flag any names for him that might be the Ten Haan woman. Arnon was frustrated and went to the airfield and worked on cleaning up aircraft parts for the evening.

He arrived at work on Friday morning feeling more relaxed than he had since he had first looked into the granny flat in the woods. As always, spending some time on the planes had been therapeutic for him. His phone message light was blinking. The first message was from Chris Janes asking Arnon to call him. Jules from INTERPOL had left the second message. Arnon would call him in about six hours.

He dialed Chris's number.

"Chris, Nick here. I take it you had a look at the Ten Haan woman."

"That was some fucked up thing there, Nick. Who did she piss off? Genghis fucking Khan?"

"Maybe. Don't know yet."

"Well they were no strangers to walking somebody through the halls of pain. They definitely flew her. The bruising on her wrists and ankles is totally consistent with that."

"I thought so too. But it's always good to get the opinion of an expert. Anything stand out for you?"

"Yeah, bud, a couple of things. Don't know if they're important. They used padded cuffs and anklets. I'd say leather lined with felt. There were bruises but no lacerations or chaffing. They clearly wanted the restraints to be the least of her worries."

"Why is that?" asked Arnon.

"The psychology of torture, buddy. A torture subject who has been thoroughly trained will focus on the constant pain of a tight ligature. If they can lock onto that, it distracts them from what the assholes are doing to them with hot irons and pliers. There are a number of institutions that train their operatives in that technique."

"Give me a list of those institutions so I can stay clear of them," said Arnon.

"Your coroner guy told me that she didn't have any dislocated joints. That means that these guys had a very good idea of her height and weight and they used first-class equipment. A pulley system, for sure, to get the final tensions just perfect. The doc said that they did her with a baseball bat. She must have been almost perfectly suspended to have not pulled apart a wrist when that was going down."

"Thanks for all this, Chris," said Arnon.

"One more thing, hoss. Even with perfect suspension - and I guess you've already figured out that they must have known all about the design of the room where they did this to have the proper attachment points - this was minimum, a three-man job."

"How do you know that?" asked Arnon quickly.

"When they did her with the bat they would have had guy holding her shoulders, a guy lifting up on her lower back and then of course, Batman."

"Seen that before?"

"Twice. Uganda. And with one of the nastier cartels that has an L.A. presence."

"It's a lovely world, isn't it?" said Arnon.

"Off to look at some weird shit that's gone down with a diplomat's family in a suburb of Washington, but I should be back on the ground here in two or three weeks. Stay in touch buddy. You have some interesting stuff sometimes."

***

A department staff meeting took place every Friday morning. Jenna resented losing two hours of her life to them.

When she got out of the meeting, the admin assistant was waiting outside of her office. She had a phone message slip upon which she had written "Robert won't be back until Sunday."

"He called while you were in the meeting, Jenna. He said there are some major changes in the company so he'll have to stay an extra day. He told me to tell you he loves you."

Jenna didn't know whether to say bitch or bastard first. She went into her office and closed the door. She had a Friday and Saturday night to fill. Jenna leafed through her very meagre personal Cardex, wondering who of her acquaintances might be free for lunch the next day.

Ing took care of Friday for her.

Her office phone rang and Ing said, "Can you meet up with my friend Tom after work Friday?"

Jenna replied that she could, about seven o'clock.

Ing gave her the name of a restaurant not far from Jenna's office building, and rang off.

***

Arnon closed the door to his office at 6 p.m. and dialed the number Jules had left him.

"Jules ici." He switched to English as soon as Arnon identified himself.

"We have identified the owner of the prints that you sent us," said Jules, "but do not let that make you think that we at INTERPOL are some sort of wizards."

"If you know who the guy was who left those prints at my murder scene already, I'd say that some sort of magic is in play," replied Arnon.

"No magic, just plain luck. It's very easy to match prints to someone when you have them in your coroner's laboratory," said Jules.

For the next ten minutes Arnon was spellbound as Jules told him what had just gone on in Germany.

That cop that had found Krohl had expedited the delivery of the body to a forensic coroner and had gone to the lab to see what might be learned. He had known this was no routine natural death when he saw the SS tattoo on the old man's arm. He called his boss who had the good sense to call INTERPOL.

Within a few hours, with the help of some other international agencies, INTERPOL knew a great deal about the body on the examination table in their lab. Tape from security cameras at Frankfurt airport and in the Frankfurt and Cologne rail stations gave them timings of his arrival and travel. Once Jules had known that the old man had arrived in Germany, he played a hunch and had the prints from the body compared to the prints sent by Arnon. They were a perfect match.

"So, who is this guy if he's not my man Walter?" asked Arnon.

"He arrived in Frankfurt using a passport in the name of Walter Danzig. His real name, however, is Erich Krohl."

"Should I recognize that name?" asked Arnon.

"You would if you were with my organization or with any number of groups that are Nazi hunters."

Jules explained that Krohl had been in hiding since just before the war in Europe ended in May 1945. He was high on the list of wanted war criminals. Not as high as Eichmann or Mengele, but up on the list near them.

"What were they after him for?" asked Arnon. "Did he run one of the concentration camps?"

"Not quite. He and a team of his colleagues were stationed at a very specialized camp just inside Poland, close to the East Prussian border. They were doing experiments in disease and the spread of disease. Dengue fever was one of the nasty bugs that they were playing around with. God only knows what else. I have a file a foot thick on my desk to plough through. Your Walter, my Erich, was one of the nastier Nazis during the war."

"I take it they were experimenting on humans."

"Well of course they were," replied Jules. "These are Germans we're talking about."

Jules explained that the 'special' camp where Krohl had worked was built in early 1943. The camp's core body of inmates was 500 healthy Jewish men and women that were directed there after selection at other camps. There were other shipments of inmates made to the camp in later 1943 and early 1944, but Jules hadn't read far enough into the file to know the details.

What he did know was that there were two huge prisoner-of-war camps nearby holding mostly Russians and Poles, but with a few hundred Frenchmen as well. Within six months of Krohl and his team showing up in the area, both camps experienced catastrophic outbreaks of Dengue fever, Typhus and some other affliction with very bizarre symptoms that survivors of the camps said the Germans called "A2".

"Was this Krohl ever seen in the POW camps?"

"Once the outbreaks occurred, survivors say he was there every day with his merry little band, but not to minister to the ailing. His gang walked around taking photos and swabbing the sick and the dead. They had bodyguards from the SS SD."

"How many died?" asked Arnon.

"From mid-1943, the body count of the two camps went from roughly 200 a month to 1000 a week. In all, about 25,000."

"Holy Christ!" exclaimed Arnon.

"Indeed. Our Herr Krohl really teed off the Russians, the French and of course, the Israelis with his science projects. Given the intelligence capabilities of those nations, it's a miracle that he was able to remain a free man and reach the ripe old age of 89. And visit your murder scene and then fly back to Germany to die of natural causes outside of the Cathedral where the vicious fucking murderer was an altar boy before the war. Quite extraordinary!"

There was a pause in the conversation.

"Jules, I can't thank you enough for this information."

"Perhaps you'll be less thankful, Nick, when I tell you that your murder scene is now part of an INTERPOL investigation. My superiors are doing the necessary diplomatic dance as we speak. We need to know a lot more about this woman that Krohl was visiting every day."

"Will you be coming over here as part of the investigation?"

"Probably. My specialty is digging up stuff on Nazi and neo-Nazi organizations."

***

Jenna found the Marienbad restaurant easily. It was an old brick building. There were several tables with umbrellas on the sidewalk in front of it and the tables were encircled by a low fence hung with flower boxes. Jenna thought it looked European.

Ing was sitting at a table outside talking animatedly to a man that had his back to Jenna. She was standing by the table before Ing noticed her.

"She's here! Jenna meet Tom. Tom meet Jenna. My work here is finished."

The man with Ing stood up and shook Jenna's hand. "Tom Robbins. It's good to meet you, Jenna."

He had very big hands. And eyes so dark brown they seemed unreal. Robert would have sneered at his sports jacket and T-shirt combination. She sensed his intensity and was drawn to it and to his obvious physicality. She felt she could listen to him talk for a very long time.

Tom asked her about her day and drew laughs from both of them as he talked about questions that he had taken during the consulting work he was doing. She realized that he had no accent.

The server came to take their drink order. Ing asked for a Mojito, Jenna a glass of dry white wine and Tom ordered a Tusker.

"You and your bloody African beer," Ing observed.

"It's a Czech restaurant Ing. I would say that Jenna is the only one who ordered in a geographically correct manner."

"Oh God! Do you think we should be geographically correct?"

"Probably impossible for you, Ing. You certainly have never shown any ability to be politically correct."

"That's quite a compliment from a man who can offend most religious groups and three races just by showing them his resume."

"You're baiting me in hopes of getting a spanking, aren't you?"

"If I want a spanking, bucko, I'll just give you my safe word and put my bottom up."

Jenna had been trying to get into the conversation. "You don't have a South African accent," she said.

"That would be because he's not a Springbok," said Ing.

Jenna was trying to figure that comment out when Tom spoke.

"I'm not a South African Springbok like our horny friend here," said Tom.

"Oh," was Jenna's reply.

"I have dual citizenship. Canadian and Rhodesian. Long story. Too long while having dinner."

"The Canadian thing explains it," said Ing. "They don't have any fucking accent at all."

"I've not met many Canadian-Rhodesians," was the first thing that Jenna could think of to say, and she would have liked to have punched Ing when she made a "duh" kind of sound.

Tom gave her a very slight smile and said, "Not surprising."

"This is quite a coincidence, actually," said Jenna. "I have dual citizenship too. Canadian and American."

"No shit!" exclaimed Ing, "I'm sitting here with two ex-pat Canadians! You two should roll around in some maple syrup and have crazy, wild Eskimo sex."

Tom gave Ing a stern look and asked Jenna what had brought her to the States.

"My husband is American."

"Ah, the polished Yank swept the young Canadian girl off her feet," smiled Tom.

Jenna didn't respond right away. Then she said, "My feet hadn't been very firmly on the ground for quite some time before I met Robert."

The drinks arrived. Jenna took a sip of her wine, Tom took a sip of his beer, and Ing knocked back several swallows of her Mojito.

"The question I have for you two," said Ing. "is which of you is going to make sure I get home tonight?"

"Why is that a concern for you on this particular evening?" said Tom, smiling.

"You bastard," said Ing, as she kicked him.

And then Jenna got it.

It put a different spin on the night once Jenna realized that they were lovers. And it intrigued her. Ing was beautiful, attractive, in her late twenties. Tom was clearly several years older than Ing.

"Ing says you have some diaries written in Afrikaans that you're interested in getting translated. Despite not having a South African accent, thank God, I do read Afrikaans. I'm off to handle some business for the next week or two, but I would be happy to take a look at one of them for you when I get back."

"Thank you so much," said Jenna. "I would really appreciate that."

Jenna was making eye contact with Tom. That was making her nervous.

"Don't think about paying me," said Tom. "I'm not going to write you a word for word translation. I'll read it to you and you can take notes. If the first one isn't too boring, we can read the rest."

Jenna was unhappy when she realized that she had to catch her train home. She reached into her purse but Tom waved her away from the tab.

***

Nils disliked James Stuart on sight. They met in James' hotel room and the Englishman had chain smoked throughout the entire two hour meeting. And he was unshaven. Nils got what he needed from the man and went back to his room to have a shower and to find out if the hotel had a laundry service.

He changed and made several calls from a pay phone on a quiet corner. Then he visited a store to buy a bottle of the heavy, sweet wine that Marcia liked.

He had called Marcia to tell her that he was back in town and to ask her if she could possibly take some time away from the preparation of her thesis to see him.

Marcia was delighted that Nils was back in town. She was 33, moving very slowly on the completion of her PhD and had had only three lovers in her life. Nils was by far the most skilled. He did things to her slim, boyish body that no one else had ever done. And he was truly beautiful to look at.

***

Jenna awakened at 4 a.m., or rather, gave up on her attempt to sleep. It wasn't unusual for her to have a sleepless night. She told herself there was a lot going on in her life and she needed to find a way to get some rest.

At Robert's insistence, shortly after they were married she had seen a sleep specialist. Robert slept like a stone. Jenna's insomnia bothered him. It did not wake him up. It simply bothered him that his wife seemed unable to sleep.

She'd had three sessions with the therapist. In the end, the specialist had concluded that there was no biological reason why she could not sleep. Jenna had known that before she had set foot in the clinic.

Jenna's mother had died when she was seven. She had grown up as the apple of her father's eye. He had been a very hard worker and he had done well with several businesses on the go at the same time. Jenna had been raised with a series of housekeepers. Generally it had been an okay life.

Her Dad was doing well financially by the time she was twelve and he got it into his head that she should go to a private girls' school. She hadn't protested much, because it seemed to mean so much to him that she would get a better education. The first such school placement ended when Jenna had stood up to a class bully and had used a roundhouse punch with a clenched fist to knock the girl down. Her Dad placed her in a more enlightened school that had a more creative approach to education. Jenna had made a name for herself as a photographer there.

Jenna had taken a couple of philosophy courses while she was doing her undergrad and had found herself wondering what her life would have been like had her mother lived, had she not been an only child, had her immigrant father had not tried to fast track her into 'better society'. She'd decided that such questions were on par with wondering what her life would have been like if she'd been a bra cup size bigger and had lips like Julia Roberts.

She made a full pot of coffee and fetched the case containing Gerta's photos. There were several packets with date labels that she hadn't yet looked at. She went through them chronologically.

Most of pictures were of scenery and wildlife. There were several group shots of usually the same people. Then she noticed a trend.

From 1975 onward, there were more and more different faces in the photos. And virtually all of the newcomers were in military uniform. The background of the photos changed as well. Frequently the people in the pictures were posing in front of tanks or large army trucks. Jenna mentally noted that she would take some of the photos with her when she met with Tom Robbins.

The last unopened packet of photos was wrapped in burgundy tissue paper and did not have a date label attached. Jenna poured more coffee and removed the wrapping. The packet contained 24 black and white photos of her Aunt, obviously professionally done. In each of the photos her Aunt was posing nude. Jenna estimated that Gerta must have been in her late thirties when the photos were taken. They were tastefully done. "You were a smokin' hot lady," Jenna said out loud.

Jenna turned one of the photos over to see it was stamped with the photographer's logo. It identified a photographer based in Pretoria. Good to know, she thought.

She carefully repacked the case of photos and disks and re-stowed it in her studio. It was still early morning. She changed into her running gear and went to do the route that she thought as her long run.

***

Jenna was sitting in the garden reading the Sunday paper when she heard the garage door open. It was 11 a.m.. Robert came into the backyard and sat in the lawn chair beside her.

Jenna said that there was fresh coffee in the carafe. Robert offered to fetch another cup for her and when she declined, he went into the house to get some for himself. When he resumed his seat, Jenna could tell that he was nervous about something.

"How was your trip?"

"It was good." said Robert. "Perhaps too good."

"Do tell," said Jenna.

Jenna recognized when Robert was 'off' because he adopted what she thought of as his sales presentation voice. And he disseminated with the voice in full play when he gave her a lengthy rendition of what has transpired during his trip. This is going to be big, she thought, when he had passed the five minute mark of his monologue.

And it was.

"I've been offered a job as regional vice-president of sales. An extra 50K a year. And two steps up the company ladder. All the guys I've been hanging around with here would be left coughing in my dust."

"Any downside to the good news?"

Robert summoned up his best presentation voice and assured her there wasn't. He said that another major plus of the whole thing was that his region would be the east coast. "We can take our pick," he said, "New York or New Orleans. The company has offices in both cities."

The ensuing discussion was conducted without heat or rancor. Jenna wondered what she would find to work at in New York or the Big Easy. Robert said that with his increased salary she could take her time to 'find something she would really like'. Jenna replied that his raise was a good deal less than her current salary. Robert said that they could cut back a bit on things. Jenna pointed out that they were not particularly good at cutting back.

Robert was really trying to make the close with Jenna. "We'll have a hell of a profit when we sell the house. It's gone up about 25% in value since we bought, and the market is hot." He realized that he had slipped as soon as the words left his mouth.

"So," asked Jenna calmly. "Have you been made an offer or have you accepted an offer?"

"I felt I had to take the offer," said Robert. "I'm sorry. I should have called to discuss it with you. But I didn't see how I could turn it down and stay with the company." He sounded like he did when he was explaining to one of his customers why a shipment would be delayed.

Jenna sat quietly for a bit and arose from her chair.

"Where are you going?" asked Robert.

"I don't know. Certainly not to New York or New Orleans."

Chapter Eight

Nils had chilled the wine that he would take to Marcia's place. He'd bought the large economy size because he wanted Marcia to over-imbibe, and more importantly, because it had a screw top. He removed that cap, poured some clear liquid into the bottle and recapped it. He knocked on the door of Marcia's apartment right at 2 p.m.

The sitting room of her small flat was as cluttered and messy as usual, but there was a clear spot on the sofa where the two of them could sit. Nils greeted Marcia with one of his most sensuous kisses and then went into the kitchen to find a wine glass for her. He selected the largest one available and gave it to her filled to the brim.

He asked her questions about her thesis, inquired about her family, and listened to a long diatribe of how wrong it was that America was intervening in Iraq. All the while he kept her wine glass filled and took only small sips from the flask that he had brought with him. When Marcia paused mid-sentence to stifle a yawn, Nils knew it was time for the main event.

He led her into her bedroom, whispering about what he planned to do with her body. She was nude under her bathrobe and when he first touched her labia he learned that she was already very wet. As he expected, she had a very intense and loud orgasm that required only minimal effort on his part. As always, she turned on her side.

Once she was snoring rhythmically Nils dressed, took her key chain from the coffee table and went out to the parking lot of the building. He had two men were waiting there. He gave them the keys and they left immediately. Nils went back inside the apartment and watched the parking lot and listened to Marcia sleep.

They were back within an hour. When Nils joined them they passed him several rolls of exposed 35 mm. film and Marcia's key chain. "I'll be in touch in a couple of days," he said.

Nils put on latex gloves before he re-entered the apartment. Once inside he carefully wiped down the key chain, the wine bottle and the glass. The handle of the door to the fridge got the same treatment. He went quietly into the bedroom and collected the condom wrapper from the floor near the bed. Nils took a note written on a leaf from Marcia's pad that he had acquired during an earlier visit and left it on her bedside table. When he left quietly through the front door Marcia was still noisily asleep.

***

Jenna drove for an hour to a beach that she had discovered about a year after they had moved to the Woods. There was no development around it and the access road was sketchy. She was relieved to see only a couple of minivans in the very limited parking area.

It was a short descent down to the water. Two families were having picnics off to the south end of the beach. Jenna walked north for about a thousand yards and sat with her back against a huge log that had been thrown onto the sand. The Pacific was moderately active with three-foot combers rolling into the beach. Jenna liked the noise of the ocean.

She had come back to her Dad's house in February of 1983 after she had finished her honours undergrad. She was one of the kids who blessedly did not have a pile of student loans thanks to her father's help. But she had felt she needed to live cheap and make some money.

Bernie's Road House was a popular spot with the lunch and after work crowd, owned by a lecherous but timid guy named George. She had a slow start, but by the middle of March she knew how to work the tables of middle-aged businessmen and was taking home a hundred or so in tips a day. And she knew that her Dad was delighted to have her around.

She'd befriended a server named Emma who was living near the restaurant with a long-haul driver. Emma got very lonely when he made trips to Mexico.

It became Emma's habit when her guy was away to spend a couple of evenings each week at Jenna's Dad's house. He'd come home to a good dinner that the two of them had cooked and then they'd watch TV. The night of Emma's birthday, they had wine with dinner and tuned into the Motown retrospective with footage of Michael Jackson's first moonwalk.

Jenna would never forget her father's laughter that night. She and Emma - no doubt alcohol was a factor - had bounded off the sofa and tried to emulate Michael's moves. Her Dad had been transfixed.

He had almost no accent by then. But that night the alcohol, the laughter and the relaxation had kicked in. "Jenna and Emma," he had said in a thick Dutch accent. "the dancing retards."

"Moonwalking," thought Jenna, "is what I've been doing since Dad died."

Her Dad had passed away three months after the night that she and Emma had nearly made him pee his pants with laughter. His chronic indigestion was cancer. He had not believed in doctors. Jenna had received a substantial inheritance. Not knowing what else to do, she had gone back to school and taken an MBA.

She'd met Robert at a conference in the States and they'd had really good sex for three days and nights. She'd gone back to Canada and applied for a working visa in the U.S. When it came through, she'd quit and gone to California.

She and Robert, she thought, were an aesthetically pleasing couple. Both were slim, fit and tanned. They'd both recognized the advantage of looking good and living healthy. They both had all the right toning to make sex good. "We're fucking Barbie and Ken," she told herself.

Jenna had rarely cried since she had watched her father slip into a coma eight years ago. She began to sob as she sat in the sand with deep, wracking sobs that shook her entire body.

Jenna listened to the Pacific crash in on the beach until about five o'clock. She drove down the coast road and found a motel that looked clean, empty and had a pay phone. Jenna called home and when Robert answered she told him that he was on his own for dinner. He told her that he was flying back to New York the next morning.

"Want me to list the house?" she asked.

"If you wouldn't mind," said Robert.

Jenna went to sleep in the motel that night with a poem running through her head. She couldn't remember the poet but "not with a bang but a whimper" was stuck in her brain. She slept remarkably well.

Jenna called her office to say that she would be delayed getting into work. She was relieved to see that Robert had already left for his new Eastern appointment. She enjoyed her shower, and in a few hours after arriving at the office had more than covered off all the things she needed to do on her watch at work.

Her colleague bought a newspaper every morning and left all but the sports section in the lunchroom. Jenna grabbed the classifieds and a real estate supplement and closed her office door. She picked an agent because she liked her photograph and because she was based at an office in the Woods. The woman would be glad to see her the next evening.

She was taken aback by the sheer number and variety of apartments that were advertised. Her criteria were close to work, two bedrooms, a full bath and a powder room, in-apartment laundry facilities, and indoor parking. None of the ads stated very clearly that they met her standards. She was thinking of hiring one of the apartment finder agents that had their ads throughout the classifieds when she noticed a two-bedroom place for rent in the Hammond Building.

When Jenna had first joined the company there was a great lady named Karen English working there. Karen was recently divorced and Jenna had gone to her apartment in the Hammond building several times for a glass of wine after work. Karen had said that it was the perfect place for an unmarried woman to live. Jenna called the number listed in the ad and took the apartment sight unseen. She said she would drop in at noon with a cheque and to sign the necessary papers.

***

Nils was becoming impatient. Stuart was, he thought, being very difficult. He had studied the photos that had been taken in the computer with great intensity for several hours. It took the Englishman most of a day to provide any information at all. And then it came in fits and starts.

He first provided a list of packaging materials he would need. It was extensive and incomplete. After the man had made multiple additions to the list, Nils confronted him. He received a lecture from the unkempt troglodyte on the complexities of shipping computer equipment around the world. Nils hated lectures.

Then the Englishman had told him that it would take days, several days, to acquire the equipment they would need to complete their mission. Nils had told him that there was unlimited money to expedite the task. The Englishman, who had very bad breath, had laughed in his face. Nils had used every bit of will power he had to not kill the man on the spot.

***

The realtor, Jenna realized, had a voice very similar to a teacher that had been Jenna's bane in grade nine. When she had mentioned decluttering for the fifth time Jenna tried to tune her out. They were in the master bedroom when the realtor got her attention again.

"Is this an end -of-marriage sale?"

"My husband has accepted a job on the east coast."

"Well, don't let him take all his clothes there with him. Buyers and other realtors, they see closets in a house this size with only a man's or a woman's clothes, they think that a divorce is happening. They think the seller is desperate. That drives the price down."

"I'll make sure there is no imbalance in the closets."

"Good. You've hired a real estate professional for advice and that's what I'm giving you. Come back downstairs with me. You and your husband have a flare for arranging your antiques in cozy little conversation nooks. It will be a family with kids that will buy this place. You need to rearrange the living room, the dining room and the TV room. Think of a couple and three young kids living here. Get rid of the nooks."

Jenna began moving furniture around as soon as the realtor left, afraid she would forget what the woman had instructed her to do. She cursed the realtor and Robert about equally as she worked. There were beautiful pieces of furniture in the house.

Cruising out to the smaller towns and finding just the right pieces for the place had been a big part of their first two years of cohabitation. They had scored some great finds including some really beautiful armoires that would be too large to have in an apartment. Jenna started developing a list of what she would want in her apartment and what Robert would be keen to send to a dealer to sell.

Robert called her at her office on Thursday morning.

"Hi, Jenna. I wanted you to know that I won't be back in town until Monday, and then I have a meeting and fly out the next morning."

"Well, if you come into the house in the dark don't stub your toes. The furniture on the main floor has all been rearranged as per the directions of the real estate lady."

"I'll just stay at a hotel at the airport. I'm catching the red eye. Obviously you got the house listed."

"Yep. She said it could sell quickly. The market is apparently hot right now."

"I hired a landscaping company to take care of the yard."

"Good. I hope you're going to at least drop by the house because there is a pile of papers on the kitchen table that you need to sign."

"I'll do that. I want to grab a couple more suits and some other stuff."

"Don't take too many clothes yet," Jenna told him what the realtor had said. "And I've left a list of things that I'd like to take with me from the house. Just cross out anything you don't agree with.

***

Arnon had not been happy when Jules told him that INTERPOL had taken an official interest in his murder investigation. He knew their involvement would complicate the situation. But he admitted to himself as he and Crane and the coroner walked to a meeting called by his boss, that he had greatly underestimated just how complicated things had become.

The conference room was designed to provide seating for 24 people. It was filled to capacity and at least a dozen people were standing behind the chairs at the table. Arnon saw that the chief as well as his own boss were there, and recognized the force's director of communications and his assistant. There were several people that had FBI written all over them. And a few of the guys wearing expensive suits, with longish hair, that Arnon couldn't figure out.

They began with a briefing from Arnon's force. His boss decided that part of the show was his and he gave a pretty thorough presentation from the police perspective. It took the FBI over an hour to say that they had nothing to report other than the fact that Gerta Ten Haan seemed to have dropped off the planet from 1965 to 1980.

***

Nils had decided that he would spare Stuart's life. In the last two days, things had come together. All of the equipment and packaging material that Stuart had demanded was on site. The troglodyte, as Nils called him, said he'd require ten hours to acid etch away serial numbers from the equipment and then it could be loaded for transport to the library.

Nils had seven men to help on this job. One was assigned to be Stuart's babysitter. One would stay with the truck. They had been briefed, briefed again, and then each had had to brief Nils on their duties. Nils was satisfied that they knew their business.

He left his men packaging up equipment as Stuart cleared it for loading and went off to make a phone call. The first was to Marcia. By the time that call was over, Marcia was in an advanced state of arousal because of new things they would try on her bed the next day.

***

Jenna put a call into Ing who was keen to know how Robert's promotion had sat with Jenna. She was about to agree to meet Ing for a drink after work, but instead she found herself telling her that she was going out to spend the weekend at the cottage that she and Robert owned. She invited Ing to come along, expecting to hear that Ing had a full dance card for the weekend. She was very surprised when Ing accepted with alacrity.

They made arrangements for Ing to meet her at the northernmost transit station of the city's transit system at 6:30 the next day. One of the perks of Jenna's job was that she could be part of the 'happy Friday' program, which ran from the first of June to the middle of September. By working an extra half hour a day during the fall, winter and spring months, Jenna got every second Friday off during the summer. She would have the day to shop and prepare for the weekend. She realized she was looking forward to the trip.

***

Chuck Holt called Sam from Los Angeles.

"Sam, I got a pretty good set-up in place for the niece. One of my women is now on the cleaning staff of Van Velt's office building. We've got eyes on her around the clock. More importantly, it doesn't appear that anybody else is watching her. She bagged off by herself to a beach and then stayed at a motel for a night. If anybody else was watching her we would have made them."

"What about the husband?"

"He's doing business out east. I didn't figure it was worthwhile to have somebody following him to watch him hire hookers dressed up as vampires. We'll be on him as soon as he gets back."

"So you're sure you can keep Van Velt safe?"

"For sure. Now do you want the bad news?"

"Give it to me."

"The LAPD is getting lots of help on Gerta's case. We have a talkative friend on the force. He says that the FBI and INTERPOL are here. There are also rumours flying around that there are some spooks attending the case meetings."

"They must have linked Gerta to Erich. How the fuck did they do it so fast? Do you think Van Velt has given them the diaries?"

"I don't know. Our guy isn't close to the case so he can't give us much more. I have my best guys finding out all they can about the coppers working this murder. We'll figure something out."

"This INTERPOL involvement worries me. I'll have Franz try to contact Joachim Maarten."

"I wish you wouldn't do that, Sam. I don't trust that bastard at all."

"Claudio, Daniel and Franz are all on their way to my place in Muskoka. I hope they are bringing a lot of good intel with them. We'll talk about Joachim then."

***

Nils' team had everything ready. One of them had bicycled off just as darkness fell. He was an expert at illicit entry and alarm suppression. He would let them in the employees' entrance of the library. The rest of the team, including the Troglodyte, was near the two vans, prepared to move at a specific time. Nils set off to meet Marcia.

As per his telephoned instructions, she was naked when she let him into the apartment. Or as naked as she could be, thought Nils, given that she declined to shave her armpit or pubic hair. He nuzzled and kissed her fervently and then introduced her to poppers.

She liked them and was soon ready to enjoy some restraint and pleasure. Nils had brought pre-cut soft, but very strong silk/cotton ties. Marcia willingly laid down on her bed and allowed herself to be tied spread-eagle. The bedstead was a lovely old oak piece that she had picked up at a local antique shop. Once she was tied, there wasn't a lot she could do about what was going on in her bedroom.

Nils blindfolded Marcia and then very quickly gagged her. She struggled at that since they had had some intense telephone talk about what her safe word would be. He administered an injection which caused Marcia to yelp through her gag.

Nils applied almost a full bottle of lube to her genitals, making sure a lot of it soaked into the bedding. He carefully uncapped another bottle and dribbled the milky liquid it contained over Marcia's genitals and thighs, pouring the dregs of the bottle onto her face and breasts. Nils inserted a dildo he had brought along into her vagina and went to the bathroom to wash his hands. He glanced in at Marcia to see that she had almost stopped struggling against her bonds. He picked up her keys and swipe card and left the apartment.

***

The kiss and ride drop off area of the northern subway terminal was chaos. Minivans full of harassed looking women and screaming children were careening about everywhere. She had to honk the horn of the car a couple of times to get Ing's attention. Ing bounded over to the car, deposited two large bags on the backseat and then climbed in beside Jenna. "How long will it take us to get to your country hideaway?" she asked.

It was a deliciously warm pre-summer evening so they drove with the windows down, and when there was a lull in the conversation they would blast some tunes from the radio.

"Let's talk about most awkward first dates. I'll go first. It was just after I got to America. I had the hots for one of the lads I worked with and I let him know it. He seemed to be more than game so we agreed to meet at his house. The place had a huge swimming pool and it was in a private yard so I broke the ice by proposing a naked swim. He looked a bit surprised at that but didn't say no."

"I got my gear off and was standing on the diving board waiting for him to peel off when the back door of the house opened and my boss walked into the yard. Turns out my young lad was the boss's stepson and he thought I had come by for a nice dinner with the family."

"Oh Christ, Ing! What did you do?"

"First I got down from the diving board. Then I resigned my position. Then I put my clothes on and walked to a phone booth and called a cab. Your turn."

"I've got nothing. I was going to tell you about going out when I had a big zit on the end of my nose. You win, Ing."

Chris Issak was singing "Wicked Games" when they turned onto the narrow dirt road that led to the cottage.

Ing fell silent as they drove through a dense forest of fir and pine trees that turned the bright evening sunlight into a sombre setting. After covering about half a mile, Ing quietly asked, "Are we there yet?" "Not much farther," answered Jenna with a slight smile.

They passed only one laneway that, Jenna explained, led to a cottage on the opposite side of the point from hers.

"So we can sunbathe to our hearts' content and get no nasty tan lines."

"It's very private here, Ing."

When they had travelled about a mile and a half down the road they could see bright light in the distance. Ing commented that she hadn't seen anything like this since her last near-death experience.

Jenna was chuckling at that when they emerged from the forest into what she called the cottage clearing.

Ing was astonished to leave the dark of the forest and suddenly enter a sunlit meadow almost an acre in size. The car, which had cooled down as they drove through the woods, suddenly became extremely hot as the evening sun hit it. Jenna parked right beside the cottage which was about twenty feet from the edge of the lake. A small dock with an overturned canoe on it was directly in front of the steps leading up to the porch of the cottage.

When they got out of the car, Ing immediately walked out onto the dock and examined the lake. She asked Jenna how deep the water was off the end of the dock. Jenna told her it was about nine feet. Without a word, Ing quickly undressed and made a running dive into the water. Jenna walked out on the dock and waited for her to surface.

Ing broke to the surface about ten yards from the dock, and the verbal barrage began. "You fucking bitch," she screamed. "You could have warned me that I was diving into the fucking Antarctic Ocean. Christ! You could use my nipples as towel racks. My pussy is so contracted that I'll likely become a virgin again." She splashed as she swam back to the ladder on the side of the dock. Jenna stood and laughed at her.

They hustled up the slope to the cottage. Ing spied a comforter on a sofa and wrapped it around her. "Does this place have a heat source?" she inquired, with her teeth chattering. "Go out into the sun," said Jenna. "You'll thaw out in no time." Ing went outside and Jenna busied herself with unloading things from the car and getting dinner on the go.

The meal was microwaved gourmet, purchased at a high-end store that Jenna patronized in the Woods. Ing had asked if she needed to dress for dinner and Jenna had said it would be a casual affair. Jenna set the meal out on a small table on the porch of the cottage. They sat with their knees touching. Ing wore the comforter, for a while.

Jenna had loaded the car with a considerable amount of personal possessions and some food and wine. Ing's two bags, it turned out, contained various bottles of liquor and an array of clothes. It appeared that she could, albeit in a wrinkled state, cope with almost any occasion. "All these clothes," said Jenna, "and here you sit naked," after Ing had dumped the contents of her luggage on the floor of the great room in search of a particular bottle.

They had drunk two bottles of wine with dinner and Ing was pouring Calvados into two well-sized snifters. "Drink up, my hardy," she said. "Because you are going into that goddamned lake tonight."

Jenna smiled at her and said "Yes I will, but I'll show you how it's done. Fill our glasses and come with me."

She took Ing by the hand and led her to the deck at the back of the cottage.

Midway through the first year that they owned the cottage, Robert had insisted on the sauna. Jenna had decided that it was the best decision he had made during their marriage. They had enjoyed sitting in it, becoming super-heated, and then running out on the dock for a quick dip in the lake fed by snow-capped mountains. Jenna looked forward to initiating Ing into that pleasure.

Jenna was pleased that Ing obviously enjoyed watching her undress outside of the sauna. Once naked, she handed Ing a large white towel and the two of them entered the heat. There was a spigot on the wall that Jenna opened to spurt a dash of cold water on the heated rocks. They disappeared in the steam for a moment.

Ing was leaning well back on the pine bench, sweating and sipping her brandy. Jenna arose from her seat, pushed Ing's knees apart, and knelt in front of her. "Shift to the front of the bench," she said.

It was the first time that Jenna had tasted a woman. The initial strangeness was momentary. Jenna found herself fascinated with the delicate folds and the soft texture of Ing's labia. She became immersed in exploring Ing and was startled when Ing moaned softly.

Jenna was aware of her own arousal. She became more aroused as she paused long enough to guide Ing to raise her heels onto the edge of the bench. Jenna took full advantage of the greater access afforded her and probed Ing's vagina as deeply as her tongue would allow.

Ing's clit was erect and protruding well out of its tiny hood. Ing yelped when Jenna nibbled it and then sighed as Jenna first sucked it and then began to rhythmically lick it. Ing came quickly, raising her hips in several thrusts against Jenna's mouth.

Jenna gently moved Ing's legs off the bench, stood up and opened the door of the sauna. "Race you to the dock" she said.

Jenna ran through the deepening twilight and took a shallow dive off the end of the dock she was well out in the lake when Ing splashed into the water. Jenna swam toward her and when they were close, Ing dove under and Jenna gasped when a hand grasped one of her breasts. Ing surfaced beside her and whispered "Let's go get hot again."

They treaded water facing each other. Ing kept touching Jenna and when she began to climb the ladder to the dock Ing's hand was on her, caressing her buttocks. They stood on the dock kissing for a time, letting the humid night air warm them slowly. Then Ing knelt and Jenna tried to maintain her balance as Ing brought her to an orgasm.

The birds awoke Jenna on Saturday morning. She was in what she thought of as the guest room. Alone.

When she arose she put on one of the bathrobes that they kept in the room and peeked into to the other bedroom. Ing was sleeping soundly there. Jenna made a pot of coffee and went outside to drink it on the porch. The sun was shining brightly and it was already a warm day. Jenna took a chair onto the lawn, tossed aside her robe and sunbathed until Ing got up.

Ing emerged from the cottage, nude, carrying her coffee. She carried a chair out to the lawn which she placed beside Jenna's. "I need to get my sunglasses." She found them and took her seat.

"This is a bit of heaven, isn't it? Sipping finely brewed coffee in the sunshine, looking at a beautiful lake, with my privates still tingling from last night."

Jenna made a sound of agreement and Ing continued "I was surprised by last night. In a lovely way. You didn't have to do that, Jenna. Just because I like to go both ways doesn't mean you have to."

"I wanted to, Ing. I have a lot of curiosity about being with a woman. Last night was amazing."

"So now your curiosity is satisfied?"

"Now my curiosity is piqued."

"Good answer, Jenna!"

They sipped their coffee in silence until Ing asked "So. How are we going to top yesterday"?

"Let's talk about that after I run some errands in town."

It was a very small town with about 11,000 people in the off-season. Jenna had only seen the place in the May to October part of the year. She thought it must be extremely desolate in the winter.

A year before, when she and Robert were having a rough patch she had spent quite a bit of time at the cottage. The executor of her father's will wound up the estate by selling a couple of her Dad's small businesses and she had received a check for a few thousand dollars. She had decided to open an account at the local savings and loan branch and had put the money there.

Jenna went into the branch and found the assistant manager to whom she had spoken on the phone earlier in the week. She signed a few papers and then was shown into a tiny room near the vault. The assistant manger gave her a key and waited to ensure that Jenna could unlock and lock the safety deposit box that she had rented and then left the room.

Jenna quickly opened the carry-all that she had brought with her and loaded the money that Gerta had left for her into the safety deposit box. Or most of it. Jenna stashed $20,000 of it in what she hoped was a safe place back at home. She assured herself that the box was securely locked and called the assistant manager who placed it in the vault. She was in and out of the branch in less than twenty minutes.

Her next stop was the hardware/department store that seemed to carry a bit of every kind of merchandise imaginable. She bought the smallest fireproof strong box they had, one with a combination lock, and when she got back to her car, she sat and carefully read the instructions on how to set the combination. She did a trial run and it opened without a problem, so Jenna put the box of discs that Gerta had entrusted to her, as well as the key of the safe deposit box into the safe and locked it. She felt a sense of relief as she drove back to the cottage.

Ing had found and inflated one of the air mattresses and was lying on the dock. She must have been dozing because she started when Jenna greeted her. Ing remarked that it was so hot she was actually thinking of going into "Lake Icefloe". "Give me a minute and I'll join you," said Jenna.

Jenna retrieved her carry-all, which now held the mini-safe and went into the cottage. There was a cranny in the bottom of the corner kitchen cupboard that she and Robert had said they should do something about. She was now glad they hadn't because the safe fit back there perfectly and was invisible unless someone were to lay on their belly with the upper part of their body deep in the cupboard as Jenna was doing. Her chores done, Jenna undressed and joined Ing in the sunlight.

Chapter Nine

The library raid went accordingly to plan. It was a Sunday and the library was closed. In a cost-saving measure, on-site security had been scrapped in the early '80s. Some of the old guard had thought that to be a very bad idea but nearly a decade had gone by without an incident, so they had stopped carping about it.

Stewart moved from place to place in the IT room, giving clear instructions to Nils' team. Nils had grilled Stewart mercilessly on how long each phase of the process would take. As he watched, first seconds and then minutes were being shaved off the estimated times.

A section of Nils' men were devoted to the demolition aspect of the operation. They were placing various chemical devices around the room, installing fuses and one man was using a very powerful electric drill to bore through the wall of the room. Once his first hole was completed, Nils led him outside of the room and showed where to bore through the outside wall of the library.

When the drilling was done, the drill was stowed back in one of the vans and its operator began to run detonation cord from the parking lot across the floor of the computer classroom into the IT equipment room. It was very hot inside the building because the air conditioning had been shut off while the library was closed.

A man immaculately dressed in the uniform of the local police force was watching the sweating ex-Bundeswehr engineer performing his task. "Hot enough for you?" he asked. The engineer told him to fuck himself and Nils remarked that the 'cop' was a pretty mouthy insurance policy.

A full thirty minutes ahead of schedule, sixteen cartons were stacked carefully by the service door, everything in the IT room looked exactly as it had when Nils' team had arrived, and it was time to go. Except that a herd of kids had descended on the parking lot and were skateboarding on the slope to the rear of building.

Nils beckoned to the 'cop', "Get rid of them," he said.

The uniformed man walked into the parking lot like Moses confronting the Red Sea. He bellowed at the kids. "I'll have all your parents fined five hundred bucks because you little fuckers are all trespassers." They scattered like sheep confronted by a pack of wolves.

Once the kids had cleared off, a motorcycle was unloaded from one of the vans. Nils' team worked quickly, loading and securing the cartons in the vehicles under the supervision of Stewart. He fussed about having the cartons well protected with movers' mats. The cartons were placed in them.

While his men worked, Nils quickly changed into leathers and lit a cigarette. The vans rolled off and as his cigarette burned down, he kicked his ride to life and casually leaned down and touched his butt to the bit of det cord protruding from the outer wall of the library. When he was sure it was burning, he torqued out of the parking lot to a street on a hill five blocks from the building.

He was gratified to see a bit of smoke emerge from the air vent on the roof of the library. He waited until he heard the sirens of the fire trucks approaching. Then kicked the bike into life and took off at a sedate pace to his next task.

***

It had been a quiet day for the 911 call centre and the bored operators were nearing the end of their shift. A call came in reporting a fire at the library in the Woods. The usual dispatch procedure was followed and the call centre people listened to their scanner with only half attention. They became more focused when the fire officer at the fire began calling in special units from outside of the area. They got very interested when he began talking about white phosphorous hazards in the burning building. One of the call centre staff who had done a couple of tours in Vietnam wondered out loud what the hell a library was doing with 'willie peter' on the premises.

The shift was about to leave when a call came in from a pay phone at the airport. A male caller with an accent told the centre, quickly and clearly, that a woman was in distress at a specific address and hung up. The man spoke so quickly that the call centre staff had to replay the recording of the call to be sure of the address. Police were notified.

They had difficulty with the shift change because another call came in reporting a fire at an auto wrecker's yard that stored old car tires for disposal. That turned into a three-alarm situation. Some of the call centre staff were very pleased to have earned overtime pay.

***

Arnon guessed he was experiencing a mild panic attack. It had been twelve months since he and his wife had separated. Today, this afternoon, in an hour, he would be picking up a woman to go on a date. Arnon had not been on a date in 25 years.

He was shaved more smoothly than he had been for years. He had done a double brush of his teeth and had a roll of breath mints by his keys so he would not forget to put them in his pocket. He had even broken out a new stick of deodorant. And he had put on some of the cologne that had been collecting dust on his dresser for years.

He had reasoned that he should dress casually for an afternoon date to see a movie. Arnon realized that he had two types of clothing. The suits he wore to work and what he thought of as his slob clothes, he wore at all other times. In preparation for the date he had had to buy a new pair of jeans and some T-shirts. The current price of jeans had left him astonished.

Teresa looked great to Arnon when she opened her front door. Arnon had only seen her in uniform or business attire. She was wearing capris, sandals and a sleeveless blouse that Arnon thought fitted her well. Clearly, as one of his male colleagues had said, she had the best rack in the Victims' Services branch of the department. She offered him a beer.

"That would be great." Arnon enjoyed watching her walk to the kitchen. He was standing looking a glass case holding some figurines when Teresa came back with the beers. She sat them on a coffee table and took a seat on a big sofa. Nick realized that she expected him to sit on the sofa with her. He thought the day was going well.

"So you collect figurines?"

"They were my mother's. When I was clearing out her apartment after she died, I hated to throw them out. I had a crappy poster hanging there so I nixed it, got out my drill and put up the showcase. They've grown on me."

"You have a drill?"

"I'm a single mom with a house to look after, Nick. I've got a lot of tools." Arnon thought that was very cool.

"This movie we're going to see. It's about sheep?"

"You don't read entertainment magazines, do you, Nick?"

"Not since I was about sixteen."

"We're going to 'Silence of the Lambs'. It's about serial killers. Got some good stuff about the FBI profilers."

"Really? It sounds great."

"Nick. I've worked around you off-and-on for over five years. Did you really think now that you've finally asked me out, that I'd be cruel enough to drag you to a chick flick?"

All Arnon heard of that sentence was "now that you've finally asked me out."

He was thinking hard about what to say next when his pager went off. Both he and Teresa sat looking at it clipped to Arnon's belt. Arnon said "I better answer the fucking thing," at the same moment that Teresa said "I guess you'd better answer the fucking thing."

It was Crane. He was on his way to pick Arnon up. As the duty detective for the weekend he was listening to a scanner. The library in the Woods was burning. Arnon said he would be waiting for him in the parking lot of a mall that was near Teresa's place.

He was very apologetic about the change in plans and even tried to make a joke about seeing the 'sheep movie' a little later. Teresa was very good about the cancelled date, but Arnon knew that she was disappointed. She agreed to a rain check. Arnon promised to call her as soon as he could.

Crane pulled into the mall parking lot in a marked cruiser a few minutes after Arnon had parked. Smart kid, thought Arnon. We'll get across security lines and parked a whole lot faster in a car with lights and sirens.

Crane gave Arnon a couple of looks when he first got in the cruiser.

"What's with you, Crane?"

"Never seen you in anything but a suit. Those are really cool jeans you're wearing."

"I needed jeans so I bought these. Something wrong with them, detective?"

"Hell, no. They're top of the line."

"Any other observations you'd care to make?"

"Not a one."

Arnon and Crane were surprised to find that police had closed off the street a full two blocks away from the library. When Crane told the uniformed cop who was standing at the line to the lift the tape, he got a negative. "This is the fire chief's show and he said absolutely nothing on wheels gets past this point. He said even if one of his guys needs an ambulance, the meat wagon stops here and the EMS folks have to walk in with a gurney. Sorry, guys."

They parked the cruiser and walked down the street toward the fire. A group of men in suits were standing under a shade tree at the corner of the first block. Arnon recognized some of the men from the meeting they had had with the FBI and State Department types. He and Crane joined them.

The men nodded as they approached. "Anybody know why the fire department is keeping us so far back?" asked Arnon. One of the FBI guys handed Arnon a pair of binoculars. "Take a look at the line where the wall joins the roof just to the left of where the hoses are working," he said.

It took Arnon a few seconds to find the spot on the wall and focus the binos. He had to look twice to understand what he was seeing. He whistled softly and handed the glasses to Crane.

"Those fucking bricks are melted. What the fuck did they have in that place?"

"It's the computer equipment room and classroom that's burning. The fire captain says he and one of his guys who were both in the service are pretty damn sure that at least two white phosphorous grenades have detonated in there. You guys have your bomb squad on route to sweep the area. Nobody but fire and bomb people get any closer than this until the area is pronounced clear," said the FBI guy.

"Somebody really didn't want us to exercise our search warrant," said Crane.

Arnon wished he had not said that.

It was turned out to be four hours before the fire was considered out and the bomb squad had deemed the grounds and building safe. Arnon, Crane and the federal people went to a café patio that was open and sipped coffee while they waited to be told they could do their jobs. Arnon sat next to an FBI agent named Jim Curtiss.

At first their conversation was forced, but then Curtiss lightened up a bit. He asked a few questions about the area and told Arnon and Crane that he had never been in California before. They told him about the nearby beaches and slightly more distant desert that were all worth seeing. Then Curtiss asked if there was some sort of air museum nearby.

Crane arose from his chair and pointed to Arnon. "This guy is a walking encyclopedia on aircraft and can tell you all about the local museum. I've heard about it already so I think I'll go play in the traffic or something."

"Are you interested in planes?" Arnon asked Jim.

"Sort of. Every heard of Glenn Curtiss?"

"Hell, yes," said Arnon.

"He was my great grandfather. I understand that the museum here has one of the aircraft his company built that's still in flying condition."

Arnon enjoyed the next two hours as they waited for clearance to enter the library. By the time they were told they could go to work, he and Jim had bonded. He promised Jim not only a look at, but a ride in the rear seat of the Curtiss JN-4 'Jenny' that they had restored.

Arnon and the others were surprised to see some of the fire department vehicles being rapidly packed up. They had decided to go back to the parking lot and were delayed in getting there because three of the pumpers that had been fighting the fire went roaring off, lights flashing and sirens wailing. "What's going on with those guys?" Arnon asked a firefighter who was standing by a roaring generator.

The fireman pointed off to the northwest and Arnon and Curtiss turned to see a giant spire of black smoke angrily climbing into the sky. "What the fuck is that?" asked Arnon.

"A tire recycling depot. It's gonna be a long fucking day," said the firefighter.

The library was in a very sorry state. The lobby and the reading room had taken a lot of smoke and water damage. The hung ceiling had been mostly pulled down by the fire fighters and the fire investigation team was swarming the place. One of the fire lieutenants called Arnon and Curtiss over to a spot near the outer wall of the classroom.

He pointed out a hole that had been drilled in the wall and a narrow dark burn mark that ran across the floor of the room. "Det cord," he said. "There's arson, and then there's God damn arson. This is Jesus H. Christ God damn fucking arson."

The computer equipment room was still off limits to them. The fire department had used foam to suppress the burning phosphorous and it would be days before they had neutralized every bit of the stuff. Curtiss said that it was a good way to keep a crime scene from being investigated.

Crane appeared at Arnon's side and it was apparent that he wanted to talk privately. He and Arnon casually moved away from the rest of the people and Crane pointed to the door that led from the lobby of the library into the computer area. It had had the hell bashed out of it.

"I asked around among the smok- eaters," said Crane. "The door was firmly secured when they entered the building. They had to break in with their axes. It's a card swipe lock."

"Anybody from the library here that can tell us about their security system?" asked Arnon.

"It's a city employee. One of our uniforms is on his way to his home to pick him up and bring him here."

"Good work, Crane. I'm going out to the parking lot on the east side of the building to get away from this smell. When your guy arrives, bring him there."

Arnon found Curtiss talking with some of his other agents. "Would you gentlemen take a good look at that door and then join me outside?" Once they were in the fresh air, Arnon explained what Crane had observed. He thought the FBI guys were impressed with their police work.

***

The 911 operator who took the call about a woman in distress was worried. Some major shit was going down with a fire in the same area and it took her a while to find an officer who could respond. It was a full thirty minutes after the call that a patrol car parked in front of Marcia's building and an officer knocked on the door of her apartment. The officer was very new to the force and when the door was not answered, he called his shift supervisor for instructions.

By the time a second, more experienced officer arrived, several people who lived in the building had gathered in the hall outside Marcia's apartment. Eventually, the super of the building came home from the bar he had been visiting and opened the door with his passkey. The older police officer directed the younger cop to stay at the door and keep everyone out. When he entered Marcia's bedroom, he was glad that he was alone.

He used his portable radio to call in an ambulance and crime scene team. The cop had a daughter in her mid twenties. What he saw in Marcia's room made him want to puke.

***

The drive back from the cottage was very different for Jenna. In the past when she and Robert had made that trip together, it was usually a time of rising stress as Robert talked about work commitments and things that he needed to get done at home. In her head Jenna had created the ten mile rule. On the least successful weekends, any sense of peace that she had achieved while at the cottage was gone by the time they had driven ten miles toward home.

The ten mile mark came and went and Jenna was content to watch the road and listen to Ing tell her about the book she was reading. It was a history by Byron Farwell titled "Queen Victoria's Little Wars." She learned that Ing was interested in the colonial history of Africa. Jenna remarked that she was surprised that Ing had left Africa to live in the States. Ing's reaction to Jenna's comment was fast and fierce.

"I like to read about Africa a hundred years ago, Jenna. But since 1948 South Africa has been an ever deepening shit hole."

"What happened in 1948?"

"That's when the fucking Boers manipulated their way into political power. That's when the country started down to the road to apartheid and made racism a virtue. That's when the new laws started to be enacted that divided the South Africans into blacks and whites and coloureds and honourary whites."

"What the hell is a honourary white?"

"It was a non-white, a Japanese person for example, who, for international political reasons, couldn't be treated in the deplorable way that other coloureds, Chinese for example, were treated. "

"That's crazy!"

"South Africa is crazy. The government is comprised of crazy men who in turn drove the rest of the country crazy."

"How bad was it to live there?"

"By the time I was 16 Jenna, it was bloody awful. By then, vast amounts of people had been forcibly moved to Bantustans. It was against the law for any of the four designated racial groups to have sexual relations with anyone from another racial group. By then, the country was a total police state."

"I turned 16 in 1979. By then the UmKhonto we Sizwe or MK, the armed wing of the African National Congress, was blowing up railways and electrical stations on a weekly basis. The South African Defence Force was out trying to stop them. And the police were running amok."

"I had gotten into a graphic design program in college in Johannesburg. There were always local artists displaying their work on the sidewalk outside of the college and some of them were really good. A lot of the stuff I've done in my work was inspired by the native art and designs I saw displayed there."

"One of the artists was a black man named Benjamin. I used to have long conversations with him about art. A couple of times cops came along and told me to move on because white girls shouldn't be seen talking to blacks for long periods of time."

"You're not joking, are you?"

"I was talking to Benjamin one late afternoon when a horde of police vans came screaming into the street and dozens of cops descended on us. All of the street artists and several people talking to them were grabbed and tossed into paddy wagons. I was one of three whites who were grabbed. The other two were guys."

"I ended up in a van with three black detainees and two big white cops. They made me sit on the bench between them and speaking Afrikaans, they said they wouldn't let the black boys touch my anties or my cuiter. That would be my boobs and cunt. I was scared shitless."

"When we got to police building we were taken inside and put into cells. I ended up in a cell alone because I was the only white female in custody. I cooled my heels there for an hour and then a cop came to take me to another room. I had had some time to think, so when the cell door opened, I refused to come out and demanded that I be allowed to phone my parents. The cop said that prisoners suspected of having dagga, that's what we called marijuana, didn't get to make phone calls until they had been searched and processed. I told him to fuck himself. Not the smartest thing to say in hindsight, but I was only sixteen."

"Two cops came into the cell, grabbed my arms and dragged me down a hall to a room where a great big old Boer matron was waiting. The only things in the room other than the big matron were a cart with a few things on it and a medical exam table with stirrups. The cops said that the matron was going to conduct a full search of me and told me that if I cooperated they would leave the room. That's when I made a second bad decision."

"I twisted out of the grip of one cop and bit the other one who was still holding me on his wrist. I was surprised when the matron waded into the fray and drove her fist into my gut. While I was trying to get my breath back, two more cops came into the room and in short order they stripped me and the four guys manhandled me onto the exam table and held my feet in the stirrups. I got to listen to them making comments about my poes, my pussy, while the matron took her own sweet time carefully looking through my clothes to make sure they weren't concealing any drugs."

"You may be surprised at this Jenna, but I was still a virgin at 16. I lost my cherry that night to a fifty something year old police woman."

Ing sat silently for several moments. Jenna was trying to think of something to say when Ing resumed her story.

"The matron slathered on some sort of thick lubricant and shoved two of her great big fat fingers into me. I had my eyes closed so I didn't have to see the cops staring at what she was doing to me with her hands. I thought nothing worse could happen but then she shoved a finger up my ass and rolled it around for a while. She finally pronounced my orifices to be free of contraband and the cops let go of me. The matron told me to get dressed and they all left the room."

"Oh God, Ing! I am so sorry!"

"When the cops and matron left the room, they rolled the cart out with them. There was nothing in there to clean up with. I was wearing a bra and T-shirt and a pair of panties and light grey stretch pants that day. I dressed but the fucking lube they had used soaked through my panties and pants immediately. And I was bleeding a bit. It took them three hours to process me in a police station with what seemed like hundreds of male cops around. That was the night, Jenna, that I made the decision to get the fuck out of South Africa just as soon as I could."

"What did your parents do? Did they sue the police department?"

"You don't understand how South Africa works, Jenna. Benjamin, the street artist that I often talked with turned out to be a trainee for the MK. About three months after my visit to the police station, he was killed by the South African air force at a training camp. My parents went to a lawyer who told them to get control of their daughter or she could expect far worse things to happen to her. He told them that body cavity searches of troublesome people was a common weapon in the police arsenal. My mom said that once the lawyer heard what had happened, he was reluctant to even talk to them."

"Christ, Ing! It must have been terrible."

"I was a good girl for the next four years. I drove myself at school. I knew exactly which American company I wanted into and when I was twenty they were bloody glad to recruit me. Once I was in, I made myself invaluable to them. And then I started to take some shots at the South African government again. The Americans were profit minded and they knew I was making them money. I did something really outrageous and they decided to fast track me to L.A. before the police came and grabbed their star artist."

"What did you do?"

"That's a story for another time, my friend. But what I will tell you now is that I made a vow not long after the night in the police station. I have told myself that my body is mine, I will enjoy it, and nothing I chose to do with my body will make me ashamed. I had to make that vow, Jenna, or shrivel into nothingness. You're becoming a good friend. You needed to know that."

They covered several miles before Jenna spoke. "I'm so glad that we have become friends, Ing."

"So am I. I look forward to hearing what vows Jenna Van Velt has made to herself. Because I know you have. And I'm going to be very much in your life as you sort out whatever shit your Aunt has gotten you into. The South African government was out of control for a long time, Jenna. They probably developed nuclear weapons in the 70's. God knows what your Aunt was involved in."

"Hopefully your friend Tom will read the diaries and tell us."

"He most certainly will. Of course Tom Robbins is a totally colonialist bastard," Ing said. "I can't believe that I let a mercenary killer like him fuck me nearly senseless." She was quiet for a moment and then giggled. "Actually I can believe it. He is a truly marvellous fuck, Jenna. If the opportunity presents, let him boff you. Trust me. It will be well worth your while. If you want a really different experience, make the two-backed beast with him. Just don't regard it as more than an intensive experience. Sort of like a ride on a really, really extreme roller coaster."

Jenna didn't swerve off the road, but she did say, "What the hell are you talking about, Ing?"

"Tom. He seems like a nice, laid back guy. Kind of thoughtful and sweet. And he certainly can be all of that. But when you two get together to read your Aunties diaries, never forget that he was a Selous Scout."

"What the hell is a Selous Scout?"

"Ask him. But he won't tell you much. I had to do some digging at the library once I saw his tattoo of the bird and got a bunch of evasive shit from him. They were an anti-terrorist unit in Rhodesian when Ian Smith was trying to hang onto the place for the whites. Very deadly. Very elite. Sort of Green Berets on steroids. Only with way less rules to follow than the Green Berets did. Utter, murderous bastards if you were the unlucky people that they were trained to hunt and kill."

"So he went to Rhodesia to be a mercenary?"

"No," said Ing. "And the story of how he got there is one of his redeeming features. And so fucking sad. He'll have to tell you that bit, Jenna. I promised him that I wouldn't repeat what he told me, and I do keep promises."

They made the rest of the drive in silence and Ing was quick to grab her bags when Jenna dropped her at the transit station. "Call me when you can, my friend," she said, and disappeared down the stairs to the subway.

Jenna was relieved to find the house empty. Robert had scrawled, "Okay with me" across the list of things that she had indicated that she wanted to take from the house. As she expected, all of the documents required for listing the house had been neatly signed and dated. Robert was big on paper work being done in a timely and accurate fashion.

***

Arnon was standing in the library parking lot with some of the feds when Crane brought a very sweaty, pudgy guy in a loud golf shirt to them. "This is Mister Juarez," said Crane. "He is a security officer for the city and can let us have a look at the logs here at the library."

The man was in a sorry state. He had smelled like he might have been opening his tenth or eleventh beer when his phone rang. He was ill at ease, very aware that he was a junior security guy surrounded by cops, and not looking good. He started to explain that he had been off for the weekend and … but Jim Curtiss cut him short.

"We're very sorry to have interrupted your time off. There's been a crisis here that requires your specific knowledge and we can't thank you enough for coming in."

The pudgy little guy straightened up a bit at that and led Curtiss, Arnon and about six others through a couple of locked doors. He opened a tiny room that housed a small desk and chair, some metal boxes, a lot of wires, and a keyboard and a small TV monitor. "What time period to you want me to check for swipe card history?" he asked.

"Let's start with the last twelve hours," one of the Feds said.

For a man who was likely well over the legal limit, the guy was pretty efficient. He had little hands with fat fingers but he knew how to work a keyboard. He very quickly brought some data up on to the screen of the monitor. There were just three lines of information.

"Joe, the janitor, swiped in at seven this morning and swiped out four hours later at eleven. That's the normal routine," said Juarez.

"Marcia swiped in at one and is still in the lab," he pronounced.

Arnon was reflecting on the fact that the guy was so drunk that he hadn't noticed the fire engines, the acrid smells and the flashing lights.

"Who is Marcia?" asked a guy from the FBI.

"One of the students with Masters level access," was the quick reply from Juarez. He was getting comfortable and beckoned his audience closer to the monitor. "See, this eleven digit number is her swipe card code. It has an "st" suffix which means student. I've met her a couple of times. She's a nice girl."

"And you say she's still in the lab?" said one of the agents.

"Yep. She hasn't swiped out and we have a 99.9 percent compliance rate with regard to card access for the computer lab. There's a lot of very sensitive and expensive equipment in there. They have stuff in there that NASA and Harvard don't have. If Marcia swiped in she would have for sure swiped out."

"Thanks very much for your help on this," said Arnon. "We appreciate you coming in and Detective Crane will arrange for you to get home. Just one last thing, do you have a log of all the people with swipe cards? For example, can you give us an address for this Marcia?"

The man typed briefly and in a few seconds had brought more data up on the monitor. He rhymed off an address and telephone number for the student named Marcia Wilson. Crane observed that her home was within easy walking distance of the library.

The firefighters and the bomb squad were beginning to bring bits and pieces from the IT room out into the parking lot and bright lights had been set up to examine them. Most of the feds were gravitating to that unfolding activity. Arnon, Curtiss and Crane decided to take a walk through the business area of the Woods to Ms. Marcia Wilson's apartment.

The three men pulled up quickly when they rounded the corner to Marcia's street and saw what seemed to be waves of yellow tape and a constellation of flashing lights. "I don't fucking believe this," said Crane.

"I do," said Arnon. "In a week this place has gone from littering and noise complaints to an exquisitely premeditated murder and an arson conducted with near military precision. Any guesses as to what awaits us in that building down the street that is likely the home of Marcia Wilson?"

"Probably not much," said Jim Curtiss, breaking into a run. "That ambulance is pulling away with lights and sirens. Somebody better get on whoever is in there before a lot of evidence gets destroyed. I'm heading for the building."

Arnon would have liked to have stayed with Curtiss at the crime scene, but he instinctively knew he'd be more effective if he followed the victim. He made a hand motion for Crane to follow Curtiss and approached a cruiser with a uniformed officer that didn't seem to be doing much. Arnon showed him who he was and told the young cop that he should do what it would take to catch up to and pace the recently departed ambulance. The kid was one hell of a driver and they arrived at the hospital in convoy.

***

Nils was very satisfied with all that his team had done. Some of the carefully packed boxes that Stuart had taken care of would be dispatched from LAX. Others would be trucked and flown from O'Hare. A few would cross the border at Detroit/Windsor and eventually leave from Canada's Pearson International Airport.

Nils had scouted out the tire dump at the auto wrecker's weeks before. The compound was partially surrounded by an old board fence. After leaving the library, it took him only minutes to ride to the tire depot and light a fuse that he had run out under the fence. Once the fuse was lit, he rode to a hillside gas station with a pay phone. As he dialed the international number to make his obligatory call to Winter, he heard the first pop of a gasoline cache explode in the depot.

Karl was at first terse until he heard that all had gone well. Nils was evasive when Karl asked what he would do next. They went back and forth a bit and finally Karl put it on the table. "Your trips to Indonesia could become an embarrassment. Everyone from the CIA to the militant Islamic groups is watching out for exploitative whites there."

"Fuck you," said Nils.

Chapter Ten

Southern Ontario, Canada

Tom was very tired he landed at Pearson Airport, but felt some energy return once he was clear of the Toronto traffic. The past two weeks had been dangerous and demanding. His legs were still covered with cuts and scrapes from trekking through the Philippines jungle. He was looking forward to spending a few hours in the little lakeside town near where he had grown up.

It was through Tom's fascination with the history of Elgin County and the lakeshore the he met Audrey Shuttleworth. She was an archivist and writer who had bought one of the most historically significant homes in Port Burwell. And she was a walking encyclopedia on the provenance of historically significant documents.

Tom first met her when he was in high school. Audrey had come to his class to give an hour-long presentation on local history. Her garb was classic 1969 and her hair was Farrah Fawcett meets Janis Joplin. They bonded intellectually as only two people who were passionately interested in the same subject could.

It took Tom three hours to drive from Pearson airport out to the little village of Port Burwell. He had driven from Pearson International airport to his meeting with a local realtor with a feeling of great expectation. When his business was done he was eager to visit Audrey Shuttleworth.

She heard him open the gate and turned to see who had entered her yard. It was just after the noon hour and the sun was high. She had to shade her eyes to see him. "Welcome back Tom," she said. "How long will you grace Elgin County with your presence this time?"

"A few hours at most. I think I've bought the Penton land."

"Wonderful news!" exclaimed Audrey. "I know how much you've wanted it. Not as much as I've wanted you to get it. Once it's in your hands there will be no fucking cookie cutter cottages or factory farms going in there."

"The realtor said my last offer would be accepted. He's supposed to be getting the Pentons' signatures late today. If all goes well, I can meet with him tonight and I'll have myself a few hundred acres of trees and sand."

"And two kilometres of wonderful beach, Tom. Don't forget the beach. Are you going to let the naturists continue to use it?" she asked.

"One can't go against nature."

"Very true," said Audrey with a grin. "And they will make your walks along the beach so much more interesting."

"You might want to use that beach yourself," suggested Tom.

"Silly man. I've been a regular out there for years. With the right sunglasses and my hair up, people have no idea who they are looking at."

"When I called I mentioned that a few crates would be arriving from France. Is it still okay if you stash them here?" asked Tom.

"Certainly. There is plenty of room in the back storeroom. There's nothing in them that will explode or cause widespread epidemics, is there?"

"I had all the plutonium, the weapons grade stuff at least, sent to a friend with an appropriately lead-lined garage."

"Very wise, Tom. We wouldn't want one of Port Burwell's most historic homes suddenly glowing in the dark."

"One of the crates is marked 'For Audrey'. Have the delivery guys loosen off the lid before they leave. It's full of documents that I would like you to sell for me. Hopefully we'll both make some money from them. I wish I could stay but I have to be back in L.A. in two days."

"That's too bad. How much of the summer are you going to miss?"

"All of it. One of the purchase conditions was that the Pentons get to stay in the place until after Labour Day. It was an easy concession to make since the earliest I could get back here would be mid-August."

***

Arnon was relieved that the ambulance had been routed to a smaller suburban hospital. He was used to arriving at the emergency entrances of the inner city institutions. This place did not resemble the abattoirs of its downtown counterparts.

The rear doors of the ambulance swung open and a female EMS worker and a female cop climbed out. Arnon stepped up to them with his badge in his hand. "Chief Detective Arnon. Is this woman Marcia Williams?"

The EMS woman was clearly pissed that some guy was interfering with her doing her job. She let the cop respond to Arnon as she sent about unlocking the stretcher. The young female cop indicated that it was very likely it was Marcia Williams on the stretcher.

The woman on the stretcher was covered in a sheet and heavy blanket. She was awake, but when Arnon got a close look at her, her eyes seemed to be rolling around in her head. He was relieved to see no obvious trauma to her face.

"What's your name, officer?" asked Arnon.

"Cole, sir, Anne Cole."

"Okay, Officer Cole. This woman is part of homicide investigation. We need to ensure that everything that happens from here on in is done totally by the book. Rules of evidence procedures are to be followed in a religious way. What can you tell me?"

"I was on routine patrol, sir. Dispatch called me to say a female officer was needed at Elm Street out in the Woods. I was the closest, so I took it. Got there just as this woman was being loaded in the ambulance. They told me to stay on her like glue."

"Is that all you know?" asked Arnon.

"The EMS says that when they arrived, there were coppers all over the place. A CSI team was working the bedroom where the victim was and they wouldn't let them in to get her for nearly an hour. The EMS folks were allowed to check vital signs and when they said she was in no danger, they got ordered out of the room for a while."

"How are the EMS folks feeling about this?"

"They're pissed, sir. The victim was naked, tied spread eagle to the bed. Cindy, that's the EMS woman, said the room reeked of semen. She thinks this has been a major gang rape. And clearly, sir, the victim has been heavily drugged."

"Okay. Thank you, Cole. Let's make sure this gets done right."

They ensured that Marcia Williams was given all the medical attention she needed. Which wasn't much. Aside from some minor chaffing on her wrists and ankles where she had been bound, there were no obvious physical injuries.

The doctor on the case was most concerned about her drugged state. He drew blood, and with Arnon's hearty support backed up by the chief of police after a couple of phone calls, ordered a whole range of analysis. The doctor also did the most thorough rape kit process that Arnon had ever seen.

All of the evidence was sent for processing and Arnon and Officer Cole sat down to wait.

***

Jenna put in her day at work, not very productively, but became energized when she pulled into the parking garage of her new home. The building was quiet, so she was able to load up her belongings in the elevator and in three trips had her car empty.

She enjoyed the process of unwrapping lamps and pictures and setting them near the places where they would eventually reside. The case holding Gerta's diaries and photos went into the walk-in closet off the master bedroom. Jenna piled a bunch of comforters and sheets over it.

She had felt a rising sense of expectation since she and Robert had tacitly decided to separate. Inside her new apartment, she felt safe but ungrounded. The whole thing with Ing at the cottage made no sense to her.

Way to go, Jenna, she thought. You spend years in a girl's school without a single lesbian encounter, and then suddenly at age thirty, you're jumping on a young woman at your summer cottage. With great results for both of you, by the way."

Once the car was unloaded, there was no reason for Jenna to hang around the apartment. She reluctantly locked up the place and made the drive back out to the Woods. She felt strange entering the house that she had already psychologically moved out of. And felt silly when she realized she could have simply stayed downtown.

The message light was flashing on her answering machine. There were several messages. A couple of her friends wanted her to join them for drinks. The mover confirmed that he would be able to take her furniture to her new apartment in two days. The last message was from St. Peter's hospital.

"Hello Jenna," said a woman with a strong Latino accent. "It's Juanita. We're full up with children and really hope you can give us some evenings. We've got some scared, lonely kids here who would love it if you would come read to them. Call me please."

Two years earlier Jenna had taken an advanced Spanish course. Her conversational Spanish was quite good, but she had felt that her reading was getting rusty. The instructor of the course had persuaded her and two other students to volunteer to read storybooks to children in St. Pete's hospital.

St. Pete's had been built before the end of World War I and had fallen upon hard times. Practically all of its patients were immigrants from Mexico and other parts of Central America. English was spoken there, but not by many. Jenna had thought she would hate her volunteering there, but went rather than piss off her instructor. The course had been over for eighteen months and Jenna was still a regular reader.

Juanita's message gave her a pang of guilt. She had not been to the hospital for over two weeks. By habit, she moved to the whiteboard where she and Robert had noted appointments and out of town travel. Then she laughed at herself and dialed the number for the nursing station of the children's floor. She left a message for Juanita saying that she would be there the next evening.

After she had been going to the hospital for several months she noticed that Robert became testy when she was there for an evening. In one of their rare heated arguments, Robert had made it clear that he thought her volunteerism was misguided. The argument had ended when Robert had suggested that it might be more appropriate for her to give her time to someone other than a bunch of 'wetbacks' kids." Jenna had told him to fuck himself. And had begun to schedule her volunteerism on evenings when Robert was travelling on business.

Jenna had been given bright orange adhesive tags to put on all of the furniture that was to be moved to her apartment. She had marked everything on the main floor that was to go and went upstairs to do the same there. Robert had agreed that she could take the bedroom suite in the master bedroom. Jenna was about to start placing tags on the items and then reconsidered. Do I really want to move the bed that Robert and I have been making love in to my new place? she asked herself. The furniture was left untagged. Jenna went downstairs, poured a glass of wine, and looked up some furniture companies downtown that would deliver.

***

Marcia Wilson started to come out of her drug-addled haze in about three hours. By that time, a female detective from the sex crimes branch was on the scene. Arnon was content to let her and Officer Cole conduct the initial interview. They were about to enter Wilson's room when Detective Crane arrived.

Crane and Arnon went outside of the hospital and found an area where they could smoke. It was a hot, humid night and Crane predicted a thunderstorm before morning. Arnon grunted his agreement.

"The CSIs are still at the scene and likely will be for some time," began Crane. "Marty Stiller is in charge. That guy cracks me up. Once the victim had been taken away he said that there was enough semen on the bed for it to have come from seven guys or one average sized elephant."

"Marty's mouth is gonna get him in trouble some day when a reporter manages to get within earshot," observed Arnon.

"No sign of forced entry. No sign of a struggle. One wine glass with some dregs in it."

"Did the place look like a party had happened?" asked Arnon.

"Nope. Ms. Wilson isn't much of a housekeeper, so the place was untidy, but it certainly didn't look like a place where half a football team had held a gangbang. There were no keys, no key ring and no swipe card for the computer lab to be found."

"Knock me over with a feather," Arnon grunted.

"Unlike the rest of the apartment, the bedroom was pretty tidy. The only piece of clothing that was visible was a woman's bathrobe," said Crane.

"So what's on your mind?" prompted Arnon.

"I'm not sure. Is it possible that she was anticipating a little bondage play with her guy, whoever he is, and he brought along some friends?"

"Anything is possible," said Arnon. "Looks to me like we're gonna have to rely pretty heavily on the CSIs and whatever our two female colleagues can get from the victim."

"They may not get much. Has anyone told you that when the first officers arrived, they found her tied spread-eagle on the bed, and tightly blindfolded?"

"Shit," said Arnon. "I had not been apprised of the little detail of the blindfold."

***

Nils was not the least bit worried about his 'desires,' as Winter called them, getting him into trouble. He was not a careless sex tourist like the weedy American school teachers and the fat European businessmen who frequented Bangkok. Nils' flight to Thailand took him to Bangkok International airport, but he did not linger in the city.

For a premium price by the going Thai standards, one could have a very different experience than the more pedestrian sex tourists. Nils was not one to skimp when it came to his luxuries. For what he considered a pittance, he could avail himself of the services of Danny Trah. Danny billed himself as the best purveyor of human flesh that was unripe and unwilling.

Danny regarded Nils as one of his demanding customers. Nils had very specific requirements which sent Danny out on pre-visit reconnaissance trips. He knew that he would need to find a sister/sister, brother/brother, or brother/sister combination to serve his client's wishes. And as always, Danny had several prospects on line.

At first Nils' visit went flawlessly. His driver delivered Nils to Danny. The man was affable and relaxed as they drove out to a town where Danny had a strong body of henchmen and where there was a great presence of Vietnamese people. Danny and Nils shared a deep appreciation of the Vietnamese bone structure. Nils selected a boy of about fifteen who was walking through the market with his sister who was about two years younger. Danny was about to park the truck and summon his men when Nils abruptly shifted in his seat and looked at the pager that was attached to his belt.

"Get me to a phone where I can get an International line," Nils said irritably.

Danny found such a place and after about fifteen minutes, Nils climbed back into the vehicle and said, "I need to get back to airport."

"Sure, buddy," said Danny. "No problem."

"What do I owe you for this?" asked Nils.

"No charge," said Danny. "But maybe you go for something really special next time."

"You're a fine man," said Nils. "I'll stay a little longer than usual next time, and I will very much want something special."

Danny hooked him up with one of his drivers and sat in his truck. "Sick fucking Joe."

***

Jenna had a busy noon hour. She made a whirlwind visit to a downtown furniture store where a sales lady quickly talked her out of buying a queen sized bed. She used her plastic to pay for two night tables, a dresser and a king sized bed. She left the store knowing that she had overbought and found herself wondering what Ing would think of the huge bed when she saw it.

Jenna's next stop was a bookstore that she always visited before a session at the hospital. Her visit took some time since she carefully vetted the books she took to read to the kids. She bought three books and hurried back to her office. It had taken her 15 minutes to spend over two grand on bedroom furniture, she thought, and over half an hour to buy three kids books. I guess my priorities are a bit askew.

Juanita looked very tired, and seemed to have lost weight since Jenna had last seen her. She told Jenna that three of their nurses had left to accept better paying jobs at other hospitals and explained that she had been working fifty hour weeks for the past month. She was glad to have Jenna there.

They went into a ward that held fourteen beds, all of them full. Juanita introduced her to a girl about five years old named Nina. The child was tiny for her age and she had the most incredible eyes that Jenna had ever seen. The child was lying listlessly on her bed and it was clear that she had been crying.

"Nina. My good friend Jenna has come to read you a story. Jenna doesn't have any children of her own yet so it would be gracious of you if you would be her child friend this evening."

Nina didn't respond.

"Someday I would like to have a little girl of my own as lovely as you, Nina," said Jenna. "But for now, can we go to the reading corner and look at a book together?"

Nina shifted on the bed and gave Jenna a searching look.

"Jenna is very good at reading, Nina, and she has brought a book about a bunny rabbit."

"Have you ever seen a rabbit, Nina?" asked Jenna.

"Once. When we visited my grandfather."

The story corner was a dilapidated old easy chair crammed between a storage cabinet and a fire escape door. After twenty minutes in the chair Nina was curled on Jenna's lap, paying rapt attention as they read through the book. She hadn't even noticed when Jenna had switched from speaking English to reading the Spanish text of the book. Nina reached out and placed her finger against Jenna's lips, and beckoned her to lean down to her. "When I am older, Jenna, I want to be a singer like Selena."

"Do you sing now?"

"No. I have five brothers who are pigs. When I sing they tease me. I only will sing for my father."

"You are very wise. I would only sing for my father too." The little girl sighed and turned her attention back to the book.

Juanita was still at the nursing station when Jenna came out of the ward. "I could take that little sweetheart home for keeps," said Jenna. Juanita smiled at her. "She's pretty easy to love, isn't she? She's the youngest of six. Her Dad is somewhere in Texas working on a ranch, her mom works 10 hours a day at a bakery and then does a shift at the Hilton as a chamber maid. The grandma looks after the family but isn't very mobile. Nina was admitted here three days ago with a URI infection. Her mom calls daily but hasn't been able to get to see her yet."

"What a shame. She is such a sweetie. Oh, and speaking of sweets." Jenna pulled a bag of candy she had bought and set it on the rail of the nursing station.

"Thank you so much, Jenna," said Juanita. She hesitated and then said, "I'm so sorry to hear that your Aunt passed away." Jenna made some appropriate noise and said she'd be back soon.

As she walked to her car she thought about the terms that people used to avoid the death word. 'Passed away' was of course the most commonly used phrase. Jenna mused about the term and concluded that it did not apply to her Aunt's situation. She couldn't come up with an alternative, though.

***

Arnon was keen to get started with his day. Since the Ten Haan murder he had been truly enjoying his job. He wondered if that meant he had some sort of moral compass malfunction going on.

The day began with a meeting of the police, the Feds and a team of four people from INTERTPOL. Arnon was interested in meeting Jules Forget face to face. It took the group over two hours to make introductions and to explain the roles of the various people in the room. Some procedures were hammered out, contact information was compiled and then the group broke up.

Arnon waited for Jules to finish a conversation that he was having with his INTERPOL guys and then invited him to join him outside. He had already had a quick word with Jim Curtiss. He joined Arnon and Jules when they came outside.

The two Americans brought Jules up to speed on the fire and apparently related sexual assault that they had responded to the previous day. Jules listened intently. He had obviously done his homework and read through all of the information that the police and Feds had provided to INTERPOL.

"Three dead and one injured. There must be something very big behind this outburst of mayhem," said Jules. "Krohl had more enemies than most people in the world. Some very powerful organizations would have been moving heaven and earth to see him dead. The Israelis, the Russians, the French, even some of the neo-Nazi groups would have taken great delight in arranging for his painful death."

"But it was the Ten Haan woman, not Krohl who they targeted," said Arnon. "This can't have anything to do with the shit he pulled during the war. It has to be related to the time period of 1965 to 1980."

"Agreed," said Jules. "Those fifteen years are the critical time. And whatever went on back then was extremely important to people who are much more powerful than Krohl and Ten Haan. Otherwise, the Ten Haan woman would have been tortured to death eleven years ago."

"Let's go see what Crane has for us about the Wilson woman," said Arnon.

Crane, Officer Cole and the cop from the sexual assault unit were waiting in a small meeting room near Arnon's office. Crane looked glum so Arnon assumed that they weren't about to hear much information. He was right.

The sex assault unit officer gave them a quick rundown on what they had. Wilson had vivid memories of her boyfriend tying her to the bed and blindfolding her. This was a prearranged game that they had agreed upon.

"The victim was blindfolded through most of the assault. She had consented to restraint and pleasure sex play with her boyfriend and suspected nothing when he tied her up. She said that she became alarmed when the guy gagged her because they had spent some time talking about her safe word. She felt a sharp pain once she had been blindfolded and gagged. That would have been the injection of whatever drug he used."

"The emergency room doctor had lots of experience with drug users and was certain that she had been given was a hallucinogenic drug. Perhaps a form of LSD. He did say that it was unusual for the drug to stay in effect for such a long period."

Crane spoke up next. He said that thus far, all the prints lifted from the scene were Wilson's. None of the lab work was done yet. The rape kit was currently being processed. A lab tech had said there were hair fibres from at least four different people.

"The thing we do have," said Crane, "is the boyfriend's name. Wilson says he's an art dealer from Copenhagen. His name is Lars Neegen. She gave us detailed description of him. They met about six weeks ago. She had seen him a couple of dozen times. She said he travelled a lot in his job. I've asked immigration to tell us what they can about him. They said they'd likely get back to me this afternoon."

"I'll get the name to my people as well. What is the extent of the woman's injuries?" asked Jules.

"Virtually none," said Officer Cole. "Bruising to her genitals. Some bruising on her wrists and ankles from the restraints. Nothing else."

"The bruising to her genital area is not consistent with a rape, and particularly not with a rape by multiple perpetrators. And there was no bruising at all to her upper thighs," said the sexual assault officer.

"Are you saying she wasn't raped?" asked Jim Curtiss.

"In the vast majority of gang sexual assaults the victim sustains a lot of physical injury. That type of assault is motivated, most often, by anger and the perpetrators have a desire to hurt and humiliate their victim. They punch and slap and often bite the person that they're controlling. Wilson sustained no more damage than a woman would during a consensual marathon sex session."

"This whole thing makes less sense by the minute," said Jules.

"Maybe Ms. Wilson is in hospital because she had a swipe card for the computer lab at the library and because she was to be a red herring for us," said Arnon. "I wonder how long her boyfriend thought we'd spend chasing down this supposed gang of rapists?"

"Doesn't matter," said Curtiss. "There have been a few hundred flights leaving LAX since the library was burned. I'm sure he was on one of them."

"But this assault, whatever kind of assault it was, serves to underline the ruthlessness of the people who are behind it," observed Jules.

"If these people are so ruthless why didn't they just kill Marcia Wilson?" asked Officer Cole.

"Because they wanted us to chase down a man named Lars Neegen," said Jules.

Arnon thanked the two female officers and he and Curtiss went to his office. Jules sat at an empty desk to call headquarters and initiate a run on the name Lars Neegen. He told INTERPOL to put a priority watch on that passport, just in case. Jules was certain that the passport had already been destroyed. In fact, Nils had left it right next to a white phosphorous grenade in the library. It had been vaporized.

***

Tom Robbins kept a small furnished apartment in one of the least fashionable suburbs of the city. He went there directly from the airport, showered and shaved and changed into a business suit. Globalization was a positive trend for Tom's business. Thousands of companies were operating in parts of the world that provided serious challenges to them. Tom was making a very good living helping the personnel of multinational companies cope with operating in unstable and violent environments.

One of his current engagements was to educate thirty staff members of a large mining company on how to remain safe as they conducted a test drilling program in the Ivory Coast. He was also advising them on which local security company - read band of mercenaries - they should hire to provide them with reliable personal protection. Today would be his first meeting with the group slated to go to Africa.

He was dismayed when he entered the room where the group was gathered to see that two of them were women. One was a bookish looking brunette about forty with the word scientist written all over her. The other was a stunning blond woman, probably in her late twenties. She would have turned heads on Rodeo Drive. Tom told the group that he would join them in a couple of minutes and asked to speak to the company's director of operations. He was told that could be arranged to take place in two hours time.

He went back to the meeting room and started to run the group through a familiarization of situational awareness. Tom began such sessions by reading part of a coroner's report pertaining to the death of a British fluids engineer who had been captured and killed by militants in Mali. They paid careful attention to what he was telling them. During the first two hour session Tom learned that the blond woman's name was Shelly and that she was a technical writer.

They took a break and Tom was shown into the director of operations office.

"Do you know what the average annual income is for the average Joe in Mali?" he began. "I'm talking about the type of guy who your company will be hiring to provide security for your people in Africa."

The director indicated that he had no idea of going income levels in Mali.

"A hundred and twenty dollars is the magic number," said Tom. "That's a good thing for multi-national companies operating there because it keeps your expenses down. However, it is a bad thing when your company makes bad decisions."

"And what bad decisions do you think we're making, Mr. Robbins?" asked the director.

"Your technical writer, Shelly, who you are planning to send over to the Ivory Coast, is worth twenty thousand dollars in U.S. cash, diamonds or gold. The man who turned her over to the very nasty people who run the human trafficking networks would get that as a minimum price. They could possibly get as much at 30K for her. She looks like she could be a natural blond. Such women are in very high demand."

"You're joking," said the director.

"I'm telling you that sending that woman into the boonies of the Ivory Coast is going to create an unacceptable security risk for your team. She's too valuable for any mercenary group you hire to not kidnap and sell."

"She's part of the team."

"She won't be for long if you send her into the field there. And her presence will put the rest of your people in danger. It would be worth it to the local bad guys to kill your entire team in order to kidnap and sell your technical writer. That's the reality of Africa, several regions of it anyway. Replace her with a male or an older, non-descript looking female."

"Do you think that is really necessary?"

"You hired me to advise your company on how to operate in a particular environment. You hired me because I have experience in such environments. I am giving you advice. I suggest you take it."

***

Arnon, Jim Curtiss and Jules went to a bar that Nick patronized from time to time. The owner's avocation was to run his own personal Andrew Wyeth art gallery. Arnon liked Wyeth's work. The owner of the bar had ensured that his prints covered the walls of the place. A few of them were signed and numbered prints and quite valuable.

Curtiss was oblivious to the deco of the bar, being intent on talking about the case. Jules, though, was intrigued and walked about in the big room having a good look at many of the hangings. When he returned to the table he asked Arnon, "Do you know who has done these?"

Arnon looked up as three young men entered the place. They wore long raincoats despite the warm weather and they had their hands in their pockets or out of sight. They were much younger than most of the people in the bar and their long hair set them apart from the rest of the patrons. Arnon quietly said, "If you have a weapon, now is the time to subtly draw it."

He had no idea if Jules or Jim had made any move because he was paying rapt attention to the three young men.

The tallest of the trio reached down and pulled aside his long coat to reveal a cut-down shotgun hanging on a tether from his neck. As he raised it Arnon shot him in the throat with his Glock. The tall man released his grip on the shotgun and spun around spraying blood all over the young server that had been standing behind him. The man tried to remain on his feet by grabbing the server but he only succeeded in tearing her blouse open as he fell.

The young man nearest the man that Arnon had shot was about fire on him with an AK-47 that had been concealed under his coat when Jim Curtiss squeezed off three rounds from a nine mm Beretta. Jim's shots all hit his target in the chest. Arnon guessed that he was dead before his body hit the floor.

To the surprise of both Arnon and Curtiss, Jules leaped forward and downed the third young man with a calculated blow to the side of his neck. The man fell to the floor but did not let go of the handgun that he had drawn. Jules disarmed him by grinding the heel of his shoe into the man's wrist.

There was some initial confusion with some of the patrons panicked and scrambling for the exits, but with three middle aged men dressed in suits and informing everyone they were cops, order was restored quite quickly. Arnon was the only one of them carrying handcuffs so he restrained the semi-conscious guy, ignoring him when he protested that his wrist was broken.

Curtiss called the incident in while Jules and the bar owner tried to comfort the blood-soaked server. "Keep her talking to you," said Arnon. "Don't let her go into shock."

The girl calmed down enough for two of the other female staff to take her into the bathroom to wash away the blood. Arnon rested his fingers on the necks of the two men who had been shot to confirm they were dead. Jules kept out of the way, standing off to the side with a perplexed look on his face.

A whole fleet of police and EMS vehicles descended on the place in minutes. Arnon and Curtiss surrendered their weapons to the Special Investigations Unit people who were on the scene as rapidly as the regular cops. They gave their statements, accepted the thanks of the bar owner and a couple of the patrons and climbed into Arnon's car.

They drove in silence for a while and then Curtiss said, "Have you ever had to shoot anyone before, Nick?"

"Yep. Twice. First time I got away with wounding the guy. Second one was too close and he had already dropped my partner. I had to kill him."

"Up until today I've only had to draw my weapon for real twice. This is the first time I've pulled the trigger. What's the likelihood of me sleeping tonight?" asked Curtiss.

"We're heading for the main station where we will each have a mandatory chat with a debriefing officer. If we're lucky we'll get to talk with one of the psychologists. If we pull a short straw we'll get the psychiatrist."

"Is this going to be a royal pain in the ass?" asked Curtiss.

"Probably. But it is helpful with getting it out there. Helps with the sleeping after a while."

As they walked into the police building Arnon said, "Do you guys want to go out and pet some airplanes after we're done here?"

Chapter Eleven

Nils had learned to travel without stress. When he felt his frustration level rising due to delays or obnoxious fellow travelers or breaches in expected service levels, he had developed a coping mechanism. The July/November English couple that he was sitting beside on the Air Malaysia flight had caused him to kick in his highest coping level.

The older man of the couple, Nils had concluded, did not really care a whit for his younger wife. Nils would hang him from an overhead beam, naked, and set to work on him with a scalpel. He would ensure that the younger wife was tied and gagged in a chair where she could observe all that took place.

Nils spent several hours of the flight telling himself in detail what he would do to the man sitting next to him. And speculating on what effect the visuals of that process would have on the mind of the woman. He was about to start thinking about what her state would be when he would turn his attention to her when the pilot announced their imminent landing.

Nils felt a vague sense of disappointment, but was glad that he was soon to be able to get to work in Mombassa. As much as Nils disliked the two men who had helped him with the Ten Haan woman, they were employees of the Cerberus Corp. and Winter had learned that they had been murdered. Nils would try to find out by whom.

***

Chuck Holt had been so surprised by the news he had received from his team of watchers that he almost called Sam Allen right away. He convinced himself that the news could wait until the meeting at Sam's cottage. But he wondered what had taken place to prompt Van Velt to move to a downtown apartment and put the house up for sale. "Perhaps she found out about some of the vampire hookers her husband likes," thought Holt.

***

Arnon awoke to begin his day with a clear head and a slight grin. The evening with Jim and Jules had been a great success. The restoration boys had treated both of them as honoured guests and the beer had flowed freely. Arnon had a couple but bowed out of the later rounds because of his status as designated driver. He anticipated that his two colleagues would be somewhat the worse for wear when they joined him as his office.

His good mood lasted until he was pulling in the parking lot. Then he remembered the reason that they were meeting that morning. They were going to be reviewing the full coroner's report on Gerta Ten Haan with all the lab results included. The lab results had been provided in record time. Amazing, thought Arnon, how things could get expedited when a bunch of Feds and foreigners were looking hard at the department.

The internal mail delivery had been made and a very thick sealed folder was in Arnon's office. Curtiss and Forget were not. Arnon checked his phone messages, poured himself a coffee and prepared to greet his guests.

It was apparent that neither Jim nor Jules were regularly heavy drinkers. Both had dark circles under their eyes, and Jim seemed to be ultra sensitive to the fluorescent lights in the office. He sat squinting for a few moments and then gave up and put on a pair of sunglasses. "You guys look like five pounds of shit in a three pound bag," observed Arnon.

"You can fuck yourself Mr. Designated Driver. I know a fucking set-up when I see one."

"Agreed," said Jules. "This morning I am questioning as to whether you are indeed a friend, Nick."

"There's coffee and water for you two sots on the table there. Are you ready to get to work?"

There were several labelled envelopes inside the file folder. Arnon took the one marked 'coroner's notes'. He pushed the one marked 'crime scene photos' to Jim and the one marked 'autopsy photos' to Jules. "I was at the scene and the autopsy," said Arnon. "I don't need to look at the photos. Be prepared. They did very unpleasant things to Ms. Ten Haan."

At one point Jim asked him if there was anything of interest in the coroner's notes.

"There are a couple things I didn't know about. Ten Haan had malaria at some point in her life. And she looks to have a through and through leg wound from a long time ago on her left calf. The coroner says it had been expertly repaired."

Jim finished going through his pile of photos first and sat quietly. Once Jules had reached the end of his, Curtiss stood up and grabbed his bottle of water. "I think I saw a picnic table under a tree outside. Why don't you bring the notes out there and we'll talk."

***

Jenna awoke after her first night in her apartment owing herself a hundred dollars. That was how much she had bet herself that she would not sleep. She slept so well in fact that the movers were buzzing from downstairs before she had gotten out of bed. She let them in the lobby door and hurriedly struggled into jeans and a T-shirt.

The deal she had made with the moving company specified that all beds would be assembled and that the crew would hang pictures and mirrors as directed. The two young guys came into the apartment with a couple of chairs, pieces for the bed in the spare room and a toolbox.

They assembled the bed in the spare room first. Jenna had marked the walls with tiny x's to show where she wanted things hung. The two young guys worked very quickly and soon they were done. When they had left, Jenna walked around the apartment looking at her new environment. It felt good. She realized that for the first time since she had been in the house where she and her Dad lived, she felt at home.

Then she sat on the floor in the center of the living room and started to cry.

***

Tom was not surprised to see that the class composition had changed after the first day. Shelly of course was gone. But so were two of the older members. There were three replacements, though, and they were all anxious to catch up on what they'd missed the first day. All were young males probably not long out of university. Tom told them that he'd hold a makeup class for them that evening at a pub.

He covered off the living arrangements that they would experience while in the Ivory Coast. The company was going to be drilling in a fairly easy geographical venue. Tom had picked up a bit of what concerned exploratory geologists, and the strata that they were going to be working in would not pose a big problem to them.

Unfortunately, they would be on the cusp of where Muslim Ivory Coast met non-Muslim Ivory Coast.

"When you are in the camp or at the mine site you are safe. The most dangerous part of your day is getting to and from the work site. I am going to run a twenty-minute movie that will show you, very clearly, what is required to keep a motor convoy safe. Watch the movie intently, take notes and then I will answer questions."

There were a lot of questions after the movie. Tom kept hammering home the concept of situational awareness.

That was the morning. In the afternoon he brought in one of his associates who gave the class several hours on how to conduct themselves should they be taken hostage. He explained a number of coping techniques and talked in detail about Stockholm syndrome. As his associate talked Tom surveyed the class. He concluded that they would all be there the next day. They had established their core unit.

He went home, made a few phone calls and set off for the Charles Dickens. His three keeners were there ahead of him and they drank beer and had an intensive two hours of talk. Tom found himself liking them and thinking back to his Selous Scouts days as he brought new recruits into his units. He was explaining the finer points of situational awareness when a tongue entered his ear.

"Hi Ing," he said without turning his head.

She sidled around his chair and wiggled onto his lap.

"Let me introduce Ing," said Tom to the three young men. They were clearly enthralled.

"Hello guys," said Ing. "Is this thoroughly bad man teaching you nasty things to do to people? He's the real fucking deal, you know. Fought in the Bush War, fought in Angola, God knows what else he's been up to. I think he was too young to have assassinated JFK but he may have been a child prodigy. Could have done it and arranged for Oswald to take the fall. He fucking hates Soviets."

"I have a deep appreciation for Ing," said Tom, "because she has a unique perspective of history."

"You bet your ass I do," she retorted. "As a woman, I realize that all wars have been fought because we have encountered phases in the history of the world when there was a shortage of vaginas. It only takes a few days for the frustration and aggression to build up among the male population and then, bingo! A war starts."

"So, I take it you've been sent to us on behalf of the UN to quell any such hormonal uprisings?"

"No, Tom. I'm here to tell you that at this moment I'm dealing with a personal hormonal uprising and that once it is over I'm coming to your home to fuck your brains out. Actually, to be more accurate young men, I'm going to his home to have him fuck my brains out."

She left them abruptly, going to the bar for a drink. Tom's students sat speechless. "I have really heavy duty cred with these guys now," thought Tom with a smile on his face.

***

Jules had asked if he and one of his INTERPOL guys could take at look at the murder scene. Arnon placed a call to Van Velt's home and the call went through to an answering machine.

He tried Crane's line, expecting him to not yet be at his desk. "I was just going to call you," he said. "I had a message from Ms. Van Velt, giving me her office number. She says that the phone at her home is to be disconnected."

"Did she say why?"

"No."

"Would you happen to have her or her husband's work numbers?"

"Yes. I have both of them."

"Good. OK, Crane, call Van Velt and tell her that there will be some of us walking around her backyard today. We'll be in the granny flat. This is a courtesy by the way; the place is still a crime scene."

"Got it."

"And please ask her if it would be convenient for her to meet with us one evening this week. I prefer it to be on Wednesday or Thursday. Don't spell out who "us" is. The guy from INTEPOL and I want to have a conversation with her. It would be best if her husband could be there as well."

Jim was first in the office. They made small talk about the weekend until the phone rang. It was Crane.

***

"I talked with Van Velt. She and her husband have split, the house is for sale, she's moved downtown and I don't think she would give a flying fuck -pardon my language- if we held platoon exercises in her backyard. Make that former backyard."

"Jesus! How did she sound?"

"Different. Different than when I went over to see her just after the murder. More confident."

"Have any early guesses as to what has brought about this tidal wave of change in Ms. Van Velt's life?" asked Arnon.

"I do, actually. The marriage was bad. The crisis of her Aunt being murdered was a tipping point. She's glad to be on her own."

"Maybe," said Arnon. "We'll see. Will she meet with me?"

"Thursday evening at 7:30. I have her new address. She's in the Hammond building."

"Thanks, Crane. Leave the address on my desk."

When Forget and Curtiss joined Arnon in his office he told them about his call with Crane.

"So help me out here. This woman, she's about thirty, has her long lost Aunt murdered in her backyard. Within days she and her hubby part company. He's a high flier and they seemed to be deeply into the white picket fence life they were living. Now she's downtown, single, and by Crane's assessment, is all the better for it?"

"Remarkable," said Jules. "Your Ms. Van Velt is becoming a person of interest, Nick."

"If Ms. Van Velt has suddenly come into money," said Arnon, "we may have just a tad more to mull over."

***

When Tom awoke to his alarm on Tuesday he immediately questioned the wisdom of holding remedial sessions with young guys in pubs. He wasn't actually hungover, but the bit of the fur on his tongue told him that he'd have a very long day.

He went back to his apartment after work with some takeout food that he picked up at a local deli. The light on his answering was flashing so he punched the play button while he ate. The first message was from Audrey Shuttleworth.

"Hello Tom. It's Audrey. I wanted to let you know about three things. Six crates that nearly gave the Fedex fellows hernias are now cluttering up my storage room. I hope you'll be back for them in the early fall. Secondly, I was delighted to see the 'sold' sign on your new home. It really is yours now, my good friend and I am happy that you will be living in Elgin. Finally, I have sent you a petition. They want to put fucking giant windmills on the cliffs around the Port. I've sent you a form to sign to help keep them out. Please sign it and mail it back to me, Tom."

Tom smiled to himself. Audrey was awesome when she had a full head of steam up.

The second message was from Ing.

"Hey, you sexy bastard. I'm long overdue for some Tom Robbins attention. And I know just what would do the trick. How about the club this Thursday?"

Tom didn't take long to think that one through. It was seven-thirty. He called Ing's number.

"Ing. I would love to go to the club with you. But some of us work seriously hard to earn a living. I'm finishing a course on Friday. Let me take you to the club on Saturday night, and I assure you that we can scratch any itch you might have then."

"I can't believe you're prepared to delay a night spent ravishing me because of work. But I have to conform to your timing since you are the only man I would ever let take me to the club. See you Saturday at night."

Chapter Twelve

Jenna looked up from the papers she was working with and was startled to see Robert standing in the doorway of her office. She simply stared at him.

"May I take you for lunch?"

"I have a meeting in an hour."

"Let's just get something in the café downstairs. We don't have to make it a long meal." They were silent on the elevator and nothing was said until they were seated at a table in a quiet corner.

"I had to call in a number of favours regarding the sale of the house."

"Why?"

"Turns out that police don't like it when you put their crime scene on the market. It's taken care of now and the sale can go ahead. I left all the papers with your lawyer. The sooner you sign them the better."

"I'll do that this afternoon."

"Good. I was at the house early this morning. You didn't take much furniture."

"I took what I have room for. Apartment living doesn't allow one to be a furniture collector."

"Are you okay for money? I know that we hammered out a separation deal, but I can help out some if you could use some cash."

"That's good of you, Robert, but I'll be fine."

"Are you sure? I know what you make a year."

"Yes, you do. But you must know that I was the frugal one."

"I do know that. You said it was your Dutch heritage."

They ate in silence and then Robert spoke again.

"I'm very worried about you, Jenna. I likely should have told you this when I first talked to our neighbour the day after Gerta was killed. She was tortured, Jenna. Whoever killed her wanted something from her."

"Why are you worried about me?"

"If they didn't get what they wanted from Gerta they may try to get it from Gerta's niece. Did Gerta give you anything to keep for her?"

"She had stored her two suitcases in the attic. When the young cop came over the day after the murder, he went up there and looked in them. They were both empty."

"I hope this whole mess is over for you Jenna. I really do."

"What's on your mind, Robert? There's something you want to talk about that you felt you shouldn't do with a phone call."

"You're right. I don't think a discussion about divorce should happen over the phone."

"If you want a divorce, Robert, I'm fine with that."

"I'm sorry that it's ending, Jenna. We had some good years."

"I'll focus on those, Robert. Is there anything I have to do for this?"

"I'll get my lawyer going on the process. Will you use the same lawyer as you have for the separation agreement?"

"I might as well."

"Okay. My guy will send stuff to your guy. It's going to cost about fifteen hundred for each lawyer. I'll pick up that cost."

"That's very civilized of you."

"I guess that's how we could describe our marriage, isn't it? Civilized."

"I'll wait to hear from my lawyer. Good luck in the East, Robert. I forgot to bring my purse with me so I guess you're stuck with the tab."

"Good bye, Jenna."

***

Nils was not fond of Mombassa. And Mombassa in mid-June was a decidedly hot and smelly place. He reckoned that it would take him several days to get all of the odours of the city out of his nostrils and memory.

He had found it surprisingly difficult to get much useful information on the murders of the Tsoba brothers. His visits to the local bars patronized by police had accomplished little more than make him a subject of suspicion. Nils admitted to himself that he was on the very whitest end of the scale of white men.

He was finally able to charm and bribe a young police department clerk who agreed to photocopy what she could of the file on the Tsoba murders. He felt that he had definitely overpaid her for the three sheets of typewritten notes that she produced. Had there been more time he would have slipped something potent into her drink and gotten his money's worth from her by other means. She left his hotel room with his money not realizing just how lucky a young woman she was.

A quick read of the pages from the file confirmed for Nils that the Mombassa police had no idea of who had killed the Tsoba brothers. He was interested to learn that aside from some bruising consistent with a struggle, there were no life-threatening wounds on the victims' bodies. Apart from the ones that had caused their death. Nils concluded that the police regarded whoever had done the killings as having performed a public service.

He ripped the pages into tiny fragments and flushed them down the toilet. He would have liked to visit a brothel that catered to men of his tastes, but he felt he had been too visible for too long in Kenya. His flight was booked and he would be back in Frankfurt early the next morning.

***

Ing was a half hour late getting to Jenna's. She came into the apartment talking at a rapid pace about having finally finished up her project with "two of the horniest old geezers with bad breath who had ever walked the planet." Jenna poured them wine and when Ing stopped to take a breath she handed her a glass and made a toast. "To Muscato and Midol."

"Oh, God! You too! Well, at least we know what we're not going to be doing tonight. Show me around your palace in the sky, fair Jenna."

Given that they were standing at the door to the kitchen, there was little to show Ing but the bedroom. Her reaction to the massive bed was predictable. "In a few days girl, I want you on that bed, naked, tied spread eagle and begging for mercy as I begin to bring you to your third but not final orgasm of the evening."

"Tied to the bed?" asked Jenna.

"Restraint and pleasure is one of the most exquisite experiences that one can have without the use of strong drugs. I am going to introduce you to it. But enough of this kind of talk for this evening. Let's get caught up."

Jenna listened to Ing talk about the trials and tribulations of the freelance business which she ran in addition to her day job for some time, and realized that she had a truly international command of profanity. It had clearly been all work and no play for Ing since their trip to the cottage. She was ready to unwind.

It was good that Jenna had gone to the wine store. Ing kept talking and refilling the glasses at a rapid rate. Jenna tried to pace herself, but by ten p.m. they were both feeling the effects of the alcohol.

As she often did, Ing suddenly changed up the conversation. "It's pretty much out there in the office about what Robert will make in his new job. It would be more than enough to provide him with the lifestyle he wants on the East coast and still maintain the leafy bower out there in the Woods. Why the move to this concrete box downtown?"

"I realized that Robert and I had been going through the motions in our relationship for a while. We were sort of a Stepford couple, I think. We looked damned good and were doing all the comfortably right things. A good part of getting there was my fault."

"Don't go down the self-blame road without some fucking good proof that the route you're taking is real. Remember who you're talking to," said Ing.

"Aunt Gerta's murder got me to step back and take stock. Robert golfed. I didn't. I loved the cottage. Robert didn't. We lived in the same house surrounded by a bunch of possessions that we had assembled. Going out and getting that stuff was our one shared activity."

"How was the sex?" asked Ing.

"We were both good at it. And if anyone had been allowed to watch, I bet we looked damn fine while we were having it. God knows we never, ever had sex unless we were squeaky clean, freshly shaved and trimmed and well rested."

"Jesus, Jenna! No drunken grab-ass sessions on the kitchen table?"

"No. They might have happened if we were sober enough to freshen up first. You know. Brush our teeth. Give the equipment a once over with a warm damp cloth."

"You're painting a picture of a nuclear winter of a sex life here, Jenna."

"It wasn't so bad. I got off a lot. So did Robert. And we were both quite horny. He travelled on business a lot but despite that, we were still good to go two or three times a week."

"You two must have gone through a lot of soap and mouthwash," observed Ing.

"When Robert first told me about his new job I bagged off to a beach I know. Among other revelations that came to me then was that I love walking on beaches. And the only time that Robert and I have walked down a beach was at the cottage to try to find some of his golf balls. Because he had been practising his drive or something."

"Had Robert proposed that sort of a walk with me, he would have had two more balls to find in the sand."

"Anyway, I realized that it was comfortable out in the Woods, but that I was coasting. In my home life, in my job, in my social life. Hell, Ing, I find I love spending time with you. But I didn't because Robert disapproved of you."

"A lot of husbands disapprove of me."

"Anyway, a second revelation that I had on the beach was that Robert really liked to leave on his business trips. And that I really liked it when he left for a few days. That's when I decided it was time to move downtown and find out what life with just Jenna would be like."

"Did you love him?"

"I thought I did at first. Once I saw how he played in his work life and who he was prepared to suck up to and who he was prepared to throw under a bus, I realized that I really didn't like him. And then I realized that orgasms aren't a proof of love."

"How is it so far, Jenna?"

"Good. Really good. I loved moving into my own space. I've stepped up at work and have a much more productive, interesting job now. And I am so glad to be away from the house. I got really spooked the last evening I went out there."

Ing asked Jenna a lot of questions about her last evening at the Woods. She listened intently as Jenna described the sense of dark and evil that she picked up from the Granny flat. She asked her if she felt safe in the apartment.

Jenna was quick to say that she felt very safe there. She told Ing that she actually had been sleeping better since moving than she had in years. And made an offhand remark about the cops coming to see her next evening with more questions about the murder.

Ing sat up straight in her chair at that news. "I thought they had already questioned you. What do they want to talk about now?"

"I've no idea," said Jenna.

"You haven't told them about your Aunt's diaries, right?"

"Of course not."

"Well whatever you do, don't tell them about them now."

"I don't intend to."

"Good. It's been several days since the murder. If you suddenly revealed that you had several books of your Aunt's life tucked away somewhere, they could charge you with obstructing justice. Probably a bunch of other stuff as well."

"I'm not going to tell them I have anything of Aunt Gerta's."

"Be a little less productive in your job and spend some time thinking about what your answers will be to their questions tomorrow night. They are obviously hitting walls in trying to find out who killed your Aunt. They are going to come in here hoping to squeeze some shred of info out of you that will make them look like they're doing their jobs."

Ing paused briefly and then said, "Where are the diaries, Jenna?"

Jenna's eyes involuntarily started to move in the direction of her closet.

Ing sat back in her chair and sighed.

"Don't do that thing with your eyes tomorrow night when one of the sneaky bastards pops a sudden question about your Aunt's effects."

Jenna suddenly felt quite sober. And she started thinking about the interview with Detective Arnon.

"Before I forget. Tom is back in town. I'm going to have a drink with him tomorrow evening. I'll remind him that you have some translating to be done. My nerd is off on another training course so the disk things will have to wait."

"I hope the diaries catch his interest," replied Jenna. "So that he'll read through a bunch of them for me. I have a lot of vacation that I've got to take or lose so I can be flexible in availability."

"Tom was whining about how hard he's been working lately. I'll get him to take me to the club and bang my brains out. That will lighten him up. He'll call you."

"You go to a club to have sex?" asked Jenna.

"Girl talk for another time my fair lady. Perhaps once I have you tied down on that mountain of a bed of yours. Now be an absolute sweetheart and call me a cab."

***

Tom had agreed to meet Ing at the Dickens at seven. Ing was fashionably late in arriving. Tom was relieved to see that she was wearing jeans and a T-shirt with a bit of paint on it. Her work clothes. There would be no cajoling to go to the club this evening.

She was almost subdued when she joined him at his table and didn't immediately launch into a torrent of stories. Tom motioned to the bartender to send them over their usual drinks. He asked her how her day had been.

"Well. It began with a hangover thanks to Jenna Van Velt and her new apartment, and ended with a call from home an hour ago."

Their drinks arrived and as usual the server proposed marriage to Ing. She brightened up at that and told the young man that he'd have to show her his unit before she could even consider his request. That got the usual laugh.

She told Tom that she had spent the past evening with Jenna and brought him up to speed on her separation, new home, and reminded him that he had promised to do some translating for her.

"The fucking cops are coming to see her again, this evening actually. They obviously aren't able to find their own asses with both hands on this case of her murdered Aunt. And you know how cops are when they aren't getting anywhere with a murder case."

Tom nodded.

"Excuse me for a moment, Tom."

Ing dropped some coins into the payphone in the bar. Jenna picked up. "Don't give the mutherfuckers anything, Jenna. You okay?"

"I'm good and thanks."

"Powerful people are looking out for you."

Ing went back to the table feeling a bit more grounded. Jenna would handle the evening with the cops.

"So friend Tom. Would you please make it a priority to hook up with her and read her some Afrikaans stories? She's withholding evidence, obstructing justice and God knows what else because she wants to know what is in those books. Will you do that for me, old son?"

"There are two things I will do for you, my dear Ing. I have a couple of things that I have to do workwise next week, but I promise you that I will arrange for a reading session with your friend Jenna."

"What else will you do, oh generous and wise one?"

"If you'd like to put on your little black dress Saturday night, I would be very keen to try to put you through whatever changes you might care to attempt."

"That would be nice, you evil, sexy bastard. That would be very, very, fucking nice. Will you book us into the club or shall I?"

"It would be my honour to make the arrangements," replied Tom. "Why don't you whisper to me what rooms we will be making use of?"

***

Arnon and Jules buzzed Jenna's apartment at precisely 7:30.

"She certainly didn't sound nervous," remarked Jules as they rode the elevator.

Jenna was standing partway into the hall of the floor of building. "Good evening Ms. Van Velt," said Arnon.

"Let's go with Jenna. It's less of a mouthful than Ms. Van Velt," she said.

"Thank you for agreeing to meet with us," began Arnon.

"It's my understanding that I have no choice with regard to this meeting," replied Jenna.

"True. But it was good of you to agree to do so in a short time period."

"I'm a 'let's get it over with' kind of person. Before we start, would either of you like something to drink? Coffee, a soft drink, water?"

"I believe I detect the scent of coffee," said Jules. "I would welcome a cup. Are you brewing Blue Mountain?"

"Good nose," said Jenna. She looked at Arnon. "How about you?"

"Only a complete fool would turn down a cup of Jamaica's finest."

While Jenna fetched the coffee the two men looked around the room. Arnon was secretly pleased that coffee was to be served. It would be easy to see if any particular line of questioning caused Jenna's hands to tremor.

Jules was doing a methodical inventory of the furniture and artwork in the room. Nothing was particularly remarkable. Except for an antique mirror that hung by the entryway. It perfectly suited that area and he could tell that it was either an expensive antique or an extremely good reproduction. He estimated that it was worth more than any six other items in the room.

Jenna set a tray with two cups of coffee and cream and sweetener and spoons on the coffee table. She went back to the kitchen and returned to her sofa seat with a glass of red wine. "I would have offered you a glass," she said, "but I know you're on duty."

Arnon took a sip of his coffee, set down the cup and reached into the pocket of his jacket for a small notebook.

"Let's start with introductions. As you know, I'm Nick Arnon with the homicide branch of the local police department. Please call me Nick, Jenna. This is Jules Forget. Jules has brought his team over here from his headquarters in Belgium. He's with INTERPOL."

"Vraiment!" exclaimed Jenna, with mock astonishment. "C'est une honore pour avez une homme de le formadible INTERPOL a chez moi!"

"Your French is very good Jenna. A Canadian accent, I think?"

"Yes, my tutor was from Trois Rivieres."

"So you lived in Canada at some point?"

"I was born there. I moved to the States when I married Robert. I have dual citizenship."

Arnon had not known that and wondered if it might prove to be important.

"So your father settled in Canada in the 1950s when the family who had adopted him moved there?"

"Yes. Dad loved Canada. Until his dying day he always talked about how good the country had been to him."

"I'm sorry that he has passed away. Has it been long?"

There's that 'passed away' expression again, thought Jenna. Eaten up by cancer was how she would have put it.

"It's been several years now. But we were very close. My mother died when I was young so there were just the two of us."

"That must have been hard," said Jules.

"He was a very good father," said Jenna, "it wasn't hard."

"When we talked before, you said that your father had visited your Aunt in Africa in 1960 and that they had a falling-out."

"My Dad did not tell me that. I gleaned that from the letters that he exchanged with Aunt Gerta. I got them out and went through them the day of the murder when you asked me to put a timeline together. She was angry that he had met with a man whose name you recognized."

"Who was that?" asked Jules. Arnon and Jules had agreed that they would ask each other questions periodically so that Jenna would feel less like she was being grilled.

"Sailor Malan."

"Who is this Sailor Malan?" asked Jenna.

"He was a South African. He joined the Royal Air Force and was a very notable fighter pilot and leader during the Battle of Britain. Legendary. After the war he went back to South Africa and strongly opposed the racist right-wing policies of the government there. He was a leader of those who fought against, among other things, Apartheid."

"Interesting. Well, my Aunt must have been a supporter of the government because she and my father cut off contact over their respective political views."

"Had your father and your Aunt been close?" asked Jules.

"Dad was five and Gerta was nine when she went out to South Africa to stay with her Aunt. She didn't see my Dad again until 1949. By that time he was fully part of the family who sheltered him during the war. They tried to stay connected, but their lives were going in very different directions."

"But they stayed in touch?" asked Jules.

"She was blood, my father was keen to point out."

"And after your father died, she stayed in touch with you?"

"Yes. She sent me her condolences when I wrote to inform her of Dad's death. We wrote a few letters back and forth."

"Did you speak on the phone very often?" asked Arnon.

"Once," said Jenna. "She called me to confirm that everything was ready for her to move into the Granny flat. It was the first time that I had heard her voice."

"When was that?" asked Arnon.

"About a week before she came here. Late January. I don't remember the exact date."

"It must have been strange to hear her voice for the first time," observed Jules.

"When I was a young kid, my Dad had a lot of Dutch friends who had immigrated to Canada. Gerta sounded like Dutch speakers when they speak English. The words were perfect but there is a softness to them."

"I know exactly what you are saying," said Jules.

"Did you find it strange that she wanted to rent your Granny flat and live in your backyard? I mean the two of you had never met."

"You've seen the place that Robert and I had in the Woods. It was a little piece of heaven. To afford it we knew we would have to generate some revenue from the Granny flat. The options were to bring in a total stranger or bring in a total stranger that I had been corresponding with for years and who was related to me. Robert and I chose the latter."

"One of the things we have to talk about this evening is the disposition of your Aunt's body," said Arnon. "The coroner's office has released it."

"Is there a bunch of forms to fill out? Do I have to prove that I'm a relative? What's the process?"

"I ask you if you are her closest living relative. I ask if you have power of attorney. I ask you if someone else should be contacted about this," said Arnon.

"Nope. I think this falls to me," said Jenna.

"Your Aunt never indicated to you that there might be someone who should be contacted in the event of her death?" asked Jules.

"For Christ's sake, Nick. You knew that Gerta had some old guy going out to see her on a daily basis. I didn't, Robert didn't. If I knew who the old fart was I would defer to him. If you know who the old fart is, I defer to him. He was obviously a hell of a lot closer to her than I was."

"That's not an option," said Arnon. "And my department would strongly advise you not to request to view your Aunt's body."

"I have no intention to," said Jenna.

"That is a very good thing," said Jules. "The people who killed your Aunt were sadists. They tortured her. They were trying to extract information from her. We believe that in the years 1965 to about 1980, your Aunt was involved in something that prompted this outrage."

Jenna was feeling her stomach starting to churn and quickly set down her wine glass. "What the hell could she have been involved in to result in a sixty-something-year-old woman getting tortured and murdered in L.A?"

"That's the problem," said Arnon. "We don't know. What we do know is that the CIA, INTERPOL and my department all view this matter as very significant. And as the local law enforcement agency with a duty to serve and protect, I worry about you. Your Aunt chose to come to your home. She died there. We have nothing to tell us that the people who did this got what they wanted."

"Do you think it's likely that the people who killed Gerta knew a good deal more about her than anyone in this room?" asked Jenna.

"That is highly likely," said Jules.

"Well I think it's highly likely too. I think that whoever killed Gerta would have been in my face long before now if they thought there was a chance that I could give them anything useful."

"I'd like to believe that," said Arnon. "I would really like to believe that. And perhaps on the day of the murder, the killers left your place in the Woods believing that they had done all they could to get information from your Aunt. Perhaps they left thinking they had a plan B to pursue."

"But?" asked Jules.

"We know the identity of the old fellow who was visiting your Aunt Jenna. We know that while your Aunt seems to have dropped off the planet for about fifteen years, her old buddy had disappeared in 1945 and resurfaced for the first time in forty-six years right after the murder."

Arnon clearly had Jenna's interest.

"The problem is, Jenna, he reappeared in the world as a dead guy on a park bench outside of a Cathedral in Germany. If he was the killers' plan B, he isn't anymore. If they are at a dead end, they just may circle back to see if they can get anything from you."

"The way you and Jules are doing here tonight," said Jenna.

"Precisely," answered Jules.

For the next hour the two men persistently questioned Jenna about her interactions with Gerta once she had moved into the Woods. Jenna gave them precious little. As the time wore on and the answers continued to yield little information, both Arnon and Jules reached the same conclusion. Jenna simply had not gotten to know much about her Aunt.

Arnon and Jules had agreed that they would signal to one another that the interview should end by standing and comment on some aspect of the apartment. Jules stood up and went to the entryway and stood admiring the mirror that he had noticed earlier. "This is a lovely piece," he remarked.

"It's old," said Jenna. "From about 1850 if the salesman is to be believed."

"Of French origin I should think," said Jules.

Arnon stood up as well. "There's just the matter of your Aunt's burial."

"Her remains will be cremated," said Jenna quickly. She walked to the front window of her apartment and peered outside intently for a moment. "Please tell your people to have her body taken to the O'Brien Funeral Home. That's it right across the street from this building."

"Had you and your Aunt talked about cremation?" asked Arnon.

"Not really. She did remark once that since her parents and siblings had been cremated by the Germans, she would follow the same route."

"I see. Thank you so much for your time and the excellent coffee," said Jules.

"Just a moment," said Jenna. She went into her bedroom for a moment and returned with a small box. "These are the letters sent by Gerta and my Dad. I would like them back as keepsakes, but if you think it would be helpful to go over them, you're welcome to them for a while."

"Thank you," said Arnon. "And I'll ask a favour. Will you please get in touch with me or Detective Crane if you notice anything unusual happening in your life?"

"I'm a recently separated woman," said Jenna. "I expect, indeed hope, that any number of unusual things are going to be happening in my life."

"Good point," said Arnon, "Take care of yourself."

As the two men walked to their car, Arnon asked Jules what he thought of the interview.

"Not at all what I'd expected," he began. "She was much more self-assured than I had imagined she would be. She certainly didn't appear to be facing a crisis over self-esteem because her marriage has recently ended."

"True, that."

"It's apparent that she's well educated," said Jules.

"And eager to show off her French to us."

"That's not that uncommon an occurrence," said Jules. "There have been occasions when I've met North Americans and they have spoken French when they learn I'm European. But she did know that the INTERPOL headquarters is in an area where French is spoken. A sign of a broad education."

"She is a very personable woman. She clearly didn't want to spend an evening talking with us, but she graciously played the hostess," said Jules.

"She sure as hell put me in my place when I suggested that she might be in some danger from the people who killed her Aunt."

"She certainly did," agreed Jules with a slight smile. "Ms. Van Velt has no trouble drawing conclusions based on a logical review of the facts."

"I am convinced that she knows very little about her Aunt. I am equally convinced that her Aunt was extremely effective at making sure that Jenna Van Velt would know very little about her."

"That would be a skill-set possessed by someone who could drop out of sight for fifteen years. I expect your Erich Krohl may have helped her hone those skills."

"What did you think of her apartment, Nick?" asked Jules.

"Nothing stood out for me. The TV is an older model. The stereo was a cheapie. She's obviously not a music buff."

"I noticed the antique mirror that was hanging in the entryway. My wife is quite an antique collector. The item hanging in Van Velt's apartment would have cost at least two thousand dollars."

"I guess she's not pressed for money. Anyway. Nothing new tonight."

Chapter Thirteen

She made an appointment for noon at the funeral home. The day had gone from hot to stifling. She was glad to step into the heavily air-conditioned foyer of the funeral home."Why the hell is a place for this purpose called a home?"she asked herself. She stood in the dimly lit room trying to let her sun bedazzled eyes adjust. She nearly jumped out of her skin when a man standing very close to her quietly asked if he could help her.

He led Jenna into a small office and she was seated at a small, almost dainty writing desk across from her host. The man spoke very quietly and slowly, beginning by expressing his condolences for her loss. He obviously had not viewed Gerta's body because he asked if her death was sudden. "As nearly as the police can tell, it lasted several hours," was the response Jenna wanted to give. Instead she told the man that it was unexpected.

He confirmed that Gerta's remains had arrived safely at the funeral. It was another what the fuck moment for Jenna. How could a murdered woman's body arrive safely anywhere?

"Good," said Jenna. "I'd like to arrange for cremation of the body."

The funeral man had a stack of documents close to hand. He first asked Jenna what sort of service she had in mind.

"I am my Aunt's sole surviving relative. She came here from Europe a few months ago and does not know a soul in the United States. There will be no service. Just a cremation."

The man was nonplussed, and after a pause gave it another try.

"You must be devastated by this death. We have some excellent bereavement counselors on staff that you might want to see a couple of times to help you."

Jenna cut him off. "A little over three weeks ago my Aunt was tortured and murdered in the Granny flat in my backyard. Since that time I have had several conversations with several law enforcement officers, none of whom seem to have the faintest idea of who killed her or why. I have had time to get my head around the fact of her death. Can we talk about arrangements for a cremation?"

The man became very matter-of-fact, presenting her with three forms to sign. He explained that her Aunt's ashes would be available for pick-up in three days time. He asked for a cheque equal to two-thirds of the fee and inquired as to how many copies of the death certificate she would like.

Jenna looked at him blankly.

"You'll need copies of the death certificate to close your Aunt's bank accounts, for the lawyer who is handling the estate, that sort of thing. Our fee includes providing you with ten certified copies. If you need more than that, there is a small fee for each additional copy."

"I'm not going to need any of those things, buddy," Jenna said to herself.

***

Friday began with a very boring briefing for Arnon, Jim and Jules. But it was necessary. The FBI, INTERPOL and the local police had no good leads and thus, no reason to stay together. Jim was flying out at 4 p.m.

Jules' flight would leave on Sunday, so he and Arnon had arranged to go to the restoration unit for Saturday. The guys out there were keen to spend some more time with a guy who had big pieces of over 15 Luftwaffe fighters in his barn.

When Arnon got up on Saturday morning it was already hot. I hope Jules will be able to stand the heat, he thought as he reluctantly shaved. Normally he would have worn stubble out at the airfield, but he thought he should keep up appearances for his European friend. Jules was waiting for him, unshaven, in front of the hotel.

Arnon and Jules were in coveralls, happily removing fifty-year old rivets from a Flying Fortress wing spar when detective Crane arrived. It was a hot day and he was sweat-soaked. "I take it you're not here to become an airplane restoration volunteer," said Arnon.

"There's a crazy thing with the library," said Crane. "The director was in deep depression over the loss of his beloved computer thingies. He must have been caressing them to give them a decent send-off. And he discovered they're not his. None of those metal boxes in the library are the ones he had. The serial numbers have been altered. Whoever got in there didn't steal information. They stole the fucking computers."

"This is significant," said Jules.

"A-fucking-men," said Arnon. "Where is this guy now?"

"Outside in my car," answered Crane.

The computer guy from the library had not gotten the memo about the hippie movement being over. He had hair down to his ass, a beard that Arnon thought could have been a home to a lot of lice, and he must have been hitting vintage shops to obtain his bell bottoms. He reeked of marijuana.

"Detective Crane tells me your name is David Dennison. Do your prefer David or Dave?"

"David, please."

"Alright, David. I understand that the computer gear in your library has been altered?"

"Yes. Actually, it's been stolen. All of the original hardware that we had is gone. The software has gone with it. It's a huge fucking theft!"

"What would you say the thieves have taken? In dollars," asked Arnon.

"At least $500,000. We had the equipment insured for more than that. Our geneology data base was priceless."

"What about this talking to other people with computers. What would the person who has seemingly stolen your equipment gain by that?"

"Everything. A good computer jock will be able to search through every file held in those computers. They will have to get around some passwords, security locks and walls, but since they have all of my fucking equipment they have unlimited time to work at that. Eventually they will be able to see everything that the computers hold."

"Did you know Gerta Ten Haan?"

"Of course. She was a brilliant woman. I couldn't believe my luck when she walked into my office back in February and started talking computer science with me. Her death is a great loss to the world. Her depth of knowledge of computers put her in the upper fifteen percentile of people in the field."

"You're saying a woman of her age was leading edge in a really new field? Did she indicate where she was trained?"

"All over the world. London. New York. Europe."

"I expect that your field is a small one. Had you heard of her before she came to the library?" asked Jules.

"No. But there's a good reason for that. Although she could have written text books because of her level of knowledge, she never wrote a thing for publication."

"Did she say why she was averse to sharing her knowledge by writing?"

"She said her knowledge was a means to an end in another field. Her primary work was in developing new pharmaceuticals. Her work in computer science was done to give her and her colleagues tools to accomplish their research and manufacture new treatments."

"So David. Please tell these gentlemen what you told me about the equipment in your lab," said Crane.

"The equipment destroyed in the fire exactly replicated every piece of my original equipment."

"So you're saying that whoever did this bought over $500,000 worth of electrical gear to leave in the library to replace exactly what you had there?"

"Precisely," answered Dennison "And this was done by somebody who is in the upper echelons of knowledge. Our system was assembled over the last six years. It would have required someone, or a team of people, with intensive knowledge and experience to even source many of the boxes that have been taken."

"Do you think that Ms. Ten Haan could have been involved in this theft?" asked Arnon.

That stopped Dennison for a moment.

"I don't see how. The only thing she did on our computers other than teach our students, was to talk on line with a friend in Europe."

"Where in Europe?" asked Jules.

"Holland," Dennison answered.

"Would there be records of Ten Haan's conversations in the stolen gear that whoever has it now could see?"

He thought hard about that and then shook his head. "Gerta was very firm about those files being totally erased out of the system. She said that she was having conversations of a personal nature. As the system administrator, I granted her permissions that allowed her to get rid of all of the data related to her conversing with the man in Europe."

"Didn't that make you a bit nervous?"

"She said she was talking to a man who was coming to live with her. I believed her."

"So whoever has the equipment now can learn nothing about her communications with the person in Holland?" asked Jules.

Dennison took some time to answer. "I was on vacation at the time of the fire. I had been gone for two weeks. There was a storage area in the system that held the addresses of any outside computers that our computers talked to. I am the only one who could access those files. Usually I would go in late on a Friday and clear the area out so that it wouldn't be using up memory."

"I have no way of knowing if Gerta used our equipment to talk to her Dutch friend while I was away. If she did, the address of that person will still be in the file."

Arnon thanked Dennison, and Crane left to drive him home.

Arnon and Jules stood looking at each other for a long moment. "Incredible," said Jules. "We go from having nothing to having a whole range of things to pursue. I'd better get to a telephone since I need to talk to my people."

***

Jenna's late departure for the cottage worked in her favour. All of the other people who had cottages in the lake area had made their trek the night before. The roads were wide open and she got to the small town near the cottage in record time.

It was four in the afternoon and very hot by the time she parked beside the cottage. All seemed well there. She threw the switch to heat up the sauna, put her few purchases inside and then stripped off and wrapped in a towel. The chaise lounge needed to be dragged a few feet to a sunny patch. She stretched out in the chair and must have dozed off right away.

The sound of a vehicle coming down the track to her place awakened her. She hurriedly wrapped the big beach towel around her and got up from her chair hoping that whoever was approaching would think that she was using the towel as a cover up for a bathing suit underneath. When the vehicle entered the clearing she saw that her visitors were driving a newer Saab.

The Saab stopped behind her car and the couple that had a cottage on the next point of land east of Jenna's place alit. Jenna and Robert had secretly referred to Steve and Deena as the poster couple for procreation because they were both almost impossibly goodlooking. She and Robert frequently had drinks with them during the summer months. Jenna realized that they were likely the only people she socialized with in the States that she had not met through Robert.

"Glad to see you've made it out to God's Country," was Steve's greeting.

"I thought that was you I saw coming out of the store in town," said Deena.

Jenna said it was great to see them and went quickly into the cottage to fetch drinks and put something on. Her shorts and top were draped over the back of the sofa.

When she emerged from the cottage with the drinks, Steve and Deena had moved three of the chairs into a patch of bright sunlight. Afternoon was turning into early evening and the humidity had risen sharply. "My God, it's sticky," said Steve as he peeled off his T-shirt.

"Is Robert working this weekend?" asked Deena.

"I think so," replied Jenna. "We've separated."

Steve and Deena exchanged looks. "I'm sorry to hear that," said Steve.

"There has been a lot happening since I saw you two last summer," said Jenna.

She gave them the highlights of the past year. Steve and Deena listened carefully as she told them about Gerta's murder, the sale of the house and Robert's relocation to the East Coast.

"Holy world turned on edge, Batman!" Steve exclaimed when Jenna finished talking. "Talk about going through wholesale life change."

"This has got to be taking a toll on you," said Deena. She was sitting beside Jenna and she took her hand. "Is there anything we can do?"

"It's good to see the two of you. When you pulled in here today I realized that you are the only people I know socially who I did not meet via Robert."

"What are you doing for dinner?" asked Steve.

"I'm embarrassed to say," she replied. "I was going to have the great Canadian fall-back meal. Back bacon on a bun."

"Comfort food is comfort food," said Steve. "I can think of three ready alternatives. One, you come over to our cottage and I'll barbeque something. Two, I'll go pick up a few things, bring them back here and we'll dine a Chez Jenna. Or three, Deena and I just go off after a couple of drinks and leave you in peace."

"I'm supporting option two," said Deena. "Jenna and I stay here and sip wine in the sunshine while Steve the superhero goes bravely forth to secure food and drink for us."

"I'm all over option two as well. But food only. There is plenty of wine and beer on hand," said Jenna.

"Wonderful," said Steve. "I'll finish my beer and go. Is your barbecue working, Jenna?"

"Yes. I checked it when I was out a couple of weeks ago."

"Well then," said Steven, taking a mighty drag of his beer, "I'm off."

Jenna had always found Deena easy to be around and today was no different. She brought Jenna up to speed on what she and Steve had been up to since the previous fall and managed to talk about the very high-end cruise they had been on without making it sound like they had been on a very high-end cruise.

Deena loved the lake as much as Jenna did and was excited that she would be able to spend most of the summer at their cottage. She had two major writing projects to do for her company and would only have to be in the office on Mondays and Tuesdays. "Imagine it, Jenna! Two day weeks after two day weeks all through July and August."

"I'm jealous," said Jenna. "Although I have so much vacation and lieu time in the bank that I expect that I'll be out here a lot as well. Not as much as you, though."

"That will be great. I've promised myself that by mid-August I'm going to have my best tan ever. I wonder what my lecherous old boss would do if he knew that his copywriter was working on his reports au naturel?"

"If he's that type," said Jenna, "he'd probably be dropping by for daily progress reports."

When Steve returned from his shopping trip, Deena told him that the summer was getting better and better because Jenna was planning to spend a lot of time at the lake. Steve was genuinely pleased about that. "That's great," he said. "You two can keep an eye out for each other. Are you nervous about spending nights alone here, Jenna?" he asked.

"I never have been. Why?"

"Well. With something as terrible as your Aunt's murder so recently, I didn't know if a cottage surrounded by dark woods might give you the heebie jeebies."

"I haven't been here alone at night since the murder. Last time I came up I had a friend with me. Guess I'll find out tonight."

"Deena and I will chat on the phone every night that she's up here alone. I'll want to talk with her anyway of course, but there is nothing wrong with a check-in call either."

"Are you going to be talking with someone on a regular basis when you're up here alone?" asked Deena.

"I hadn't planned to."

"We're having a phone hooked up next week," said Steve. "I'll drop the number off. Shove it under your front door. Do you have a phone here?"

"I have to get it activated."

"Can we get that number?" asked Steve. "It would be great if Deena could have it while she's here this summer."

***

Tom Robbins had arranged to pick up Ing at 10 p.m. at her apartment studio. She looked stunning. Her hair hung over her shoulders in a dark silken mass. Her little black dress fit her perfectly, showing off her lithe figure. She was braless and wore black stockings with a pronounced pattern. She'd done her makeup to suit the low light conditions of the club. "You're an enchantress," said Tom as he kissed her cheek and held the car door for her.

The club was located in an industrial area north of the city. The owners had taken over a three-story furniture factory and converted it into a facility of a completely different nature. It wasn't for everybody, but as they walked in from the parking lot it was apparent that a fair number of would-be attendees had already been turned away from the very security laden front doors. The club operators were unabashed about their policy of only letting in the most physically attractive customers.

As they approached the door two of the security guards stared fixedly at Ing and beckoned to her and Tom as they were about to take their place in the line of about a dozen couples. "What you got for me, man?" one of the guards asked Tom.

Tom slipped him a wad of fifties. "And where in this den of inequity might this young beauty be seen tonight?" asked the guard.

Ing looked him in the eye and said, "One of the smaller viewing rooms. You find out which one. I guarantee it will be worth your while."

"I'm sure it will be, beautiful lady," he said as he unhooked the chain to let them pass into the club.

The first thing that assailed the senses when one stepped into the club was the sound. A DJ with seemingly half the speakers and amps in the city at his disposal was cranking out some new hip hop that was getting radio air time. Strobe lights were plentiful. They stood inside the door without moving for a couple of minutes to let their eyes adjust to the darkness.

A hostess approached them and Tom gave her the entry fee in cash. She was wearing black spike heels, a wide black leather belt with a cash pouch on it, and there was a small dildo hanging on a chain around her neck. She assured herself from a ledger mounted on a stand under a small reading light that Tom and Ing were indeed booked to use a viewing room and gave Tom a small sealed plastic bag which he slipped into his jacket pocket. The hostess then said, "Please go in, unless you wish to try me first."

Tom watched Ing intently since whatever she chose to do in the next few seconds would tell him what the night would be like. She gave the hostess a fixed gaze for a moment and then lifted the dildo and chain from her neck. "Turn around and put your hands on the seat of your chair," said Ing.

The woman complied and Ing used her foot to indicate that she wanted her legs further apart. When she was satisfied with the hostess's stance Ing leaned forward and deeply probed the woman's labia with her tongue.

When Ing felt the hostess was wet enough, she moistened the small dildo with her saliva and inserted it into the woman's vagina, leaving the chain hanging down. "You can ask the next guests to remove your toy for you," Ing told her. She took Tom's hand and they walked into the main part of the club.

Ing chose a high stool at the bar and Tom stood beside her, trying to catch the attention of a bartender. It took time, but eventually he got them drinks. When he handed Ing hers, she was gazing raptly at the dance floor.

Just in front of them, a very tall shapely blond woman, likely about forty, was being undressed by two men and a woman. She was down to a very tiny thong which came off to the cheers of a number of observers. The woman who had been helping to strip her dropped to her knees and explored her mons and labia with great enthusiasm. After some time, one of the men tapped the woman on her shoulder and she reluctantly allowed herself to be helped to rise.

One of the men had moved behind the naked blond woman, bracing her. The other man unzipped his trousers and lifted one of the woman's legs. A bystander helpfully held her leg as the man entered the woman and began to thrust wildly. The woman made noises that were audible over the sound of the music at each thrust and there was much verbal approval from members of the crowd. "Must be her birthday," said Ing. "Let's move on to our room."

The viewing room was not very large but it was very specifically equipped. Once inside, Tom unzipped Ing's dress and hung it on a wall hook. She looked superb in black garters, black stockings and her heels. Tom added a black blindfold to her ensemble.

"Which one tonight?" asked Tom.

"Oh my dear Tom, it has to be only one?"

It was the answer Tom expected. He led her to the sling, secured her hands above her head and then proceeded to complete the process with the leg straps. Her choice of sling predetermined the position she would be in. Once all was fastened Tom pressed his mouth against her ultra-exposed genitals. Ing was very wet. "I am going to come quickly, my darling," she whispered. "So that I can get on with it. I want all the lights."

Ing was true to her word and she bucked and cried loudly as Tom enjoyed her fragrance and wetness. As she had insisted, Tom then arranged for all the small but intense spot lights mounted on the walls of the room to shine on her body. He then opened a shutter which had covered a 18 X 18 inch opening that permitted anyone in the club to look into the room. Ing had chosen to be suspended only four inches from the window opening. Her exposed buttocks were about four feet off the floor. Tom took up a position beside Ing where he could observe and intervene if necessary.

It was nearly three in the morning when Ing said weakly, "It's perhaps time to go home, dear Tom."

He helped her to stand and slide into her dress. She was silent, nearly asleep he thought, as he drove her home. About two blocks from her apartment she said quietly, "Are you coming up to boff me and cum? God knows you've earned it."

"I'll let you get some rest tonight, Ing. Rain check?"

"Always, Tom." There was a long pause and then she said, "Fuck, that was a trip! I think I'll do a little self analysis about that this week." She fumbled her key out of her tiny evening bag and walked carefully to her door. Tom waited until he was sure she was safely inside and then went home.

***

Arnon, Jules and the rest of the cops had suddenly become busy. Arnon's first job was to contact his boss and tell him that the arson at the library was actually a bizarre robbery. He had to brief his boss at poolside with some sort of office party for his wife's staff going on. Arnon knew his captain well so he led with the numbers.

"We've learned that whoever burned the library stole over $500K of gear and replaced it with exactly the same gear."

"Say what?" was the captain's response.

"Detective Crane had a talk with the head honcho of the computer lab this morning. The guy is an absolute freak about his wires and boxes. He was going through the ashes inventorying things to make an insurance claim when he notices something funny about the serial number on one of the pieces. He says that all of the serial numbers he can read are wrong."

"That's crazy," said the captain.

"Well. It sure as hell gives us a lot more work to do," said Arnon. "We now know that we've got people with big money and access to huge expertise who wanted whatever information was in the library's computers. "

The captain was looking across the pool where his wife was making 'what the fuck are you doing' faces at them.

"I'll get out of your hair," said Arnon.

"Thanks Nick. Good work! And good work to that detective too. What's his name?"

"Rob Crane. He's gonna be a useful cop some day."

"I'll remember that," said the captain.

***

Nils was very glad to be back in Cologne. But he was feeling on edge. Luckily for him, all of his connections had worked, so he had a full six hours before his meeting. He went to his apartment, set his alarm and crawled into bed. It was unusual for him to feel fatigue, but he had felt vulnerable in Mombassa. He did not do vulnerable well.

Nils awoke to a feeling of disaster. Such awakenings gave him a murderous feeling. He wished he were in some of the more sketchy spots that he had visited, the Democratic Republic of the Congo, perhaps. One could find many ways to express one's self in such a setting.

Instead, he was at home in Koln. He was about to commence shaving when there was a pounding at the door of his apartment. Outraged, he snatched the door open with his hand on a Beretta pistol in the pocket of his bathrobe. Two large policemen told him that he must evacuate the building immediately. It did not improve Nils' mood to spend three hours in a transit bus while the authorities unearthed and loaded a thousand pound British aerial bomb onto a truck to be taken to a safe place for demolition.

When he got back into his apartment, the message light was flashing on his phone. It was a message from Winter demanding that he call immediately.

Nils dialed the number. When it was picked up he said, "It appears that the British have at some time bombed Koln. I've been evacuated to a bus. I am now in my home, apparently allowed to make use of all of the facilities."

"Well, make use of them quickly," was the answer. "And then mount that ridiculous Harley whatever it is and get here by backstreet and alley. The city is paralyzed by the discovery and transport of this fucking wartime explosive. A pox on the Allies!"

"He's pissed!" thought Nils. "That is a very good thing. When he gets pissed he gives me greater freedom of action."

Nils was in such a good mood that he contemplating masturbating during his shower. But he decided to hold back in case greater opportunities presented. He hadn't been feeling himself lately. A new opportunity wouldn't be amiss.

He pulled on a leather jacket, picked up his helmet and descended to the street where his Harley was parked at the curb. The main routes were in gridlock because so many of the major streets had been closed to allow the movement of the convoy carrying the British bomb. Nils took to the back streets and alleys.

He entered an access lane behind a row of bars and pawnshops. Two men were in the process of beating up a woman who, from her attire, Nils deemed to be a hooker. The two men stopped their assault as Nils rolled up and he probably would have simply rolled past had not one of men, in poor German said, "Just keep going, motherfucker."

Nils stopped his bike about ten yards from them, dismounted and walked back toward the two men. Predictably they both pulled knives and one of them let go of the girl and advanced threateningly toward Nils. "I can't believe how much better the morning has become," thought Nils. He smiled pleasantly at the man nearest him.

When they were about eight feet apart the man went into the classic knife fighting crouch. He had started to take a step forward when there was a loud smack and he collapsed to the ground. A blood pool started to form under his head instantly.

The cosh that Nils had just swung so accurately had been lovingly handcrafted by a master leather worker in Argentina. One of Nil's ancestors had been a Prussian cavalry officer during the Napoleonic Wars. At the battle of Leipzig two French canister balls had smashed into his leg. Once removed, the two projectiles had become treasured family heirlooms.

Nils was practical man with a limited sense of sentimentality. Each of the lead canister balls weighed two ounces. He had them mounted on the end of seven feet of exquisitely braided leather. And he practiced frequently with his toy.

The man on the ground had two deep indentations in his skull. It was likely that he would die in a few hours, never regaining consciousness. Few surgeons had the mix of skill and speed necessary to save a person bearing the horrible crushing head wounds made by the cosh.

The second man had released the hooker and was backing slowly away from Nils. It was clear that he had not seen the lightning fast whip of the cosh. "I ain't got a gun," he said.

Nils continued to walk toward him, keeping a close watch on the man's hands and his eyes. They were ten feet apart when the man's eyes flickered and Nils tensed for the next move.

The man turned and started to run. Nils moved very quickly and again there was a loud smack, followed by a snapping sound and a scream. The second man fell to the ground with a compound fracture of his right leg. He was almost certainly going to beg for his life, but Nils had an appointment. The cosh whirred through the air a third time and the left upper side of the man's skull seemed to implode.

Nils admired his handiwork as he carefully wound up the cosh. He tucked it with precision into the special pocket sewn into his leather jacket. The hooker was crying and saying "Danke," over and over as he walked back to his motorcycle. Nils approached her and when he was very close he leaned forward and loudly said, "Shut up."

"You are a life-support system for three orifices and a pair of tits. Nothing more. Next time I feel like killing some vermin, it could be you."

The girl quickly stepped back from Nils but he was already striding to his bike.

He parked in front of Winter's building ten minutes later. He was whistling softly to himself when he entered Winter's office, which annoyed the older man. "What has put you in such a cheerful mood?" he asked curtly.

***

Tom's phone rang the day after the visit to the club.

"Good morning," said Ing.

"Have you looked at a clock yet, beautiful woman? You've missed morning by a good three hours."

"Did I have five orgasms last night, Tom?"

"Seven actually. That's counting the one with me. And the female security guard was merciless. You had two from her. I kept listening for your safe word, but you just kept begging her to stop. I think you knew how much that was turning her on."

"Oh shit. Yes. It's coming back to me with a bit more detail."

"How are you, Ing?"

"Profoundly tired. And despite some tenderness and bruising, profoundly horny. Would you care for some gentle, slow, careful love making tonight?"

"That would be lovely."

"Why don't I come to you? And if you don't mind, I'll sleep in your spare bedroom tonight. I have a feeling that if I were here alone the demons might come a-creeping."

"Absolutely."

"I'll see you about nine. And sometime today, be a super love and call Jenna."

"I will do that."

***

Jenna was at first annoyed to see the message light on her answering machine flashing when she entered her apartment. She hit the play button expecting to hear Robert's voice. Instead it was the deep mellow voice of Tom Robbins asking, "when it might be convenient to meet and go over the diaries".

"Anytime," thought Jenna.

She checked her day timer and then dialed Tom's number. Her call went to his machine.

"Hello, Tom. It's Jenna Van Velt calling."

She paused a moment and then said, "It's great that you have some downtime. I will as well, starting this Wednesday …"

The need to visit the bathroom had brought Ing out of her deep sleep. Tom knew her quite well and was sure that she was up for the day. By the time she emerged from the bathroom, having no doubt availed her of his toothbrush, the kettle had boiled and the French press was ready to yield some excellent coffee.

The moment that Ing heard Jenna's voice coming from the machine, she dived for the phone and broke in on the message that Jenna was leaving.

"Leave no message my sweet friend, talk to us in real time. We need to arrange to get those fucking diaries read as soon as we bloody can."

After a pause Jenna said, "Is that you, Ing?"

"It is. I am drinking coffee and recovering from a hangover at Tom's place. I'm glad you two are finally connecting to deal with your Aunt's diaries. Are you inviting us to go out to your cottage to read them?"

Jenna surprised by Ing's question but quickly answered yes. Ing and she made some arrangements about meeting at the market in the town of Bayfield on Wednesday.

"This is going to be a blast," said Ing. "It's always for the best when I make Tom's social arrangements for him. Did you want to speak to the dear man, Jenna, or can you wait until Wednesday?"

Jenna felt the only answer to that question could be "wait until Wednesday" she said goodbye to Ing.

When Ing got off the phone she was smiling impishly. "Who is clever enough to secure a lovely spot for a few days vacation?" she asked.

"That would be such a good place to go through those diaries, Tom. I've been out there and it is beautiful. Private, right on the water. We'll have a great time!"

"Does your friend Jenna think she's being put upon, Ing?"

"Not at all. She is a really good person, Tom. I've gotten to know her well. The sooner that she finds out what her mystery Aunt was involved in, the better for her. I worry about her."

"How many of these diaries are there?" asked Tom.

"I think quite a few. Probably a few days worth," Ing sipped her coffee and then smiled. "She is now a single lady, Tom. And she has a great body. This could be the beginning of a beautiful friendship," said Ing, doing a terrible impression of Bogart.

"I don't think that the prim and proper Ms. Van Velt and I would be on the same page when it came to carnal activities," said Tom.

Ing gave that some thought. "Maybe not. Or she maybe in need of a Svengali. God knows I've taken on that role with her a bit."

Tom was only mildly surprised at that. He arose from his chair. "Enough of this. I want you in the bedroom with your delectable ass in the air. Now!"

An hour later they were lying wrapped tightly, damply together. "I am always amazed at how fucking wonderful you taste," said Tom.

"And as much as I love lying here feeling your cum trickle out of me," said Ing, "I have work to do. Must clear things off before our cottage vacation."

***

Nils was feeling on top of his game. His meeting with Winter had gone well. The older man was in a state of anxiety about the shipments of the computer gear from the library in America. Nils explained to him that the need for subterfuge meant the equipment would not all arrive on a neat pallet at one location.

The upshot of their meeting was an agreement that Nils would visit each of the receivers of the equipment personally. He had managed to make Winter believe that this was an onerous task and had secured the promise of serious remuneration and resources for doing so. Winter was somewhat mollified about the whole project when Nils laid out his itinerary for the next several days.

It was summer in Europe, the weather was perfect and Nils was being paid handsomely to ride his Harley across Germany and into France. None of the shipments were sent to Koln. His first stop was to his contacts in Hamburg.

Because it was closest to Koln, Nils had had the shipments from LAX directed there. His contact assured him that all had arrived and had been dispatched to their terminal destination. Nils took the man for a good lunch and slipped him an extra thousand U.S. dollars for his efforts.

***

When Jenna got to her office, she had a telephone message from Tom Robbins, asking her to give him a call. He answered on the first ring.

"So, we actually talk to one another," said Tom.

"It's almost a miracle," replied Jenna.

"Jenna, you may have noticed that Ing can sometimes be just a touch impulsive. We don't have to horn in on your vacation to go through those diaries. I can meet you in town."

"Well thank you, but I think Ing has had a brilliant idea. There would be no better place to read them and learn about my Aunt. And a few days by the lake would likely do us all good. If you're a runner, I have a five mile route laid out through some lovely scenery."

They talked a bit longer and Tom became convinced that they would be welcome at the cottage. He explained that Ing was a bit foggy on the meeting-up arrangements and had no idea at all of how to get to Bayfield.

Jenna gave Tom directions to the little town and explained that there was only one market to shop at there. He asked for a description of her car and they agreed on a time to meet in the parking lot. Tom told her what he would be driving.

"Can I ask a favour?"

"Sure," Jenna replied.

"If you have a working barbecue, may I cook dinner Wednesday night? I'll bring everything that's required."

"I would be insane to turn down that offer. Thank you. By the way, what do you like to drink?"

"I like to drink what I will bring in abundance."

"Tom. As well as the diaries, my Aunt had a lot of photographs. There are pictures of lots of military trucks and several army tanks. Would they be useful for you to look at?"

"They would be very interesting, Jenna. Extremely interesting. Please bring them."

Jenna ended the call, excited about the coming days.

***

Jenna awoke on the first day of her vacation with a feeling of great anticipation. She had the remainder of the week away from the office as well as the entire following week. It would be the longest stretch of time she had taken away from a job since she had graduated from university.

She had loaded most of what she planned to take the previous night. Once the coffee was brewing, she filled a cooler with food and ice packs and took it to the car. She drank a coffee and made another trip down to the garage, this time with a canvas carry-all that held Gerta's diaries and photo collection. She left an hour and a half early, unable to stay in the city any longer.

When Tom and Ing pulled into the parking lot to meet Jenna, Tom said, "I love it when a plan comes together. I'll follow you to your cottage."

As Jenna drove with Tom and Ing following along, she reflected on what it was going to be like to be a third wheel for the next few days.

It was three when Jenna parked. Tom pulled his Jimmy in beside her car. "This is just crazy beautiful," he said as he walked to the lake.

Ing got out of the car and gave Jenna a long, tight hug.

"What's it called?" he asked as they joined him on the dock.

"McCrimmon Lake. It was named for the Army surveyor who mapped this area."

"Lucky surveyor! I've always wanted a lake named after me. Not gonna happen, but one can still have the dream. Do you know Lake Erie?"

"The Great Lake?"

"That's the one."

"My Dad and I and some friends camped at a place called Turkey Point once."

"That was Lake Erie. Not the best part of it, but it was Lake Erie. I guess we should see to the logistics."

"Jenna," said Ing. "How do I turn on your sauna?"

"Sauna," said Tom. "It's eighty freaking degrees!"

"Well, friend Tom. When you dive into Lake Hard Nipples out there, you will feel a sudden tightness in your throat. That is how far and how rapidly your balls will retract when that water contacts them. I intend to sunbathe and swim. But I must be able to ward off hypothermia."

Once Tom had the ribs marinating they took drinks to the chairs in the sun. Jenna wore a bikini, Tom bathing trunks. Ing had gone out to the lawn ahead of them and was busily arranging deck chairs for maximum exposure to the sun. She was nude.

Tom and Jenna stood awkwardly watching Ing at her self appointed task. She looked up and asked, "Are you two going to stand there getting tan lines or are you going to get with the Lake Hard Nipples program? Don't either of you try to play coy. I've seen you both naked and I know you don't lie in the sun with bathing suits on."

Tom glanced at Jenna and said, "Ing wasn't raised in Canada, Jenna, so she doesn't understand our sense of propriety."

"Oh, for God's sake! Canadian propriety! Get 'em off, you Eskimos, or I'll get them off for you. This is California, not the Great White North."

Ing crouched and moved toward them with a very twisted smile on her face. Jenna hurriedly undid her bra and dropped it beside her chair. "Okay," said Ing, "That's a move in the right direction. Now on three." Tom didn't wait for her to finish the count and Jenna followed suit quickly.

"Good," said Ing. "The ice is broken. Let's get on with learning everything there is to know about Aunt Gerta."

Jenna had the tote bags with the diaries and photos in it. Tom had taken a seat in a deck chair and Jenna was very self conscious when she walked over to him to hand him the bundles of photos from the bag. It did not help that Ing made an appreciative comment about her bum.

Tom had said that picture was worth a thousand words. He took a pull from a cold can of beer and started to look through the photos. Jenna watched him closely and she could see that he was deeply interested.

He extended three of the photos for her to look at. Jenna took them and realized that they all had army tanks in them. "Those are Oliphants," said Tom. "British built Centurion tanks which the South Africans modified. Damn Interesting. I can't make out the unit markings."

He kept shuffling through the stacks of pictures, stopping from time to time to carefully scrutinize a particular shot. His beer was left untouched. He was into a stack from one of the later years when he swore softly.

"Shit! I knew this guy."

He leaned toward Jenna and showed her the photo. He placed his index finger on the chest of one of the uniformed men in the photo who was standing next to Gerta. "That is Major Andreas Van Trup. He was an INTEL officer who worked with the South African armoured units."

"Wow," said Jenna. "My Aunt hung out with army guys."

"Your Aunt hung out with hard-core army guys. Van Trup was a seriously involved guy. This has to be in Namibia."

"Namibia!" exclaimed Ing. "All sorts of unrighteous crap happened there when it was the grey zone."

Tom was engrossed in the photos, paying careful attention to each one. It took him an hour of intense concentration, which Jenna did not disturb, before he had two piles of pictures on the arm of his deck chair.

"This stack of photographs," said Tom, tapping the smaller pile," is a unique visual record of the South African presence in Namibia in the sixties and seventies. There are several hundred politicians of various political stripes, from many nations who would befoul their drawers if they knew these photos existed."

"Why?" asked Jenna.

Tom shuffled through the deck of photos and selected one. It was a group shot of Gerta, another woman and six men, four of them in uniform. Tom tapped one of the men and said, "South African Army." He indicated a second uniformed man and said, "French Army." And then he placed his fingers on the last two uniformed men in the photos and said, "American Army and Air Force."

"What's so important about my Aunt being in Namibia, whatever the hell that is, with these army people?"

"When did she disappear?"

"I beg your pardon?" said Jenna.

"I think you or Ing told me that she seemed to have dropped out of sight for a time. When was that?"

"About 1965 to 1980," said Jenna.

"Oh, damn," exclaimed Tom. "I am looking very forward to reading these diaries."

"This is going to be fascinating," said Ing. "I think we're about to find out some of the evil deeds our lovely government was involved in back in the bad old days."

Tom shuffled back and forth through the small stack of photos for a time and then took a swig of his beer. And he made a face because it had become very warm. He arose and walked to the cottage.

"I need a cold beer and to get the ribs in the oven," he said.

"Should I get the diaries out?" asked Jenna.

Tom attended to his cooking duties in the cottage and returned carrying a small cooler that he had brought along. He put the cooler on the ground near Jenna's chair and took a beer out of it. "I put your wine bottles in here," said Tom. "No sense in making constant trips back to the cottage. We are on vacation, after all."

Ing told him that he was a clever boy.

"What I'm going to do is read a few paragraphs and summarize them for you. If we get to a point where your Aunt is talking about something that seems quite important, I will give you word for word as best I can. That work?"

Jenna nodded and picked up the notebook and pen that she had fetched when she brought out the first two diaries. Tom was focused on the first page, squinting as he read the fine handwritten script. He whistled softly.

"Well, here's the first revelation. It's April 6, 1965. Your Aunt is saying that Hector Verwoerd is leading the team off on their great adventure. And that her name is now Johanna Buist."

"What?" exclaimed Jenna.

"Jesus," said Ing. "She's going all James Bond on us!"

"She's talking about her new identity papers and having to get used to being called Johanna. She says she doesn't know anyone in the party other than this Hector guy. There is one other woman in the group who she has just met for the first time at the railway station. Her name is Christine."

"Christine is named on the back of many of the photos," said Jenna.

Tom read for several minutes, turning a few pages. "She's a detail person. The past four pages have been descriptions of the countryside that the railway is running through. She hasn't said where they are yet, but from what she's describing I would say it has to be southern Namibia."

He went on reading, noting it was "still about the countryside," several times and then he loudly said, "Bingo! Their train is taking them through the Kalahari Desert. They are for sure in Namibia."

"I miss the Kalahari," Ing observed wistfully.

Tom went through several more pages and set the diary aside and rubbed his eyes.

"Your Aunt writes in a lovely hand, as my dear old grandmother used to say, but it isn't easy to read. She's treating the train ride as a safari. Describing all of the wildlife and vegetation in detail. She has just noted that they'll be stopping for the night at a camp and she hopes that she will get to talk with some of her new colleagues over dinner."

Tom arose from his chair. "And speaking of dinner, I'd best get to work on ours." He took another beer from the cooler and went into the cottage.

When he was gone Ing asked, "Does he have a nice cock, Jenna?"

"I didn't notice," Jenna answered, which caused Ing to blow half a mouth full of wine out of her nose.

"You liar," she managed to blurt out. "You were sitting there, trying not to look, wondering what it would look like when it was angry."

"I was not," said Jenna.

"Liar. I hope you understand, Jenna, that Tom and I fuck but not just with each other."

Jenna made no response.

They talked about the fact that Gerta had lived under a different name for several years, and Ing and Jenna went through the small stack of photos that Tom had set aside. Most were group portraits with Gerta and soldiers in them. Jenna was aware that the proximity of Ing's nude body was very pleasant to her.

About thirty minutes later Tom called out that dinner would be ready in 10 minutes.

During dinner, Tom asked her questions about the lake and the surrounding area. Jenna couldn't give him much. He said that he'd like to see if there were any local history books for sale in Bayfield. He had donned a barbeque apron for the duration of the meal. Jenna was glad there was no chance of Ing blurting out anything about where Jenna's eyes were directed. She and Ing were nude and she cursed the mirrored sunglasses that Tom was wearing.

She told him about the five mile route that ran through the woods and along the beach and Tom said he thought it would be a good way to start the day tomorrow. Ing told them that were both crazy and she would be sleeping in. They ate the meal quickly since they all wanted to get back to the dairies.

By the time they had covered a quarter of the first book, the only two important bits of information were that Aunt had assumed a new name, and that she was excited about the "work" they would be doing. It was still warm but the light was fading, so Tom put the diaries in the cottage, asked Jenna and Ing if he could get them anything and settled into the chair beside her with a Jack Daniels and water.

They speculated on what her Aunt might have been doing in Namibia for a time. Clearly, whatever it was required a high degree of secrecy. They agreed that a full day of reading after their morning run would likely bring them a lot of answers.

Ing had been quiet, concentrating on the sinking sun. She speculated that the sauna must be up to heat. Tom commented on the heat of the evening and questioned again why a sauna might be necessary. Jenna pointed at the lake. "Mountain meltwater. Trust me. A short swim and you'll be running to get into the sauna."

Ing arose from her chair and picked up a towel. "C'mon you two. It's time to take the plunge." When she reached the dock she made a running dive. Jenna told Tom that the only way to get in was to simply run and dive and followed suit. When Jenna surfaced she got a glimpse of Ing swimming quickly for shore. Tom surfaced a short distance from her, cursing loudly.

"For the love of Christ! What perverse entity created a body of water this beautiful and this fucking cold?" he asked no one in particular.

"Swim for the dock," yelled Jenna. "Before the polar bears come to investigate the splashing noises."

She had a good head start, but she and Tom reached the ladder on the dock at the same time. He deferred to her and she was sure he enjoyed the view as she climbed out of the lake. He came up the ladder quickly and they ran for the sauna.

Ing was already there, lying on her towel on the uppermost bench where the heat was the most intense. "Give me five minutes and I'll fetch us drinks," she mumbled. "Any problems with shrinkage?" she asked Tom.

"I'm more worried about it just snapping off," he answered.

"That would be a shame," said Ing. She got down from the bench somewhat unsteadily and left the sauna.

And here I am, thought Jenna. Sitting naked in my sauna with a naked man that I have seen at dinner once before today. The door to the sauna swung open violently to Ing's kick. She came in carrying one of the coolers. "Everything we need is in here," she said.

The three of them sat quietly with their drinks for some time. The alcohol was clearly taking the edge off Ing's constant frenetic energy. When -as Tom put it- the heat had restored life to all body parts they went outside to the lawn chairs.

It was still a warm, humid night but after the sauna, it felt cool. Ing and Jenna wrapped their towels around them. Tom seemed to enjoy the feeling of the comparatively cool air. Ing had switched from wine to some sort of liqueur that she had brought with her. Jenna wasn't sure that it was meant to be consumed by the water tumbler-full.

Ing abruptly arose from her chair, letting her towel slip to the ground. "I'm going to bed," she announced. Tom and Jenna watched her walk unsteadily to the cottage. "I wonder which bed she'll choose?" thought Jenna.

They sat in silence for a time and then when Tom was pouring a bit more Jack Daniels, Jenna quietly asked, "How did you happen to become a Rhodesian, Tom?"

He didn't say anything for a long moment. He stood up and as he walked to his SUV he mumbled something that Jenna couldn't make out. When he returned he had a pack of cigarettes.

Chapter Fourteen

"I'm originally from southern Ontario. My family farmed tobacco in a fairly big way in Elgin County. I worked the farm during the spring, summer and fall but in the winter there was really nothing to do. So I would pick up some extra money working in construction. Usually in London, which was the largest city close by."

"There is a big university, the University of Western Ontario, in London. I was on a job there in the winter of 1972 when I met Terri. She was the most beautiful, interesting girl I had ever seen. Completely unlike anyone I had known. You have to keep in mind that I was a twenty-one year old farm boy from Ontario so I didn't have a whole hell of a lot of life experience."

I was taking a smoke break when she walked up and asked for light. Western was a pretty snooty place and the students seldom noticed, let alone spoke to, the hired help. I lit her smoke for her. I still remember the next thing she said to me.

"She said, 'It's nice to have a smoke with someone who works for a living'."

"I was not a smooth conversationalist back then. But I knew in that moment that I wanted to go on talking with her for a long, long time. So I blurted out the first thing that popped into my head. If you want to see people working, you should be on our farm when we're harvesting the tobacco."

"And Jenna, I had said the perfect thing."

"Terri had come to Western because she wanted to take economics from a guy named Gull from England and Medieval English history from a prof named Lambert. She was desperately homesick and totally put off by, as she called them, 'the entitled brats' in her classes. And our Canadian winter was depressing the hell out of her."

"She could talk a mile a minute. Faster than our friend Ing. Over that first cigarette I learned that she was from Rhodesia, that her family ran a big beef and tobacco operation there, and she extracted a promise from me to take her out to our farm. I was working laying cement blocks up three stories that day. I think I just flew up there after my break because I don't remember climbing a ladder to go back to work."

"She was the first person I had ever met who had green eyes. Although sometimes when she was excited about something, they were a gray/green colour. I loved her accent. I loved her outlook on the world. She was totally unlike any girl I had ever met."

"She truly loved Rhodesia. Certainly as much as I loved Ontario. We were very similar in that regard."

"When she graduated I went to Rhodesia with her. Her family liked me, I liked them, and I was in love with Terri. Then she got pregnant."

"She hated what Ian Smith was doing to the country and was all for extending the vote to the blacks. She said that was the only way the country would ever survive. She said that if things got too much worse in Rhodesia and she had to leave, she would be done with Africa. We had some serious talks about what it would be like to live in California."

"We went to see government people and they told me that I had two choices. I could go back to Canada, apply for immigrant status, likely wait two years for an answer, and that I might get in. I didn't have any post-secondary education or special skills, so I would not be fast tracked. Or, I could immediately join the Rhodesian Army, stay in the country and after a year's service, I would be granted full citizenship. I felt that I had just been presented with a no-brainer."

"In 1972 the Bush War had started in Rhodesia. ZAPU, the Zimababwe African People's Union was the political group sworn to take out Ian Smith's white dominated government. ZIPRA was their military wing. It was a very dirty war with all sorts of nasty shit going down. I found myself neck deep in it, serving as a private in the Rhodesian Light Infantry."

Tom had been sipping his drink steadily as he talked. Jenna took his glass and went into the cottage. She returned with drinks for both of them.

"Anyway," Tom continued, "the Rhodesian army turned me into a soldier pretty quickly. I'd do ten to fifteen days on duty and then would get five off. We were operating close to Terri's family's farm so I always got back there to see her and help out on the farm. The day my daughter was born, I was deep in bad guy territory conducting an ambush.

"On my eleven month anniversary of joining the RLI, I got promoted to master corporal and was sent off on a training course to become a senior non-commissioned officer. It was a six week course held at quite a distance from the farm. I only got home once during the six weeks to see Terri and Kathryn. When I finished the course I was told that I was fast tracked to be promoted to sergeant and given three weeks leave."

"Those were the best three weeks of my life up to that time. Terri's parents had friends who owned a place a stone's throw from Victoria Falls. We took Kathryn there and holed up for most of my three weeks. Terri was beautiful, Kathryn was beautiful, and that part of Rhodesia was extremely beautiful. It was hard to take them back to the farm and report for duty."

"I was deep in the bush a week later on the track of a group of ZIPRAS that had blown up some electrical pylons and shot up some farms. Rhodesia had an elite anti-terrorist unit called the Selous Scouts. My unit linked up with theirs and we went way deeper into the bush than I had ever been. I'm pretty sure that when we caught up with Terrs, we were in Zambia."

"One of our guys got hit in the legs and a Scout was badly wounded in the chest. When a helicopter came in to pick them up, there were orders for me to evac with them. I found out that Terri and Kathryn were dead when we landed back at the base hospital."

Tom sat silently for a long time, quietly sipping his drink.

"I am so sorry, Tom. What happened?" asked Jenna.

"Terri was in her Dad's Land Rover driving a few miles to visit a friend of hers. A civilian contractor to the army was returning from a fuel run in a big tank truck. He was drunk and hit the Rover head on at speed. The tanker blew up and the driver, Terri and Kathryn just disappeared in the flames."

"Oh my God," breathed Jenna.

"I said other things. The army gave me two weeks and then I had to report back. The first thing they did was tell me that my year was up and that I was officially a Rhodesian. Then they said they were going to make me a sergeant."

"I was totally adrift. My sole reason for being in Rhodesia was Terri and Kathryn. They were gone. I didn't have a clue of what I would do next."

"The Selous Scouts had an ultra-rigorous admission standard that included some of the most brutal training in the world. I had heard horror stories about it. It seemed to be a good way to get my head away from Terri and Kathryn, so I blew off my rank in the RLI and applied to join the Scouts. And I was right. Once I embarked on that training, there was nothing in my head but thoughts of survival for the next two months."

"How long were you in with them?"

"Four years. Saw a hell of a lot of things that would keep me awake at night if I thought back on them. But I made some very, very good friends. I stayed around after the war ended long enough to get issued with a Zimbabwean passport and left the country."

"Not to go back to Canada, I would guess," said Jenna.

"I tried. I tried very hard to go home." Tom lit another cigarette.

"I had lots of dollars in my pocket because after Terri was killed I pretty much soldiered and banked my pay. I spent the summer in a little cottage in Port Stanley, a beach town near where I grew up, mostly taking home girls who looked a bit like Terri for a night or a weekend. That got very lame very fast."

"I was drinking way too much. One night in August I was in one of the bars in Port Stanley when a woman gave me a look. I was showing some interest when her boyfriend, a great big biker bastard appeared and told me he was going to cut me a new asshole. That's a bad thing to say to a former Selous Scout. I hurt him badly."

"The next morning an old buddy of mine who had joined the OPP, the provincial police force, showed up at my cottage and told me that I'd just pissed off a fairly large bike gang. He suggested that I should take a long vacation abroad."

"Earlier that week I'd had a letter from one of my guys that I'd led in the Scouts. He wanted me to come back to work with the South Africans. I dropped by to see my mother for a few hours and a day and half later I was in Johannesburg."

"And on that note, I think it's time for bed," said Tom.

They went into the cottage and Jenna was surprised to find Ing in her bed. She slid under the sheets as carefully as she could, but Ing sensed her presence and snuggled up to her. Jenna drifted off into the deepest of sleeps.

***

Arnon's phone began to ring at 4:30 a.m. Thursday. He rolled over, picked it up and said, "Whoever is calling better have a lead on who assassinated JFK. Otherwise, I'm coming for you."

There was some laughter from the caller, then Jules said, "Nick, we've caught a break!"

Arnon came wide awake and listened as Jules, with glee in his voice told him that a bunch of computer equipment that had been shipped from LAX had been seized in Marseilles. Jules was laughing when he told Arnon that two drug sniffing dogs had homed in on three boxes. The customs people had set the boxes aside and waited for someone to come and claim them.

"Did you get anyone?" asked Arnon.

"Mais, oui," said Jules. "A very small-time thug from one of the bigger Marsielles gangs. He's in custody, not talking. Eventually he will."

"You've got to secure that equipment like it's Fort Knox," said Arnon. "You know what these people will do to get it."

"No fear, my friend. It's under the escort of one of our best army internal security units on the way to our most secure location. It will be safe and our best computer people are enroute to see what secrets these boxes hold."

"Do you have any serial numbers or anything? I want to talk to our dope smoking computer priest here to see if he can tell us what you've got."

"Get a pen and paper, my American friend," said Jules. "And thank God that your computer priest likes to smoke marijuana and hashish!"

***

Jenna awoke to some very slight sounds coming from the main room of the cottage. During the night Ing had snuggled close to her. Jenna slowly and carefully moved away from her and once clear of the bed, arranged a sheet over the sleeping woman. She quietly slipped on underwear, shorts, socks and a tee shirt and grabbed her running shoes. Tom was making coffee when she stepped into the main area.

"You look like you're ready for a serious run," he said in a whisper.

"Not until I've had a coffee."

They sat on the porch and sipped their coffee. Tom asked her about the property and was interested to learn that her lot was actually several acres, mostly of bush.

He began telling her about his place in Ontario, giving her a detailed description about the long beach and the sand dunes. When Jenna asked about the house, Tom was at a loss. He finally confessed that the house had seemed large but he was unsure how many bedrooms and baths it had. Jenna found that very funny.

They left Ing a note saying they were going for a run. Jenna led off setting her usual pace with Tom following about five yards behind her. The day was becoming warmer and they both sweated profusely. Tom didn't seem to be winded, though. Not bad for a guy who had smoked half a pack of cigarettes the night before, Jenna thought.

Well into the run, Jenna led Tom up a very steep path which led to the top of a rocky hill. She stopped at the top so that they could take in the view. Tom could see Jenna's cottage and the lake about a mile distant. He had brought a water bottle along and he uncapped it and offered it to Jenna.

She drank and gave it back to Tom. He drank off the remaining water and commented on the beauty of the area. Jenna asked him if it measured up to his place on Lake Erie. He assured her it did, in a different sort of way.

In the past, when Jenna had done this run with Robert, this hilltop was the place where he customarily turned it on and left Jenna either struggling to keep up or trailing behind. She half-expected Tom to do the same. When she started on, he fell into his station behind her, and when she glanced back he was looking from side to side, enjoying the landscape they were running through. Jenna always felt that the last mile of the run was the best scenery.

They emerged from the woods into the clearing about four hundred yards from the cottage. Tom edged up to run beside her for the last stretch. "There were some pretty good hills on that trail. Please tell me that the shower in the cottage is operational. I don't think I could stand a dip in the lake this early in the morning."

"The shower works just fine," said Jenna. "And you can have full use of it right after me."

Ing was lying on a deck chair in the sun when they got back. She sat up and looked at them for a moment. "You two are sweat hogs."

***

It was 5 a.m. when Arnon got off the phone with Jules. It would be three hours before he could expect Crane or any of the others to be into the office. He threw on some jeans and went through a nearby drive-through for a coffee and returned home.

He sat at the small kitchen table in his apartment and carefully transposed the notes he had taken down during his call with Jules. The words that Jules had given him were likely brand names but he had never heard of the companies. Each of the items that INTERPOL had seized seemed to have a half dozen model letters and numbers and the serial numbers of the pieces were multiple digits as well. "I hope this isn't a picture of the future," Arnon thought.

He had an uncustomary leisurely shower and a shave and picked up another coffee on his way to work. It was 7:40 a.m. when he entered the parking lot, but Crane's car was there. Crane was at his desk reading the previous night's report summary when Arnon walked into his office. Arnon quickly filled Crane in on the call from Jules. The younger man had a broad smile by the time Arnon had finished recapping the call.

"Here are the numbers and names of what they've got," said Arnon, handing Crane the list. Get your computer guy from the library out of bed, and have him go over this and tell us what the guys in Belgium have. Make a couple copies of this for me before you head out to meet the guy."

"I think it would be a good thing if the INTERPOL guys didn't start in on this equipment until David has a look at this. I'm learning a bit about this computer stuff, and they can put all sorts of codes and crap in their software. David is a smart guy and he may have files set up so that they just go away if someone tries to open them up the wrong way."

"I didn't understand a fucking thing you just said other than I think you want me to tell INTERPOL to not jack around with this stuff until you talk to your guy."

"That sums up what I just said."

"Alright. Call your guy and tell him you're going to pick him up and bring him here. Have him go over the list and match it to his inventory so that he is absolutely sure what it is that Jules and his people have laid their hands on. Then get him back here as fast as you can."

"You got it," said Crane.

"Does David happen to speak French?"

"I would be astonished if he does."

"Alright, get on your way and I'll alert Jules that he needs a guy that speaks both English and computer on his end of the phone."

"Nick, it's Jules."

"Have your guys done anything with the computers yet?"

"No. They aren't going to be here for another half hour or so."

Arnon told Jules about Crane's fear of information being lost. They agreed that his guys would call back to be briefed by the library guy before doing anything with the equipment.

***

Nils rode into Marseilles mid-morning and immediately went to Italian restaurant that was far off the normal tourist routes. When he went inside, the four men there abruptly cut off their conversation. One could have cut the hostility with a dull knife.

The largest man in the group, obviously their leader, got up from his chair and walked toward Nils. When he was two feet from him he spat in his face and called him a bastard in French. Nils' only reaction was to wish him a good morning and ask about his shipment.

This time the man told him that he was a diseased cocksucker. And he said that the Capo would soon be putting a price on Nils' balls which he, personally, was looking forward to removing and delivering to the Capo.

"Ruffo, what has happened to sour our long friendship?"

"You ass licker," replied Ruffo. "You didn't tell us there were drugs in the shipment. If we had known we would have made the proper arrangements. Instead I have one of my men in jail. And he is a baby shit. They will likely make him talk."

"I supervised the packing of the boxes. There were no drugs in them."

"Well then, your fucking crew must have been puffing away on some good shit as they worked," said Ruffo.

Ruffo had been totting up some figures when Nils had arrived. A pad and pencil were on the table near them. Nils bent over the table, picked up the pencil and tore a page from the pad.

"Give me the name of your man and my organization will use our resources and have him out before the end of the day."

"No you fucking won't," said Ruffo leaning over to shout at Nils. "Fucking INTERPOL has taken your shipment. You don't spring guys when fucking INTERPOL is in the fucking game."

Ruffo didn't notice that Nils was holding the pencil between his two middle fingers with the point extended outward and the eraser resting in the palm of his hand.

"You're right, Ruffo," he said as he straightened up and drove the pencil through Ruffo's left eye, through the thin bone of the eye socket and into the frontal lobe of his brain.

The three goons that Ruffo had with him were not ready. Everything they had witnessed had made them think that Ruffo was in control of the situation. Nils shot two of them in their bellies and the third one - who had succeeded in drawing his gun - in the shoulder. The three shots had sounded very loud in the restaurant, but this was a neighbourhood with no cops and frequent gunplay.

Ruffo was lying on the floor making animal noises and apparently having a seizure of some sort. Nils screwed a silencer onto his gun and shot him in the head. Then he turned his attention to the other three men. It took seconds for him to pistol whip them.

Nils turned the sign on the door to 'Ferme' and then found an abundant amount of telephone wire in a pantry. He secured each man to a sturdy chair, pulled down the trousers and underwear of one of the belly shot victims, and gagged the other two men. Then he revived them with slaps and sluices of cold water.

Nils had put the three men into a tight semi-circle and had pulled up a table and chair so that he sat facing them across the table. He had lit three candles and had laid a wooden handled ice pick that he had found behind the bar and an old wicked looking meat cleaver from the kitchen on the table. He had taken a very expensive looking pen from his pocket and sat with Ruffo's pad of paper in front of him. He flipped to a fresh page.

Nils pointed the pen at the ungagged belly shot victim with his nether regions exposed.

"I am going to ask you some simple questions," said Nils.

"Fuck you," said the man.

Nils smiled and very deliberately heated the end of the ice pick. The steel was cheap and porous and soon the tip of it was glowing red. Nils arose, walked over to the man and drove the ice pick through his flaccid penis.

He put the toe of his shoe on the tip of the man's dick so that he could withdraw the pick. Nils very deliberately went back to his chair, sat down, laid down the ice pick, picked up his pen and said, "I'm going to ask you some simple questions."

The first man was tough. Nils had to heat the pick up three times before the he was willing to end the pain. And Nils did ask simple questions.

"Tell me about your two friends here. Their names, their addresses, whether they have kids."

Nils took meticulous notes as the man responded to him. Then he arose and gagged the man he had just tortured with the gag that had been in the mouth of the other belly shot victim.

"Did you see what I did to your friend with the ice pick?"

The man nodded.

"I am going to do similar things to your wife and your children, with an ice pick just like this one. I know about your wife and children because your friend there with the dick with all the holes burned through it told me all about them. Are you ready to answer some simple questions?"

The man nodded.

"Do you know why I heated up the ice pick before I stabbed it though your friend's cock?" asked Nils.

The man shook his head.

"I did that because if I had just stabbed his cock several times with it he would have bled to death. By heating it up, I was able to put holes in his cock and cauterize them at the same time, thus saving his life."

"Where does your Capo live?"

The man did not answer. Nils got up from his chair, picked up the cleaver and went to the man who had been stabbed and burnt. He grasped the man's scrotum and penis, stretched it out from his body and severed his testicles and penis. He dropped the flesh on the floor in front of the chair of the second man and went to the sink in the kitchen to wash his hands. When he returned, the first man was unconscious. The smell of fresh blood filled the room.

"Where does your Capo live?"

The third man, the one with the shoulder wound, began to try to talk through his gag. Nils arose from his chair again and stood in front of the man.

"You're either going to tell me something useful or tell your friend to never reveal where your Capo lives. If you tell me something useful, I will kill your friend and no one will ever know you talked. If you tell him to remain silent, I will use him to show you what I'm going to do to your son."

Nils removed the man's gag and was quickly given an address.

He replaced the third man's gag and retrieved the gag from the man who had bled to death and gagged the second man. They both had wallets in the breast pockets of their suit jackets. Nils took his time going through them, dropping whatever money that was in them on the floor but keeping any ID with addresses. He arranged the photos they carried on his table and studied them carefully.

Nils patted down Ruffo's body and removed his wallet, which he slid in his pocket. Ruffo had a nine-millimeter Browning automatic in a shoulder holster and a small .22 Beretta in an ankle holster. Nils loved to have extra handguns for contingencies, so he took both of them.

By this time both of the men had lost a lot of blood. Nils was able to take his time exploring the property. He found a lot of cooking oil, many pounds of lard and a can of gasoline beside a small emergency generator. All of this material was poured or placed on the floor by their chairs.

Nils went outside through the front door of the restaurant and got his motorcycle running. And waited.

An old man came shuffling down the street, puffing on his pipe. Nils called out to him, pointing at the restaurant.

"There's a boss in there buying drinks for everyone."

The old man smiled, said "merci" and headed for the door. Nils rolled the bike up the street about forty yards and stopped.

The restaurant blew its front wall onto the street as soon as the old man's pipe ignited the gasoline fumes. Nils thought he saw the old man being hurled across the street as the oily smoke from the lard and oil started to roil. He had trouble controlling the bike as he rode away because he was laughing so violently.

Chapter Fifteen

They made more coffee, settled on chairs in the sunshine and Tom picked up a diary. "Miss Jenna VV's reading circle," Ing said, making a bad attempt at a Georgia accent.

Tom read only a couple of pages before he started to summarize. "Okay, get your pen ready, Jenna. Gerta, or Johanna, is sitting between the woman called Christine and a German dude named Walter."

"That was the name of the old guy that visited my Aunt," said Jenna.

"Your Aunt has been having a good time. She likes both Walter and Christine. She says they've been attentive to her."

"Give us a bit on attentive," said Ing.

"Your Aunt is frank with her diary, Jenna. Obviously this was written for her eyes only. She clearly thinks that both Walter and Christine are attractive."

"Oh, Lord," said Jenna.

"I like this theme," said Ing.

"Walter is a biochemical genius according to Gerta. Christine is a medical doctor and guru on symptomatology. They are all excited about the work they are going to be doing."

Tom read a couple more pages.

"They're having dinner at a fortified South African Army base camp. Oh! This is good. Walter is telling them to shun the military people there since they will all want to have their way with two such lovely women."

"Isn't that pretty much the case for soldiers everywhere, Tom?" asked Ing.

"Pretty much," agreed Tom, as he continued to read.

"They're going to somewhere in northwest Namibia, in the bush, where an installation has been put in place. They're talking about what will be there. Walter is telling them everything is 'world class'. And now he is describing the countryside. There's going to be ample opportunity to see all sorts of wildlife. Your Aunt is eating this up, Jenna."

A few more pages went by. Tom had mumbled, "still at dinner a few times." Then he said, "Holy shit."

Both Jenna and Ing were rapt.

"Walter had his foot on your Aunt's calf. And Christine had her foot on your Aunt's other calf. I shouldn't be surprised. This is happening in the sixties. But Jesus! This gets any hotter and I'm going to have to take a swim."

"Is Gerta expressing any feelings about this?" asked Jenna.

"Yes," said Tom.

"Well, for Christ's sake Tom, spill!" said Ing.

"She's not opposed to anything that's going on," said Tom.

"Go, Gerta girl," said Ing.

"Are the two of you making this up?" asked Jenna.

"It's all right here in the book," said Tom.

"It's clear," said Ing, "that you, Jenna, are meant for a lot more than a simple boy/girl relationship. Your Aunt's diaries are going to reveal this to you. I hope that you will open your soul and psyche to these lessons."

"Fuck you both," said Jenna. "Does anyone want anything from the cottage?"

"I'll take a cold coke,' said Tom.

"One of the wine coolers in the fridge door wouldn't hurt," said Ing.

Jenna strode off to the cottage with all the dignity that a naked woman whose Aunt had just revealed herself as a hot-blooded vixen could muster.

***

It was about ten-thirty when Crane arrived with David. He had verified to Crane that the gear that Jules' people had grabbed was very serious stuff. Arnon was keen to hear how serious it was.

When the two of them came into his office it was clear that Crane was being the good cop. David was at ease. Arnon gave that a bit of thought.

"David. Some of your stolen equipment has been recovered."

"I know! And you've got some of the key pieces. My CPU and the main server and a memory array! This is magnificent! I can't thank you enough."

"You do know that you won't have it back any time soon?"

"What?" asked David.

"People have burned out your lab. Stolen your gear. Murdered people. We need you to work with us on this."

David said that he was in.

"Did Detective Crane tell you how your equipment was recovered?"

"No," was the answer.

Good fucking job, Crane, thought Arnon.

"The stolen equipment had been shipped to Marseilles, France. When it was coming through French customs one of their drug sniffing dogs homed in on it. Can you shed any light on why there was a bag of hash inside of one the pieces?"

"Do I need a lawyer?" asked David, glancing at Crane.

"No David," said Arnon. "We need you. If the hash was yours you've lost it. However, because it was inside your machine, it's allowed us to recover some of the stolen goods."

Arnon stood up. "Unless you commit felonies, I don't give a fuck what you do in your spare time. In fact today, right now, I am grateful that you are a hash smoker. If you weren't, the French drug dogs would be wandering around aimlessly pissing on fire hydrants and the stuff stolen from your library would be gone forever."

Arnon pointed at his desk. "That phone is going ring in about two minutes. The call will be coming from Europe and you'll be talking to computer guys over there who need to access everything in the equipment they've recovered as quickly as possible. Are you willing to help them out?"

"Of course," said David. "I'll enjoy talking with them."

"That's good," said Arnon. "Now, in the equipment that we have, could there be stuff related to what Gerta Ten Haan was doing when she used your lab?"

"Sure," said David. "My server will hold the record of what computer she was communicating with. And hey, if Gerta didn't do her usual erase, her messages might be there as well."

"What's the chance of her not having done this erase thing?" asked Arnon.

David thought about that for a bit. "She knew I was on vacation for a couple of weeks, and it was a lot of work to wipe out the stuff. She might have decided to wait to do it until a couple of days before I was due back. Gerta was a very efficient type."

Arnon looked at Crane. "I think your friend David here is going to be a very useful part of our team."

The phone rang.

***

When Jenna returned with the drinks, Tom indicated that she should pick up her pad and pen. He had read ahead a few pages while she had gone to the cottage and tucked blades of grass into the book to indicate the passages he thought she would think were worth noting. "Okay, Jenna. Your Aunt says they stayed that first night in tents in the army camp. They caught a train again, early in the morning and she says it will take them to final destination in North East Namibia. Walter is sitting with her, pointing out landmarks and things of interest. It's clear that he knows the area quite well."

"She shared a tent with this Christine woman for the night. No hanky-panky although they did talk way past their bedtime. Christine is 27 and has only been a doctor for a few months. She's South African, born and bred."

"The train journey took them all day with no stops. They ate a lunch that the army cooks had prepared for them. It was getting dark as they got close to where they were going. This Walter guy pointed out two satellite camps when they were about two miles from the main camp."

"They arrived in the dark and she and Christine were shown to the room that they would share. They were relieved to have their own bathroom with running water and a shower stall. Your Aunt won a coin toss and got to shower first."

"So, Tom. Claiming the shower first runs in Jenna's family. Explains why you had to hang around as a sweat hog after your run this morning," said Ing.

"So now we start the entry about the first day in the base camp. You ready to write?"

"Sure," said Jenna, taking a quick sip of the ice water she had fetched for herself.

Not surprisingly, the next several pages were a detailed description of the installation. There were 12 buildings in all, all South African pre-fab pattern army barracks that had been brought in by rail and erected within the past three months. Two big diesel generators enclosed in a heavily sand-bagged revetment provided power to the place. Two others in a separate protected enclosure were on hand for an emergency.

"This camp they're in is the real deal. Concentric fences, razor wire, guard towers with machine guns. Very serious fortifications. She is saying that first thing after breakfast they are to have a safety lecture."

Tom read on for a while and looked up from the diary with a slight smile. "Your Aunt is a detail lady, Jenna. I take it you don't care what she had for brekkie?"

"Alright then. The safety lecture. As we have all deduced I'm sure, the elaborate perimeter fences are meant to keep out more that roving packs of hyenas. Hector and a captain from the South African Defense Force are delivering a lecture on terrorists."

"Oh fuck," chuckled Tom. "This is hilarious. The army captain is speaking in officialese. He just used the term 'in a situation of controlled violence'."

"What the fuck is that?" asked Ing.

"War," answered Tom. "But this slick from the army public relations department isn't using that distasteful word. In fact," said Tom, bursting into laughter "he has just told them that there is a minor insurgency in nearby Angola that might overflow into their region on occasion."

Tom lowered the diary and took a long swig of his pop. "I killed at least twenty people during the first minor insurgency that I got caught up in."

He went back to the diary. During the next hour, only a few tidbits made it onto Jenna's note pad. Her Aunt would be given training in how to fire a handgun. Once trained, all staff would keep their issued weapons with them at all times. Each staff would be assigned a post to which they would go in the event of an alarm.

"This is interesting," said Tom. "There are mine fields, extensive mine fields around the base camp and the two satellite camps. Only a very few people - they know who they are - are allowed to go to the satellite camps. Anyone else trying to go there will be removed from the project."

"Sounds like the main event, whatever the main event is, isn't taking place at the base camp," said Ing.

"What the hell are they doing out in a war zone?" asked Jenna.

"That would be a situation of controlled violence zone to you, dear girl," said Ing. "I rule that we finish this diary and go through one more today, and that is all the work that gets done. You two carry on while I go prepare us a delicious lunch. I should tell you that some of my best creations occur when I am working sans apparel."

"Want to finish this one?" asked Tom.

Jenna nodded and prepared to write.

The rest of the book they were going through was all about the first day in the compound. Gerta/Johanna had noted all procedures in the greatest of detail. Jenna and Tom speculated that she might have wanted to use the diary entry as an 'aide memoire'.

Tom was surprised to read that in the evening a bar was opened in the dining hall offering a full range of beers, wines and spirits. He explained to Jenna that the Afrikaans were very religious and straight-laced. He remarked that providing an open bar in such an environment was more like something the Europeans or Americans would do.

They had only just finished the diary when Ing emerged from the cottage carrying a large tray. Tom arose quickly and took it from her. Once free of her burden, Ing curtsied to Tom and said, "Thank you, kind sir."

The tray held three bowls of what Ing said was Cape Town bisque, a plate with a freshly sliced baguette, a small tub of butter, flatware and napkins. Ing had slung a small cooler over her shoulder and from it she produced a bottle of chilled South African white wine. "You are about to have a Tabletop Mountain experience, Jenna."

"Tabletop Mountain is probably the most famous picnic spot in South Africa," said Tom.

"The first thing to do, Jenna, is to select a piece of baguette and butter it," said Ing. Tom was already working on his.

"Then take sip of this very cold wine." Ing sipped and passed Jenna the bottle. Jenna took a sip and passed it on to Tom who did the same.

"And now," said Ing, "a small spoonful of the bisque."

When Jenna first tasted the soup she detected a subtle flavour of oysters and oranges. Followed immediately by a very great sensation of heat in her mouth. As her eyes began to water she realized that both Tom and Ing were taking small bites of their buttered bread and were gesturing for her to do the same.

When she did the burning was gone almost instantly. And she was left with the aftertaste of the soup.

"Okay, Jenna. Now you understand why South African wines are so robust. Now let's do it again. Sip wine. Take a spoonful of bisque. Bite of bread. This meal is like the whole Tequila, lime, salt thing."

They established an efficient rhythm of passing the wine bottle and in due course the soup and bread was gone. Jenna felt satiated without feeling full, and then a great warmth arose in her body. "I won't soon forget this meal," she said. "That was lovely, Ing. Where did you learn how to make it?"

"It was very good," said Tom. "Did you hang out with the oystermen and steal their recipe?"

"As a matter of fact I did."

"We must be careful of her," said Tom to Jenna. "In Africa a woman with her talents would be deemed to be a witch."

"Oh, dear Tom and Jenna. I'm a witch here in America as well."

***

The call from Belgium went on for two hours. They had the INTERPOL people on speakerphone and David and Crane seemed to be very interested in all that was being said. Ten minutes into it, Arnon wished that he could pry his aviation magazine out from under the computer guy's elbow since he had surrendered his desk to him, so that he could be closer to the phone mic.

David and the guy on the other end of the line, who spoke English flawlessly, might as well have been talking in Swahili. All Arnon understood was that David was giving the guy in Europe very detailed instructions of how to do certain things with the computers. An hour into the call there was an 'aha' moment.

"We have the address of the destination computer," said the guy from Europe.

David was almost bouncing in his chair. "That's huge! Will you be able to do anything with that?"

"It will take some time, but we well may. Now, how do I access the messages file?"

For the next half hour David talked the guy through a bunch of stuff that to Arnon sounded like total gibberish. Even Crane looked bored. Then came the moment.

"There are seven messages here. Quite lengthy. They are written in Dutch I think, but I don't read it."

Arnon heard Jules speaking in the background. He was telling someone to fetch someone.

"Give us a few moments," said Jules into the phone.

Five minutes elapsed. Crane sat patiently, David picked at his cuticles, which were in grave need of attention, and looked at the ceiling-level cobwebs in the four corners of his office.

"Hello in America," said Jules suddenly.

"Yes," said Crane eagerly.

"The messages are from Gerta Ten Haan to an unnamed man. They are obviously speaking in veiled speech. Critically though, she almost threateningly tells the man that she has the disks with all of the formulas."

"Well," said Arnon. "We may not know what these disk things are, but we can assume they got her killed."

"Equally important," said Jules, "is that the man who she is corresponding with demanded to know if she had destroyed her 'infernal diaries'".

"And she said," asked Arnon.

"Fuck you. We're killing thousands of people. It is time to do the right thing. That is a verbatim quote."

"What else?" asked Arnon.

"Sadly, that is all we have, my friend. We'll fax transcripts of the conversation to you within the hour. Thank you to Detective Crane and Mr. Dennison. This is all so very helpful. I will be in contact the moment we learn anything about the address of the correspondent. Even if that means waking you up, Nick."

"I have a couple of things that I want to follow up on, Jules. I may wake you up!"

They ended the call and all of them sat silently for a moment. Then Arnon asked Crane if he had some cigarettes with him. Crane said he did. Arnon asked David if he had anything that he liked to smoke along. He nodded yes.

"Into my car," said Arnon.

***

Ing insisted on clearing up from lunch so Tom and Jenna went back to the diaries. The first book had covered only two days. Gerta described long days in her little office which was adjacent to an air-conditioned room that housed the computer equipment that she was in charge of. She mentioned that the equipment room was the only air-conditioned area in the camp.

It was clear that she and Christine were becoming close friends. Equally clear was the fact that Gerta was becoming attracted to Walter. Near the end of the second book, she had devoted four pages of the diary to discussing with herself if there was any merit in having a relationship with a man twenty-five years her senior. No matter how much she admired his intelligence.

"Good God," said Jenna when Tom translated that passage. "He's truly old enough to be her father."

"If it happens," agreed Tom, "it will definitely be an early summer, mid-winter arrangement."

Nearly a third of the way into the second book Tom noticed a trend. At more and more of the evening dinners military people were present. Most only stayed for a meal and a couple of drinks. Tom remarked that the South Africans must have been stepping up their presence in Angola.

It was three o'clock by the time they got through the second book. Ing had been lying on a deck chair near them, immersed in a heavy looking tome. She looked up when Tom pronounced the second book finished. "It's three in the afternoon. We're sitting naked in the sunshine beside a lovely lake. But something is wrong with this scene."

"You're right, Ing. I'll fetch drinks," said Jenna as she arose from her chair.

"Would you be offended, Tom, if I described to Jenna how I spent last Saturday night?"

"No. Just so long as you make it clear that the proceedings were your idea and that you derived a benefit from the evening."

"Of course. How could I convince her to step out of her tight little sexual envelope to explore greater benefits if I don't share with her the ones I've gained?"

"How indeed," said Tom.

When Jenna returned with the drinks Tom took a beer and asked if any trails ran through a section of woods about two hundred yards east of the cottage. Jenna assured him none did, Tom excused himself and went to his SUV. Jenna and Ing watched with some interest as he assembled an elaborate looking bow and slung a quiver of arrows over his shoulder. With some difficult he wiggled a large cardboard target with a line drawing of a charging soldier on it out of the back of the vehicle.

"I'm going to get in some much needed target practice," said Tom. He hiked off across the clearing.

They watched him set his target up against a tree and then Ing said, "Jenna, let's talk sex."

***

Nils had made several visits to Marseilles and knew the city quite well. The Capo's house was in an older area of big houses sandwiched tightly together. Nils concluded that the Capo had chosen to live in the neighbourhood where he had grown up because he felt he could trust his neighbours.

There was a man sitting smoking in the shade beside the front steps of the Capo's house and two other guys were idling across the street by their parked motorcycles. They watched Nils closely as he approached on his motorcycle but lost interest in him as soon as he passed by without slowing down. Nils turned right at his first opportunity and sized up the back yards of the row of houses where the Capo lived.

There was a lane that ran behind the houses and the walled back gardens all had a gate to the lane. When Nils rolled by the end of the lane he could see that two men were sitting on chairs at the gate that led into the Capo's garden. The lane was narrow and garbage strewn. Nils concluded that the Capo would enter the house through the front entrance when he came home. He parked in a shaded area to reflect on his tactical problem.

***

Arnon drove the three of them to a park a few blocks from the police station. "Let's walk, gentlemen," he said, and got out of the car. Crane and David followed him as he entered a heavily wooded trail.

Once in the woods he held his hand out to Crane, fingers extended. He took a cigarette and accepted a light from Crane. David was concentrating on packing a small pipe. Arnon was content to smoke his cigarette until David had his pipe fully alight and had taken a couple of deep drags.

"David," said Arnon, "did Gerta Ten Haan ever ask you to store anything for her?"

"No. Never."

"These disks that have come up in the conversation. Do they take up a lot of space?"

"Not at all. Floppy disks are four inches by four inches and each one can hold the equivalent of 500 textbooks. You could put as much information on 300 of them as the average library in a small town would hold and store them in a shoe box."

Arnon took a little time to digest that statement. Then he looked at Crane.

"Given that Ms. Van Velt seems to have gone through a significant metamorphosis since we first met her, what do you think are the chances that she has a bunch of her Aunt's computer disks and a stack of her Aunt's diaries in her possession?"

"We certainly can't rule that possibility out. She doesn't seem like a person who would conceal evidence, but maybe her Aunt was closer to her that she admits."

"Well," said Arnon. "If she does have them, she has a lot more gumption than I would have given her credit for. I mean, she knows what happened to her Aunt."

"True," said Crane. "What are we going to do?"

"I'd like you to take David home and then come back into the station. I've read your reports and you are good at writing. Let's put our heads together and find out what we can about Ms. Van Velt. And then maybe we'll try to persuade a judge to let us search her new digs downtown."

***

Nils' planning session while sitting in the shade astride his motorcycle ended abruptly. His pager began to vibrate. He cursed and rolled off on his motorcycle to find a payphone. Someone had vomited a lot of wine onto the floor of the little cubicle and Nils had to fight to not be sick. He dialed Winter's number hurriedly.

When Winter answered Nils' call, his voice was stilted with concern and anger.

"Do you know about the shipment to Marseilles, Nils? Are you aware that INTERPOL has that material in their possession?"

Nils answered yes. And he felt the anger in him rising.

"Given that you know that, I have to assume that the sudden demise of four of the Marseilles gang is your work."

"No one can prove that. Or even show that I have been anywhere near Marseilles."

"Keep it that way, Nils. Get on that motorcycle of yours and head north. Andre will meet you at the safe house in Limoges at ten a.m. tomorrow. Be there. If you get within a metre of anyone connected to the Marseilles gang, even the lad who delivers their fucking new papers, you will be expelled from this organization."

Nils was appalled at that. He muttered something in agreement and rang off.

He took Ruffo's wallet out of his jacket pocket and went through its contents carefully. There were several photos. They showed an attractive dark haired woman and two girls. Nils carefully stowed them in his wallet, along with the ID card that held Ruffo's address.

A pimply teenaged boy approached the call box and rudely motioned for Nils to get out of his way. Normally Nils would have hurt him badly. Instead, he stepped out of the box and let the young lad use the phone. He felt paralyzed.

Nils fumbled around in his pocket and found a small jack knife. He was well practiced in its use and without removing it from his clothing, he opened out the awl that was about half the size of a pen. Nils shoved it three times into the hard muscle of his outer thigh. The blood trickling down his leg calmed him enough for him to mount his motorcycle and head north.

***

Ing began her talk with a series of questions.

"Jenna, have you ever tried restraint and pleasure sex games?"

"Since I don't know what you're talking about, I will say no," was her answer.

"Have you ever been getting it on with a partner and wondered what you should do with your hands?"

"Come again?" said Jenna.

"Okay. You're lying on your back and your partner is going down on you. Has it ever felt awkward because, for example, you don't know what to do with your hands? Should you have them relaxed by your side? Should you be playing frantically with your nipples? Should you grasp your lover's hair and force their face deeper and harder into your pulsating pleasure palace?"

"I'm not convinced I have a pulsating pleasure palace, Ing."

"Oh you do, Jenna. You do! Have you forgotten about our adventures already? Anyway, Jenna, when having sex there can be awkward moments when you're having something done to you, and you don't know how to respond with your eyes and other parts of your body. How wide should I spread my legs? How high should I raise my ass off the bed? Should I watch my nipples being nibbled or should I stare at the ceiling?"

"I'll admit to some awkwardness," said Jenna.

"Now let's talk about distractions. We have five senses. Agreed?"

"Sure. Except for clairvoyants, who have six."

"Clairvoyants are lousy in the sack, Jenna. Trust me on that. So we regular-type humans are working with a toolbox that contains five tools. Think about that while I get us drinks."

Ing found the largest wine glasses and brought them each a brimming glass of South African white wine. It was deliciously cold.

"So, five senses. One of the things that restraint and pleasure does is remove the distraction of some of the senses."

"You'll have to explain that, Ing."

"When you're blindfolded, you aren't distracted by visuals. You aren't worried about where you should be looking. You aren't glancing at your partner to see what they are looking at and worrying about whether they like what they see. You also can't watch to see what or where they are going to do something next."

"Then there is the audio."

"Christ, Ing, are we talking about a blindfold and earplugs?"

"I'm not so extreme as to use earplugs, but good on you for thinking of it. No, I'm suggesting that very loud music, the right loud music, blocks some of the other distracting sounds. Have you ever been really, really wet and then the fucking starts and it sounds like somebody is trying to unclog a stubborn drain?"

"I hate the squidgy noises."

"Do you like the slurpy noises when your pussy is being eaten?"

"Not usually."

"Well there we go then! A blindfold to take away the visual distractions, the right loud music to cover the distracting noises, and then there is the elimination of what to do with one's body. That is where the restraints come in."

"I personally favour having my partner tied with their hands above their head. Whether tethered to an overhead point or to the headboard of a bed, it is the most flattering position for a woman. The breasts are pulled up and the nipples made totally available. From there, the dominant person can do as they like. Position legs as they wish. Roll the person over to access their ass. It's all good. And the restrainee need not worry one whit about what they should do. The dominant decides all that for them."

"It sounds perfect," said Jenna. "Except that once one is blindfolded and tied up, what if the other person starts doing things that hurt or are disgusting?"

"Simple," said Ing. "The person who is tied up says the pre-agreed upon safe word."

"And do you really think that the person who has you tied and helpless is going to stop because of a safe word?"

"The whole essence of restraint and pleasure, Jenna, is trust. You would only enter into such a situation when you know that the person or persons you're with want to give you pleasure. And you would have to trust them implicitly. They'd be the sort of people that you would reveal to that you are a felon, withholding evidence from a murder investigation, just to give an example."

Ing had drained her wine glass and motioned for Jenna to do the same. She walked back to the cottage for refills. Jenna sat with a hundred thoughts bouncing through her head from the conversation and watched Tom in the distance, apparently having some very successful target practice.

Ing returned with more wine and watched Jenna watching Tom.

"I guess we're on pretty much the same cycle, Jenna. I'm ovulating and I'm so horny I'd fuck just about anyone of the same species right now. I want you. I want Tom. And I know that Tom would like both of us. I propose that this evening you have your first restraint and pleasure experience. "

"With both of you?" exclaimed Jenna.

"Give that some thought. Two mouths and two sets of hands to pleasure you. All you do is remember your safe word and let us enjoy your body. Did you like the taste of me in the sauna?"

"Yes."

"I think you would like to taste me even more as Tom fucks you while I straddle your face. And if I'm being graphic, well, sometimes graphic is good."

Ing fished around on the ground for her watch which she had removed to avoid tan lines. "It's four, Jenna. Give this some thought. If a safe word pops into your head by five today, you'll know that it's an experience you should try."

Ing arose from her chair. "Is the sauna still on?"

Jenna nodded.

Ing ran along the dock and dove into the lake. As she passed Jenna on the way to the sauna with her teeth chattering she mumbled that her nipples were "fucking turning blue." Ing was lying on the hottest bench of the sauna when Jenna entered, deeply chilled from her own swim.

"Metamorphosis," said Jenna.

"What?" asked Ing.

"Metamorphosis," said Jenna. "That's my safe word."

"Go have a shower, Jenna."

***

Franz Von Hesse settled back into his seat in the first class section of a Lufthansa jumbo jet. He hadn't been out of Europe in years and he was looking forward to spending a few days in Canada. He loved Muskoka in the summer, and the Allen's summer home there was one of Franz's favourite places to be.

The flight was uneventful, the passage through Canadian Customs was fast, and the Otter float plane was waiting on the apron with the engine turning over.

"We should be taxiing up to the dock in Muskoka in forty minutes, Herr Von Hesse," said the pilot.

"Excellent," replied Franz.

As the Otter circled to land, Franz saw two people leave the front verandah of the house and make their way down to the dock. He was certain that one of them was Sam Allen. As they taxiied in from the lake he recognized the second man as Chuck Holt. The Americans have arrived first, he thought to himself.

He deplaned and embraced the two Americans. They started to walk to the house but Franz paused on the dock. He stood for a full minute, looking around at the rocks and the trees and the waters of Lake Muskoka. "I have been away from here for too long," he observed, then turned to follow the two Americans.

The three men took seats on the huge front verandah and Sam gestured to a table where glasses, an ice bucket and two bottles of scotch were laid out. "We decided to break out a couple bottles of the good stuff. Franz poured himself three fingers, neat, and took a sip. "I'll soon be ready for anything," he commented.

Claudio was the next to arrive after a much longer flight in a pontoon plane that had brought him from Long Island. Daniel Sterling landed about two hours after Franz's arrival. Franz observed that of all of them, Daniel seemed to age the least. They were all sixty-one years old.

Sam, as host and chairman took over the day.

"I am very happy to see you gentlemen here. It has been too long. I know the it's best for security to not have the Legacy Organization meet face to face, but I can tell you that I miss seeing each of you. The friendships that our fathers forged have been passed down to us just as surely as the responsibilities have."

"We'll have dinner at seven. We've all been travelling today. I came in from Atlanta, Chuck from L.A. Let's have some of this fine juice, get caught up on what we've all been up to, and get to bed early. Then it's down to work early tomorrow, gentlemen."

***

Nils used every bit of his skill as a rider as he roared through southern France. He took the lesser known roads that had more hazards but fewer police. Andre was impressed when he arrived at the meeting place hours earlier than anticipated.

Nils was at first glad to see Andre. But when they went into the inner office and he saw the Dokter seated by a coffee table with Winter, his spirits sank. "It's good to see you safe and sound," said Winter as he arose from his chair. "We'll leave you with Simon for awhile."

Simon had come into Nils' life when he was thirteen. Nils had reached puberty early. Which was the time his unusual urges began. At age fourteen, several Roma families had encamped on one of the Winter's estates. His family was fretting about how to move them on.

Nils had decided that he could solve the problem. He went to the edge of their campsite with candy and a bottle of Jagermiefter. A boy and a girl from the Roma tribe were intrigued. Nils stabbed the boy to death and then raped the girl. Several thousand marks changed hands and the Roma went away. And Nils' family realized his potential.

Dokter Simon Kepp was fascinated by Nils. The young man had soaring intelligence. He registered high into the genius range. Physically, he was a lithe and strong specimen. He stayed fit by rigorous workouts with weights and long runs. His reflexes were uncannily fast which is what made him such a good motorcycle racer. And he was, as the Americans said, "very easy to look at."

But, Dokter Kepp reminded himself, he was also a born psychopath. Nils could not begin to understand suffering other than his own. And should he be bored, he did not have the slightest regret in causing suffering to another if it might alleviate his boredom.

Nils had interesting relatives. They were all very connected, very old money, very old Europe. All of them, Nils included, had titles. The whole lot of them had been causing suffering on a widespread basis for hundreds of years. And that had served them in good stead.

"So, Nils. It's good to see you again. Can you tell me what you've been up to in the last few days?"

As always, the presence of Dokter Kepp had its effect on Nils. He told the perfect truth. From killing the pimps in Cologne to his reception in Marseilles. The Dokter winced when Nils told him that Ruffo had spat into his face. He listened attentively as Nils told him what had happened in the bar.

Doktor Kepp gave Nils three small capsules and stood over him as he took them. He stayed with him until Nils' eyelids were drooping; then he called in a very large older man. "Sit with Nils awhile. I have a meeting." Nils knew the big man well and respected his capabilities.

Doktor Kepp went to Winter's office and tapped lightly on the door. He was asked to come in immediately. "What is going on with him?" asked Winter.

"A fellow named Ruffo spat in his face. You know what the outcome of such an action had to be. A violation of his space and honour of that nature would be huge for Nils. He was in genuine danger and he responded accordingly. Nothing was pathological in his initial response."

"Go on," said Winter.

"He tortured the other men."

"To what end?" asked Winter.

"That's where he started to slip," replied the Dokter. "He was behaving logically until then. He wanted the name and location of their boss in case he tried to do something offensive to this organization. But then he slipped into a very pleasurable place. Torture and mayhem for the sake of gratification. Pleasure."

"Can he be used anymore?" asked Winter.

"Oh, of course," replied the Dokter. "He's still a hugely effective weapon. He's just had some drugs that will bring him to a very secure place. From there, he will be a very valuable person for you again."

"You've known him for a very long time, Herr Dokter. When can we use him again?"

"Soon. Within a few days, I should think. He'll be your man again when the drugs wear off about seven tomorrow morning. Rest assured, Herr Winter. I've known him since he was thirteen, shortly after he committed his first murder and rape. He is brilliant, and you and your colleagues have found the perfect employment for him. And he is fiercely loyal to the Cerberus Corp."

"I can't thank you enough," said Winter.

"Oh, trust me," said the Dokter, "you thank me enough. By the way, Nils also killed a couple of pimps in Cologne before he left on his road trip. It was a totally random encounter. I doubt that anything will come of it."

"I wonder what the total body count of his activities is?" said Winter.

"Nils has a photographic memory. I can ask him if you really want to know," said the Doktor.

"Don't bother. It's not important."

***

Jules sent the transcripts of the messages from the computers by fax. Arnon and Crane pored over them for an hour and Arnon told Crane to call Jenna Van Velt's home again. The call went straight to her machine.

"Let's go to her office," said Arnon.

The admin assistant provided the detailed information to Arnon and Crane about Jenna's location without hesitation.

"So Ms. Van Velt owns a cottage in the mountains," said Arnon as they left her office building. "I wonder what sort of artifacts of her Aunt's she might have in that location?"

"It is a damned interesting development," agreed Crane.

"Well, we can't kick the door of her apartment. What say we find the captain and see if we can get a warrant for this retreat of hers?"

"Worth a try," said Crane.

They didn't do so well with the captain. Granted, he was responsible for over half a dozen high profile cases including one involving some serious misbehaviour of a congressman's kid. He told them to execute the apartment warrant and if that came up empty, then to try for some paper for the cottage.

Arnon had a gut hunch. "I feel like a drive in the country, Crane."

"Sure. Need a navigator?"

"Thanks for the offer. But two guys in blue jeans with our haircuts would sorta stand out, out there in cottage country. Draw me a camera with a good telephoto lens and some film and I'll drive out there myself."

"I'll leave the gear on your desk," said Crane.

***

The five men who had gathered in Muskoka had breakfast together on the east porch. All of them claimed to have slept like babies. None seemed to be nursing a hangover despite the amount of fine scotch they had consumed the previous night. As their host had said, it was very smooth.

At ten they trooped downstairs to what was called the lower hall. It was a huge room, sixty feet long and thirty wide. A pool table was at one end of the room. A lovely old oak table was in the very center of the hall this morning, well lit from overhead. The walls of the room were covered with an array of edged weapons and firearms. There were showcases holding artifacts from five generations of the Allen family's military service. Sam joked that the room was the "best goddamn American military museum in Canada."

During his first visit to Sinclair House, Franz had asked Sam why so many priceless mementos of his family's history were housed in Muskoka rather than at one of his homes in the States. He had never forgotten Sam's reply.

"Good question ,Franz. My Dad, my Grandad and I were all involved in one way or another on the Intelligence side of things. I was in Black Ops for a while. Hell, even old D'Arcy was involved in stuff during the Civil War that has not seen the light of day. We've got a lot of stuff in this room that we're either not supposed to have or that people don't know we have. It's much safer up here in Canada where it's less likely that anybody will come snooping around. I couldn't have this stuff in any of my houses in the States given the sorts of people I have coming by for dinner."

They took their seats at the table. At each place was a pad, some pens and an exquisite crystal liqueur glass filled with an amber liquid. Sam picked up his glass and held it aloft. "I know it's early in the morning gentlemen, but tradition is tradition. To the Legacy Organization," he toasted.

All five men drank off their glasses and placed them back on the table.

"To work," said Sam.

Franz had the floor first. He concisely told them that he had received a call from a panicked Erich in the late evening, German time, in late May. The old man had described the state that he had found Gerta in, and indicated that he was in his 'safe' apartment. He told him that he was certain his main residence was being watched but felt that the safe apartment was still secure.

Franz had spoken with him for some time, trying to calm him down. Gradually he could hear Erich's breathing get back to something like normal. They ran through a checklist of options and decided it would be best for Erich, using his Danzig papers, to get to Cologne as soon as he could. He directed Erich to go to the address of one of the apartments that the company held for visiting VIPs. Franz said he thought it would be calming for Erich to hole up in his hometown. He was confident that Erich had made it to the safe house without attracting attention. "Regrettably, he died within minutes of arriving."

"We know it was a heart attack, right," said Chuck Holt. "Nobody hit him with a dart or some other sneaky poison shit?"

"We have very good sources within the Cologne police," replied Franz. "It was a heart attack. Although I'd like to make an observation."

"Yes?" Claudio.

"Walter was no doubt absolutely grief-stricken over the death of Gerta. He may have simply given up once he was in our hands".

All of the men around the table had heard about the relationships that had been formed during the covert years in Africa. Gerta had been the love of the life of more than one of the men of their previous generation.

They all sat silently for a moment and then Daniel Sterling quietly asked Franz to continue. Sterling had been listening intently to Franz and his hands had never stopped moving. He was busy knitting as he always did during meetings. Franz told them that Erich was very clear that Gerta had been tortured. Her body was naked, lying on the floor of her apartment. He described very local deep bruising and deep round burns all over her. He said that she had been bleeding from her vagina and anus. Erich was crying as he described the scene.

"He's not the only who'll be crying once we nail down who did this," said Sam.

Franz went on, explaining that he had a very good source who was providing them with all the information that was available. INTERPOL had made the identification quickly, likely due to Erich's SS tattoo. They had made a link between Erich and Gerta's murder, which Franz said he found astonishing.

They discussed how INTERPOL might have made the American connection so quickly. Nobody at the table had any insight.

It was Sam's turn to take the floor. As always, when speaking to a group he paced back and forth.

"Some unholy shit has been unleashed here. We had Gerta and Erich buried just about as deep as a person can be. The minute I heard what had happened, I put our guys on all of the known assholes that the Cerberus Corp have used."

"The Tsoba brothers arrived in Mombassa a couple of days after the murder from the U.K. They were in a whorehouse a couple hours after landing, telling the ladies about their trip to California and bragging about drinking with Brad Pitt. Back to you, Franz."

"Sam and I discussed things," said Franz, "and we felt we had to hit back quickly."

"How so?" asked Daniel.

"The Cerberus Corp. received a package a day ago. It contained a photograph of the Tsoba brothers with each other's cocks in their mouths," replied Franz.

"Do you think that will shock them?" asked Daniel.

"I think it will," said Sam. "You see in the picture, the boys are sitting side by side, both facing the camera, tied to chairs."

"Our people took the photo while they were both still alive. They stayed long enough to be sure they had both bled to death," explained Franz. "We know that fucking Nazi Winter enjoyed living vicariously through those two wastes of skin. That pleasure has now been denied him."

Chuck Holt described the steps he had taken to keep Gerta's niece under surveillance and safe. He said that he was working on a way of obtaining good information on how the police investigation was progressing. "When we checked out the niece and her husband before Gerta went to live there, my team nearly died of boredom. This is a whitebread squeaky-clean couple. The hubby likes to hire hookers when he is away on business and he might have had a side thing going with a secretary, but that was it."

"What about the niece? Did she have any side interests?"

"Nope. She was truly a lady with nothing to hide."

"That's good," said Daniel, stopping his needles for a moment. "Should we need to bring her to talk with us, she likely won't pose us much of a problem. She certainly doesn't sound to be very worldly."

"I am very interested in confirming that it is Winter and Cerberus Corp. that killed Gerta. It's time I think - and I've spoken with Franz and Chuck about this - that we try to make contact with Joachim Maarten. Chuck votes no on this. Franz and I say we contact him. Daniel, we need you and Claudio to weigh in on this."

"The worst that could happen is that Joachim tells Winter that we've made contact. I say do it. It could be useful. What do you think, Claudio?"

"I'm a doctor. Our creed is to do no harm. If reaching out to Maarten will do no harm and it could be useful, I think we must do it."

"I am learning more and more about this AIDS epidemic," said Claudio. "The virus resembles, but is not the one our team developed in Namibia. It's highly likely that the South Africans, specifically 7 Medical Battalion, got their hands on some of the data from our project and created a virus similar to what we developed. Clearly, they didn't take the painstaking precautions that our team did. If they had a way of controlling or destroying the virus, they surely have done so by now."

"Do you think the disks that Gerta has entrusted to her niece hold information that could end this outbreak of disease?" asked Daniel. He had again paused his knitting.

"Very likely."

"So, Chuck. You are our key man now. Find out if the niece of Gerta has turned this information over to the police. If she has not, we will have to arrange a meeting with her as soon as possible."

The meeting in Muskoka was over by 3 p.m. Claudio and Daniel shared a float plane ride back to Toronto. Chuck left in a different plane to go back to the States. Franz had pretended to the three men who were leaving that he was catching a flight out in the early evening. Instead, he stayed on, as he usually did after a meeting of the group. Sam, he knew, wanted to talk.

The two of them went back down to the lower hall. Franz could tell that Sam was filled with restless energy. He occupied himself looking at the artifacts on the walls while Sam collected the liqueur glasses used for the toast. Eventually Sam was ready to talk.

"I still can't believe that Gerta had all the data from the work they did in Namibia," said Sam.

"It's astonishing," agreed Franz. "Hopefully we can retrieve Gerta's belongings and find a place for this information. It's clear that we need it."

"Yes we do, and all because of that asshole Winter," said Sam.

"Karl Winter has been a very large thorn in our side for a very long time."

"He's obviously had something force his hand. He's got good security around him. But he knows that only can go so far. I would give a lot to know what happened to make him kick the beehive."

"Claudio and his team will turn up some news. We need to know a good deal more about what's happening before we make any more decisions," said Franz.

"My old man was there in Namibia when old Hector Verwoerd threw Winter off the team. Dad said it was like a scene from the Old Testament. Hector raged and stormed and cursed Winter to seven sides of Sunday."

"Pity the group hadn't listened to Erich instead. He wanted Winter's throat cut and then have him fed to the hyenas," commented Franz.

"There were some compelling reasons not to do that," said Sam. "Not that I don't agree with you. But we did need the support of the South Africans for a few more years and they would never have agreed to Winter being killed."

"True enough," said Franz. "And Erich - scientist and genius that he was - could only see things in black and white. Erich despised Winter, you know. Felt he was mentally inferior and reckless."

"Pretty much everybody was mentally inferior to Erich. But he had the personality of pet rock. My Dad valued his work but he thought he was a pretty poor excuse for a human being."

"My father described him as a creature of his time. Nazi Germany was a very bad place to be if you had talent. The Nazis either harnessed it or destroyed it."

"Seems to me Erich did a pretty slick job of harnessing the Nazis' resources. From everything I've read or been told, he fit the bill of psychopath pretty damn precisely."

"When Erich and Gerta first told us last fall that they had all the formulas, should we have gone and taken them, Sam?"

"I doubt that we would have got them. The two of them were fanatical about the work they had done. I think Gerta just proved that."

"Well, what they achieved in Namibia and proved they had achieved, had never been done before."

"The trick," said Sam, "was to find people immoral or desperate enough to take advantage of their breakthrough. When Verwoerd realized that he had such a person on his staff, he threw out Winter."

"The formulas from their work filled 270 pages. Winter was stripped naked and body cavity searched before they threw him out of the compound. There is no person alive- not even an idiot savant, which Winter is not - who could memorize that much data."

"I know," said Sam." I just hope the reckless motherfucker hasn't tried to do something with the bit he might have been able to recall. And we have to stop him and everybody else in the world from getting their hands on those disks and Gerta's diaries. None of us know what's in them. She may have fucking named names."

Sam had arranged for Franz to be driven to a nearby healing lodge to chat with some of the aboriginal elders. Like many Germans, he was fascinated by North American 'Indians.' Once Franz had gone off on his road trip, Sam had some business to take care of.

It was his first visit to Sinclair House since his father had died. There was a standing intergenerational agreement within the Allen family that a man's 'drawer' had to be expunged. Sam's father had been one of General Patton's young Turks and had advised the Kennedy brothers during their administration. When he opened his father's drawer he expected to be faced with destroying some very interesting bits of American history.

There were just two items in the drawer. The first was a thick sheaf of papers that Sam realized were the operations orders to send two divisions of the army and two divisions of marines crashing ashore on Cuba if the Missile Crisis worsened. "Cool", thought Sam and he lost an hour reading them. The other item was a series of photos shot by a photographer in Pretoria. Sam had a quick look at them and thought, "You old bastard."

There was a fireplace in the lower hall. Sam got a good blaze going and fetched some brandy. He sat sipping and tossing pages of the plan to invade Cuba into the flames. From time to time he alternated pages of the operations plan with photos of Gerta. He regretted burning every piece of paper.

***

When Nils awoke in the morning his mouth had a harsh metallic taste and he had a sharp pain in his neck from sleeping in the chair. The Doktor was sitting at a table in the room, quietly reading a newspaper. When Nils first stirred, the Doktor pushed a button on the intercom near his elbow and asked that coffee be brought to them.

"How are you feeling, Nils?" he asked.

"Groggy. And my neck feels like it's broken."

"You slept awkwardly. I prescribe coffee, a hot bath and a shave, and then Angelique will be in to give you a massage to get the kinks out. Have you been following your exercise regime?"

"I'm due for a long run. Haven't had time during the past few days."

"Excellent. After Angelique has worked her magic, Andre will be your pacer on the high trail. Then come back to join us for a late breakfast. Does that sound alright?"

"That will be fine," said Nils as he arose to take a coffee from a servant that had entered the room.

When he left, the Doktor went to Winter's office. Winter was seated exactly where he had been the previous evening, making the Doktor wonder if he had been to bed at all. Winter looked up when the Doktor entered the room.

"How is he this morning?" he asked.

"Fine," said the Doktor. "Angelique will join him soon and then he and Andre are going for a long run. He'll join us for breakfast in an hour and a half relaxed and ready to hear about whatever you have planned for him."

"So these drugs you gave him have acted like the reset button on an electric power tool?"

"Certainly the drugs have their function. Nils is full of restless energy which Andre will see is drained out of him on the run. Angelique will ensure that any sexual tension that he is experiencing is dealt with. She is very skilled."

"Skilled, yes," said Winter. "I agree. I'll see you at breakfast at eleven."

Chapter Sixteen

When Jenna emerged from the sauna, Ing was with Tom by his SUV. He was nodding as she spoke and once she turned away from him, he began to very efficiently put away his archery equipment. Ing rapidly walked to Jenna and said, "Gonna have a nice shower?"

Jenna nodded and went into the cottage. Ing followed her inside and went into the master bedroom. What the fuck is she doing? thought Jenna as she adjusted the water temperature and stepped into the shower.

In one area of Jenna's mind she was very aware of what she had agreed to. She took time with her shower and shaved carefully. She wondered if she should emerge from the bathroom draped in a towel. Since all of them had been naked all day that seemed silly, so she came out of the bathroom naked. Ing was waiting for her.

The bed in the master bedroom of the cottage was queen-sized. Ing had found the cupboard that contained the extra bedding and had made it up fresh. When Jenna entered the room, Ing arose from the floor where she was doing something and hustled Jenna out to the porch of the cottage. She fetched Jenna a glass of wine and told her to enjoy the view in the shade of the porch. Tom was nowhere to be seen.

Jenna was nearly finished her wine when Ing opened the cottage door and beckoned her to come into the cottage. She led Jenna into the bedroom and asked "Metamorphosis is the word, right?" Jenna nodded.

"Okay," said Ing. "Let's get started."

She directed Jenna to lie on her back on the bed. Once Jenna was positioned to Ing's liking, she straddled her and used a silk tie that she had affixed to one of the spacers of the brass headboard to tie Jenna's hands together. Ing tied a very efficient knot and when Jenna tested it she was very aware that she could not escape.

Ing then leaned down to Jenna. "Raise your head, sweetie," she said. Jenna did and Ing very firmly affixed a blindfold to her. The world went black.

"Any questions?" asked Ing.

"No."

She was startled when the stereo started to blast out loud music. She wasn't aware that anyone was in the bedroom until a warm hand drew her face to the left and kissed her deeply. Then another hand drew her to the right and kissed her even more deeply, her mouth being thoroughly explored by his or her tongue.

Tom and Ing touched and kissed and fucked her incessantly for what seemed like hours. Jenna had two orgasms in the bedroom and then they led her outside and fastened her hands to the porch overhang. She uttered her safe word when she had had a third orgasm.

They released her from her bonds after that and removed her blindfold. As she stood between the two of them on the porch, blinking her eyes to focus her sight, they hugged her and Ing said that she would get drinks. Tom took Jenna's hand and led her to the deck chairs.

"Go to your car and get your fucking cigarettes," said Jenna. "I want one."

Tom returned with cigarettes as Ing stepped onto the porch balancing three drinks. Jenna took one from her. When she sat down, Tom lit a cigarette and gave it to her.

"I didn't know you smoked," said Ing in surprise when Jenna took a drag on the cigarette.

"Oh, yes, I always crave tobacco after group sex."

"Technically it was a threesome, Jenna," said Ing. "You need five or more to call it group sex. I could go into town and try to find a few other people if that's what you'd like to try next."

"Shut the fuck up Ing. I'm sitting here trying to figure out how I can have a normal conversation with two people who have just had their tongues in every part of my body. It's awkward."

"But judging by your responses during our little play session, it was also pleasurable," said Ing.

Jenna sipped her drink and puffed on the cigarette, not making eye contact with either of them. She stood abruptly and walked onto the dock. "I need to think about what just happened to me." She dove into the lake, swam back to the dock, and walked quickly past them to the sauna.

"Think she's pissed?" asked Tom.

"No. She's dealing with the guilt that was embedded in her during a typical middle class North American upbringing. It was hard for her to deal with the first time she and I had sex. It 's going to take her some time to process the reality that she just had three orgasms in short order as part of a threesome."

"Hopefully we haven't rocked her world too badly," said Tom.

"Jenna and I have talked a lot. Her world needs rocking, a lot of rocking. Without some new experiences she would have bumbled into a relationship with a guy who would be just like her husband. She needs to enlarge her boundaries a bit. Step outside the white picket fence. Given that her murdered Aunt was tortured to death after having lived covertly doing God knows what in Namibia, our friend Jenna may well have some very bad people interested in her."

"Well, Ing," said Tom arising from his chair, "I believe we have accomplished that goal. It's getting late. I'm going to cook us something."

He walked to the cottage and Ing sat in her deck chair wondering if she should help him fix dinner or join Jenna in the sauna. She mixed drinks for all and took two with her to the sauna. When Ing opened the door Jenna was sitting on one of the benches. She wordlessly reached out and took a drink from Ing.

***

As he was sitting in his office waiting for Crane to drop off the photography equipment, a thought struck Arnon. He searched in his wallet briefly and was pleased to find Teresa's business card. He called the number, expecting to get her answering machine. Instead she picked up on the second ring.

"Hi Teresa, it's Nick Arnon."

"Well hello. I wondered if I'd hear from you again. How are you?"

"I'm fine. And sorry I didn't call you sooner. I've been up to my butt in swamp creatures."

"I expect that you're busy with all that crazy stuff going on out in the woods. One more murder or rape and maybe the property values will go down enough for me to be able to afford something out there."

"I don't think working cops like us would be a good fit on most of the leafy avenues out there," said Arnon. "How have you been?"

"Busy. I thought that victim services would be a nice break from the bunko squad but it's just depressing. I've asked to be transferred back to fraud."

"That's likely a good thing," said Arnon. When he had first met Teresa he had been taken aback to learn that she was in Victims' Services. He didn't know anybody who had been able to do that job for long.

"So, here we are talking on the phone," said Teresa. "What's up?"

"Would you like to mix a bit of business with pleasure?" asked Arnon.

He told her a bit about the Ten Haan case, enough to realize that she was really interested and explained that he wanted to drive out to the Bayfield area to get a look at the property that the victim's niece owned. Teresa was all in on that. They covered off the details for the next day and Arnon hung up.

Crane came in with a camera bag and set it on Arnon's desk.

"Are you going to try to talk to her when you go out there?" asked Crane.

"I don't know. If I see her sitting all alone by her cottage guiltily sorting through banker's boxes of papers, maybe. I more want to get a feel for what sort of money she has in her property out there. She and her hubby seemed to be pretty well-heeled."

"Drive safe," said Crane. "See you Monday."

Arnon left the office shortly after Crane and went home. He rummaged around in some of the boxes that were still not unpacked from his move to the apartment. In the third box he found his pair of German binoculars.

Arnon gave some thought to the attire for the trip the next day. It was bloody hot and he would have liked to wear shorts, but he had been living in suits and had no tan at all. You're working too much, asshole, he told himself as he laid out jeans and T-shirt.

***

Although he did not show any sign of distress, Winter was aghast at the sudden turn of events in Marseilles. The fact that INTERPOL had some of the equipment that Nils had stolen from the library in California left him with an icy feeling in his stomach. He had kept things on track and hidden for so long that he could scarcely believe that his plans were possibly in jeopardy.

Stuart was methodically analyzing the rest of the computer equipment. They had him working in a very secure location only a few miles from where Winter sat. Thus far he had uncovered nothing of interest and when he had been told about the INTERPOL seizure of equipment, he had theorized that the 'boxes' that the organization wanted had now been lost to them. Winter found Stuart to be almost as annoyingly analytical as his former colleague Walter Danzig. How I hate that man, thought Winter.

It had been going so well in Namibia. Winter was quietly working as part of the team, doing his job and taking copious notes. He had found ways to access most of the data he needed and had managed with great stealth and effort, to obtain a copy of the key to the room that they all called the 'Hessenkessel' - the Witch's Kettle- where that oversexed little bitch Johanna Buist/Gerta Ten Haan worked.

The war in Angola was spilling into the area. The MPLA and the FNLA had both raided in the areas near the compound. There were South African Army personnel around the camp all the time and there had even been a visit by a group of Americans that he was sure was all soldiers or spooks. He decided that he must act.

He had gone to Buist's office at three in the morning. The compound was dead quiet. His key had fitted the lock perfectly and he turned it slowly, quietly. The lock clicked open but when he pulled the door expecting to step into a dark room, there had been soft desk lights on. And Buist and Danzig were lying naked on the sofa that had been put in the room to allow her to rest between batch runs.

Danzig had arisen from the sofa seething with anger and had landed a very solid punch on Winter's jaw before he could really take stock of the situation. If Winter had brought a weapon, he would have killed them both; instead, that crazy Buist woman had snatched her pistol from her desk and stood over him, naked, until security people arrived and handcuffed him.

He had been frog-marched into the dining hall and all of the staff had gathered. Hector issued several orders and before very long, all of his belongings were brought to the hall. His large cache of illicit notes had been quickly unearthed by the security people and became the focus of attention.

Danzig, Buist and the others, who he thought of as the Boers, had scanned the notes and quickly concluded that he was on the verge of stealing their work. Hector paced the room as they examined his belongings, from time to time having whispered conversations with the South African Army Colonel who seemed to be his chief of staff.

Danzig gave an impassioned denunciation of Winter and demanded that he be killed on the spot. No one in the hall objected. Hector had listened to Danzig impassively. He stood quietly for a full minute and then had roared, "Strip him!" to the security people.

They had kept him hand cuffed and used their bayonets to cut his clothes off. Through a combination of fear and cool night air, his penis had shrunk to a ridiculous size. There was a visiting American present who made a disparaging comment about his 'dick'. Hector ordered that a fire be built outside of the hall.

When the security people had a huge fire burning, Winter had been led outside. Hector ordered the guards to conduct a body cavity search, which they did very roughly. Winter thought that he would be thrown alive into the fire.

Instead, several of the staff had carried his belongings out and cast them into the flames. He watched as all of his clothes and many cherished personal possessions were burned. Then Hector had raged at him as the lot of them stood staring at him.

Eventually, the South African Army officer with the help of the security staff beat him until he could barely stand. Then they took off the handcuffs, hung a satchel over his shoulder and dragged him to the entrance of the compound. Hector was there and as the gates opened, he shouted, "We cast you out."

As Winter had staggered away from the place he could still hear Walter Danzig/Erich Krohl urging the guards to shoot the pariah while they still could.

Winter walked to a south facing window and picked up a pair of very good field glasses. He scanned for some time and finally caught sight of Nils and his pacer as they came over a rise and started into the last three kilometres of their run. Winter was looking forward to giving Nils his next assignment.

***

Jenna had sipped half her drink before either of them spoke.

"You okay, Jenna?" asked Ing.

"I don't know," was the reply.

"What's going around in your head?"

"I'm wondering how the hell I agreed to act the whore for you two. Not each of you, one at a time, both of you. All at once, for Christ's sake!"

"Whore? For Christ's sake. My God, they certainly did a number on you!"

"Who did a number on me?"

"Your preacher, your teachers, your peers, their parents. Sounds like you've been with the snowy white bread crowd for all your life."

"What are you talking about?" asked Jenna

"Guilt , Jenna, and societal standards. Standards that leave you feeling like a whore because you've enjoyed intensive sexual pleasure in a consensual situation with two good friends."

"Are you saying that I should have a nice little tie-up sex game with two other people and pretend that it was no more than if we'd played a game of cards?"

"Actually, Jenna, thank you for that analogy. That is exactly what I'm saying."

"Well from where I come from, that's not the way it rolls."

"That's my point. Other people in your life have built a whole construct about what you should and should not do with your own body. Once you realize that you really do own your body and that you can decide what you want to do with it, the guilt will go away."

"You're not religious," continued Ing. "You don't believe in the Bible or the Koran or any of the 'holy' books. Neither do I. What we three just enjoyed was not a sin. Leonard Cohen got it right. 'When they said repent, I asked them what they meant.'"

"I'm not there."

"Nor should you be. Maybe you'll never be. But maybe you'll get part of the way there. And getting out from under that fucking great rock of guilt that society puts on our shoulders is a good thing, Jenna. Society says that it's okay to make love. Well, you know what? It's okay to fuck, too!"

***

When Arnon picked up Teresa she was wearing shorts and a red T-shirt. Arnon realized that he was going to have some problems staying on task during the business part of their trip.

For the first hour of the drive he and Teresa talked about the case. She was interested and she was a trained cop. Arnon wanted her to know as much as he felt was appropriate to tell her because he wanted a second set of eyes and ears.

Once they got into the mountains the talk shifted to remarks about the scenery they were seeing. By the time they reached Bayfield, a town that neither of them had ever visited, Arnon was feeling like a tourist. He parked on the main street and they got out and walked along to find a real estate agent.

They found three places they wanted to visit in the first hundred yards of walking down the main street. Teresa collected Depression glass and was delighted to score a couple of wine glasses in an antique shop. And then there were the almond tarts in the bakery. Arnon was really enjoying following Teresa around as they shopped. He liked her shorts a lot.

In the second block they found a real estate office. There was a man in his late seventies who came from behind his desk to greet them. He was wearing a golf shirt and shorts. I could get to like this kind of living, Arnon thought.

On the way to Bayfield, Arnon and Teresa had agreed that they would pose as a couple interested in buying a cottage in the area. The real estate guy had no trouble believing that. He surprised them both with his response to their inquiry about water front property.

"If you'd walked in here two years ago I'd have had a dozen reasonably priced properties to show you."

"What's happened in the last two years," asked Teresa.

"Computers," said the old man.

"I beg your pardon?" said Arnon.

"There're all these new companies in the valley. Bunch of young people makin' money hand over fist. They've been comin' out here for the last two years in their Corvettes and Benzes, buying up every cottage and house that's near the water. I sold a cottage to a retired couple two years ago for a hundred and twenty-five thousand. I sold it again yesterday for just over six hundred thousand."

"Holy crap!" said Arnon.

"You got that right. Until two months ago I was the only realtor in town. It's a small place. I know everybody including the summer people. Or did until this boomtown in the valley started up. I was making a reasonable living. In the last two years prices have gone crazy. So have the commissions. I'm a wealthy man because of all these newly minted millionaires from the valley."

"Well, good for you," said Teresa.

"I hate it," said the old man. "One of the big real estate chains has opened an office down the street. I'm gonna retire as soon as the few listings I have sell or expire. Real estate sellin' doesn't feel like an honest livin' anymore."

"So, if I'd bought something here just over two years ago it would have been affordable and I would have increased my money five times over if I sold now?" asked Arnon.

"Absolutely! And you wouldn't have even had to have painted the goddamn place to get that kind of money, pardon my language ma'am. Hell! We've got a pool, sauna and spa construction company in town now. There are six perfectly good lakes around here. And these new people all want pools and spas to dip their butts in! At the risk of repeating myself, I hate it."

Arnon and Teresa left the office and found an outdoor patio to have a late lunch.

"I know from Jenna Van Velt's very talkative admin assistant that she and her husband bought their place out here more than two years ago."

"So, she's likely sitting on a piece of property that is more valuable then when they bought it."

"Clearly. Kinda skews things though. She's now got an unexpected asset but it wasn't acquired through any great skill at investing. And she certainly didn't have to lay out a whole bunch of cash to get it."

Arnon had drawn a one over twenty-five thousand military map of the area from the police library. He had matched it to the directions that he had written down. He was pretty sure of his route.

He and Teresa were both city dwellers and weren't ready for the long, tree-shrouded road. Arnon was watching the odometer of the car intently, but even so, he came upon the barely discernable lane to Van Velt's property with a start. He quietly backed down the road about a hundred yards and found a place on the shoulder where he could pull off the road.

"Ready for a walk?" he asked Teresa.

"Are there any fucking bears here?" was her answer.

Fortunately it was a very mature, open forest. They made good progress through the woods. A dense band of thick underbrush told them they were nearing the edge of the forest.

Arnon realized they were much too landward when he got his first glimpse of the clearing. They went back into the forest and moved five hundred yards further south. When they carefully re-entered the thicket of brush they were only about four hundred yards from the cottage.

From their vantage point they could see that there were three people in chairs, sipping from what appeared to be coffee cups. At the distance it appeared that two were women and one was a man.

"Are they all naked?" asked Teresa.

Arnon fished into his carry-all and brought out the binoculars. He scanned the group for a time, adjusting the eyepieces and the main focus. He handed the binoculars to Teresa.

She peered through them for a moment. "That is one ripped guy and two very attractive ladies. Maybe we should buy a six hundred K cottage out here, Nick."

"I'd like to know a lot more about her friends," said Arnon. "The muscle man is interesting. Let's try to get a bit closer."

They moved through the bush, but to stay undercover the best they could do was a little over hundred yards. From behind Arnon a vehicle horn sounded and the three people they were observing were galvanized into action.

In a trice, they went into the cottage and emerged wearing bathing suits. After a short interval an SUV entered the clearing and trundled up to the cottage. A man and a woman got out. They were both wearing bathing suits. In a few moments Arnon realized that he was having trouble keeping track of Jenna Van Velt because the woman who had just arrived by SUV looked so much like her. Jenna in blue bikini, new woman in red bikini, he reminded himself.

The property, Arnon reckoned, was about six acres. If the real estate agent they had spoken with was to be believed, it would be worth a couple of million. He wondered if Jenna Van Velt knew what she had. He and Teresa watched the five people adjourn to lawn chairs and pour drinks.

"They're settling in for the evening," said Arnon. "Business part of the trip is over. Want to start the drive back to town and get some dinner?"

***

Winter had carefully staged breakfast. There were smaller, more intimate places to dine in the safe house, but he wanted it to be as formal as possible.

"Excellent," exclaimed Nils. "I love it when cook prepares her Tribute to Cholesterol breakfast."

Winter ignored his remark and the doctor asked how his run had gone.

"Not nearly as well as my massage. Angelique is a wonder. I feel like a new man."

"I'm glad to hear that," said Winter. "We need you to pull together a team to go to America."

"How soon?" Nils asked. The doctor felt the question wasn't asked with much interest. Good, he thought to himself. Nils would have been much more eager for a job if his bloodlust was still up.

"I am not certain yet. We have some people gathering information for your team to act upon now. I hope that we will have what we need soon. You'll probably go within two weeks."

Nils nodded and continued to eat his breakfast without comment.

"You may have a free hand in who you decide to use this time. Needless to say, they have to be clean enough to cross borders."

"What's the job?" Nils asked calmly.

"You're going to have the same sort of conversation with Ten Haan's niece as you did with her Aunt."

Nils nodded and extended his coffee cup to the elderly man serving for a refill.

"Initial reports indicate that your subject is a woman about thirty years of age. Quite attractive, I'm told. And we have learned that she and her husband separated not long after you visited her Aunt."

"It couldn't have been much of a marriage to have fallen apart so quickly after a tragedy," observed the doctor.

"We have learned that she owns a summer place on a lake in the mountains about two hours away from where you met her Aunt. It is very private and quite remote. I think you will be able to take all the time you need to question her."

Nils was showing a little more interest in the conversation.

"Is she alone at this retreat of hers?"

"Possibly. We know that she is there now and that another couple is staying with her. That may well change. In her workplace all people who are going to be on vacation must enter the dates they will be away on a bulletin board. She is tentatively scheduled to be away for a week in two weeks time. It is likely she will spend that time at her cottage."

"I take it the people you have on the job there know what they're doing?"

"Of course," Winter answered curtly.

"I need lots of good information and will also need some extra lead time and a passport that gives me dark brown hair and brown eyes. A lot of people saw me during my last visits there and that insipid student that I was fucking will likely have provided the police with a very good description of me. I'll fly into an airport a couple of hundred miles from that area and drive to the cottage without going anywhere near Los Angeles."

"That seems prudent," said Winter. "I, of course will need to know who you are going to take with you."

"The Spaders."

"I think they are a good choice for this work."

Chapter Seventeen

When they arose on what would be their second last day at the cottage, Jenna, for the first time since they had gone there, sensed that there was urgency in how they would spend their day. Tom obviously had the same feeling because when she stepped onto the porch with her first coffee of the day he was already engrossed in one of the diaries.

"Roust Ing," said Tom. "There's a lot of stuff in these next two diaries that I want you both to hear." Tom had put several place markers in two of the diaries. Jenna awakened Ing with some difficulty and lured her out to the porch with a cup of coffee. "I read these two before you got up this morning, Jenna. It's mostly about the research they'd done. They're putting in twelve hour workdays most of the time. She is mentioning data coming in from the satellite camps more often. These two diaries take them up to the end of the second year in the bush."

Tom opened one of the books to a spot he had marked. "These dozen or so pages are all about a safari that Gerta, Walter and two of their friends went on. The four of them were out of the camp and living rough for six days. Your Aunt was quite the outdoors person. And she knows a hell of a lot about the species in that part of Africa."

Ing was showing some signs of life. "What else?"

"Well, your Aunt was truly a free spirit of the '60s. She and Walter and the other pair thought nothing about getting jiggy on river banks, under shade trees, in the one tent that they shared. And it wasn't just Gerta doing Walter. There's nothing to indicate that guys were doing each other, but that would be the only variation that wasn't mentioned."

"Good God," said Jenna. "Is she writing details about the sex?"

"Yes. Yes, she is."

"Crap! I so wish I could read Afrikaans," said Ing. "Read us some of the juicier bits, Tom. Slowly."

"Later. We've got a lot to cover today. Maybe those parts can be your bedtime story tonight if you are good today."

"This book," said Tom, picking up a third volume, "takes them through the first four months of the third year at the camp. There's a lot of detail about her work. And it's getting nasty."

"What are they working on?" asked Jenna.

"They're trying to develop biological weapons. Viruses, it seems."

"My Aunt was involved in developing weapons?"

"I wanted you to hear this, Ing, because you're South African and know how fucked up the place is. Most people who haven't been there have trouble grasping the whole concept of Apartheid."

"Nothing will surprise me about the government in South Africa at that time," said Ing. "They were a bunch of racist demons."

"Agreed," said Tom. "And as I read through these diaries, I am getting a picture of just how evil they were. I'm sure that in this book or in one of the next ones, going chronologically, we're going to find out that whatever they were working on was being tested on humans. Prisoners of war from the Angolan mess most likely."

"You're not joking, are you?" said Jenna.

"As I said, Jenna, these diaries are telling the story of some very secret, very evil stuff."

"And my Aunt was part of it. I don't know if I want to go any further with finding out what is in these diaries. Maybe we should just get a good fire going and destroy them."

"There are a couple of reasons why you can't do that," said Ing.

"Why? Only we three even know these diaries exist. "

"Why do you think that someone went to a lot of trouble to torture and kill your Aunt, Jenna? You can be certain that someone else knows about these nasty little books. And will certainly want them gone. The whites in South Africa are about to lose their power and Apartheid is about to end. I think some of the people that have run South Africa are anxious to cover their tracks from the last thirty years. Whatever your Aunt was up to in Namibia is likely to be a high priority for them to make sure it remains secret."

"So you think it was the South African government that killed my Aunt?"

"Why not? They've killed thousands of other people during the past few decades. What do you think, Tom?"

"It's a real possibility," said Tom. "It's not likely the government as a whole made the decisions. Just the politician most connected to the stuff that was going down with this camp in Namibia."

"Let's read on as fast as we can," said Ing. "We need to know all we can about who has been involved in this."

Tom pored over the rest of the diary that he had been reading from. He gave Jenna some dates to note that were associated with data that Gerta was compiling on three differently numbered batches of tests. He mentioned that Walter and several of the other scientists were spending more and more time in the satellite camps. Then Tom let out a soft whistle.

"Okay. Here it is," he said. "She's talking about a couple of South African army engineers that joined them for dinner. They have a troop with them, equipped with heavy road building gear. They are driving a road out into the bush to establish an isolated grave site."

"Those fuckers," said Ing.

"Your Aunt loves her data. She's noting how much earth has to be moved to bury a hundred bodies."

"This is making me sick," said Jenna. "I need to take a break."

"Give me your notebook. I'll do a bit of work for a change," said Ing.

Jenna walked to the dock and stood looking out at the lake.

"Gotta be tough to learn that your Aunt was involved in something this dirty," said Tom, watching Jenna.

"Gonna be a lot tougher if the people who want these diaries come to ask Jenna about them," said Ing. "Let's keep going. Maybe there's the name of their government contact."

The rest of that diary was just more talk about the work. Tom noted that one of the batches they were working with was abandoned by the scientists as being too unstable for their purposes. He finished that book and looked at the stack of diaries on the table. "Halfway through," he said.

Early in the next book Tom began to focus more intently on the pages. After a moment he called to Jenna to come back and join them. She did so reluctantly.

"What now, Tom? Has she implicated herself in the J.F.K. assassination?"

"Not so far. But some VIPs are visiting."

"The government contacts?" asked Ing eagerly.

"Nope. An American, a German, a Brit, and a Brazilian."

"What the fuck," said Ing.

"Yep. This is an international outfit they've got going. These four visitors are observing every aspect of their work. Trips out to the satellite camps, meetings with this Hector guy who is running things, long sessions reviewing data with your Aunt."

"Is she using names?"

"She is. Mr. Allen, Mr. Mendez, Herr Von Hesse, and Mr. Sterling. Let me get through a few more pages of this."

Tom read for about twenty pages without speaking. Then he set the book aside, rubbed his eyes and sat looking thoughtful for a minute or so.

"Okay. These visitors are clearly mega VIPs. The American guy has become close to your Aunt. So close that he has arranged for them to leave the camp and hole up in a five star hotel in Johannesburg. He and your Aunt just returned to their suite after a photo session in a studio."

"Just a minute," said Jenna. She went into the cottage and rummaged around in her carry-all. The small bundle of nude photos was still in its wrapping. She gave them to Tom.

He flipped through them quickly and passed them to Ing.

"There were two sets of prints made. The American guy, who she is now referring to as Bill, kept one set; she kept the other. They were shot in 1969, Jenna."

"My Aunt was quite a piece of work," said Jenna.

"Put it in context. 1969 was the year of the Woodstock concert. The hippies were promoting free love and peace and drugs. The late sixties and early seventies were a very different time," said Tom.

"I find it hard to believe that Gerta was doing this free love thing. My Dad was very conservative."

"Yeah, Jenna, but he was raised in Canada by Dutch immigrant farmers. Academics and scientists were out on the leading edge of all things new and crazy in the '60s," said Tom.

Tom read steadily, only telling Jenna points that were out of the ordinary. They were well over three quarters of the way through the pile of diaries by noon. Without being asked, Ing mixed everyone a drink. "The breakfast of champions," she said as she handed them around.

"Grab your pen, Jenna," said Tom. He was speed-reading, and went ahead several pages.

"The compound was attacked by a group of what your Aunt refers to as Angolan terrorists. It was a night attack and it's clear that the security people were caught with their hands on their dicks. At least twenty of the terrs got into the compound. Gerta and her female friend ran to a slit trench because mortar rounds were being dropped into the compound."

"She's indicating that she caught shrapnel in her calf and that the other woman was badly hurt. She's bound her leg with the sleeve off her blouse and is trying to help the other woman. Now she hears someone approaching and she's cocked her handgun."

Ing had been gathering up glasses from the night before to take into the cottage. She sat down quickly.

"Holy crap! You Aunt just shot a terr, Jenna. Hit him square in the chest and he's fallen into the trench on top of her. She's pinned under him and says she's afraid that more terrs will be along to kill her. Now security troops and Walter have arrived and they're hauling them out of the trench."

"She and the other woman were taken to the infirmary. Doctor on hand has cleaned out the hole in her leg. The shrapnel went right through, so there's nothing to dig out. She's had an X-ray. The other woman is going to be operated on to remove splinters, but she will be okay. Walter is staying close to her in the infirmary and is being a wonderful support."

"Now she's writing on the morning after the attack. It's November 10, 1973. Jesus! Seventeen of their security people were killed during the raid. And there were a dozen dead terrs inside the compound. They've got three wounded ones in custody and the South African army has killed or captured another thirty terrs outside the wire."

"Her female friend came through her operation just fine and is sleeping off the anaesthetic in the bed beside her. Hector, the head guy has come in to see her. So has the army major who lead the troops that swept the terrs outside the wire. He has told them that they were from a sub-group of the MPLA called the "Lions."

"Stop there, Tom," said Jenna. "Something that my Aunt put in a letter to me that was left with the diaries now makes sense. She said that I should hang on to the computer things that were in her suitcase and only give them to someone who would tell me that they were with her when she shot a lion. I thought she was talking about a real lion."

"Great," said Ing. "Clearly some of these mad scientists who were in Namibia with her know she had all the disks and will be coming to see you to get them."

Tom was sitting looking troubled.

"Where are these things, Jenna? Somewhere secure, I hope," said Tom.

"We need to get my computer whiz to look at those, Jenna. I'll give him a good screw when we get back to town and spend an evening at his house. He says he has a hell of computer set-up," said Ing.

"They're here," said Jenna. "Well hidden. I'll get a few of them to take back for Ing's friend to look at. Let's go on with Tom," she said, gesturing toward the diaries.

Tom read forward a page or two and began to talk again.

"She's out of bed with a heavy bandage on her leg and is using crutches. The other woman is in pain but will be fine. There is going to be a memorial service and burial of the security people who were killed the next day. Gerta remarks that it is appropriate because that will be Remembrance Day. The army guys are preparing a burial site. Shit!"

"What?" said Ing.

"They are going to bury the security people in the bush," said Tom.

"So?"

"These are mainstream human beings. Not members of an opposing rag tag army."

"Okay?"

"This fucking operation is so covert that the dead guys don't get to have a funeral and be shipped home for burial in the family plot. They are being quietly put into the ground in some hastily made clearing in the Namibian bush. That's real CIA type bullshit."

"These people were doing something really crazy bad," said Ing.

"Four books left, Tom. If I make my famous eggs benedict for lunch and you have a break while I cook, do you think we can get through them this afternoon?"

"I think we have to," he said.

"A-fucking-men to that," said Ing. "This whole scenario keeps getting scarier by the minute. It's a good thing that your new friend Tom Robbins is a security consultant, Jenna. Because you sure as fuck need one!"

***

Sam was glad that he had decided to stay on in Muskoka after Franz Von Hesse returned to Germany. The days were long and demanding since he was running his usual array of companies as well as coordinating the efforts of the other members of the Legacy Organization as they worked to formulate a plan to deal with deaths of Gerta Ten Haan and Erich Krohl and to recover the information that they had disclosed that they had.

All of the communication that Gerta and Erich had with the LO - which was how Sam and the others referred to the Legacy Organization - had been via the ARPNet, computer to computer. The LO had gone to a great deal of trouble to assist Gerta and Erich in hiding them from all of their enemies. A virtually untraceable means of communication had been needed.

The system had worked well, although it meant that Franz had to carry a heavier load in trying to manage Erich and Gerta. From 1983 on, both of them had become more difficult. They had lots of money, lots of time on their hands, and they were watching the developing epidemic in Africa like a pair of cats that had cornered a mouse.

Both of them felt they had an axe to grind with the South African government, and Gerta, against the explicit instructions of the Legacy Organization, worked some of her contacts in the South African army. They had started to prod the LO about the work of the South African 7th Medical Battalion. Somehow, Gerta had obtained a tidbit of information about the South Africa's Operation Coast.

Erich had been loath to leave Africa when the project in Namibia was shut down, but the LO were blunt with him. Take our direction or you are on your own was their ultimatum. Gerta had not been so defiant and was a useful incentive to get Erich out of Africa and safely tucked away in Holland. Although once in Europe, he was forced to live the life of a hermit, posing as Gerta's elderly and disabled husband.

As the 1980's drew to a close, the two of them had become more and more troublesome. They constantly badgered Franz, demanding that the LO use its knowledge and resources to intercede in the efforts being made to halt the new epidemic that was plaguing Africa. The LO met in Muskoka in '86 to come up with some plans to deal with their increasingly erratic behavior.

Some veiled threats were delivered to them by Sam and Daniel Sterling in 1988 which shut them up for a while. But as more research came out about the disease and its origins, the messages to Franz began again. Then in 1990 Gerta crossed the line.

Franz was a noted industrialist, investor and philanthropist. He made many public appearances in support of a range of causes. As he was leaving one such event in Hamburg, he was confronted by a well dressed, attractive woman who demanded to speak with him. He had not seen Gerta for years and was so taken aback that he hustled her into his waiting limo. The paparazzi who were about in abundance had loved it.

It was fortunate that this occurred at a time just after Franz had ended his third marriage and had not yet started dating the woman who would become wife number four. But the magnitude of the security breach had sent all of the LO members reeling. Gerta and Erich were whisked off to Brazil and held under what amounted to house arrest in one of Claudio's houses in the mountains.

A great deal of negotiation ensued. After six months in Brazil, a deal was struck and it was agreed that the two would live in the United States. All felt that there was less chance of anyone recognizing Erich in California, thus giving him the chance to move more freely. Gerta seemed to be experiencing some need to connect with her past since it was her idea to live in a flat on her niece's property. The phone call that Franz had received a month before her death had shed some more light on why Gerta wanted to establish some ties with a relative.

***

They ate their lunch quickly and went back to the diaries. "Okay," said Tom. "It's the morning of the funeral. The whole team is gathered in the clearing. There are ten chairs for the wounded and the rest are standing. Your Aunt's female friend and three others are back in the infirmary with a couple of staff and an army security unit. Everyone else is there."

"She says the smell of the crushed trees and shrubs that the army bulldozed out of the way to make the clearing is making her feel ill. All of the bodies have been sewn into white shrouds and a team of eight army guys is laying them in the burial trench in a row. Hector is standing at the head of the trench, holding his Bible. She says that with his black clothes and huge beard he looks like a prophet."

"Hector is saying words over the dead. He's speaking in Afrikaans. Now he's said a couple of sentences in Gaelic. Three of the security people were apparently Scottish Mercs."

"Mercs?" asked Ing.

"Mercenaries," replied Tom. "Probably in their fifties. A lot of Scots couldn't stop soldiering just because World War Two ended."

"Hector is done talking and now an army chaplain is reading scripture. He's done and a bugler is playing the Last Post. They are silent and of course, the bagpipes have started. And now they are all singing "Abide with Me." Your Aunt is crying.

"Now they're headed back to the compound for a reception. Your Aunt observed that there were bulldozers in the clearing and is thinking about the machines moving forward to cover the bodies. She thinks that is very uncool. Walter is holding her hand and trying to comfort her."

"The South African army has moved into the area in earnest. As they get back to the compound, your Aunt is seeing that they are dug in around the place in depth. There is a heavy mortar battery just outside the gate and a troop of four Oliphants inside a partially constructed camouflaged laager nearby. The reception is in the dining hall. There are more soldiers than civilians."

"Hector has called for the attention of all and has singled your Aunt out. He describes how she made it to the slit trench despite her wound and then shot a terr. There are resounding cheers from all present. She says that many of the people are getting drunk."

"An army captain who she has never met before has approached her and proposed marriage. Two of his colleagues have led him away. Damn, I've done that so many times!" said Tom.

"Aren't you glad I've never accepted?" said Ing.

"Don't answer that, Tom," said Jenna.

"Your Aunt is now in bed in the infirmary. She's thinking about the lonely, unmarked graves of the security people. She writes that she will be cremated if at all possible because she can't tolerate the thought of being put in the ground. She wants to be in the sun, feeling the air."

"Did that for ya, Auntie," said Jenna. "Just have to figure out where to sprinkle you."

"Three more books to go," said Ing.

"We've fast forwarded. It's 1975. Gerta apologizes for having been away from the diaries for so long. Work has been intensive. The army presence has changed things to a more results oriented, less academic environment. Walter is all for it. They are making great progress on whatever they are doing."

"We're moving quickly now. It's '76 and there has been a disaster! They are down to working with one formula. Formula 65b has turned rogue. That's the word she used. They all have had to leave the compound and a bunch of people, she thinks they were army, in hazmat suits have hosed the whole place down with chemicals. Their whole team had to strip naked, leave their clothes in a pile, and walk about a mile to a disinfecting site."

"They are back in the compound, which smells horrible from the chemicals and are eating army rations. Three of their colleagues are gone. Presumably sick. Hector has lost a bit of his aura of being God-like. Your Aunt and Walter are having a tryst in her office. Holy fuck!"

"Some German guy named Winter has just opened the door to her office and caught them doing the deed. Walter has decked him and your Aunt is standing over him, naked, covering this Winter guy with her sidearm."

"Hector and security and the army are all in it now. This guy is some sort of traitor, trying to steal their research. Walter is calling for his immediate execution. Your Aunt is angry and embarrassed since she was naked and post coital when Hector and the security folks arrived."

"The whole lot of them is holding a sort of trial about this guy. Your Aunt thinks they're going to execute him. She's disappointed when the army intercedes and he's packed out of the compound with enough gear to maybe walk to safety. She and Walter have gone back to her office to debrief, and debrief, if you get my drift."

"I admire her spirit," said Ing.

"Damn straight," said Tom, "and with a game leg into the bargain."

"Both of you shut up," said Jenna.

"It's much more austere at the compound. Food is worse, work is more intense; no one is having much fun. Hector is crabby and has learned that your Aunt is keeping a diary. She has been told to burn the books and to cease and desist. She is supremely pissed."

"Walter and Gerta have managed to get their hands on a bunch of notebooks. They have soaked them in gas and have called Hector out to a fire pit. Your Aunt has tossed a match on to the pile of books and they are blazing away merrily. Hector is pleased."

"Your Aunt has carefully packed all of her real diaries into a box. She has let a lieutenant of the South African Army Service Corps play with her boobs for half an hour; he's drunk, and now the books are on their way to Johannesburg where they will go into storage."

Tom sat the last book down and said, "I need a really big drink."

***

Chuck Holt was employing over twenty people to handle surveillance and fact finding regarding Jenna Van Velt and her husband. Two of his people were deeply connected to the LAPD, one of them a personal friend of Arnon's boss. He was somewhat relieved when his two sources reported that the cops felt that Van Velt deserved a 98.5% rating on the boring person scale.

He had briefly hoped that the guys had been right and that there was a suitcase or parcel sitting unopened in the couple's house that would be handed over to the LO's designate when they showed up and claimed to "have been there when Johanna killed a lion." The last few days had banished that hope. He called Sam Allen.

"I have a whole shitload of things to talk about, Sam."

"I'm listening."

"First of all, Van Velt has moved out of the marital home and it's for sale. Her hubby has taken a new job in the East. Secondly, she has spent the last few days at her cottage with a man and a woman. They spend their days stark naked swimming, sunbathing and the guy reads aloud to them from a stack of notebooks."

"So she found somebody who reads Afrikaans."

"That's what it has to be. So now there are three more people on the planet who know what we were up to in Namibia."

"How the hell did she get on to these people? You can't just go to the yellow pages and find a number for a place that rents South Africans."

"We're doing everything we can to find out who these people are. The guy is in good shape and yesterday he spent a couple of hours tweaking his archery skills. Combat archery. My people were impressed by what he can do with a bow."

"Are they still at this cottage of hers?"

"They are. Last evening my guys were entertained when the guy and woman led Van Velt out onto the porch. Her hands were tied to a bench, she was wearing a blindfold, and the two of them very thoroughly did her."

"Could your guys tell if this was a consensual session?"

"The three of them poured drinks afterward and the guy and Van Velt had a post-shag cigarette, so my guys think it was just a sex game. But it gets better, Sam. Two days ago my guys watched the cop from LA who's in charge of the case sneak through the woods with a woman in tow. He watched Van Velt and friends through binos for awhile while the woman took pictures with a long lens."

"So the cops think Van Velt is holding out on them?"

"For sure."

"So we can now be certain that Van Velt has held onto the disks and knows what was in Gerta's diaries."

"I'd bet a lot of money on that. Which leads me to money. I'm spending a lot, Sam, and I'm going to have to spend a lot more."

"Why?"

"We're not the only ones watching Van Velt. There are a bunch of guys lying low in the woods near here. I sent two of my best recon guys in as close to them as possible. They were speaking German."

"German? Not Afrikaans?"

"My guys know German when they hear it."

"Which confirms that this is Winter's show."

"Absolutely. Sam, I need to put a bunch more guys in the field here. We will have to intervene if they make a play to grab Van Velt. If we have to do that, I want the odds very heavily in our favour."

"Do want you need to do, Chuck. I think it's time for me to give Joachim Maarten a call."

"Glad it's you and not me who has to talk to that scumbag. Talk soon."

***

Tom, Ing and Jenna had several big drinks as they talked about what they had learned from the diaries. As usual, Ing had done most of the talking. Tom did the least.

"The murderous bullshit that she was involved with in Namibia, judging by the visit by the VIPs, had international backing," said Ing. "She managed to hide out for 11 years after she stopped being Johanna Buist. That is not an easy thing to do. Someone was giving her a lot of help. And something changed last year because suddenly she was coming to live at your place."

"Maybe the help stopped," offered Tom.

"Maybe. But she still had lots of money to pay her rent, get her hair done and so forth. And so apparently did this old guy who visited her every day. He's almost certainly her lover from the camp in Namibia. The age is about right. It could be that whoever was helping her helped the old guy to hole up somewhere around here as well," said Ing.

"There is, of course, the awkward question of why the hideout in Jenna's backyard didn't work out so terribly well for her," said Tom.

"I'd guess that whatever happened to make her want to come to California also led to her cover being blown," said Ing.

"What's most fucking important to note, though, is that you have a dead Aunt, a box of diaries and photographs and a stack of computer disks. We three may be the only people on the planet who know they exist, but there is at least one other person who suspects that they do. And that person is extremely unpleasant."

"Ing makes a helluva good point," said Tom.

"Well, what the hell should I do? Call the police and tell them that when I was unpacking from my move I realized that my Aunt had stashed some of her stuff in the attic? Then if the cops don't arrest me for withholding evidence I could take out a newspaper ad saying, dear person or persons who raped and killed my Aunt, the police now have everything you were looking for so leave me the fuck alone."

"I don't think the Times will let you use the word fuck in the classifieds," said Ing.

"I think the top priority is to have Ing work her magic on her computer guy. It would be good to know what's on those disks. I'm guessing it's the 'work' they were doing in Namibia. Let's make that our job for an evening as soon as we can."

"Alright," said Jenna.

"Ing. Do you have to fuck this guy before he helps us take a look at this stuff or will he accept a promissory note, so to speak?"

"He'll do whatever I ask him to do."

"Great. So let's eat, drink and be merry for the remainder of our time in this beautiful place. Then we shall hie off to the city to delve deeper in the mysteries of Gerta Ten Haan," said Tom.

The three raised their glasses in a toast. Ing knocked her drink back, remarking that it was perhaps best the drinking would end for a few days. She declared her bedtime was imminent. Tom helped her into the cottage.

"I've bedded Ing down in the spare room for tonight. She is a tired and drunk lady. She thinks that she can drink like a sailor on shore leave but she doesn't have the experience or the body weight."

"I can't figure out if she likes drinking or if it's self medication," said Jenna.

"I'm on edge tonight," said Tom. "What your Aunt wrote in her diaries is TNT on steroids. My life is assessing risk. I rate you to be at a very great risk factor. I don't want to spoil this lovely evening or scare you, but you are the holder of some seriously sensitive information. Someone wanted it from your Aunt and didn't get it. It's a certainty that they will want to pose the same questions to you as they did to your Aunt."

"I'm beginning to understand that. Where do you think I should run?"

"You never run unless you have to. You make a plan. You estimate what the bad people might do. And you take counter-measures."

"That works for me."

"I don't want to come across as a pervert trying to take advantage of you, but it might be a good idea if I stayed close to you while we have a look at what's on the computer disks. I have some pretty good experience in helping people disappear for a few weeks when there is a need to."

"It's funny, Tom. My Dad was a Dutch Jew who became a Canadian Calvinist. My Aunt was a Dutch Jew who became God knows what. I've spent all of my life wondering who the hell I am. And here I am, desperately in need of a new identity."

"There are a lot of options. Have you had this place appraised?"

"What, the cottage?"

"Yes."

"No. We bought it a little over two years ago. Do you think it's worth something?"

"It's worth a lot. A big lot. You might want to list it. I can show you how to sell it without bad people knowing where you are when you receive the money from it."

"That makes me sad," said Jenna. "I understand that my world has changed forever. But leaving this place makes me sad."

"Places are places. Experience makes places valuable. You can find new places. Most of the great wars in this world have been fought over spots that weren't worth the cost of the gunpowder."

"I think, Mr. Tom, that I would like to bed you. Take you to bed and make my body available to you. Experience you without a blindfold and my hands tied. That is my plan for the rest of the evening. Does that work for you?"

Tom stood up and took her hand.

Chapter Eighteen

Winter had agreed when Nils suggested that the Spaders be asked to come to the chateau which Cerebis Corp. used as a headquarters as soon as possible. Once that was agreed upon, Winter left immediately since he could not stand to be around the Spaders. The team in America that was keeping tabs on Jenna Van Velt was calling with updates on a daily basis. Nils was a great believer in planning and wanted the Spaders to be part of the process.

Nils was not one to spare expense when preparing for a job. He had had 1/25000 scale maps of the area around the Van Velt woman's cottage shipped to him express. Each day when he spoke to the team leader in America he had a list of further questions to be answered. He kept the information he was receiving highly organized. Few people knew that Nils was an excellent typist.

The Spaders arrived in the late afternoon the day after Winter had departed. Nils felt excitement as he watched Hanna get out of the car that had brought them. He had given a lot of thought to introducing them to Angelique.

Hanna hugged him tightly as he greeted them and Alan Spader shook hands with his customary grip of steel. It was their first visit to the chateau and Nils could see that they were impressed with their surroundings. Both of them had clawed their way up to a life of some comfort, but opulence was not something they were familiar with. Nils had a staff member show them to their suite and asked them to join him in the gym/indoor pool area as soon as it was convenient.

A couple of large folding tables had been set up in the gym area so that Nils could use it as a planning room. This was where Angelique had a massage table and she was there when Nils entered, using the treadmill. Nils greeted her and said that a couple of guests would be coming into the gym soon, but urged her to finish her workout.

Nils had not told the Spaders that there would be anyone but him in the gym. He was watching carefully as they entered and was delighted to see that both of the Spaders were like hunting dogs that had spotted a pheasant when they saw Angelique. He led them over to where she was working out on the weight machine. Angelique stood up to shake hands and Nils said, "Alan and Hanna Spader, may I introduce you to Angelique."

"Are you a guest here?" Hanna asked Angelique sharply.

"No, I'm the masseuse," she answered.

"Well, I hope that I may avail myself of your skills during our stay here," said Hanna.

On the morning of the Spaders' arrival, Nils had received his first packet of photos of Jenna Van Velt. All were shot with telephoto lens while she was on the move, so the detail was far from studio quality. But it was clear that their subject for this particular job was about five feet seven inches tall with shoulder length dark hair. One of the photos had been taken as she was doing her morning run near her apartment and her level of fitness was apparent.

"Tasty," remarked Alan.

Nils took them through an hour-long briefing, explaining that they would be interrogating the woman about some unspecified articles that had belonged to her Aunt. He made it clear to them that the woman had no covert or military service and thus, no training on how to resist interrogation. Then he led them to the map.

Alan had served four years as a squaddie with a Highland regiment before joining the Hong Kong police and Hanna had done her basic training, so they both were familiar with topographical maps. When Nils pointed out the long trail leading to the isolated building in a sea of green colour on the map, they both smiled.

"How old is the map?" asked Alan.

"Only five years," Nils replied.

"That's nothing," said Hanna.

"What a lovely place to have a chat with this lovely lady," said Alan.

"America is the land of opportunity. Do you think we will have several days with her?" asked Hanna.

"It's quite possible," said Nils.

***

As usual, it was Tom who awoke first and Jenna and Ing came out of their beds, drawn to the aroma of coffee. Tom was standing on the dock when they emerged from the cottage with their mugs. The sun was already hot and there was a bit of mist over the lake.

"Is the sauna still up to heat?" Tom asked.

"I haven't turned it off yet".

"Great," he said as he set down his empty mug and dove into the water. He swam to shore and headed to the heat. Ten minutes later Ing and Jenna did the same.

They sat in the sauna talking about the beauty of the place. Ing remarked that there seemed to be plenty of room in the sauna even with the elephant in the corner. Tom told her that he would be "keeping an eye on Jenna for a bit."

"Thank fucking Christ!" said Ing. "We've been very blasé about the shit Tom's read to us from these diaries, but it's time to stop the bullshit. Thanks to your Aunt, Jenna, you're sitting on a pile of dynamite and someone is going to come and try to shove a couple of sticks of it up your ass. Stay fucking close to Tom and let him teach you how to watch your back."

Tom reminded Jenna that they needed some of the computer disks for Ing's friend to go over. Jenna grabbed a flashlight and slithered into the space where she had hidden the small safe. Getting the disks had taken much longer than it should because once she was contorted into a vulnerable position, working the combination of the steel box, Ing had unfastened her shorts, pulled down her underwear and mercilessly played with her. Tom had finally intervened by telling Ing that he had heard Jenna utter her safe word. Jenna emerged from the hiding place pissed at Ing.

Jenna took the lead in her vehicle as they drove back into the city. The entrance to her laneway was still heavily overgrown. In the past, Robert had trimmed the trees back. She made a mental note to call the man in Bayfield who did odd jobs around the cottage to trim the trees which nearly obscured the entrance to her lane. She was amused to see that Tom's larger jeep had acquired some random branches that clung to its roof racks and underside.

Once they were on the highway, Tom told Ing that he had a big favour to ask of her.

"Ask away, Mr. Tom. If you want me to stand up with you and Jenna at your wedding, I'm in."

"I'll keep that in mind," said Tom. "Thanks. Actually, I wonder if you might be willing to take an all expenses paid trip with me to Zimbabwe. We'd have an old, very physically sick guy with us."

"I'm getting wet just thinking about it. Tell me more."

***

There were four of them at dinner: Nils, Hanna, Alan, and Doktor Kepp. Nils had told the staff to serve the meal in the study, which was a small intimate setting. He insisted that a fire be lit in the room despite the season.

Hanna and Alan had spent the past six months working for two large organizations. They had been doing research into the ways and means to improve the results of 'urgent interrogations'. Specifically, they were trying to develop chemical tools that would allow them to quickly extract time-sensitive information from subjects. Getting reliable information that could be acted upon instantly was a notoriously difficult task.

"You know the problem," said Alan. "You capture a subject on a battlefield, say, and all you need the wanker to do is to tell you where the artillery position that he passed when he came up to his slit trench that morning is. If you could get him to give you that information within fifteen minutes of his capture, you'd have a useful tidbit to pass on to the air force or the counter battery blokes and bingo! Their artillery takes a pasting."

"But almost anyone can convince themselves to hold out against their interrogator for fifteen minutes or half an hour," said Hanna. "And a soldier or a trained operative can usually hold out more much longer. That is why it is nearly impossible to get useful tactical information from a subject. No matter how much pain is quickly inflicted."

"Yes. I have read that a psychological change must take place in the subject of the interrogation before they will betray secrets. A change that only occurs after there has been a considerable aggregate of pain and humiliation," said Doktor Kepp.

"Correct," said Hanna. "Alan and I are very excited to tell you that we have discovered a way to make a subject give us timely and valuable information in a very short time period. We've proven this method works on a number of subjects."

"Will you be bringing this to the States with us?"

"Of course. Alan calls it Love Potion Number 9."

***

When Jenna returned to work on Monday, she was delighted to see on the whiteboard that her vacation had been approved. One week back in the office, then two weeks off. Jenna decided she could embrace that sort of schedule.

Tom had arranged to meet Ing Thursday evening to get photos of her taken so that he could get documents in place for their trip to Zimbabwe. He was surprised to get a call from her Tuesday morning asking him to meet him at their pub that evening. When he agreed, she ended the call.

When he got to the pub she was already there, nursing a beer. Tom grabbed a drink from the bar and joined her at a table in the 'quiet' part of the place. Ing did not look well.

"Are you okay?" asked Tom.

"Not so much. My mom has taken a bad turn, Tom. She's really sick now. The docs have confirmed that she has something very bad going on. But the dense buggers still don't know what it is."

"I am really sorry, Ing. Sorry for your mom. Sorry for you. What are you going to do?"

"My company is being really great about this. They've agreed to transfer me back to the Capetown office for as long as I need to be there for my mom. They're not too nervous about the government chucking me into prison since it looks like apartheid is about to go the way of K-tel records. I've assured them I'll be too busy with my mom to get into trouble shooting my mouth off."

"I'm glad they're treating you well in all this, Ing. Think you'll become a Springbok again?"

"God, no! I'll stay there until things are sorted out with mom and then it's back to sunny California for me. Dear old South Africa is going to see some trying times, methinks. I want to get back here to do you and Jenna at her lovely country place."

"When do you go?"

"Tomorrow afternoon. I'll call Jenna when I get home to say goodbye." Ing took an envelope from her bag and gave it to Tom. "Jenna's Aunt's disks. I didn't have time to connect with my nerd."

"I'll get them back to Jenna."

"Sorry to stand you up for your trip to Zimbabwe."

"I always have a plan B, Ing."

"If plan B involves a former Canadian woman, you make sure you take damn good care of her."

Chapter Nineteen

"Sam Allen."

"It's Chuck. Van Velt is back in town at her apartment. We still don't know much about her guy but the woman is named Ing Stoller. One of my guys is on the plane that she's taking to Capetown."

"And who the hell is she gonna meet with there?"

"We'll know when she lands, Sam. Got people on it."

"Anything new on Winter's people?"

"We've got a couple of good things in mind to fuck them up. When the time comes we'll thin the herd pretty quickly. I'm thinking that things could get very serious very soon."

"I've been onto the others. If you need to grab Van Velt and get her to some place very safe, Daniel has it all set up. Scotland."

"We'll see. Their deployment pattern at Van Velt's cottage is atypical. Usually these former East German guys do things the way they were trained. These boys are way up the road. I don't like things I don't understand."

"She okay, though?"

"Sam. I swear to God that it would take some major zodiac event for her to come to harm. I just am not sure what the fuck Winter's guys are doing. It makes no sense. They've got their people in weird places all over the woods up in cottage country, but it seems they've stopped their close watch on Van Velt here in town."

"Stay on it. Let's get through what's going down in your neck of the woods and then I want you all back here in Muskoka."

***

Jenna had agreed that they would take Tom's jeep out to the cottage. He gave some serious thought as to how he would pack the vehicle. His bow case went in last, after a Glock, an M16 and some white phosphorous and fragmentation grenades. Two spools of twenty-pound test fish line rested on top of the load.

He drove to Jenna's apartment building and used the parking card she had given him to pull into the garage downstairs. Jenna was ready with a pile of bags, coolers, etc. He remarked that he thought they had agreed that they would buy food and booze once they got to Bayfield. Jenna told him they would, but there was this evening to think about.

Chuck Holt's watchers were good, but they had never seen Tom's jeep before. It had heavily tinted glass so they could be forgiven for having missed that Tom and Jenna had left the building. There was no tail on them as they drove to the cottage.

***

Nils was pissed off when his people let him know that the woman was at her cottage early. He left his maps and notes and tables and scrambled onto a plane that would take him to an airport less than a hundred miles from the target. Fortunately the flight was under-booked and he had a row of seats to himself.

He was met by the commander of the team that Winter had put in place. The man had been in the bush near the cottage for the past twelve days. He gave Nils several grainy photos of the woman taken as she did various tasks outside of the ultra-modern building.

The team leader drove Nils to a small inn where the Spaders were staying. Both of them had been taken down the wooded road to the cottage. Alan assured Nils that it would be very easy to conduct a blitz attack on the woman. She had set routines and would be unprepared for anyone to suddenly appear on her property. Nils relaxed. His team had hidden a vehicle deep off the wooded road that was equipped with a phone, so they were in constant touch. They were too far east though to see the jeep that crept up the road and then pushed through a small hole in the brush.

***

Jenna laughed as Tom drove the jeep through the thick brush that shrouded her laneway.

"I'm sorry, Tom. I meant to call the guy in Bayfield who takes care of the grass and have him trim things up. Robert always did that job. He had an obsession about keeping the entrance to the laneway cut and open."

"It's not like it stopped us," said Tom. "I'm just amazed that you could find the place."

"It's easy. I just watch for the big beech tree close to the road and the laneway is twenty yards past it. I kind of like the whole camouflaged entry way thing."

"It should keep away the religious door knockers. Hide it, and no one will come," said Tom.

***

Sam was in a deep sleep when the phone rang. He took a couple of deep breaths before he picked it up. Chuck Holt was on the line.

"Okay Sam, this is getting really fucking weird. Van Velt and her guy arrived at her cottage at about seven. They've unloaded a hell of a lot of stuff from a jeep, which I assume is his. The barbecue is lit and it appears that it's business as usual for them."

"Okay," said Sam.

"Up the road we've got Winter's people moving in tighter to the big new cottage east of Van Velt's and my guys have just told me that a guy who looks like Nils Witt, only with dark hair and brown eyes, is motoring this way. And one of my other guys has pretty much for sure put the Spaders in Bayfield."

"The perfect storm," said Sam.

"It's tense, buddy, I'll keep you posted. My guys have lots of firepower."

***

"I'm curious, Jenna," said Tom. "What possessed you to not give the diaries and disks to the police when they began their investigation into your Aunt's murder? You knew that they were there."

Jenna walked to the cupboard over the stove, felt around, and withdrew a tightly folded piece of paper. She handed it to Tom. It was Gerta's letter to her. "Read that," said Jenna. "What the hell else could I have done?"

Tom read the letter. And read it again.

"Okay. How much would you give, right now, to have the opportunity to have given the diaries and disks to the cops about five hours after they began their investigation into Gerta's murder?"

"I don't fucking know. From the time I opened her suitcase and took out the packages, I've been dealing with fucking shit! If Robert wasn't who Robert was, I would have talked about it with him. Ing told me to just hand them over when I told her about them. You're a security guy and you think I've got several pounds of dynamite up my butt." Jenna glanced at her watch. "I've got to call Deanna up the road. She's there alone and we've agreed to check in with each other."

Jenna dialed the number and Deanna answered right away. "Deanna, it's Jenna. We're here at the cottage."

"Wonderful! Do you have Tom and Ing with you?"

"Ing has had to go back to South Africa. Her mother is sick. So it's Tom and me this weekend."

"I'm sorry to hear about Ing's mom. Is it serious?"

"I don't think Ing knows yet. Is Steve coming out tonight?"

"No. The bum has a golf tournament tomorrow, so he isn't coming until Sunday morning. He's taken Monday off, so he'll be here until Monday afternoon."

"Deanna is obviously enjoying her alone time out here in the wilds."

"Good," said Tom. "I don't want to presume anything but at the same time I would like to be up front and say that I would enjoy some together time here in the woods with you."

A couple of hours later they went out on to the porch, Tom naked, Jenna with a sheet draped around her since she found the night air cool. They took their chairs in time to catch the last of the daylight. Neither of them seemed to want any alcohol.

They enjoyed a good deal of silence and looked at the starry sky without having to remark on it. Tom was about to start telling Jenna about his friend Ed Cromwell when he heard something that was out place for the venue. It was a distant sound and very faint. He'd heard it before in other places, and he gestured for Jenna to be quiet as he walked off the porch to the lawn to listen more intently.

He stood motionless in the darkness for what seemed like an eternity. There was some light because the full moon was rising in the east. Finally there was sound again and this time he recognized it for what it was.

"Jenna," he whispered. "Into the cottage. Dress in your darkest shirt and jeans. Find the darkest jacket you have. Get a tote bag and stuff some bottled water and granola bars in it, if you have any. Then stay low to the floor and away from windows until I come to you."

Jenna immediately did as he had directed. Tom cursed the white sheet she was wearing until she had disappeared into the cottage.

He moved swiftly to the jeep and opened the back hatch. He had long ago modified the vehicle's lighting system and there was no illumination as he uncased the Glock and it slid into the shoulder holster. The M16 was uncased next. He placed it on the ground with some webbed bandoliers. Tom put two fragmentation grenades in the case with his bow and arrows and went back to the cottage with all of the gear.

Jenna was dressed in dark clothing.

"What have you got on your feet?" Tom whispered.

"My jogging shoes."

"Perfect! Do you know anything about guns?"

"They kill people."

"Guns don't kill people, Jenna. People kill people."

Tom took the Glock out of the shoulder holster and cocked it. He moved a chair so that it faced the door of the cottage and told Jenna to sit in it. Once seated, he carefully placed the weapon in her hands and gave her an aiming point at the center of the screen door, just above the wooden cross bar.

"If anyone approaches the door to the cottage they will be silhouetted by the light reflected off the lake. If someone appears at the door, squeeze - don't pull the trigger- squeeze it. The idea is to have the gun pointing at the spot it's pointing at now when you fire. Got it?"

"I don't think I can do this," said Jenna, trying to seem calm.

"I'll be two minutes," said Tom.

To Jenna's relief he was back quickly, fully dressed in black clothing. He left Jenna holding the Glock while he put on heavy boots. Then he gently eased the pistol out of her hands.

"You know that rocky knob of a hill that tears at our chests as we're finishing our runs?"

"Yes."

"We're going there. I'll lead. You stay right behind me. Within touching distance."

"Okay."

"Where's the bag with the water?"

Jenna pointed to a knapsack.

"You get to carry that. Get it on your back so your hands are free."

As Jenna struggled into the knapsack, Tom put on the shoulder holster and tucked the Glock firmly into it. He did a check of the rifle and then took something out of the black leather case lying on the floor. He closed the case and slung it over his shoulder.

"Give me your right hand," said Tom.

When Jenna did Tom placed a small heavy object in it.

He made sure that a lever on the thing was firmly against the palm of her hand and closed her fingers around it. Then he twisted aside a metal clip and straightened the spread ends of a pin.

"If something bad happens to me," said Tom. "like my head suddenly explodes, you need to pull this pin, toss this thing in the direction of whatever seems to be most threatening and then run like hell in the opposite direction. You got that?"

Jenna nodded and was able to say "Yes".

"Stay right on my ass, Jenna. Go when I go. Stop when I stop. Go when I go."

Tom put on a headband with drop-down eyepieces that Jenna thought looked like the eyes of the Sand People in Star Wars.

"A minute for my eyes to adjust and then we move," said Tom.

***

Sam snatched up the phone when it rang.

"I wish you were here to help with the decisions, buddy," said Chuck Holt.

"What now?"

"Nils Witt and the Spaders spent an hour in their room with two of the goombas that Winter has out here. Undoubtedly they were being briefed about the local situation. It is now dark here, but with a full moon that is gonna be lovely. They have driven down the road where Van Velt's cottage is and their vehicle has been concealed in the bush, ready to make a crash exit."

"Think they plan to snatch Van Velt?"

"They have left the vehicle and are moving east along the wooded track. Well east of Van Velt's place. Sam. I think the stupid fucks have the wrong cottage."

"You're shitting me!"

"My guys tell me that from a distance Van Velt and the woman in the cottage up the lane look remarkably similar. I think Winter's guys have used old maps and have been watching the wrong woman. That would explain why they took their downtown surveillance off Van Velt."

"In-fucking-credible!"

"It gets better. Van Velt and her friend were having some nice, probably post-coital time, sitting naked on the porch of her cottage when the guy suddenly went all bird-dog. Then they disappeared into the cottage and emerged dressed in black. The guy was packing a handgun in a combat shoulder holster, carrying a M16, and had a big bag over his shoulder. Van Velt was wearing a knapsack and had something clenched in her hand. Oh, and the guy was wearing night vision glasses."

"You have to admire a man that comes fully prepared for a weekend in the country."

"Yep. So Sam, you were a two star general and I was only a lowly colonel. I want to run my assessment by you."

"It can never hurt for a Marine to seek advice from an Army officer."

"It would seem like Van Velt's boyfriend has her protection well in hand. And as best we can tell, all of Winter's people are up the road getting ready to do all sorts of devilry at the wrong place."

"That's what it sounds like to me, Chuck."

"I'm inclined to tell my guys to let Van Velt go into the bush with the guy. He's armed to the teeth, likely has all the skills he needs to keep her safe, and if my guys get too close to him, it's very likely some people are gonna get killed."

"I concur."

"So the big question is what do we do with the crowd at the other cottage? Witt and the Spaders are headed there thinking that they are going to have a lively question and answer session with Jenna Van Velt. That ain't how it's gonna turn out. But do we care about what happens to the woman they're about to lay hands on?"

"Nope. We don't care at all, Chuck. But it would be just fucking awesome to hit Winter hard on this one. Kill as many of his people as possible and leave very messy bodies for the cops to find all over the place. Do your people on site have anything to plant?"

"We've prepared for that contingency."

"Alright, my friend. It takes two of five votes in emergency situations for the LO to authorize extreme prejudice. I cast a vote in favour."

"So do I," said Chuck. "Watch the news from north of L.A. tomorrow, Sam."

***

Despite the jet lag and the rather chaotic situation, Nils was enjoying the scenario. At three hundred yards their subject, who was moving around her ultra modern cottage, looked very enticing. Nils had a penchant for women with dark hair.

Nils wanted the Spaders into the cottage first. A classic blitz attack.

It went well. The woman had not locked her door and one of the watchers had snatched it open. The young woman had been astonished as a couple had entered her summer home, grabbed her, and injected her. Furniture was moved, pillows were shifted, and very quickly she was stripped and in the position. Nils entered the room, full of anticipation.

"Is she in the state?" he asked.

"Give it another couple of minutes," said Hanna. "If you look at her labia you will see them getting more engorged and redder as the seconds pass by."

Nils thought that those were some of the most arousing words he had ever heard. He turned to Alan Spader to congratulate him on the flawless capture. Glass showered the room and he ducked as Alan's head dissolved into red and white mush.

Nils and Hanna had well-honed survival instincts. They dropped to the floor. The sniper was still there, no doubt, looking for another target. But now the other gunmen started. Spraying rounds high into the room. Distraction fire. They didn't want to kill the cottage owner.

Nils and Hanna had a quick conversation and rapidly concluded that this would not be a hostage situation. He would have loved to shoot the woman, but Hanna advised that they may have need of every round and in any case, they still needed to interrogate Van Velt at some point. He and Hanna kicked out a basement window of the cottage and snake-crawled thirty yards into the bush while his protection and watcher teams bought them some time and were efficiently killed by Holt's men.

Nils and Hanna were both in superb condition and there was a full moon. In less than an hour they had run to a cottage owned by a middle-aged couple. They dragged them out of bed, got the keys to their SUV, their IDs, their ATM cards with passwords, and then they killed them.

Nils had noticed that Hanna had been cradling her right arm as they had run through the bush. He asked her if she had been hit. She nodded yes.

Nils guided Hanna into the bathroom of the cottage, which had no outside windows, closed the door and flicked on the light. The back of her shirt was soaked in blood. He found scissors in the medicine chest and cut the shirt off her. There was a deep gash just under her shoulder blade with a shard of glass protruding from it.

"You've been hit by glass," said Nils. "Stay here."

He found the bedroom used by the cottage owners. The woman they had just killed had been very petite. None of her clothing would fit Hanna. He found a couple shirts that had belonged to the man and took them into the bathroom.

"We have to get moving," said Nils, as he used the scissors to cut a bath towel into strips. He fashioned a pad with a couple of facecloths and then bound it lightly over the gash on Hanna's back. "We'll do a better job on this when we find somewhere well clear of here."

***

Chuck Holt's team carefully removed and replaced various items on the bodies of twenty men they had killed. Photos were taken of Alan Spader's body. They left the young woman - unharmed except for the injection and superficial cuts from flying glass - restrained in the cottage. There had been enough gunfire to ensure that 911 had taken a raft of calls.

***

Jenna and Tom were tucked away in a sharp, deep cleft of rocks when the gunfire began. It had started with a single deep distinctive report, followed instantly by a sharper bang. The two shots told Tom that a sniper was at work.

Jenna reacted to the automatic weapons fire by crouching low. Good instincts, noted Tom. He listened intently to the firefight. It lasted no more than twelve minutes. Professionals, he concluded. But one group must have had far better intelligence than the other.

"That is a very major gun battle going on," he whispered to Jenna. "When we were sitting outside the cottage I heard the sound of radio static a couple of times. One group of armed people with radio communications has obviously just taken on another group. Sounds like the fight is at your friend's place."

"Why the hell would someone be after Deanna?"

"I don't think they are. I think they intended to visit you."

"Oh fuck! So it's started."

"It started long before your Aunt came to live in your back yard."

When he heard the sirens of approaching police cars, he leaned down and asked Jenna for the grenade. She was glad to offer it up. He crimped off the pin and managed to get the safety clip back in place as well.

"Let's get back to the cottage and pretend we've been in bed," he said. "We'll put on PJs because the cops are going to visit us soon."

Amazingly, it was hours before someone from the local police force discovered the entrance to their laneway. Jenna and Tom were ready for their questions. Tom had slipped out during the night and made his way to the roadway. He had shinned the pole that was hidden by trees and had used side cutters to sever the phone line to Jenna's cottage. His breakfast had been some potato chips and the salt in his mouth when he licked the severed connection had caused it to develop a patina almost instantly.

Tom had spoken first and his information had captured the cops' imagination. He had described hearing deep gunshots and then higher ones, occurring rapidly. His description of what they had heard translated nicely into what the cops already thought had gone on.

Jenna wasn't of much interest to the cops. She told them that she had simply stayed in the cottage during the gunfire. Jenna mentioned that she had tried to call 911 but that their phone line was dead. A cop was dispatched to check the line and came back to report that the line had been intentionally cut at the pole near the road.

The cops paid more careful attention when Jenna asked about her friend Deanna. Once it was clear to them that Jenna knew the woman who owned the cottage up the road, they had a lot of questions for her. One of the cops scribbled furiously in his notebook as she told them the name of Deanna's husband and told them where he worked. They were tight-lipped when Jenna asked how Deanna was. When Jenna persisted with questions about Deanna, they cut off the conversation.

When the cops left, Jenna sank into a chair on the porch. Her voice was shaking when she said, "They didn't know about Steve. Do you think Deanna has been killed?"

"Jenna, I hope not. She could be injured and in shock. Let's go with the idea that she is alive and getting whatever care it is that she needs."

"Whatever has happened to her is because of me and my Aunt's fucking diaries."

"I have a proposition for you," said Tom. "I have a pisspot full of money waiting for me in Canada. If you still have any of the money your Aunt talked about in her letter to you, now's the time to lay your hands on it. There are big forces at play here that have thankfully fucked up. We can't count on them to fuck up again."

"So the dread that I started to feel when we learned what Gerta had been up to in the camp in Namibia is now here, front and center?"

"Your life has changed, Jenna. Mine too. And Ing's as well. Because we all know about your Aunt's nasty little secret. And dangerous people want to know the secret too. Or they just want to make sure we don't tell anybody about your Aunt's science project."

"Are you serious about going to Canada?"

"Yep. Today."

"Jesus, Tom! How the hell do we do that? I have job and an apartment and this place. I can't just leave."

"You heard the shooting last night. We'll read about it in the paper today. The cops won't have told the media people much. But that was a major event. There were at least a couple of dozen people shooting at each other. Did you notice anything special about the cops that just talked to us?"

"No."

"Exactly. They were all local force uniforms. If one of the groups doing the shooting last night was FBI or some other government group, there would have been a guy in a suit talking with us as well."

"So?"

"So. Two non-government groups were in the bush around here last night, probably with you as their target. We have a big problem, Jenna. Too big of a problem to go to any cops and hope they'll take care of it for us. We need to get a long way from here and go to ground while we try to figure out what we can do to make these bad guys go away."

"I don't have my passport with me."

"That's the least of our worries. Can you access any money?"

"It's in a safe deposit box in Bayfield."

"That's good news. If you have a better plan, Jenna, I'm keen hear it. But to my way of thinking the only thing we can do now is run and hide."

"I'll start packing."

"Be quick. We have to get to the bank before it closes and I want to be many miles north of here by nightfall."

Jenna went into the cottage and began putting clothes in bags. She was sobbing and packing when Tom entered the cottage. He hugged her tightly for a minute and then wordlessly gathered up his belongings and started carrying things to his SUV. Jenna helped him retrieve the computer disks and Tom placed the ones that Ing gave back into the safe. They and the diaries were the last things loaded into the vehicle.

***

Chuck Holt sent his team off in four directions after they ambushed Winter's men. Chuck's guys were pros and he didn't worry much about any of them attracting unwanted attention. Sam, Chuck knew, would be chomping at the bit to hear from him. But Chuck wanted to be well clear of the Bayfield area before he placed any call to Canada. It was four hours after the firefight when Chuck got to one of his company offices and commandeered a phone.

"It's Chuck," he said when Sam picked up. "We've just finished a fine re-enactment of the Vietnam war, minus the airpower."

"How did it go?"

"One of my guys took a round in the leg but our medic has him taken care of. He'll be fine. We left twenty of Winter's guys dead in the bush or the cottage. Alan Spader is in the cottage with most of his head blown off. Witt and the Spader woman got away."

"I wish that little fucker was part of your bag, but all in all, this is pretty frikkin' good news."

"It's very bad news for anybody that Witt and Spader woman tap for assistance. I have my people working their contacts to find out if there are any murder-robberies in the area of Bayfield. Witt is gonna need wheels."

"What about the woman in the cottage?"

"She was alive when we cleared out. They had her naked, tied in the classic torture position and they had drugged her with something. My team all wore balaclavas so she can't identify any of us. She had a few superficial cuts from flying glass. Other than that, and some pretty heavy duty psychological trauma I expect, she seemed okay."

"How about Van Velt?"

"I pulled all my guys way out of the area because the local cops are sweeping the bush with a fine-toothed comb right now. We know what her friend is driving and I've got people watching her office and her apartment. Once the cops pull back a bit on their investigation, I'll get eyes back on the cottage."

"Do you think they'll stay there? The guy knew enough to head for the bush last night. He and Van Velt obviously know they're being hunted."

"Depends on what the cops told them to do, I think," answered Chuck. "They may have directed them to stay put. The cops are trying to figure out why there was a bloodbath in their jurisdiction. They may have things clamped down thinking there are still shooters in the area."

"Maybe. I'll feel better when your guys get eyes back on them."

"We left some interesting bits and pieces on Winter's dead guys. Some of Herr Winter's associates in the 'States are going to have some very difficult conversations with law enforcement over the next few days. The Feds are sure to be involved given the weapons that Winter's guys were using. Winter's outfit is going to find it very hard to get up to no good in the U.S. for some time to come."

Chapter Twenty

Arnon and Teresa were sipping coffee when the phone rang. It was his captain calling.

"Nick. Did you say that woman whose Aunt was murdered in The Woods has a place up Bayfield way?"

When Arnon said yes, the Captain told him to turn on the news. Teresa cleaned up the breakfast things while Arnon hurriedly showered. He dropped her off at her apartment on his way to his office.

His phone was ringing as he arrived. Arnon was not surprised that it was Jim Curtiss on the line.

"Nick, Jim Curtiss here. How are you?"

"Fine. I am just getting ready to take a drive to cottage country."

"So you've heard. Good. How soon will you be out to Bayfield?"

"I should be there in about two hours. Are you going to be there?"

"I'm calling from our van. We should be there in about three hours. We're bringing a large team. It takes a lot of manpower to investigate a scene with twenty corpses."

"Christ! The media obviously doesn't know the extent of the slaughter yet."

"And I sure as hell hope the locals can keep it that way. Early indicators are that most of the dead guys are Caucasian. This was not some sort of Latino drug battle."

"I'm going to head straight to Jenna Van Velt's cottage," said Arnon. "That's where you'll find me when you get on the ground."

"See you in about three hours."

The duty officer had located Detective Crane and he was waiting outside of Arnon's office. He had gotten them a marked cruiser and they put the lights on as soon as they were out of the city. Arnon could tell that Crane was enjoying the drive.

***

Nils and Hanna Spader drove for twelve hours with one quick stop at an out of the way gas station for fuel. Hanna had been quiet for most of the trip, sitting awkwardly sideways in the passenger seat. She had nodding off briefly a couple of times. She stirred when Nils slowed the vehicle to pull into a long farm laneway.

"It's time to change vehicles," said Nils. Hanna simply nodded.

The farm Nils had chosen was seedy. The barnyard was choked with weeds and there had apparently been no cattle for years. A late model pickup truck was the only thing visible that looked to have any value. Nils parked behind the pickup and got out of the car. Hanna remained seated.

An elderly man came out of the clapboard farmhouse that was badly in need of a coat of paint. The old man had a bottle of beer in his hand and he used his other hand to shade his eyes to see who his visitors were. Nils walked up to him carrying a map.

"California plates, huh," said the old man. "You folks lost?"

"We could use some advice," said Nils. "You and your wife live way out here by yourselves?"

"We do. I can't stand the city."

"Well it must be peaceful. There's nobody within two miles of this place is there?"

"Nope. We've got this whole square to ourselves. Where are you wanting to get to?"

Nils used the handgun that he had concealed in the map to pistol whip the old fellow. He made sure the foresight caught the farmer on the cheek so that it opened up a superficial but bloody wound. He grabbed the back of the old man's shirt and propelled him to the house. Hanna got out of the car and followed the two men.

There was an old woman working at the kitchen sink when they entered the house. She screamed when she saw the blood streaming down her husband's face. Nils shoved the old fellow into a chair and motioned with his gun for the woman to sit at the table as well.

"Do you two have children that you go visit?"

The old couple was so stunned that neither answered. Nils asked the question a second time.

"Yes. We've got a daughter that we go see in Montana."

"Where will I find a pen and some paper?" asked Nils.

The woman directed him to cupboard drawer. Nils found a large note pad and pen that he placed in front of the woman.

"What's your daughter's name?" he asked.

"Evelyn," was the reply.

"Write on the paper, gone to visit Evelyn. Be back on Friday."

The woman did as she was told. Nils politely thanked her and then pointed at a key ring that was sitting on the table.

"Are those the keys for your truck?" he asked.

The woman nodded.

"Do you have a first aid kit here?" Nils asked.

The woman pointed at another cupboard. Nils opened it and saw that it contained an array of first aid items.

"We're going for a walk outside now," said Nils. He walked the two back toward the big, dilapidated barn. There was a large liquid manure tank behind it. The tank was nearly full of foul smelling, dark water. The two old people were walking ahead of Nils and did not see him pick up a length of two by four that was lying on the ground.

Nils' first blow was to the old man's head. The woman turned toward Nils with a look of horror and his second blow caught her full in the face. Both fell to the ground unconscious.

Both of the old people were quite scrawny but Nils was sweating heavily by the time he had dropped them into the manure tank. He used the two by four to hold them under the surface of the tank for several minutes. Then he went back to the house.

Hanna had found some tape and had fastened the note the woman had written to the inside of the windowpane in the back door. Nils took the keys to the truck and moved it into a drive shed, closing the door of the shed. Then he drove the vehicle they had arrived in to another ramshackle shed and closed it up. When he got back to the house he could hear a shower running.

Nils busied himself searching through the rooms on the ground floor of the house. The woman's purse and the old man's wallet yielded seventy dollars in folding money and some credit cards. A twelve gauge shotgun was stashed behind the door of a small room used as an office. There were about two dozen shells for the gun in a bag hanging on the doorknob. Nils set them on the kitchen table as Hanna walked into the room, naked.

"Let's see what we've got," said Nils and led her over to where evening sunlight was streaming in a through a window.

The piece of the window glass that Holt's men had blown out at the cottage was protruding from Hanna's back. Nils was relieved to see that there was enough of it sticking out for him to grip with pliers. Blood and clear liquid was seeping around the jagged piece of glass and trickling down Hanna's back.

"Sit while I get some things together," said Nils.

Nils rummaged through the drawer holding first aid stuff and made a compress out of gauze. He set out a roll of gauze as well, and opened a jar of anti-bacterial cream. A door in the kitchen led to a single bay garage. Nils searched the workbench area and found some pliers.

Hanna stood up when he came back into the kitchen and walked to the well lit area and grasped the edge of the cupboard with both hands.

"Make it quick," she said. "And if getting it out starts a major bleed, promise me you'll douse my body with gas and torch the house. I don't want any fucking cops looking at me."

Nils rummaged though more cupboard drawers and found one full of clean tea towels. He placed a stack of them on the cupboard near Hanna. He took another close look at her wound and reasoned that the glass would have struck her from a high angle.

"Crouch down a bit, Hanna," he said.

She flinched when he grasped the protruding glass with the pliers and let out a yelp of pain when he pulled the glass out of her back. The piece was about half the size of a dollar bill. Nils wasn't happy to see that that there was a bit of cloth deep in the wound. There were tweezers in the drawer with the bandages. Hanna was sweating profusely and had turned very pale by the time he was satisfied that the wound was clean.

Hanna had caught a break. No major blood vessels had been opened up. Nils bathed the wound with clean water and dabbed the area dry with tea towels. He packed the cut with antibacterial cream and again dabbed the edges of the wound dry.

"Just a bit more pain, my lovely Hanna," he said.

He had found a tube of Super Glue on the workbench. He uncapped the tube and applied it liberally to both sides of the cut. Hanna growled in pain as he pushed the two sides of wound together and held them for a couple of minutes. The edges remained together when he finally released them.

Nils guided Hanna to a chair and then went into the bathroom and drew a bath. He had her stand in the tub while he washed away the blood that flowed when he had removed the glass. He towelled her dry and led her to what must have been the old couple's guest room. The bed was a bit musty, but clean. Hanna lay down on her stomach and was asleep in minutes.

***

Tom and Jenna found a motel about four hundred miles from Bayfield. He left her in the room sorting through her hastily packed bags and went shopping. He came back with a stack of road maps, two coolers loaded with bottled water, juice, and food. He also had a bottle of wine, a six-pack of beer, some stationary supplies, and a disposable camera.

Jenna had all of her bags open and clothing covered both of the double beds in the room. She was making a list on the motel stationery.

"I have lots of summery casual clothes, a plethora of bathing suits, and thanks to my having mistakenly grabbed a bag of clothes that Ing had left at the cottage, a vast assortment of vulgar undergarments."

"We'll go shopping once we get to Canada," said Tom. "Best to just have clothes suited to the season with us. Sometimes people get snoopy, so it's good that we're not carrying winter boots."

"I did mention that I don't have a passport with me, right?"

"That's something we will start dealing with right now. Up against that wall, Jenna."

Tom took several head and shoulder shots of Jenna with the disposable camera. Once he was satisfied he addressed an envelope and put the camera in it.

"I'll be back in a few minutes," he said.

By the time he got back, Jenna had most of her clothes repacked. Tom opened the bottle of wine, poured some into one of the flimsy plastic cups provided by the motel and opened a beer. He took a small notebook from his pocket.

"Now to work," he said.

Tom explained to Jenna that when he had checked them in, he had told the motel staff that he had just learned of the death of his brother. He had given the hotel clerk two hundred dollars and asked him to let him know when the long distance calls that he needed to make were nearing that amount. The motel staff put his calls through without any issue.

The first call was to Ing's mother's place in South Africa.

"Ing. Don't worry. It's Tom calling. The Springbok government isn't stalking you."

"Why the hell are you calling here? Not that it isn't lovely to hear the voice of a friend."

"How's your mom?"

"Not very good. The frustrating thing is that the docs still can't say what's wrong with her. Just an endless series of tests."

"I'm so sorry. I wish there was something that I could do."

"Hell, I wish there was something I could do. As you know, I only like to feel helpless in very specific circumstances."

"I hate to do this to you, Ing, but listen carefully. Jenna and I are on the run. We're heading for Canada just as fast as we can move." Tom told Ing what had happened the previous night. Ing listened intently without interrupting him.

"So, Ing," Tom concluded. "Do not go back to L.A. If you want to link up with Jenna and me, come to Canada. Get a pen and I'll give you some contact information."

When she had written down the information, he silently handed the phone to Jenna. She and Ing talked for several minutes, then Tom made a 'time' sign. Jenna got off the phone, looking sad.

Jenna sipped her wine and listened as Tom placed a number of phone calls. He was all business until the last call. It was clear to Jenna that his last call was to a friend.

"That was Audrey I was talking to," said Tom. "Lovely lady. She spent her career as an archivist for the government and then in some universities in Canada. She's retired now, but she runs the local history chapter of Elgin County with an iron fist and has a thriving antique business in Port Burwell. I think you'll like her."

***

One advantage to being in a fully equipped squad car was the radio. Arnon played with different frequencies as Crane drove at a very fast speed. Eventually Arnon found the frequency being used by Bayfield police. There was a lot of chatter. It was clear that a major search operation was still underway.

As they approached Bayfield, Arnon radioed back to his own headquarters for information on where the Bayfield police had their command post. He wasn't surprised to learn that it was at the junction of the road to Jenna Van Velt's cottage and a main county road. Once they got close he gave Crane instructions on where to turn.

The Bayfield chief of police was a practical man and his department focused on the meat and potatoes of community policing. His command post was his own family Winnebago. He and two of his lieutenants were standing under the RV's awning looking at topographical maps laid out on a folding table when Arnon and Crane pulled up.

"LAPD! Lord, boys, we must truly be in a fix if LAPD is sending plainclothes cops in a marked car to our crime scene. And they're here before the F-fucking-BI. We are truly having ourselves a time, aren't we?"

Arnon had been ready for that sort of reception.

"Both Crane and I are ex-army, Chief. We heard that you were having a rehash of the battle of Gettysburg here, so we wanted to come and pitch in."

"Gettysburg? More like Bunker Hill. Our coroner is a guy who emigrated here from Belgium. Speaks good English. He's had a look at most of the bodies. Says a lot of them have European style dental work. Makes me want to go to France or Germany and find out how it's done over there. Maybe not so fucking painful as the asshole I deal with."

""I'm Nick Arnon, senior homicide detective. This is Crane. We've been working a murder case in LA. A weird one. An older lady from Holland and South Africa. She was tortured and killed. Her niece - who has not been the most forthcoming of informants - has a cottage up this road."

"Our vic's name is Deanna Brown. Until last night I think she's had a pretty nice life. It's shame what happened to her last night."

"Good looking. Dark hair. About five feet seven," said Arnon.

"Yep."

"Pretty much a carbon copy of our lady. Have your guys interviewed the people in the first cottage up this road?"

"First thing this morning. They had heard the shooting but didn't call 911 because their phone line had been cut. We didn't even know they were there at first. The end of their laneway is pretty much grown over."

"Chief, could I talk to your guys who interviewed them?"

"I'm guessin' you should. I'll be there, of course."

"Of course."

It took twenty minutes for the locals to get the cops who had talked with Jenna and Tom to the command post. The senior guy was a corporal named Lambert.

Corporal Lambert was used to small town community policing. Trekking around through the woods looking for people who had just fought a deadly gun battle did not suit him. His uniform was bedraggled and Arnon could scent fear on him.

"I understand you talked with a couple in the first cottage up this road this morning. How did they seem?" asked Arnon.

"Pretty normal, considering that they had been close to a major gun battle."

"Who did most of the talking?"

"The man." The cop consulted his note book." Tom Robbins. Forty years old."

"Did you get a look at the woman in the cottage where all the bad stuff went down?"

"Yeah."

"Did she look at all like the woman your guys found at the other cottage up this road?"

The cop thought about that for a bit.

"Yeah. She looked a lot like her."

"Anybody know if this couple is still at their cottage up the road?"

One of the cops that had come in with Lambert spoke up.

"They went into Bayfield hours ago. I stopped them at the roadblock. They said they would be coming back through in a few hours."

Arnon turned to address the senior cop.

"Chief, if they come back here, be prepared for monkeys to fly out of my butt. These twenty homicides in your jurisdiction are directly related to my murder in LA. I know the FBI is on the way and we need to all work very fast to sort out what the hell went down here. This isn't your problem. Actually, I don't think it's an LA problem or an FBI problem. It's way fucking bigger than that."

"Detective Arnon, I like to hear the words 'it's not my problem'."

***

Jenna was working very hard to get onto the changes that had happened in her life and kept pressing Tom to tell her what would happen next.

"We're driving to a place called Algonac, Michigan. We'll stop in the next town with a car lot and I'll use some of your money to buy us a new vehicle."

"What should I do about my job?" she asked.

"You're on two weeks of vacation. Sometime between now and the end of that time we'll figure out a place where they can send you the last of your pay and so forth. We'll get you set up with a realtor in Bayfield to sell your cottage. You're sitting on a pile of money there. We'll be able to deal with all of that once we get to where we're going."

"I am having a very fucking hard time with this, Tom."

"I know. You must feel completely adrift. But being on the run like this is something you will get used to. And once we're in Canada we'll be a lot safer and things will stabilize a lot."

Jenna sat staring out of the window at the cornfields that stretched to the horizon. Tom let her cry quietly as he concentrated on covering as many miles as possible. He made a quick purchase of a used Jeep and got them back on the road. He reckoned that they would be near the western border of Illinois with twelve more hours of driving.

***

Nils called Winter.

'If you can shed any light on what just happened in California, I would be most grateful," began Nils.

"I'm sorry," said Winter. "We've had a setback."

"You're the master of the understatement."

"We have some information. It was the Legacy Organization that attacked our team."

"Of course it was. Only attacked is another of your understatements. Annihilated would be a more accurate description of what took place."

"The surveillance team leader got out unharmed. He has been in touch."

"Was he the only survivor? Alan Spader is dead."

"I did not know that. I take it that Hanna Spader is with you."

"She is. We need money. A lot of money. And we need it quickly."

"How are you, Nils? How is the Spader woman?"

"I'm fine. A couple of superficial cuts from flying glass that are easily concealed. Hanna has a more serious cut on her back but I've taken it care of it. We need money and we need to get to Canada."

"Documents?"

"We're fine. We had what we needed with us."

"The leader of the surveillance team watched the Legacy people going over the bodies of a couple of our men. He was certain that they were planting things on them. We must assume that much of our network in the United States is compromised."

Nils was silent as he thought that over.

"The Americans will have to follow all of their legal processes as they act on whatever they find out there in the forest where the gun fight took place. We'll have a couple of days to act."

"Agreed," said Winter.

"Have your man in Chicago bring me a couple of hundred thousand dollars. He needs to leave right away."

"I will arrange that, Nils."

"He will have no idea that we had anything to do with the incident in California."

"Of course not."

"Good. Get him moving toward the west. Have him call you in about twenty hours. By then I will be able to give you details of where he should meet us."

"You'll be good enough to kill him after he gives you the money, correct?"

"Of course. And before you feel the need to ask, I will kill Hanna should her wound become a problem."

"One last thing, Nils. The Van Velt woman, what is her status?"

"We left her tied to a table with her lovely ass in the air. Unless a stray round hit her, she is still on our list of people we would like to know."

"Goodbye, Nils. Keep yourself safe. I'll look forward to your next call."

***

Chuck Holt called Sam again in the late evening.

"The media people aren't being given much by the cops. And they can't get in to the area to snoop around because of the roadblocks and the terrain. The local cops even have patrols out on the lake keeping the boaters out. The press is not happy about this. They are reporting that the FBI is on the scene."

"I bet they are," said Sam.

"I've got two guys - who were totally not there last night - out in Bayfield. They can't get out to check on the Van Velt cottage. Likely won't be able to for days. We've got watchers on her apartment. Nothing going on there."

"I hope like hell the cops have them roadblocked in at the cottage."

"Amen to that!"

"We've found out that the Stoller woman has been transferred to her company's office in Capetown. Her mother is in Capetown and is sick. It's looking like she has gone to South Africa for personal reasons, Sam."

"That seems innocent enough."

***

When Tom was too tired to drive, they pulled into a restaurant in a little town whose entrance sign proudly claimed to have 12,000 citizens. Neither of them was hungry but the homemade tomato soup was good. It was 8:30 p.m. Jenna pointed out a two-story motel across the roadway from the restaurant.

"I think you need some rest, Mr. Robbins. Let's check in there and talk about the plan for tomorrow."

"We'll make for the border. A buddy of mine will meet us in Algonac. It's a small town with a ferry connection to Walpole Island in Ontario. He'll give us your new passport and head back with a few things that I'll want to have with us in Canada. Then we'll catch the next ferry."

"Thinking about it is making me crazy!"

"I already have a back-up passport. My new name on it is Tom Roberts. When you can, you always get new papers that are close to your real name."

"So who the hell am I about to become?"

"Jennifer Roberts, I hope."

"Was I asleep or drunk when that happened?"

"Will you please be my wife as we cross the border into Canada?"

"I was actually going to give you a mercy fuck to relax you after all your driving. That is a rapidly fading possibility now that you're my husband."

"I am deeply saddened. But I respect your decision."

"Liar," said Jenna, pulling him close.

Chapter Twenty-one

The chief, Arnon and Curtiss spent some time talking about the murder of Gerta Ten Haan and its probable link to the shooting

As they talked a semi rig pulled up with the reefer machinery running full blast. The chief broke off their talk to speak with the truck driver. The driver got back in his cab and the noise of the rig's refrigeration unit abruptly diminished to a low hum.

The chief walked back to the map table shaking his head. "That crazy bastard had his reefer turned up to the coldest setting. I told him we needed the bodies kept cool until an autopsy could be done. Not fast frozen for shipment to a burger joint."

As soon as the reefer arrived, the chief's men started bringing out the bodies. They came four at a time, lying on the bed of two pickup trucks. A local National Guard unit had dropped off a bunch of body bags.

Arnon, Crane and Curtiss looked at the first few bodies that were brought out. As the chief had said, they were all men in their prime. All of them but for the body of the man from inside the cottage were dressed in the same type of fatigues. Curtiss was quite certain the fatigues were standard East German Army issue.

Arnon realized that there wasn't a need for him and Crane to hang around since the local police and the FBI had the situation under control. He and Crane got into their cruiser to drive back to L.A. At least we know Van Velt's boyfriend's name and address, he thought.

***

They stayed in another motel, well away from any big city, that Jenna thought hadn't changed its décor since Eisenhower was president. In the morning Tom said he needed time to make some phone calls. "What's our destination for today?"

"Toad Lake Resort. It's near a place called Union City in Michigan. It's an easy drive from there to Algonac on the Michigan-Ontario border."

"Why that specific resort?"

"I've been there. It has a great pool, wooded trails to run on, quite a good little restaurant, and it would be the last place anyone would look for us."

"Why?"

"Because it's a nudist resort."

"Now, just a goddamn minute, Tom! I'm feeling completely adrift, insecure as hell, afraid of what each new hour will bring, and you want me to go hang out with a bunch of sex-crazed naked people?"

"Calm down Jenna. Let me tell you a bit about naturists."

***

They executed the search warrant for Jenna's apartment as soon as they could. Arnon, Crane, and two crime scene people comprised the team. The superintendent of the building let them in. He remarked that he had never seen a search warrant before. The only thing of interest they discovered was that Jenna Van Velt had left her passport in her apartment.

"She clearly wasn't planning any international travel," was Crane's observation.

Arnon went back to his office and after some delay got the chief out in Bayfield on the phone. Arnon asked him how he was bearing up.

"Well, Nick. There was a murder here in Bayfield when I was a rookie patrolman. A jealous wife gave her husband a beer laced with pesticide and then cut his throat. That was 31 years ago. Since then, until last night, we haven't had a homicide in this town. Now I've got twenty. And I expect more are coming now we know that there are likely some ruthless fucking fugitives out there."

"We searched the Van Velt woman's apartment this morning. Nothing, really. I wish I had something that would be useful."

"Thanks for that, Nick. Your FBI buddy wants to talk to you."

Curtiss came on the line.

"How's it going, Nick?"

"There was a packed-down place on the carpet in Van Velt's closet. Likely a box filled with something heavy. Books, maybe."

"Books. Maybe notebooks. Maybe containing information that got her Aunt killed."

"And nearly got her killed."

"She and her boyfriend are gonzo. We're trying to find out everything we can about him. Do you know anything about the other woman that was out here with them?"

"Nope."

***

Chuck Holt called Sam early in the morning. I've got to educate this jarhead about time zones, Sam thought.

"Sam. I've got the superintendent of the Van Velt woman's building on retainer. I personally went through her apartment. Nothing there of interest to us. A couple of hours after I went through the place, four cops presented a warrant and searched her apartment. When they left they weren't carrying anything."

"I'll take that as a good sign. Chuck, I'm getting some really crazy shit from Claudio. He's been working all of his academic colleagues in South Africa. There's this 7 Medical Battalion Group in the South African Army that was going in the 80s. Lots of hearsay about it. And something called Delta 6 Scientific down there. They seemed to be getting damned desperate, my friend."

"Their world has been ending for a long time, Sam. People don't like it when their world is ending."

"Claudio has picked up that they deployed a nerve agent called 'BZ' a few times. It scared the shit out of them and they stopped using it."

"All those fucking nerve agents are scary. We should find the guys creating them and make them and their ideas disappear."

"Well, Chuck. I think Winter took a little knowledge way too far."

"Anyway, can we pick up the pieces without getting dirty?"

"It's at the point where we have to. The LO wasn't created to do harm. We've always been around to try to regulate things when parts of the world went crazy. Winter and his crew are definitely making it go crazy. They are depopulating Africa."

"Not intentionally, maybe. But for Christ's sakes, Sam! It's time to intervene."

"Agreed. And Gerta's niece, whoever she is, whereever she is, is likely to be in possession of all of the scientific data we need to do that. I wonder if she has the slightest clue of what her Auntie passed on to her."

"I have no idea what Gerta Ten Haan wrote in her diaries but her niece and the boyfriend have read them. And probably have a fairly solid idea of how Ten Haan spent fifteen years of her life. And if what they read didn't tip them off to what's at play here, the gunfight near their cottage sure as hell did. I have everything ready to go into that cottage and snatch them but I think they may be on the run now."

"Ever hear about 'Operation Infecktion', Chuck?"

"Nope."

"I want everybody here in Muskoka in three days. Claudio has some stuff to tell us. Keep me posted."

***

They were passing through Great Falls when Hanna pointed out the hitchhikers. They were a boy and a girl who both looked to be about fourteen. Nils pulled over and the two of them scrambled into the back seat of the crew cab.

"Where are you headed?" asked Hanna.

"Choteau," answered the boy.

"Are you from there?"

"Yep."

"We're headed to a hunting camp near there. Do you know of one?"

"Must be Black Bear Lodge you're looking for," said the girl.

"That's the place. Have you ever been there?"

"My girl guide troop went out there once a few years ago. The old guy who owns it is really creepy. He was supposed to show us deer and bear tracks and stuff. I think he wanted to show us his dick instead. Our leader got us back on the bus pretty fast."

"Is the place pretty run down?"

"It looked pretty ghetto to me," answered the girl. "We didn't go anywhere but the main building. It smelled bad."

"Can you tell us where to find it?"

"Sure. It's on its own road before we get to Choteau."

"You aren't gonna dump us out there, are you?" asked the boy. "It's a good eight mile hike from the turn off to the Black Bear to Choteau."

"Don't worry. We'll take you right into town," said Nils. "Just point out the turn off to the lodge as we pass by it."

"Okay, Mister. Thanks."

They drove for several miles with the two teenagers whispering and giggling in the back seat. Hanna took a note pad from the side compartment of the jeep and wrote three sentences in German on it. She passed it to Nils and he read it and nodded, with a slight smile. Five miles up the road they pulled into a truck stop.

"We have to make a rest stop. Do you two want to come in?"

"We'll stay here if that's okay."

"Would you like a milkshake or a soda?"

Both of the kids wanted a chocolate milkshake. Hanna bought the shakes while Nils called Winter. The call was very brief. He told Winter to send his money man to the Black Bear Lodge near Choteau. Winter said the man could likely be there in six hours. Nils said that timing was acceptable.

The kids were necking in the back seat of the truck when Hanna and Nils returned. Hanna passed them the shakes and they politely thanked her. Nils was impressed. He had developed an opinion of American kids during the time he had spent earlier in the Woods. These two weren't rude little bastards like the ones that had hung out around the library back in the L.A. suburbs.

Hanna turned in her seat as they got back on the road and engaged the kids in conversation. They told her that both sets of their parents were away so they had caught a ride with a friend into Grand Falls to buy some CDs and hang out in the city. Their friend had taken off so they were very grateful for the ride home.

Nils asked if they knew the name of the road that led to the Lodge. The girl said she didn't but indicated that it was about forty miles up the road. She recalled that there were signs on the highway indicating where it was. Both of the kids were getting very sleepy and were having trouble carrying on their conversation with Hanna. When they had both dozed off Hanna turned in her seat to face forward again.

"I feel like we have Hansel and Gretel with us," she said to Nils in German.

Nils smiled and nodded.

***

Jenna was feeling bewildered and self-conscious. It was a lovely hot day. She was leaning against the front fender of the jeep. Tom was inside a small building, booking a cabin at the Naturist Park. How the hell did he talk me into this was the main question on Jenna's mind. Where am I going to look when the first naked people start talking to me was another question. She had actually posed that one to Tom but his answer hadn't been helpful. "Just leave your sunglasses on," he had said.

She heard a whirring sound and gravel crunching and against her best judgment she turned to find the source of the noise. A golf cart had pulled up and parked next to the jeep. Two older people, a man and a woman, got out of the cart, greeted her cheerily, and walked toward the camp store that was beside the registration office. Both were stark naked.

Tom came out of the office carrying a key.

"We're all fixed up," he said smiling.

"Did you see that?" Jenna whispered, looking toward the store where the elderly pair had gone.

"Yep. I think your mental picture of this place being filled with hardbodies intent on engaging in all forms of group sex is going to change rapidly, Jenna. I would hasten to point out that you have probably just seen two of the younger and slimmer members of this community. Let's go get some groceries. The cabin has everything we'll need to do our own cooking."

Jenna was relieved that the store clerk was wearing clothes. Not so for any of the eight or nine other shoppers who came in and out of the place while she and Tom gathered up what they would need. The youngest person she saw aside from the teenaged cashier was a very fit and tanned woman who looked to be in her fifties. Jenna realized that she was feeling self conscious about being dressed. This is crazy land, she thought.

It was a relief to her to be back in the jeep. She was amazed as they drove through the village of permanent residents to see all manner of yard work and home maintenance being carried out by people wearing, at most, sneakers and sun hats.

Tom had secured them the cabin furthest from the built-up area. It had a small open porch with four outdoor chairs. Inside everything was clean and compact. There was a queen-sized bed shoehorned into a very small bedroom, a full bath room with adequate space and the rest of the place was one big room with a kitchen area in one corner.

They put the groceries away and Jenna went to shower. Tom said he would have a glass of wine waiting for her on the porch. When she emerged from the shower, Tom was standing outside talking to a couple that had obviously been jogging. Tom was nude, the man was wearing high end jogging shoes and a sweatband and the woman had on shoes and a sport bra.

She stepped out on the porch, wrapped in a towel. Tom introduced the couple who were from someplace in Texas that she had never heard of. They were telling Tom about the three mile running trail that threaded through the wooded areas of the park. Tom asked if the whole trail could be done without clothing. The woman assured him that it was a clothing optional trail and said that she only wore a sports bra to "keep the girls under control".

Nobody seemed to think it strange that Jenna remained wrapped in a towel. She eventually sat down and took a couple of healthy sips of her wine. The couple invited them to drop by their cabin later in the evening to sit by their fire.

***

The girl sleeping in the back of the SUV that Nils was driving had been correct. The entrance to the road leading to the Black Bear Lodge was clearly signed. The two teenagers didn't awaken as Nils drove the SUV down a wooded, rough and narrow road.

The narrow road ended abruptly in a clearing. Nils parked in front of a large log building with a sign that said "Lodge" helpfully placed over the double front doors. There was a huge man who appeared to be in his sixties cutting a small tree when Nils had pulled into parking lot. He shut off the chainsaw he was using and began to cross the clearing.

"How can I help you?" said the man.

"That looks like hard work," answered Nils. "I hope you've got some help."

"The young folks around here aren't worth paying minimum wage to. I do the work myself. How can I help you?"

They were about ten feet apart. Nils swung the cosh and the owner of the Black Bear Lodge died on his feet. Hanna was beside Nils before he was aware of her.

"I am impressed," she said.

Hanna administered an injection to each of the kids. The boy stirred momentarily but then settled down. Nils and Hanna explored the main building of the lodge. There were eight surprisingly clean bedrooms with baths upstairs. Nils carried the two kids upstairs, placing them in different bedrooms. Hanna used heavy twine that she found in a workshop attached to the main building to tie them to their beds.

Hanna kept watch while he got three hours sleep. She awoke him when she saw the lights of a vehicle coming down the road. Nils walked out on the porch of the cottage to greet the visitor.

Winter's man in Chicago had some ties to a group in the Middle East that was violating a bunch of laws regarding the illegal harvesting of marble. He had a thriving business in high-end kitchen counter tops, made more profitable because of the origin of his shipments. He had no idea of who the man in Germany who had provided him with some excellent and profitable business connections really was.

Nils greeted him warmly and invited him into the lodge. They sat at a table and the man presented Nils with a briefcase. It was full of well worn U.S. twenty and fifty dollar bills.

"I hope that our mutual associate had adequately compensated you for this long trip you've taken," said Nils.

The man assured Nils that he was very happy with the arrangement. Nils leaned forward across the table as if he was about to share a secret. Instinctively the man leaned forward as well. Nils grasped both of his wrists in an iron grip and Hanna dropped a necktie over the man's neck and tightened it.

Nils searched the man carefully and removed everything from his person that might help someone identify him. He was delighted to learn that the man was carrying about two thousand in cash and a handgun.

"Why don't you check on the children," said Nils to Hanna.

The lodge owner's body had already been placed in his battered pickup truck parked in front of the building. Nils had pulled down the lodge owner's trousers and underwear. He placed the Chicago man in the passenger side of the vehicle and bent his body over so that his face was pressed against the flaccid penis of the other man. He smashed out the driver's side window of the truck with a convenient rock. Safety glass showered over both of the dead men.

He was putting all of the money, and some other useful items that he had found around the lodge in the developer's car when Hanna joined him.

"They are both out for at least another ten hours."

"Good," said Nils."

"I took the liberty of looking at the girl. She shaves away all of her pubic hair. These American kids grow up so fast."

"They do indeed," said Nils. He picked up the phone that sat on a counter in the lodge and dialed 911.

"911. What is the nature of your emergency?"

"My buddy and I get on the phone and talk about doing pervy things to kids. I don't really mean it but I think he does."

"Why do you think that, sir?"

"Tonight he told me that he's got a couple of kids in his place and he was describing all the things he is going to do to them."

"Do you think this he is serious, sir?"

"He says he's got some hot shot in from Los Angeles and that they've got a young boy and girl there, drugged. I don't like this."

"Where is he, sir?"

"I've only talked to him on the phone, never met him, but he told me he has a hunting lodge just south of Choteau."

"Please stay on the line, sir," said the operator.

Nils hung up and he and Hanna climbed into the Chicago man's Audi and headed for the border. They had been back on the highway for ten minutes when they met three police cruisers, lights and sirens on, heading south.

"I liked those children," said Nils. "They were polite. Hopefully the government will send them to school or something because of this ordeal."

"You are such a sentimentalist," said Hanna.

Chapter Twenty-two

"Sam, it's Chuck. Our contact on the force out here tells me there is a lot of craziness going on out at Bayfield. The cops don't have a clue about what happened."

"That's a good thing."

"On the downside, the Van Velt woman has definitely left the building. The cops and FBI now really want to talk to her some more and are pissed that she's gone."

"Do you have any thoughts on that, Chuck?"

"Well the cops now know that her boyfriend 's name is Tom Robbins and they left the cottage driving a vehicle registered to him. I have guys all over this and I think we're a bit ahead of the cops because they are pretty busy with all the dead bodies. This Robbins guy has a security consulting business here in LA. One of the mining exploration companies that I do business with uses his services to prepare their teams to go in to dangerous shitholes in Africa."

"His background?"

"Interesting. Dual citizenship. Canadian and Zimbabwean. His resume shows him in the Selous Scouts and then with the South African Defence Force. With his experience he will be a dangerous and difficult man to find. I expect he's already got Van Velt to Mexico."

"Why there?"

"Closer. Any money they've got would last a lot longer. And there are those fucking Canadian winters, Sam."

"Canadian winters? Do you think they're going into a long hide?"

"I sure as fuck would, if I were them!"

"So. Our best bet is the Stoller woman?"

"I think it is," said Chuck. "I've asked Claudio to put more people on her and I'll go there to take a direct role as soon as we're done in Muskoka. If we're going to ever talk to Jenna Van Velt it's going to be because of her. Claudio has set up the team watching Stoller but I know he's more interested in his research about the epidemic there. What's he saying, Sam?"

"We'll talk when we meet here. I know it's a risk but it's necessary."

***

"How are you adjusting to this place?"

"It's not as weird as I thought it would be. The people are certainly friendly. I'm glad they almost all wear mirrored sunglasses. At least I don't know where they're looking."

"Feel comfortable enough to take a drink and sit by our neighbours' fire for a while?"

"Now that it's dark I think I'm okay with that."

The couple that had been out running were their hosts. They were the only ones remotely close to Jenna's age. One of the women by the fire complimented Jenna on her sandals.

"That's the usual conversation starter in a nudist resort. I mean really, what the hell else can you talk about?"

"I like it when people compliment me on my boobs," said another woman.

"We know, sweetie. And we know you paid a lot for them. Not everyone likes compliments on their body parts until they have gotten to know the crowd." There was a lot of the good-natured banter. Jenna was sorry when it was time to leave.

They spent most of the next day lying in the sun and talking about the next few weeks. Jenna asked Tom if the idea was to simply hide out.

"I wish it were that simple. We can run, but we can't hide for long. Whoever wants your Aunt's stuff has a lot of resources behind them. There were a lot of people shooting the other night at your cottage."

"I'm scared, Tom. Not as scared as when we were out in the bush when the shooting was going on. But I'm scared. This feels like being trapped in one of those nightmares where you're constantly running away from something bad."

"I'm surprised at you. I thought this, right now, would feel like one of those nightmares where you're making a speech to a roomful of people and you suddenly realize you're naked."

"You're an asshole. If we can't hide, what do we do?"

"Try to find who your Aunt wants you to give the discs to."

"Given that it was likely some of those people who were shooting up the woods by the cottage, that would seem to be risky."

"Yep. I am trying to come with a plan B."

Tom went to get more wine, beer and some firewood. The second night they had a fire and hosted four other couples. One of the men who came was eighty years old and had commanded a company of infantry that had landed on Omaha beach on D-Day. He and Tom had a deep conversation. At times Jenna forgot that the people sitting around the fire were all naked.

They left the park the next day. Jenna felt she was leaving the only peace she had felt in days.

***

Winter was unhappy. Three of his organization's important associates in the United States had been in contact to say that the FBI had paid them visits. They all indicated that they considered themselves to be under surveillance and expected their phones would be tapped soon. None of the calls lasted long. Winter was concerned that he had only heard from three of his contacts.

Nils had not called to verify that he had met with the organization's man from Chicago. Winter was anxious to hear that the money Nils required was safely in his hands. He knew it was unlikely that he would hear from Nils until he and the Spader woman were safely in Canada. He did not like waiting.

Angelique was at the chateau. Dr. Kepp had provided good advice, and the intimate dinner that the two of them enjoyed in one of most splendidly decorated rooms of the giant building had gone well. Winter needed a distraction so he told one of his aides to ask Angelique to meet him in the pool area.

As he changed into a robe he could feel his anger rising. The humiliation that had been inflicted on him by his European colleagues in Namibia was always close under his skin. The people who knew him best believed that he was a man driven to acquire great wealth. Everything that he had done in his life since leaving Africa had resulted in substantial financial gain. Not even Nils or Dr. Kepp had the slightest sense of his primary motivation.

Revenge. He wanted revenge on the people who had thrown him out of the camp in Namibia.

He visited the wall safe before he went downstairs to the pool area. There was a particular ring there that had come into his possession during the war. It was beautiful and the blue diamonds in it were extremely rare.

Angelique lusted after jewellery. She studied jewellery. She coveted jewellery.

"I'm so glad you could join me," said Winter when he entered the pool area.

Angelique was wearing a rather dowdy bathrobe and he expected that she was probably feeling slightly bored and put out at having to be available to her patron on short notice.

"It is so good of you to come down here, Angelique. I would like tonight to be somewhat different. If you will put up with the whims of an aging man, I would like you to have this."

He gave her the ring case and was delighted to see her pupils dilate as she intently studied the ring.

"It's lovely," she said. "Are you giving it to me?"

"Are you willing to indulge me tonight?"

"Of course."

"You are sure? Without reservation?"

"Yes. Yes, of course, Herr Winter," and she dropped her robe to the floor.

An hour and a half later Winter left the pool area and told his aides to see to Angelique. He was sorry to probably be losing a faithful employee, but he felt much better. More in control. And he had come to a decision.

He wondered what Nils would think when his next orders would be to bring Jenna Van Velt to the chateau. It was time to stop living vicariously through Nils. Winter was envious of Nils' visit to Gerta Ten Haan. He would be present when her niece was made to atone for the sins of her Aunt.

***

Tom had promised Jenna an interesting lunch. They arrived in Algonac in ample time and had sat on a bench looking across the St. Clair River to Canada. Jenna said that she had only been to Southwestern Ontario once before when she was young.

An hour slipped by and then a tall and slim man approached them. The tall man reached inside of his shirt and gave Tom an envelope.

"It came the day before yesterday. To my general mailbox at the store on the island. Nobody fucks with that, Tom."

Tom placed the envelope on the bench beside him. He went to a hotdog cart and returned with three sausages. The tall man ate his silently and arose from the bench.

"The cove across from Sombre?"

"Yes, please," said Tom. "And we'll meet you in the parking lot of the CBD club in Wallyburg." He slipped something into the tall man's hand.

"See you in a bit," said the tall man and he walked away from them.

"How did you like your lunch?" asked Tom.

"Not bad street meat," said Jenna. "Not up to LA standards, but not bad. Was this dog supposed to be the interesting part of lunch?"

"Nope," said Tom. "This was."

He picked up the envelope that the tall man had given him and tore it open. He took out a very authentic looking Canadian passport, opened it and studied the front pages carefully. After looking at it very intently for several minutes, he handed it to Jenna.

"The Grave Robber has done his work. Welcome to my world, Jennifer Anne Roberts. You'll notice that your maiden name was Skeates."

When Jenna looked over the document she was astounded to see her photo affixed to a very official looking passport. She stared at it for some time and then looked up at Tom.

"I think I'll continue to call you Jenna," was all he said.

They caught a tiny ferry a couple hours later, on foot, wearing their backpacks. The sleepy customs agent on the American side paid no attention to them at all. On the Canadian side of the river it was a relaxed passage through customs. It seemed clear that they had nothing to declare and a battered taxi happened to be waiting about three hundred yards down the road from the ferry dock.

The tall man was in the parking lot of the club. Tom gave him an envelope that the man tucked inside his pocket without opening it. There was a jeep for them, a couple of years newer than the one they had driven across the States in, and Jenna was surprised to see all of their bags and belongings in it.

"I've booked us into a place a couple of hours from here. A great big old dignified country house that's been turned into a hotel." He leaned over and pecked her on the cheek. "Welcome back to Canada, Jenna."

***

Ing Stoller felt her life reeling out of control. South Africa was in turmoil. Distrust and paranoia filled the air.

She had settled into a routine that was demanding and soul numbing. She had long days at work which were followed by nights of being the primary caregiver of her increasingly helpless mother. With some moments stolen during the day to badger the health care system to get something done to alleviate her mother's suffering. Ing was exhausted.

She was completely unaware that her every move was being intensely scrutinized. Her fatigue and preoccupation with her mother's health worked in the favour of the team that had the LO put in place. She had totally become a creature of routine. The men and women watching her liked routine in a subject.

There was still no clear diagnosis. Ing had given her mother her evening medication and meal and was about to go to bed when the telephone rang. She was going to ignore it, but wondered if it might be one of the doctors calling. Tears welled up in her eyes when she heard Jenna on the line.

"Ing, how are you? How is your mother?"

"Oh Jesus, Jenna! I so needed to hear from you. Are you two okay?"

"We're fine. We're close to where we need to be. But come on, Ing. How are you?"

"I'm pretty fucking nearly done," said Ing. "Mother just gets weaker and weaker each day and nobody seems to know what to do about it. The capper came today. The doctors want me and my brothers to go to a lab tomorrow to have blood samples taken. They are now wondering if there is some chromosomal issue going on with Mom."

"Oh God, Ing!"

"I know. Just when you think you've hit rock bottom, some fucker throws you a shovel."

"I am so sorry, Ing. Would you like me to come there to help out?"

"Jenna. That is the sweetest thing that I have heard since you and Tom and I were together at your cottage. But no. Mom is going down quickly. My brothers are actually being a bit helpful. I'll stay here to see her off."

"Christ, Ing! It's that bad?"

"It's that bad, Jenna. I'll deal with this and then I want to come to see you and Tom. I know where to find you."

"We'll be waiting for you," said Jenna.

Ing ended the call.

And one of Holt's listeners in Africa was on the line to Chuck immediately. "The Stoller chick just took a call from Jenna Van Velt. She knows where they're going."

"Stay tight on her."

Chuck would be meeting Sam and the others in Muskoka soon so he didn't bother to call and wake up Sam with the news.

***

When Winter answered his phone a voice said "Bonjour, Monsieur L'Hiver."

"Why French, Nils?" asked Winter.

"Because I am calling you from 'la belle province'. We are about to board a direct flight from Montreal to Paris. Would it be possible to have someone at Orly meet us and bring us to the chateau?"

"Nearly everything is possible," said Winter.

"Except, apparently, an adequately researched appraisal of how best to have Ten Haan's niece join us for some meaningful conversation. Have we figured out what the fuck happened?"

"Our intelligence team on the ground made some errors. The terrified young woman whose genitals you contemplated at the ultra modern cottage was someone named Deanna. She is an acquaintance of Van Velt and looks a lot like her. I would punish the whole team that made this mistake, but of course, the Legacy Organization has taken care of that for me."

Nils was silent for moment, which told Winter that he was doing a rapid risk assessment.

"We have obviously exercised all precautions during our trip."

"Clearly the Legacy people are at war with us. You need to be extremely careful. Things have slept for years, but now the wounds have been torn open. I am about to order 'waterfall' to begin."

"I would not do that yet."

"That is not your decision to make."

"Fuck you, then, and the ride from Orly."

"Nils!" said Winter. But the line was dead.

When Winter realized that Nils had ended the call he felt his rage engulfing him. He fought to gain control for several minutes. An aide came into the room at his summons.

"Ask Doktor Kepp to join me," commanded Winter.

***

When Nils had ended the call with Winter, he had a brief conversation with Hanna. Twenty minutes at the airline ticket counter resulted in them changing their destination from Paris to Edinburgh.

Nils spent a long time in a telephone booth once they reached Edinburgh. He was quite sure that Winter did not know that Angelique had provided him with the telephone number of the tiny apartment where she stayed when not in attendance at the chateau. He called the number expecting to get her answering machine. His plan was to leave instructions for her to be at the phone in two days' time. He was very surprised when Angelique answered his call immediately.

"allo".

"Angelique, this is Nils calling."

"Nils!" He could hear excitement in voice. "Why are you calling me?"

"To find out how you are. I understand that Winter is acting strangely."

Angelique's description of what had transpired in the exercise room and later in what Winter called 'the silent room', caused Nils to experience an great feeling of coldness, starting in his chest. He cared not a whit for what the young woman had experienced at the hands of Winter and two of his minions. But he cared deeply about what those actions revealed about Winter's state of mind.

Nils did his best to calm Angelique and when the time was right, he asked her if she had any money. She assured him that she did. Nils had expected that would be the case because Winter would have bought her silence. Nils told Angelique that she was undoubtedly being watched by Winter's people and then gave her very explicit instructions as to how to leave her apartment and meet with him. When he was certain that Angelique knew what steps she needed to take to rendezvous with him in two days, he ended the call. Hanna was waiting patiently on a nearby bench.

"Have you found us a place to hole up for a couple of days?"

"The woman in the tourist information kiosk tells me that there is a Hilton hotel quite near here and that it is next door to a large department store." Nils and Hanna split up when they entered the department store and arranged to meet near the check-out area in half an hour. Nils told Hanna that he would select luggage for both of them.

They cashed out of the store about forty minutes later and Nils led Hanna to a secluded bench outside. No one paid any attention to them as they packed all of their purchases into the suitcases and carryon bags that Nils had bought. As soon as they entered their hotel room, Nils stripped off all of his clothing and rummaged in his new suitcase for the toiletries he had bought. Hanna did the same.

"I'll just be a moment, and then I'll go out and make some calls."

When Nils emerged from the bathroom Hanna was lying in bed.

"You must make me get up to shower, Nils. I feel that if I fall asleep I won't ever wake up again."

"Turn onto your stomach. I want to look at your back."

There would be a scar. But the doctor in the small town that Nils had held at gunpoint had done a very good job. The wound was dry and there was very little redness around it.

Nils gathered up all of the clothes that they had worn on their trip through the States and Canada, and all of the wrapping from their recent purchases and stuffed them into one of the carry bags.

"There's a pub nearby with a phone. I'll be some time. Shower and get some sleep."

***

It was a beautiful summer day when they drove into Port Burwell, and as Tom had expected, Audrey was in her garden. When Tom called out to her she set aside the shears that she had been using and walked to greet them. Tom introduced Jenna as his friend from California and Audrey led them to her porch, told them to be seated and went into the house briefly to get them cold drinks. Tom was delighted to see a can of Tusker on the tray. Jenna noticed the can of African beer and remarked that she must know Tom well.

"I'm not sure that there are many people who can claim to know Tom well, Jenna. Perhaps on some sort of sliding scale, I might fit into that category. Have you come from far off today?"

"Not far at all. We spent last night at the Elmhurst Inn near Ingersoll."

"That is a lovely old place, with quite a history as well. I'm glad that you haven't been driving all day Tom, because you have some business to attend to."

"What's up?"

"You need to go see your lawyer. The people you've bought the place from have decided that they'd like to give you possession as soon as possible."

"That's amazing," said Tom. "They fought tooth and nail to hang onto possession until after Labour Day when we were negotiating the sale. Jenna, I'll leave you here in good company."

They watched Tom march rapidly up the street to the small business area in the town.

"Have you known Tom a long time?" Jenna asked Audrey.

"I met him when he was still a teenager. I'm active in the local history society. It became customary for someone from our group to give a talk to the grade thirteen history class. I think Tom was the only one who stayed awake during my presentation. How about you?"

Jenna realized that she was suddenly out of her depth. She and Tom had not discussed what story they would give his friend in Canada. She didn't know what Tom might have told her when he had called her. She opted for the truth. "Only a couple of months."

"Well, there must be something special about you, Jenna. I've known Tom since he was eighteen. I've never seen him so at ease with himself."

Jenna sat silently thinking about that statement.

"Please tell me something about you! In all the years I've known him, Tom has never brought anyone around to see me".

"I'm not intriguing. I grew up north of Toronto, in Thornhill. My Dad was an immigrant from Holland. My mother died young so it was just the two of us from the time I was eleven. Dad worked hard. I always knew I was his priority and that he loved me deeply. He just wasn't around a lot to show me that."

"You just said that you were his priority and then you said he loved you. I admire your honesty in saying that. It says to me that you just spoke from your heart. You speak of him in the past tense so I assume that he is no longer with the world."

"He died six years ago. I miss him a lot. I've felt like I'm adrift with him gone."

"I like you. Wait here."

When Audrey returned she was carrying a cut glass decanter and two tiny crystal glasses. She poured a dark coloured liquid into the two glasses and gave one to Jenna, and offered a toast.

"To all of the good people we've lost."

They gently touched their glasses.

"I was sad when Tom fell in love and left Canada. It was like someone had blown out a candle in a dimly lit room."

"So he was very connected with people here?"

"He was before he went to Africa. I'm about the only person left around here that he is in touch with now. "

"I am in a lot of trouble. I don't know if Tom has told you about that, but he is helping me out."

"Of course he is. Do you think I would let a scalliwag like Tom put his probably ill-gotten gains in my home if I didn't believe he was helping damsels in distress?"

Audrey refilled their glasses. The dark liquid was sweet and fiery.

"What are we drinking?" asked Jenna.

"Elderberry wine. A family of rogues outside of this village makes it. They say it's wine but it's actually a cordial."

"Are we going to be drunk when Tom comes back?"

"Possibly. But Tom will understand the need for me to have gotten us into such a state. Jenna, I would dearly love to have been in one of the army units that he has led over the years. He says little, but I am a student of politics and history. Our Tom has likely caused some bad people to have some very bad days. In many cases, I would say the worst days of their lives."

"I have seen that happen," said Jenna.

"No!" Audrey's eyes widened. "And?" she said softly.

The shadows were lengthening when Tom pushed opened the gate to Audrey's garden and walked to the back porch. He could hear Audrey and Jenna's laughter before he rounded the corner at the back of the house. They seem to be getting along well, he thought.

He pulled up short when he saw the decanter on the table. Tom knew all about Audrey's evil elderberry moonshine. Her truth serum as she called it when she had had a few glasses. He knew that it would be hitting Jenna like a speeding freight train.

"What are you two sots up to?"

"I have to say, Tom, that I thoroughly approve of your taste in female companions. Your friend Jenna here is delightful. And from what she's told me, she's brought all sorts of intrigue and skullduggery and danger and all those other things that you seem to hold so dear into your life. You've apparently made a flawless choice!"

"Except, of course," said Jenna. "He didn't get to make the choice. I chose to drag him into my newly crazy world."

Audrey leaned forward to pat Jenna's knee reassuringly. "Trust me, Jenna. Tom requires women to be his catalyst for change. He'd be a tobacco farmer sipping tea at the historical society meetings had it not been for a woman."

Jenna found Audrey's remark to be hysterically funny and arose from her chair, crossing her legs. Audrey gave her barely understandable directions to the bathroom and then was incapable of speech because of her own laughter. Tom stood regarding her with an eyebrow cocked.

Audrey eventually regained some sort of control and was about to address Tom when Jenna came outside.

"My pants are still dry," she remarked brightly and unsteadily took a seat.

Audrey promptly lost any composure that she had regained. Jenna resumed her chair, watching Audrey intently. As Audrey's spasm began to subside, Jenna realized why Audrey had been laughing and suddenly lost it. That provoked the two of them to stand and hug one another. Tom watched the shoulder of Jenna's T-shirt darken with Audrey's tears of laughter.

"You two need to eat something. I'm calling in the Lighthouse bicycle boy."

Chapter Twenty-three

Nils had grown up in the Cerberus Corporation. And as the years went by he had learned that it was not a corporation in any normally understood sense of the word. The younger generations, the post war people, did not carry the hate that Winter and the other members of his generation did.

Nils, with his intelligence and willingness to engage in appalling violence, brought some talents that they needed. But they valued blind obedience. Which was not part of Nils' make-up. For the past five years his contact with the upper management of the collaborative had been minimal. He had become a sort of special arm of the group, accountable only to Winter.

The senior members of Cerberus were all of the World War II generation. Winter was the youngest of this upper echelon of people. All of the them were members of the Winter, Witt or Harpt families. None of them would act on their own initiative. They would always wait for an order from Winter.

Nils thought that most of them should have been put out to pasture long ago. But they still had their historical positions of authority in the structure of the Corporation. Soon they would start to receive orders from Winter and would actually be expected to do things. They would make mistakes.

By the time he had finished his calls, Nils knew where most of the senior members of Cerberus could be found during the next few days. When he returned to the hotel he ordered room service and awakened Hanna.

During their drive through the States and across Canada Nils and Hanna had had ample time to talk about the failed mission in California and about the Corporation. Their conversations so far had focused on the shortcomings of the organization. Nils wanted to take the discussion further.

"We'll go out in an hour or so," said Nils. "There are a couple of things we need to pick up, and of course we need to rent a car."

"I take it we aren't going to fly into Germany?"

"No. Winter would expect us to do that because he knows I despise slower means of travel. We will drive to a place on the coast, Rosyth, and take a ferry to Zeebrugge in Belgium. The chances of him having thought to put watchers there are very small."

"And once we have used our current passports for this trip we'll change our appearance and obtain new documents?"

"Certainly. Once we are back on the continent with new papers and some extensive changes to our appearance, we should be very safe and able to move freely."

"And then what?" asked Hanna.

"That's up to you. Once we're in Germany I can access a good deal of money that Cerberus does not know exists. Enough to compensate you for your efforts and the inconvenience you experienced in America. Then if you wish, you can go on your way."

"Given that we have a powerful group that opposes the Corporation in full cry trying to kill us, and knowing Cerberus has very little to gain by letting me continue to breathe, I really don't have many ideas of where I might enjoy a semi-retirement."

"The current situation is problematic," conceded Nils.

"I've gotten used to working with a partner. It would be strange, and given that I am a woman, perhaps dangerous to go back to working with several of my former clients. Some cultural groups have bizarre ideas about unattached women working with them."

"I plan to use this war that that Cerberus has gotten itself into to effect some change in the organization. If you would like to take part in that change process, I would welcome the opportunity to work with you."

Nils outlined the broad concept of his plan to Hanna as they walked two miles to a car rental company. By the time they had taken a car and visited a wine and spirits store, he had covered off the key points of his plan and had identified what Hanna's role would be in several parts of it.

"Let's go back to the room and we'll fuck to seal our partnership," said Hanna.

Once in their room, there was a great deal of tension. It was greater than anything they had experienced since the shoot-out. Nils took the lead and stripped. Hanna followed suit. They stood naked, staring at one another for a time, wondering what the nature of their alliance would be.

"Make it intense," said Hanna.

Nils was deeply affected by that statement.

He removed the sashes from their bathrobes and used one of them to tie Hanna's wrists behind her back. He used the second sash to bind her elbows tightly together. When he was satisfied that she could not move her arms he stepped in front of her.

"Spread please," he said, tapping the inside of one of her ankles with his toe. Once her feet were far apart he knelt in front of her and began to lick her exposed labia. Hanna made a sort of purring noise that stopped when Nils abruptly forced three of his fingers into her vagina. She gasped and struggled to maintain her balance as Nils roughly fucked her with his hand. When he stopped the assault and stood up, Hanna saw that his penis was fully erect.

Nils went to his suitcase and opened a small box. Hanna saw that he had a bottle of personal lube and said "You won't need that."

Nils poured a generous amount of the lubricant into his hand and then quickly stepped behind Hanna and hugged her tightly with his left arm.

"I'm very certain you'll be glad that I have some of this," said Nils.

Hanna started as Nils slapped his hand into the crack of her buttocks and began to rub the lube on her.

"You bastard!"

"You're right about that. Father fucked mother on a whim and was shocked to learn he'd made her pregnant. He was appalled, but both families were delighted. It was a brief and dynastic marriage with me the only progeny. So common among the lesser noble families in Europe. I am going to very much enjoy myself for the next while, Hanna."

Nils penetrated her anus with two fingers, withdrew them, then penetrated her again, forcing lube inside her. When he was satisfied with the slipperiness of her ass, he released his grip on her and grabbed her shoulders. He propelled her to the foot of the bed and forced her to kneel on its edge, her forehead on the bedspread, her ass in the air.

"No noise now, my lovely Hanna. We mustn't disturb the other guests."

Nils forced his way into her roughly. Hanna fought to relax her muscles as he thrust quickly and repeatedly. Tears were welling in her eyes and she wanted to hurl a string of obscenities at him. She instead whispered "you fucker" repeatedly.

Nils slowed the pace of his thrusts and forced himself as deeply into her ass as he could. He was holding her tightly with his left arm wrapped around the front of her body just above her hips. Hanna groaned when he started to fumble with her labia with his right hand.

He found her clitoris and squeezed it tightly between his thumb and forefinger. Then he began to roll it between his thumb and finger. Hanna clenched her teeth and tried desperately not to come. But the contractions started and she moaned loudly as Nils, uncontrollably aroused, thrust into her violently.

He withdrew from her while still erect. She had hoped he would be become flaccid so that she could tense her muscles and make it difficult for him. He untied her wrists and arms and then stood away from her. She would have struck out at him but it took time for feeling to return to her arms.

"Let's shower," said Nils.

***

There was no small talk when the Legacy Organization took their places in the meeting room. Sam made the obligatory toast and said, "I've asked Chuck to start off. A lot of what he has to tell you is time sensitive."

"I know that you've all been told about the shoot-out that my team had with a group of guys who were attempting to snatch Gerta's niece. We think they were all ex-East German Army. I think we got all of them plus Alan Spader."

"The world is well rid of that particular blight. Good work," said Franz.

"On the negative side, Nils Witt and Hanna Spader got away. Once the police came streaming into the area we couldn't attempt a pursuit of them. Our contacts within the police department are working well. There has been a string of murders and abductions across the mid-western states. We are sure that Witt and Spader are headed for Canada."

"Is that what the cops think?"

"Yes. They know from blood they found in the first car that Witt stole that one of them is wounded. A doctor was abducted from some small town and found dead a hundred miles up the road a day later. The gunman who took him matched Witt's description except for hair colour. The doctor was ordered to bring a supply of drugs and instruments with him."

"So the Spader woman presumably caught a bullet," said Daniel. "Not surprising given the amount of shooting your men did."

Sam jumped in quickly. "I made the decision with Chuck to hit Winter's men as hard as we could."

"You know me, Sam. I'm all for killing off some of Winter's hordes. I just prefer to do it quietly and in smaller batches." For a few seconds the only sound in the room was the clicking of his needles as Daniel knitted furiously.

"Neither we nor the cops have any idea what identities Witt and Spader are using. I expect that next time we hear of them is when Daniel's people see them back at Winter's place. I have a team standing by if they're spotted. I think we should deal with Witt - and Spader if they stay together - as soon as we can."

"Europe is not the wild west, Chuck. There can't be a repeat of what happened in California, in Germany or France," said Daniel. "I will take care of Witt if he is spotted in Europe."

"What's the status of the search for Van Velt and this mercenary that she has taken off with?"

"We know more than the cops. They have no clue where she has gone. We at least have her friend in Capetown under tight surveillance. We have Ing Stoller's work and home phones tapped. We know that she plans to join up with Van Velt and this Tom Robbins guy as soon as her mother passes. That's our best chance of finding them for now."

"And you believe that Van Velt has the diaries and the disks with her?"

"We know quite a bit about Tom Robbins now. He reads Afrikaans. She not only has the diaries. She now knows whatever Gerta chose to write down about the work in Namibia."

"When do we discuss what we will do with Ms. Van Velt once we find her?" asked Daniel.

"We need to find her first. Once we know where she is, we'll decide how to handle her," said Sam.

"The critical point is that until Chuck fought his battle in cottage country, nobody in the States knew that there was anything related to the epidemic in Africa except for us and Winter's Cerebus Corporation and Van Velt and her buddies. Now INTERPOL, the FBI, the CIA and probably a dozen US police forces are turning over rocks trying to figure how Gerta's murder relates to twenty or so dead guys in the mountains in California. Winter started this and we have to deal with him. Can we do it with the attention that this whole goddamned thing has attracted?" Daniel was knitting furiously.

"We have to. We have to stop Winter and get to the Van Velt woman." It was first time that Claudio had spoken during the meeting.

"I've been in South Africa for the last week. Despite the chaos they're in, I have had some private conversations with several scientists there. We know that Winter went to work for the South Africans, the research arm of their 7 Medical Battalion, after he was thrown out of our operation. I have been shown some of the work he did for them. The bastard was clearly able to smuggle some of the data that our team produced in the earlier stages of their work."

"What did he do with it?" asked Franz.

"He and the South Africans tried to replicate our efforts to develop a bio-weapon."

"And?"

"They have inadvertently started this plague called AIDS. But here's the thing. Our team in Namibia had developed not only a virus, but also medication that could control the disease as well as a vaccine that could avert it. Erich and Gerta have told us the formulas for all three are on the disks that they had."

"Are you saying that the disks could contain information to stop the AIDS epidemic?"

"Possibly. Winter and the South Africans leaned heavily on the work he had stolen from our team. We should - without too much trouble - be able to adapt our work to deal with Winter's rogue virus."

"So Winter has made the same conclusion. Which is why he's started this war with us."

"I visited several hospitals while I was in Africa. The death toll from AIDS is rising at an unimaginable rate. The company that finds a cure for AIDS will be a very, very rich company."

There was a lot more discussion before the meeting ended.

***

Tom and Jenna had spent a quiet day sunning on the beach of the property he would take possession of in a few days. It was late afternoon when Tom suggested they pack up and walk back to where they had left the jeep.

Port Burwell was not the beach for sunsets. Tom knew that they would hike for the jeep with long shadows in front of them. There was a slight breeze coming up though and Tom hoped it would cause a slight ripple on the water. He wanted Jenna to see the diamonds.

"Jenna. When I was in Rhodesia I became close friends with a guy named Ed Cromwell. We've been through some dangerous things together. A few months before I met you, Ed asked me to meet him in France. I learned a lot of things I didn't know about Ed. And just after I met you, I used information given to me by Ed and I came back to Canada with a lot of money. A stinkin' lot of money. I owe Ed big time."

"What do you need to do to settle that debt?"

"Ed and his wife loved Rhodesia. It literally killed her to leave there."

"I've often wished there was some place that it would kill me to leave," said Jenna. "I haven't found one yet."

"Well. In five days I'll show you the place that I don't ever want to leave. You'll have to see what you think of it. I just wish I could be certain that I'll be able to stay here and enjoy it."

"Why wouldn't you?"

"I've made a promise to Ed. He's dying of cancer and he is bound and determined to die on his former land in Rhodesia. I told him that I would make sure that he and his wife's ashes go into the ground on his old farm. It's a promise that I have to keep."

Jenna started to say something but Tom excitedly interrupted her.

"Look, the lake is going into diamonds!" said Tom excitedly.

Lake Erie was getting choppy from the breeze with little wavelets rising everywhere. The sun was low on the horizon. The sinking sun was lighting the deep green of the lake. The tips of the wavelets were turning a silver gold colour. There were millions of them. Stretching to the horizon. Jenna smiled when she saw it.

"So, Jenna. Ed wants me to call him tonight. I know he's going to tell me that we need to make the trip to Africa soon. It's a trip I have to make."

"Are you worried about what would happen to me if I were left here on my own?"

"Not at all. I called a buddy back in LA when we were on the road. I'll speak with him again tonight. He is solid and is picking up the contract I should be dealing with tomorrow. He also drinks with the cops in that area all the time. I hope he'll have some news of what the hell went down the night we bailed out of the Bayfield area. But whatever the news is, I think we've shaken off the bad boys for a while."

"I've come to understand in the last few days that 'safe' is a relative term. Are we presently safe?"

"I believe we are," said Tom. "If I didn't have the obligation with Ed that I have, I would say we hunker down and try to figure out what the hell you are dealing with. The problem is there is now something I have to do."

"Then you have to go do it. I'll be fine here."

"Sure you will. But we need information about this Legacy Organization and this guy Allen. And we are lucky enough to know a retired archivist with connections from hell. What would you say to some days in Toronto with Audrey?"

"If it can help us get out of this fucking mess, I'm in."

"I'll speak to Audrey. I will fly out of Pearson so I can drop you two at a hotel in Toronto. Fair warning. Audrey will work your pretty ass off once you get to the library there."

***

Winter was becoming increasingly concerned about the absence of Nils. He had issued a lot of orders. In some ways it felt good to be engaged in operations. But he had come to depend upon Nils to coordinate the lion's share of the covert activities of the collaborative. He had relied upon an Austrian based contractor to do the surveillance of the Van Velt woman, sending in his team of European based gunmen at the last moment. Nils had vetted and approved the team from Europe but had had to rely on the Austrian's work at the site. That had proven to be a disaster.

***

They went for dinner at the Lighthouse restaurant. Tom stayed at the table long enough to order, then went to the payphone. He came back about fifteen minutes later just as their dinners arrived.

"Note to self. Go to bank tomorrow and buy rolls of quarters. Damn it's expensive, not to mention a gigantic pain in the butt to call California from a payphone."

"What did you find out?"

"Let's get some nourishment first," said Tom.

Tom ate quickly and used the chewing time to think about what he would tell Jenna. He reasoned that keeping information from her could possibly put her in greater danger.

"The shooting we heard was at your friends' cottage. A whole bunch of people burst into the cottage, stripped and tied Deanna up and gave her some sort of injection. Before they could do more, a major gun battle started and one of the guys in the cottage got dead with a head shot."

Jenna simply stared at Tom.

"The cops responded as quickly as they could. When they got to the cottage, there were dead guys in soldier clothes all over the place."

"When the sun came up, the cops found a total of twenty dead bodies scattered around the Brown's cottage and in the woods. All of them but the dead guy inside were in the same kind of camouflage clothing and all of them were armed to the teeth with sidearms, assault rifles and grenades."

"Oh God, Tom! How is Deanna?"

"She must be relatively okay. She is definitely talking to the cops. That's a good thing."

"And everything that happened to her should have happened to me?"

"No, Jenna. Everything that happened to her was meant to happen to you. But none of it should have happened. Nobody should have killed your Aunt, either."

"But it did."

"It did. We're going to have to find a way to stop this."

"I have no idea how it started, Tom, so how the hell do we go about stopping it?"

"It started in Namibia. We have the diaries and we have a shitload of computer disks. And the most important thing we have is the letter that your Aunt left you. That's the bit that gives us a way to end this."

"I'm not following you."

"Okay, Jenna. We know that your Aunt was involved in some ultra-secret, heavy duty research that was ninety-nine percent likely to have been for bio-warfare shit. Right?"

"Okay."

"And we know that people tortured her and murdered her. Clearly somebody wants the information that she had tucked away in your attic. And clearly she was determined not to let them have it."

"I think so."

"The gunfight that sent us off on our road trip. The twenty dead guys were likely working for the same people who killed your Aunt. They think that she passed on the information she had to you."

"I get that, Tom."

"What we need to do is to make contact with the people who killed those twenty bad guys. I think they have to be part of that Legacy organization that your Aunt named in her letter to you. You and Audrey will find us what we need to get in touch with them when you're going through the library in Toronto. One of those people will walk up to you and say they were with your Aunt when she killed a tiger."

"A lion. And once we give them the disks, it's over and life can become sane again?"

"I wish it were that simple, Jenna. The toughest part in all this is surviving making contact with the guys who killed the bad guys."

"Why?"

"Because we know what they were doing in Namibia. And I would bet my whole collection of edged weapons that they don't want anybody to know about that."

"You have a collection of edged weapons? What the hell are edged weapons?"

"This will all be revealed to you, Ms. Van Velt, when I take possession of my new home and various cartage companies are called to bring my belongings from hither and yon."

"Is there any way we can get in touch with Deanna to see how she is?"

"Don't even think about it," said Tom. "Jenna. There are a couple of things I think you should do."

"What?"

"First, I think you need to send a letter of resignation to your employer. The last thing we need your company to do is for them to file a missing person report for you. The second thing is for us to get the keys to your apartment in the hands of some lads that I know in L.A. They can move your stuff out of your place and into storage. Hopefully the cops won't have people watching for that."

"Resign my job?"

"We're not going to be back in L.A. for the foreseeable future, Jenna."

"God I hate this!"

"I know. It sucks. But it is what it is. And you need to write a letter to your ex. The cops will be bound to contact him as they look for you. You can tell him that you've decided to be the public relations manager for one of the big resort chains in Mexico. Please think about what I've just said."

"If we start sending letters and the police are looking for me, won't that let them know we're in Canada?"

"I'll mail a package with the letters in it to a contact of mine in Mexico. He'll mail your letters from there. I actually would hope that your boss would notify the police that she's heard from you and give them the letter."

Jenna fell silent.

***

Nils and Hanna caught a train into Brussels and Nils made a couple of calls from a phone booth. They took a cab to a salon and in two hours Hanna became a short haired blond. Nils had his head shaved, and was fitted for contact lenses that turned his icy blue eyes dark brown.

Within an hour they had had their photos taken and it would be a matter of a day before their new papers were ready. They sat in an outdoor café sipping Stellas.

***

Winter was coming under increasing stress. His contacts in America were disappearing. Calls weren't being returned. The lack of information was distressing. Winter knew it could become deadly.

The man who had survived the gun battle in California had managed to get back to Europe via a circuitous route. He would be joining Winter in under an hour. Two trusted senior staff of the Corporation would be with Winter in that meeting.

He was concerned about Nils' continued absence. This was the longest time that Nils had ever remained out of contact. The previous evening he had awakened suddenly and realized that he had been dreaming that members of the Legacy Organization had captured Nils. It had taken some time for Winter to drive the that thought from his head and he did not get back to sleep for hours.

***

Nils and Hanna rented a car. They drove for less than an hour to an enchanting house/castle on the Belgian/French border and Nils rapped on the door of the place. The woman who opened the door didn't recognize him. She had been his surrogate mother for the first six years of his life.

When she turned to walk down the hall to tell the homeowner that he had visitors Nils moved swiftly behind her. He and Hanna had stopped at a music store and Nils had bought guitar strings that he had modified slightly with lead fishing line sinkers. He nearly decapitated her in the main hallway with the garrotte that he had made and went off looking for his beloved uncle. Although Uncle Gerd was a voting member of the Collaborative, Nils doubted that Winter would have called him yet.

As Nils had anticipated, Gerd Witt was in the workshop of his home, surrounded by partially completed stuffed animals and birds. His passion was taxidermy and on this day he was working on a large wild boar. The arrival of Nils and Hanna annoyed more than surprised him.

"Well," he said. "I think it's been more than five years since I've had a visit from my dutiful nephew. What brings you to my part of the world, Nils?"

"You obviously haven't heard from Karl Winter."

"Why should I have?"

"Because Winter has declared war on the Legacy Organization. He's launched 'Waterfall'. The bodies are piling up quite rapidly. Unfortunately so far, most of the bodies in the piles have been provided by our people."

Gerd Witt set down the wicked looking tool that he had been using and moved to a sink to wash his hands. While his back was turned Hanna picked up a pair of glass eyes that were intended for the wild boar and slipped them into her pocket.

"So Winter has sent you to me to bring me into this conflict?"

"No. He feels it would be best if you remain outside of the main actions that are taking place. He only asks for some financial and other material support for now. He sent me because we want you to appear to have had no contact at all with Cerberus Corporation."

The relief of the old man on hearing Nils' words was palpable.

"Of course. I have plenty of money here. What is needed?"

Nils gave the old man an amount and indicated that some of the handguns and ammunition that had been stored in the house by the Corporation were also required. Gerd said that he would be relieved to have the weapons gone from his home. His safe was cleverly hidden in a support arch in the cellar outside of his workshop. In short order Nils and Hanna were awash in cash and armed to the teeth.

"How will I know if this war you speak of is going in our favour if I am to be kept out of it?"

Nils was focusing his attention on loading a semi-automatic Browning pistol. He didn't reply at first, but then he raised the handgun he had been working on and aimed at Gerd's chest.

"If someone comes into your house and points a firearm at you like I am doing, Uncle Gerd, you can assume that things are going off the rails."

The old man started to say something but Nils fired two rounds quickly into his chest and the man reeled backwards and sprawled over the carcass of the boar he had been working on. Nils walked to him and rested his fingers on his neck. There was no pulse. Nils suddenly let out a yelp of laughter.

"What do you find so funny?" asked Hanna.

"Dear Uncle Gerd was a swine and a pedophile. It's fitting that his last breath was taken as he was draped over a dead pig. We'd best be going. No one will have heard the shots, but we have some driving to do to make our next meeting."

***

As usual, Tom was awake long before Jenna. It was a hot, humid, sunny morning as he took a long run along the beach. Lake Erie was churned up with whitecaps stretching to the horizon. In just over two hours, Tom would visit the lawyer's office to pick up the keys for his new home.

He showered and was sitting on the small porch of the cottage sipping his second of cup of coffee when he heard Jenna stirring inside. Tom went to the kitchen counter, poured a cup for her and placed it on the table close to the sugar bowl. He was about to go back outside when Jenna stepped out of the bathroom wearing the small tee shirt that she had slept in and nothing else. Tom had trouble taking his eyes off her.

"Good morning. In less than two hours I get to show you my new place."

"You're excited about it? It's good to get excited about a thing as important as taking ownership of a place you've wanted for a long time."

"I am that. I'll let you hit the shower. I'm going to run out and pick up a few things and get the keys from the lawyer. I should be back here shortly after ten."

There were only half a dozen documents to sign, which Tom did, trying not to show too much excitement. The lawyer smiled and gave Tom a big handshake when the formalities were completed. He handed Tom two key rings with tags attached by string to them identifying what each of them would open.

Tom drove back to the rented cottage in a hurry. Jenna was ready and waiting on the porch. Tom would have been disappointed had she not been.

He got out of the jeep and walked to the passenger side and opened the door.

"Ms. Van Velt. It would give me the greatest of pleasure to hand you into my vehicle and escort you to my new and hopefully last home."

"Thank you, kind sir," said Jenna.

They spoke little on the drive out to Tom's new place. Jenna could feel his excitement. When they reached the long laneway, Tom drove slowly, looking at the woods to each side. When she first saw the house, Jenna let out a cry of surprise.

She had thought that Tom would have bought an old heritage property. Instead she saw a three story stone and glass structure. The two lower floors were quite conventionally modern in design, but the third floor seemed to defy construction technology. The roof appeared to be supported by nothing but glass. The view from there would be spectacular.

"What do you think?" asked Tom as they drew closer to the house.

"It's magnificent, but not at all what I expected."

"I know. I wish it were a hundred and fifty year old conventional brick farmhouse. But I wanted this land and it came with this house. There is a lot of redecorating to do, Jenna."

"Bit too modern for your taste, Tom?"

"The previous owners fancied themselves to be Wiccans. I can't wait to show you the stone circle back there in the piney woods. There are many murals inside the house that have to go. I may leave the sound-proofed black room in the basement intact for a while. As a conversation piece."

Chapter Twenty-four

The teleconference with INTERPOL was intense. Arnon was allowed to attend at the back of the room. The people in charge were clearly rattled. Arnon's captain had had to get assertive to get them both into the meeting.

"We have looked at everything on these computers. The bulk of the transmissions are conversations between the murder victim and her older friend and a fellow in Germany named Franz. They discuss the research they were doing in Namibia. They were working on genetically racially based, biological warfare applications."

"That's huge," remarked one of the more senior American members on the call.

"What is most important, we think," said the senior man from INTERPOL on the call, "is that these biological weapons they were working on may be the origin of the Acquired Immune Deficiency Syndrome."

That statement stopped all conversation for several seconds.

"What makes you think that?" asked the senior state department guy on the call.

"Keep in mind that we only have about two weeks of messages. But there were several exchanges between the Ten Haan woman and a man called Franz each day, four days a week. In each of the exchanges Ten Haan is pleading with Franz to come and get their data because it might have had the potential to stop the AIDS epidemic."

"Might have had the potential," exclaimed someone on the line.

There was an FBI guy in the room where Arnon was listening to the call. "What sort of fucked-up scientists create a bio-weapon without having a viable antidote first?"

"I believe I can answer that," said another voice on the INTERPOL end of the call. "Ten Haan and Krohl both kept referring to the outcast. This was a scientist who had been fired off the project team and it is clear that this man Franz knew all about that. The pair in California said he must have tried to recreate their work and had gotten it wrong."

Another long silence ensued. Someone from the European end of the call asked if the connection had been broken. The senior man in the room assured him that they were still on the line.

"As I understand it, you have no way of detecting the location of the computer used by this man Franz?"

"There is a slight chance if we could engage him in a conversation when he is on-line. However, we are using our very best technicians and we have not seen that computer on the Arpnet since we started to search for it. It is likely that this man Franz knows that Krohl is dead, that Ten Haan is dead, and has switched off the computer. Actually, we think that if the person knows that Ten Haan is dead, his computer has likely been melted down to make beer cans."

***

Tom parked the jeep and dismounted. He walked around and took Jenna's hand as they walked to the house. He looked at the paper tags, identified the one for the front door and unlocked it.

"Be ready to be amazed, Jenna."

The front door was overly wide and had been handcrafted of oak. Tom swung it wide open and Jenna stepped into foyer that was about ten feet square with closets on both side on it. Tom edged past and found the light switches for the great room.

"Step in here, Jenna. We need the lights on so you can get the full effect."

Jenna walked into a large room. The ceiling was high. It was a beautiful space, stunning at first glance, until one saw the murals.

"Oh my God, Tom!"

"I don't think that God can help us here, Jenna. What we need is a small army of house painters. They're booked for this afternoon."

"What were the previous owners thinking?"

"As I said, they were practicing Wiccans. The murals aren't to most people's taste, but you must admit that they are well executed."

"Oh they are, Tom, with great attention to detail. I mean, the sheer artistry of that penis about halfway up the wall entering that vagina is breathtaking."

"Yes. Yes, it is. When I first toured through the house the realtor explained that the north wall depicts a typical Wiccan Summer Solstice rite at Stonehenge. The same artist did the west wall which is of course, a larger than life rendering of a black mass of some kind."

"Thank God the south is mostly glass and the east wall is mostly the staircase!"

"Wait until you see the ceiling of the master bedroom."

"Oh God! What's painted there?"

"No paint, Jenna. But it is going to take eight workmen to get the mirror down."

"Jesus wept!"

A door led off the west side of the great room to a powder room, a large well equipped kitchen and a big dining room. Tom said that the realtor told him that the witches entertained a lot. Off the east side of the great room was a large study lined with bookshelves and a smaller sunlit room.

"Is this a breakfast room?" asked Jenna looking around the space that had not a stick of furniture in it.

"This was the studio of the female witch. She dabbled in oils and acrylics"

"It's lovely."

"Good. I'm glad you like it. You figure out what use it should be put to and what furniture we need in it." Jenna thought about the words "we need in it" as they moved on through the house.

They went to the second floor, climbing the curved staircase that was a feature of the east side of the great room. Upstairs, the layout was more conventional. There were four bedrooms, each with their own ensuite. The master bedroom was huge, with a soaker tub in the ensuite and a massive walk-in closet.

"Strange that people who seemed to spend a lot of their time on a nude beach or in black robes would have such a huge closet," observed Tom.

"When does that mirror get taken off the ceiling?" asked Jenna.

"All in good time, milady. All in good time."

"Pig," said Jenna.

"Let's go up to the top."

The staircase to the third floor was at the end of the second floor hall. The stairs were much wider than usual and light streamed down the stairwell. Despite knowing that she was entering a room that was mostly glass, Jenna was not prepared.

The person climbing the stairs was facing south when they reached the third floor and until they were fully up them and had taken a few steps across the room the only thing they could see was the sky and a vast expanse of Lake Erie. The moment she stepped into the room Jenna knew why Tom had coveted the land.

They both stood in silence, taking in the view.

"On a clear night we can sit up here and see the lights of the American cities across the lake. Can you imagine how beautiful the view from here will be when the leaves are turning?"

"It would be wonderful to be up here during a lightning storm. Actually, I can't imagine when it wouldn't be wonderful to be up here."

"The previous owners had this room furnished with bean bag chairs and futons. I think it was likely the scene of many witchy orgies. They offered to leave the furniture but it looked sort of sticky. There's probably some unsuspecting bastard at a thrift store as we speak, thinking he's scored a bargain."

"Eww!"

They lingered in the room for some time, neither wanting to leave. Finally Tom led Jenna downstairs saying they had work to do.

There were several outbuildings. Tom and Jenna walked to each of them and Tom removed the padlocks on each of the doors and installed new locks.

"Chances are there are many members of the witch crowd that had keys to all of the doors at this place. A locksmith should arrive soon to change the locks on the house."

"I've saved the second coolest thing for second last," said Tom smiling broadly.

The last building to be visited was a frame single car garage. When Tom first opened the door, Jenna wasn't sure what she was looking at.

It was a green, open vehicle with six seats moulded into its body. It had a boat-like shape but there were three small wheels with fat tires on either side of it. There was a small instrument panel and very small windshield, but Jenna couldn't see a way of steering it.

"What is it?" she asked.

"It's an Argo. Amazing piece of machinery! And I made sure that it was in perfect running order before I agreed to buy it. It's an amphibian. Land. Water. Makes no difference to this bad boy. And Christ is it fun to drive!"

"I'll take your word for it. Where's the steering wheel?"

"No steering wheel on this baby, Jenna. It rolls with tiller bar controls. Just like a tank! We'll go on an outing later."

As they walked back to the house, a van rolled in. Tom gave the locksmith some directions and then they went into the study. Jenna looked at the many bookshelves and remarked that Tom was going to need to buy a lot of books. He assured her that he wouldn't have to.

The wall of the study that faced the bookshelves was bare. Jenna contemplated it for a while and then asked Tom if it would be a wall for paintings. He shook his head and said "showcases". Jenna was intrigued but didn't pursue that because it was clear that Tom still had something to show her.

The walls of the study were paneled in oak with raised detail in a very symmetric pattern. Tom ran his fingers along the edge of one of the raised sections of the paneling at the north end of the room and there was a sharp click. A whole section of paneling swung out to reveal a staircase. Tom made an attempt at an evil professor type laugh, took Jenna's hand and led her down the stairs.

When they reached the bottom of the stairs they were in a small area that made Jenna feel claustrophobic. There were three doors leading out from the area. Two were very ornate. The third was utilitarian.

"Alright, Jenna. Door number one, door number two, or door number three?"

Jenna pointed to the very plain door.

"You wussie," said Tom.

He opened it to reveal a two piece bathroom.

The first of the ornate doors gave access to a dungeon lined with faux stone walls and lots of restraints.

"I wasn't kidding," said Tom.

"If what you're showing me is what you think is the coolest thing about this house, Tom, I may be getting on a plane very soon."

He laughed and opened the third door.

Jenna had not realized that the ground to the east of the house fell away. They stepped into a ground level greenhouse. It was filled with tropical trees and plants. The center of the large glass room was a large pond.

"This is the hot tub room, Jenna. I'd propose a dip now but we have the painters coming."

"I'm blown away."

"So was I. I am looking forward to living here. Want to try it as well?"

Jenna stood silently. Tom noticed that she had become teary-eyed as he placed his arm around her shoulders.

"There's another staircase leading to the other half of the basement where the furnace and laundry room are if that might help your deliberations," said Tom.

Jenna punched him in the chest and they went back upstairs.

***

Nils did not say that he was anxious, but Hanna could feel his tension. She knew that they had one more member of Nils' family to remove, but he had not told her much about him. They took a room in a rundown hotel about ten miles from the home of Nils' last surviving uncle. The sex that night was bizarre.

The next day they drove to wooded hilly area and Nils left Hanna in the car and walked off through the woods. When he returned his mood was light and he was almost playful as he drove them a short distance to "call on Dear Uncle Tomas' wife". Hanna did not ask him what had taken place during the hour that he had been away from the car.

Chapter Twenty-five

The man had been frisked and had passed through a metal detector. Winter took no chances with employees that had recently experienced severe trauma. He had learned that from his superiors during the fighting in Normandy.

Winter began slowly, asking the man to detail every step he had taken to prepare for the assault on the cottage of Jenna Van Velt. The man provided a detailed summary of the preparations, consulting notes that he had brought. The questions they posed to him were answered without evasion. Winter knew that the man was speaking the truth.

"What counter-measures did you take the night of the attack?" asked Winter.

"All of our counter-measures were directed to avoiding detection by law enforcement. No one had apprised us that there might be any other threat."

"So you had no one looking behind you?"

"We did not. We achieved our mission of assaulting the cottage without attracting the attention of any police or local civilians. That was the mission we had been given. There was no intelligence provided to us indicating that some para-military force outside of the law was stalking us, so we did not look for it."

Winter sat silently letting that last statement sink in. It was absolutely true. The Corporation had not known that they had been detected and then targeted. And the man sitting before him was competent. He was struggling with making a decision of keeping the man in his employ when the man made it for him.

He lunged from his chair. Winter threw himself sideways and though the man missed Winter's heart, he was able to drive his dagger deep into Winter's shoulder. The pain was excruciating and Winter felt cartilage being severed. Before he passed out he heard gun shots.

Winter awoke to find several people in his bedroom. The doctor from the village was there as was Doktor Kepp. The two men who had been with him at the interview with his assailant were nervously keeping a close watch on everyone. One of the female servants was keeping her distance from the bed he laid on, waiting to be given orders by the others.

He made a move to sit up and the doctor from the village quickly said, "Non, monsieur" and placed a hand on his chest. Kepp explained to him that the wound was serious and would require surgery. Pressure bandages had slowed the bleeding but any movement would have negative effects.

Winter ordered everyone but Kepp and his two men out of the room. When he was sure the others had gone, he told the men with him to come closer to the bed.

"The man who tried to kill me. Was he working for the Legacy Organization?"

"I think not," said the older of Winter's assistants. "Before he died he said that he wanted to kill you because it was your carelessness that caused the death of his men in California. I believe that he was sincere."

Winter was silent. They could hear the siren of the approaching ambulance.

"Has Nils been in contact?"

"No," said Doktor Kepp.

"The minute he is heard from, he must be told to come here. And Adolph Harpt must be told to come here as well. You three are my witnesses. I place Adolph Harpt in the role of chairman of Cerberus until I can return to that position. Is that understood?"

"Doktor Kepp, I ask you to make contact with Nils' uncles. You have met both Gerd and Tomas Witt?"

"Yes, Herr Winter "

"Contact them. Tell them what has been happening. I was planning to summon them to the chateau today anyway. We need them here. Have the staff make the necessary preparations."

"We will take care of this, Herr Winter. Now the doctor from the village needs to give you an injection so that you are better able to travel."

The ambulance left the estate slowly to minimize the discomfort that the slightest motion might give Winter. Doktor Kepp sent the servant girl bustling about a dozen tasks. He used Winter's desk phone to call Adolph Harpt. Harpt said that he would immediately head to the chateau.

Kepp was surprised to get no answer when he rang up Gerd Witt. According to Winter the man was virtually a recluse. It seemed strange that there was no one available to answer his call.

A male voice answered the phone when he called to Tomas Witt's home. When Kepp asked to speak with Tomas the man on the phone curtly asked him to identify himself. Kepp did so reluctantly and explained that he was calling Witt on behalf of one of his business associates.

"Herr Tomas Witt appears to have been the victim of a homicide. We will want to speak with this man that you are calling on behalf of. When will he be available to speak with us?"

Kepp told the police officer that a medical emergency would prevent them from speaking with Herr Winter for several days. The cop took down detailed contact information and requested directions to the chateau. As Kepp spoke with him, he felt his anxiety level increasing dramatically. The world seemed to be falling apart around him and Winter and the Corporation.

Kepp felt exposed. It seemed to him that the Legacy Organization was in full attack mode. Had Winter been operating at his usual level of efficiency, Cerberus would have known within hours that one of their members had died violently. Kepp knew only that something sinister had happened at Tomas' home.

He was about to have a glass of cognac when Winter's private phone rang. Kepp hesitated but hit the button on the third ring with the receiver to his ear. He noticed that his hands were shaking.

"Hello. It's Nils."

"Gott! It's Doktor Kepp. Are you nearby?"

"I'm in Northern France."

"You must come to the Chateau immediately!"

There was no response.

"Nils, Winter is seriously injured and in hospital. He has appointed Adolph Harpt as temporary chair of the Corporation. Willem Harpt is on his way here as well. Winter wants you here urgently."

"What happened to Winter?"

"The man who survived the shootout in California was briefing Winter. He had concealed a dagger in his clothing. He stabbed Winter in the shoulder. He obviously was trying for his heart."

"Are the metal detectors at the chateau no longer working, Doktor? How did he manage to bring a dagger into the chateau?"

"Bosch says it is a very unusual weapon made of ceramic. The detectors didn't pick it up."

"How badly is Winter hurt?"

"The wound is serious. He was stabbed deep in his shoulder. The cartilage is badly damaged. He will have surgery tomorrow."

"Where is the dagger the man used?"

"I have it here."

"Good. I take it the man who attacked Winter is dead?"

"Yes."

"Are the police involved?"

"No. We convinced the local doctor that Winter fell on an implement in the groundskeeper's shed while he was on a ladder looking for something."

"This man, the attacker, is he Russian?"

"East German. He was with one of their elite military units."

"Who was with Winter when he was attacked?"

"Spracker and Bosch."

"Do they think this man was working for the Legacy Organization?"

"No. They are both convinced that he attacked Winter because mistakes were made in America and many of his men were killed. He told them that as he died."

"Have my uncles been ordered to the chateau as well?"

"Winter told me to contact them to come here. So far I have not been able to reach Gerd. But Nils, when I called Tomas a policeman answered. He told me that Tomas has apparently been the victim of a homicide."

Nils remained silent on the call. Kepp thought he must be in shock. He could not see the gleeful grin on Nils face. Nils had to struggle for composure before he spoke again.

"I think you should tell Spracker and Bosch to re-evaluate their belief that Winter's attacker was simply on a mission of revenge. For God's sake, you tell me Uncle Tomas has been murdered and Winter nearly has been. This is war with the Legacy Organization!"

"Yes. I agree."

"I'll get to the chateau as soon as possible. I have been travelling carefully since the debacle in California. Clearly I must be even more careful. Hopefully I'll see you in a couple of days."

Nils ended the call before Kepp could say anything else, hung up the receiver and then fell backwards on the bed, helpless with laughter. Hanna watched him, wondering if he had suddenly become mad.

***

In the absence of Winter and in the face of the incompetence of Adolph Harpt, Doktor Kepp was being thrown into the role of leader of the Collaborative. They expected some sort of attack from the LO at any time. At Kepp's urging, Harpt had brought in additional security and the chateau had a cadre of armed guards placed discreetly on the grounds around the clock.

He had been delighted when Nils had contacted him and felt that the news about Winter and his uncle would have driven any remaining tendencies to negative behaviour directed at the Corporation. After that call, he had felt more optimistic than at any time since he was called to find Winter bleeding and unconscious in the study upstairs.

Kepp's mood improved even more when he was called to the phone and spoke with the surgeon attending to Winter. The surgery had gone well, the cartilage had been repaired to a considerable extent and with a long regime of physiotherapy, Winter should regain almost total use of his arm. The surgeon said that he was resting comfortably and would likely welcome a visitor for a short time in about twelve hours.

Kepp found Adolph Harpt and gave him the news of Winter. Harpt was clearly relieved. Kepp was rapidly concluding that Harpt did not have the capacity to run a small bicycle shop and longed for Winter to be back in control. It appeared that Harpt felt the same way.

The improved mood that Kepp was experiencing evaporated with the next telephone call he took. It was from a neighbour of Gerd Witt asking to speak with Herr Winter. Kepp convinced her to speak with him. She had little to say other than that Gerd and his housekeeper had been found murdered a day ago. Kepp ran to Adolph Harpt's room to give him the news.

* * *

Tom and Jenna spent several days getting settled in the house. They were in the study where Jenna was watching Tom unpack the last crate of edged weapons that had been brought to the house by a storage company. From time to time she asked him to explain what he was handling. Each time she asked, he gave her a complete history of the weapon. Jenna was developing a healthy respect for Tom's memory.

She asked him about the upcoming trip to Africa.

"I'll fly from Toronto to Heathrow and put up in a hotel for the night. Ed is coming up from Devon with his daughter. Our flight from London to Pretoria hopefully won't tire him out too much. The upside is that I'll have access to business centres in the airports at Heathrow and Pretoria. I can call Ing and give her some instructions on how to get to us once her mom is gone."

Jenna thought about that for a time.

"Why can't we just call her from here whenever we want to?"

"Ing was an anti-government activist before her company shipped her off to L.A. It's possible that her phone is tapped."

"Okay. But we won't be talking with her about anything subversive."

"True. But if she is under government surveillance, they will note every call she gets from a foreign country. And I'd rather not have the South African Government know that she has a Canadian connection. It was likely fine to call her last time, but by now the locals will be monitoring her. Far better for me to call her from England and Pretoria."

"Does she know her phone is tapped?"

"She'll suspect it is. Don't worry. I'll get her ready to make the dash here safely when the time comes."

Chapter Twenty-six

It was another early morning for Nils and Hanna. He told her that they would collect Angelique and then drive like mad to a town about ten miles from the chateau. Hanna and Angelique would take a hotel suite there and Nils would go on to the chateau.

When he rolled up to the gated entrance to the place, he was pleased to see that there was added security. But of course the fact that he could see the added security made him angry. He had hoped that the deaths of his two uncles would have galvanized the Collaborative into taking effective actions.

Doktor Kepp greeted him like the Prodigal Son and Nils was astonished when Adolph Harpt was obsequiously cordial as well. He was also taken aback by the barely concealed sense of panic in the two men and how their demeanour had seeped into all of the other people in the great house. Even Spracker and Bosch were affected.

Nils wanted to dramatically assert himself, so, with as many staff and Collaborative members present, he demanded to see the weapon that had laid out Winter. Kepp fetched it to him.

Nils examined it closely and then beckoned Kepp, Harpt, Spracker and Bosch to approach him.

"This is a ceramic blade, which is why it was undetected by the sensors. But see here at the tip. A hole has been drilled an inch deep. It's easy to do with a high speed drill. Once one has made a cavity, one can insert anything one wishes in there. Poison, bacteria, whatever. A tiny bit of beeswax seals it off."

"Mein Gott," said Kepp.

"Has Herr Winter developed a post-op infection?" asked Nils.

"The surgeon was on the phone a few hours ago and said the operation went well. I will call the hospital for a status report," said Kepp as he bustled off.

"The East Germans had lots of tricks up their sleeves that the Russians taught them. This is pure KGB. Stab someone in the arm with one of these loaded with the right plague and the arm falls off. Let us hope that Karl survives."

Everyone in the room, including the Harpt brothers, stood looking at Nils. After a long silence, Nils turned to Adolph Harpt.

"I understand that Winter has appointed you as chair of the collaborative. What are my tasks?"

As Nils had hoped, Harpt had not thought of any tasks for him. Everyone in the room watched as Harpt stumbled out the need for a meeting as soon as Nils had settled into the chateau. Nils told him that there was no time for settling in and proposed that he and the Harpts meet immediately. The two brothers followed him into Winter's office.

***

Tom drove Audrey and Jenna to the Four Seasons hotel in Toronto and made sure they were settled in before leaving for the airport. Audrey was pleased that they were staying so close to the central library and the University of Toronto. She handed Jenna a notebook and began to list the things they would be doing during the next several days.

***

Tom got to his hotel near Heathrow in the late evening. The flight from Toronto to London had taken over nine hours. He called Ed's daughter.

"I'm finding this hard. We're here in the hotel, Tom. The drive up tired Dad out. He's sleeping now."

"I don't know what to say, Sara. Other than we're all doing what we can to meet his last wishes."

"It's so hard to let him go. See you in the morning, Tom."

***

Arnon was surprised when Jenna's boss called him to say she had received a letter of resignation from Jenna Van Velt. He asked if he could see the letter and the woman agreed immediately. Arnon went to the building where Jenna worked.

The letter was short and to the point. Van Velt apologized for not providing adequate notice of her resignation, which she indicated was for personal reasons. Van Velt's boss was reluctant to give him a copy of the letter because of company policy. She was happy to let him have the envelope it had arrived in.

Arnon was headed back to his office to call Jim Curtiss when a thought struck him. He drove to the apartment building where he and Jules had interviewed Van Velt. As he had expected, her name was no longer on the call panel in the lobby. Arnon buzzed the superintendent of the building and they had a short conversation.

He went to his office and called Curtiss.

"Jim. I've just read Jenna Van Velt's letter of resignation. And talked to her former landlord."

"Really? Interesting that she bothered to resign."

"Or maybe she's being coached by somebody who is good at disappearing."

"I'm not following you, Nick."

"If she hadn't resigned it is possible that her employer or her co-workers might have reported her as a missing person. That would have given us license to plaster her picture everywhere. That would make it much harder for her to travel."

"Good point. You're right. Her travelling companion is coaching her."

"The landlord got a letter from her as well. The building she was in only will do a month-by-month arrangement with their tenants for the first year. Helps them get rid of any riffraff, the super said. Anyway, he got a letter from her with a check paying up to the end of August but with instructions to let a particular moving company in to remove her belongings. That took place three days ago."

"Your guys didn't notice anything?"

"I haven't had anybody watching the place for days, Jim. Budget wouldn't permit it. But even if I had someone there, it's not likely they would have learned anything. They would have just seen guys loading a truck with stuff from one of a hundred apartments in the building."

"True."

"For what it's worth, I've got the envelope from her resignation letter. It's got a Mexican stamp and postmark on it. Her super didn't keep the envelope from the letter she sent him, but he said it had come from Mexico. Clearly that's where they want us to look for them."

"Did he have anything to say about the movers who picked up her stuff?"

"Only one of them spoke English. The super figured that the crew were illegals like most of our labour force in this city. The guy gave him a note signed by Van Velt and he had the keys for the apartment so the super let them clear it out."

"She's getting good advice on how to make stuff like this happen."

"How much longer are you going to be at Bayfield?"

"We're packing up all our shit now and will pull out tomorrow morning. We interviewed the Brown woman again and got nothing new. There's no point in us hanging around here any longer."

"The whole mess is going cold on us, isn't it?"

***

Ed got early boarding status. Tom had hired a nurse to travel with them and by pre-arrangement she went to sit beside Ed. Tom had fed Ed a line about them not being able to get three seats together and said his 'girlfriend' would sit by Ed.

They were somewhere over the Sahara when Tom went forward and tapped the nurse on her shoulder. Ed was dozing and didn't even realize that the nurse had left his side.

"How did that go?" asked Tom.

"He's doing okay. I went over the package of meds he has with him. There are some strong narcotics that should keep him going for the next few days."

The nurse went down the aisle to her seat and Tom slid carefully into the seat beside Ed. Tom was staring at the back of the seat ahead of him, lost in thought.

"What the hell kind of airline is this?" said Ed. "I doze off sitting beside a beautiful young woman and I wake up beside a dangerous-looking bastard."

"How are you bearing up?"

"I've got a few days left in me. Where are we?"

"Probably at the south edge of the Sahara. Couple of hours left before we land in Pretoria."

"Can't come too soon. I'm looking forward to stretching out for a while. I get tired sitting or standing. It's pathetic."

"It's what's to be expected, my friend. Not that that makes it right."

"That's a lovely young lady you've brought along, Tom. I like her. I'm kind of surprised she's who you picked for this job."

"How so?"

"Well, old son, she either plays things close to her chest or she has no military or paramilitary background."

"Christ, Ed! We're not making a raid on Zimbabwe. She's along to make us look like a happy little family group. We're going to avoid trouble. That's why we're going in through Bierbridge. All the old hands from the bush war are on the eastern border or in Harare getting fat. Nobody is going to recognize either of us down south."

"I hope you're right. Ben Harris doesn't think it will be that easy."

Tom questioned Ed intently for the next hour and realized that the crazy old bastard had set him up.

Chapter Twenty-seven

They got Ed settled into his hotel room in Pretoria and Tom took the nurse to a bar for a drink.

"What's your best guess for how long he's got left?"

"A few days at most. He's living on adrenalin. The drugs he's brought will help."

Tom gave the nurse a good deal of cash and wished her godspeed back to England. He checked in on Ed again and then took a cab to a business center at the railway station to call Ing.

***

Jenna felt like she was back in school. Audrey was an absolute dictator when it came to research. The central library was undergoing a major overhaul of its catalogue system. Audrey took one look at the array of keyboards and monitors and beckoned to Jenna.

"I am far too old to be expected to use these television things, Jenna. You are at the perfect age to take on some adult learning. You can figure how to work them."

"I hate computers, Audrey."

"I know you do, dear, which makes it a noble thing you're about to do."

"Crap, Audrey, this is going to be painful!"

"There are many ways to accomplish a task, Jenna. If you were to unfasten the top button of your blouse and ask that young man sitting at that desk over there for some help, you will be through your assignment before I am."

***

Sam Allen was placing calls to the other members of the LO on a regular basis to coordinate the information flow. His first call was to Chuck Holt.

"What the news from Capetown?"

"Stoller's mother is still hanging on. She's following her usual routine, which the watchers like. Got her foot cut in some sort of street riot that she blundered into, but otherwise it's all good. The stuff we planted on the dead guys at the cottage is having its effect. There are a hell of a lot of Winter's associates in the States that are having awkward conversations with the FBI."

"Alright. I will be talking with Daniel and Franz right away. If they have anything important I know where to reach you."

***

"Gutentag."

"Franz, Sam here. Things are good with the Stoller woman. Any sign of Witt or Spader?"

"Neither Daniel or I have found out anything. But I have what is possibly very important news. There are rumours that we're trying to confirm that Tomas Witt has been found dead at his home."

"Found dead? How did he get that way?"

"That's what we're trying to find out. Certainly neither Daniel nor I have sanctioned any actions of that nature."

"Alright. Find out what you can. I take it you and Daniel are in close touch now?"

"We're talking regularly. Sam, has there been any word from Joachim Maarten?"

"No. I reached out to him through a mutual acquaintance. He hasn't seen fit to contact me."

"I guess the bastard is still getting a significant amount of his income from Cerberus Corporation."

***

Once they were sequestered in Winter's office, Nils addressed Adolph Harpt.

"Well, Herr Harpt. I assume that you have called this meeting to address what steps we must take to counter all the mayhem that the Legacy Organization is wreaking on us."

Nils' statement was helpful to Harpt since he didn't have any idea why he had called the meeting. He knew only that there was a great need to take some sort of steps to make the nightmare that he was trapped in stop.

"Yes," Adolph said. "We must take steps to stop these attacks by the Legacy people."

"I say we kill all of the bastards," said Ernst. "Especially that swine Sterling."

"That seems like an excellent plan to me," said Nils to Ernst. "How do you plan to kill Daniel Sterling?"

That question brought on a prolonged period of silence. Finally Nils spoke.

"Herr Harpt," he said, addressing Adolph again. "Would I be correct in assuming that both of you gentlemen are somewhat rusty on planning and organizing covert activities? You know. Arsons. Assassinations. Car bombs. That sort of thing."

The Harpt brothers agreed that they had been away from that kind of work for a long time.

"I would like to propose a division of labour for the next few weeks," said Nils. "I suggest that I take charge of everything we need to do that will happen outside of the walls of this estate. You two take charge of the security arrangements here, you handle the business affairs of the Corporation, and you receive and distribute the intelligence that is gathered by the network that Winter has put into place."

The brothers were trying to think that proposal through when Nils presented them with something else to mull over.

"During the whole history of Cerberus Corporation, whatever initiatives were being undertaken, we have always worked on the principle of mixed family teams. For the last few years it has predominately been a Winter/Witt effort. I know that there was a time when your father worked closely with mine for some years. That was during some of the Collaborative's early work in Africa. Am I correct on this?"

Ernst Harpt spoke up in agreement.

"I think, Herr Harpt, that we should maintain that principle. Do you agree?"

Adolph nodded his head, but his face registered confusion.

"Each of you gentlemen has one son. Thus far, because of the early death of my father, I am the only full member of the Corporation of the new generation. I would like to suggest that your sons begin their apprenticeship in anticipation of their joining Cerberus in the future. I further propose that Herr Winter's nephew, who he has designated as his family's future representative, be summoned to become involved. That way, your sons can work with me in the field, Winter's nephew can work here with you, and we preserve the principle of mixed family teams."

"I believe that to be workable suggestion," said Ernst before Adolph could respond. Ernst deeply distrusted Nils and had been trying to think of a way to not allow him to have a free hand. Nils had just solved that problem for him.

Adolph had also been trying to think of some ways to keep some control on Nils. He readily accepted the suggestion as well.

"How long will it take your sons to get here?" asked Nils, knowing full well that Ernst's son was on a prolonged holiday, surfing in Australia.

"I'm sure that both of our boys can be here in five days," said Adolph.

Nils frowned when he heard that and muttered about the delay at least giving him time to do some preparatory work.

"Will you be contacting Winter's nephew?" Nils asked Adolph.

"Yes, of course. I am going to the hospital to visit Karl in an hour and I'll mention this to him. Then I'll call young Andrieas."

"It's a pity that neither of my uncles had sons," said Nils. "It appears that I'll be the last Witt to serve in the Collaborative."

The Harpt brothers were feeling more comfortable now that there was a plan and there seemed to be some sort of control mechanism shaping up that would not see Nils running amok.

"You will find a girl with good big hips and make some sons, Nils," said Ernst.

Adolph thought the concept of Nils breeding was the most appalling thing he had heard since he had been notified of the death of the two senior Witts.

"Herr Harpt. As chair of the Corporation you are the one who directs our intelligence operations. I have a good many questions for Joachim Maarten. Should I route them through you or will you speak with Joachim so that I can deal directly with him? There is a great deal of work to be done if we are to move against the Legacy Organization."

Adolph did not like the phrase, "a great deal of work." He hurriedly agreed to call Maarten and arrange for him to work directly with Nils.

The Harpts felt the meeting had gone extremely well and were somewhat confident for the first time in days. Nils left the meeting looking very serious and managed to maintain that façade until he got to his room. Once inside the bedroom, with the door locked, he burst into laughter and repeatedly punched the mattress of his bed. When his composure had returned, he left the estate to call Hanna Spader.

"How are you and your guest getting along?"

"Splendidly. Our suite is very comfortable, the room service is excellent, and Angelique is enjoying being pampered. She is quite an aficionado of bad soap operas though."

"This must be hard for you."

"I shall soldier on, Nils. Angelique has said that our time together is rather like a prolonged pyjama party. I'll have to take her word for it since I have never been to such an event."

"I think you'd like to attend one," said Nils. "Is she becoming compliant?"

"Oh, Nils. You are again the object of her affection and desire. She sees me as your business associate. Earlier today, after she had bathed, I gave her a leisurely pedicure. She became quite flirty. I tried to strike a balance between friend and lustful older woman. Which was difficult, Nils, because she let her bathrobe fall open and she was wearing only white cotton panties."

"You are truly a paragon," said Nils.

"She is in the exercise room now. She says she is about to ovulate. I think we will remain only friends until tomorrow night. Then, after a bit of wine, I'll show her just how good a friend I can be."

"She is a lucky girl!"

"Now tell me. How has your day been so far?"

"Better than expected. The Harpts are dithering fools and have put me in charge of all of the outside operations. Winter was stabbed with a ceramic knife tipped with something nasty so he is not out of the woods, and I have been given direct access to the Corporation's intelligence source."

"Well done, Nils! Could things be any better?"

"Things are better, Hanna. The Harpts have given me their sons and they are bringing Winter's nephew into the estate to work with them. "

***

The trip north went well. Ed's medication seemed to be working and he did not tire as quickly as he had on the flight. He talked endlessly about the days in Rhodesia before the Bush War began. Tom regretted that he had not seen the Country when it was in a state of peace.

They were about an hour south of the Zimbabwe border when Ed began to search his pockets and shift in his seat.

"What's up Ed? Forget your condoms?"

"No, you young smartass!"

He kept searching and finally took a small lavender coloured sheet of paper out of the chest pocket of his shirt and handed it to Tom.

"This is pretty," said Tom. "Are you inviting me to the prom, Ed?"

"You're an asshole! And now you're an asshole with a Swiss bank account."

"Say again."

"My share of the loot from Pinatubo, Tom. I figured that you would be too busy shagging Canadian girls so I marketed it. It was easier to do it in Europe because that's where the high-end dealers are."

"How did you make out, Ed?"

"I got a couple hundred grand over thirty-two million U.S."

"Glad to see that you're still a fucking bandit."

"I gave each of my girls four million, Tom. Made 'em swear that they'd keep the money secret from their husbands. The other sixteen million is in a bank in Switzerland. This paper tells you which bank and how to get at the money."

"Thank you, Ed. As you know, I've always preferred high end hookers."

"As I said before, you're an asshole."

They drove in silence for a time and then Ed spoke again.

"You know me as a man who wants value for money, don't you, Tom?"

"Absolutely. You're the only guy I've ever known who had a herd of five udder cows."

"And you must have thought that I was getting senile when I told you that I'd invited Ben Harris along on our trip?"

"Something like that."

"Have you ever thought that I might be checking my investment?"

"Checking your investment?"

"There's sixteen million dollars that you can now access. On that slip of paper are also instructions of how to get into a safe deposit box in a bank in near Heathrow. There is a list of ways I want you to use the money."

"Okay. We talked about that right after we divvied up the Pinatubo booty."

"This trip is a test for you, Tom. I wanted to see if you still have what it takes to carry through on what I want done. I'm keen to see how you manage to pull off getting me to where I'm going."

"You realize that this test of yours might just prevent that from happening."

"Tom. If you get me inside the border of Zimbabwe, I'm happy. If some Zimbabwean soldier shoots and kills me a hundred yards inside the border, I'm happy. You're talking to a man who is going to be dead in forty-eight hours, one way or another. I want to know before I die, if you are still a Selous Scout."

They drove in silence until they were twenty minutes from the border crossing.

"Alright, Ed. Let's not fuck this up. What's your name, what's your relationship to me, where have you been living in Canada for the last ten years, and whose wedding are we going to and where is it?"

Bierbridge was as Tom had expected it would be. The border security people were young and bored. The young man who checked their passports became animated when he saw that they were from Canada. He had a lot of questions about the country and said that he hoped to live there in the future. He asked about the winter.

"Have you ever been to the top of Kilimanjaro?" asked Tom.

"Yes"

"The Canadian winter is like the weather at the top of Kilimanjaro, often for three solid months."

The man gave them back their papers and they passed through the border point without incident. Except, Tom thought, he left behind a young man who regarded him as an outrageous liar.

***

Adolph Harpt returned from his visit to Karl Winter thoroughly rattled. He had expected to find Winter improving. Instead, he was running a high fever and the medical staff were earnestly assuring him that Herr Winter was receiving the best care. When normally arrogant doctors became solicitous and earnest, Adolph knew it was time to worry. Adolph had tried to talk with Winter, but Karl was speaking gibberish.

Nils had spent an hour in Winter's office speaking with Joachim Maarten, the freelance Intelligence specialist that the Corporation used frequently. Maarten knew that Nils did a good deal of operational work for Cerberus. He was intrigued by the questions that Nils was asking and the information he wanted. They were close to wrapping up the call when Nils posed a last question.

"Do we, at this point in time, know where each of the members of the Legacy Organization is?"

"We do not. Franz Von Hesse and his wife flew to Pearson airport in Canada a couple of days ago. Our best information is that they immediately boarded a chartered float plane. We believe that they have gone to somewhere in New York State."

"And the others?"

"Charles Holt was last seen in California. He may still be there but it is unlikely since he doubtlessly arranged for the group that attacked you and the Spaders. Our estimate is that he had gone to one of his homes. The one in Texas, perhaps. We have no idea, as usual, where Sam Allen might be. And trying to get any handle on the two Americans is now virtually impossible since your supporters over there are being mercilessly shaken down."

"And finally, Joachim, where is that grave digger Sterling?"

"Given what has happened to your uncles, we believe that he is in Germany."

"Please respond to the requests I've given you, and do try to find Sterling before he finds us."

"Yes, Herr Witt."

Chapter Twenty-eight

The most recent meeting of the Legacy Organization had left all of the members feeling depressed and edgy. They decided that Daniel would go to Europe first. Franz would go back to Germany in two days, giving Daniel lots of time to put the necessary security arrangements in place.

Sam would go back to the States and take charge of things there while continuing to be the communications hub. The steps that Chuck had set in motion in the States to hamper the allies of the Corporation were having an enormously positive impact. Sam needed to be in his home in Alexandria, Virginia, where he had optimal access to communications and politicians. His main goal was to ensure that the influence of Cerberus Corporation in the United States would be entirely destroyed.

Chuck and Claudio had the big jobs for the moment. Claudio would continue to have his teams pillage and raze the archives of South Africa. He main task was to engage two former members of the South African 7 Medical Battalion Group who were eager to leave the country and settle somewhere on a different continent. Both of those men had assured Claudio that they could tell him exactly what Winter had brought to their projects after he had been ejected from the LO's work in Namibia.

Chuck would go to South Africa as well. His visit there had a twofold purpose. He would take over the surveillance and eventual abduction of Ing Stoller. And he would conduct an assessment of how unstable the situation in South Africa was likely to become.

***

Ing's mother went down quickly. Her brothers had been badgering her for weeks to move their mother to a hospital. Ing's mother liked the idea of dying at home but had expressed the view that perhaps the people in the hospital would take better care of her. Ing, making sure that all the homecare people were present, caved in to her brothers' arguments. The homecare workers were dismissed and her mother was transferred to the hospital by ambulance.

The watchers that Claudio had put in place were dismayed and immediately contacted his executive assistant to tell her what had happened. His executive assistant was up to her ass in alligators, handling expenses and travel vouchers for five teams of people moving around the world. As she had been instructed, she gave them the number of Chuck Holt's Executive Assistant.

Chuck had planned to call his EA to tell her that there would be a bunch of new people calling her from Capetown. He had been so caught up with hounding the Cerberus people in the States that he forgot to make the call. His EA was unprepared for the call and a very big intelligence lapse occurred for the Legacy Organization.

***

The first of the new generation of the Collaborative to arrive at the chateau was Tony Harpt. Nils was appalled when he met him. The young man was a pallid, untoned, two hundred and forty pound monster.

Joachim Maarten was feeding him useful intelligence. The assault on all things Cerberus in the United States was continuing unabated. Nils didn't give it much thought.

"Do you have any idea where the members of the Legacy Organization are?" asked Nils.

"To some degree. Sam Allen is at his principle residence in Virginia. Not good news because that is where he conducts his most intensive business."

"Charles Holt is in South Africa. Pretoria, actually. We'll try to find out what he's doing there."

"Any sign of that motherfucker Sterling?"

"No."

"He must be found," said Nils. "He's just taken out two of my uncles, one of my Aunts, a housemaid, and whatever the fuck the woman who lived with Ernst was. By the way, has it been determined how Gerd's wife and maid died?"

"There was a lot of non-consensual sexual activity. No semen. Gerd's wife was whipped. Brutally. It appears that there were three women involved. One them obviously an assailant. That worries me. The two women died by electrocution. The cord of a table lamp was applied to their bodies. They were found in sexually explicit positions. Each of the women had a glass eye, the type used by taxidermists, inserted into her vagina. It would appear that their killer had visited your uncle Gerd prior to assaulting them."

"Appalling," said Nils. "Why does it worry you that there was a female assailant?"

"That is not how Sterling works. He does his best to spare women and children."

"Well," said Nils. "We all alter our methodologies by necessity. I want whoever you have available to carefully watch Sterling's home. I need to know the moment we confirm that he is actually there."

***

Teresa was giving Arnon's chest what she called butterfly kisses when his phone rang. She reluctantly moved from being astride him to let him pick up the phone. It was Jim Curtiss.

"How was your call with our European cousins, Jim?"

"Very fucking intense, Nick. Ever heard of the Cerberus Corporation or the Legacy Organization?"

"Nope. Sounds sort of John LeCarre-ish."

"You got that right. There were times on this last call where I thought that Ian Fleming may have written INTERPOL's script. An ex-Marine named Chuck Holt is possibly a member of the Legacy Organization. It's almost for sure that Lars Negan, the guy who arranged for the phony gang rape of the girl out in the Woods, is actually a German named Nils Witt."

"This Witt guy is in this Legacy outfit too?"

"Nope. He's with the Cerberus guys. And the two organizations don't get along. In fact, in a thirty-six hour period in Europe, two of the key members of the Cerberus Corporation were murdered, as was the wife and housemaid of one of the guys, the live-in poke of the other guy, and the number one man of the corporation is in hospital, maybe dying, because somebody stabbed him."

"So it would have been the Legacy guys who shot the hell out of the Cerberus guys up in cottage country."

"It looks that way."

"Anything we can do on our end?"

"We'll have a Federal warrant to go over the Van Velt woman's cottage with a very fine-toothed comb. I'm sending my best team out there. Would you be willing to go out there, give them a detailed rundown on what you saw and what you know about the Van Velt woman?"

"Tell me when and I'll try to clear it with my Captain."

"Trust me, Nick, that won't be a problem."

"Want me to bring Teresa? She was with me when we watched the cottage a few days before the shooting started."

"Please do. My people want every scrap of memory that either of you have."

"When?"

"Tomorrow."

Curtiss gave Arnon the name of a hotel where the FBI had already taken a block of rooms and gave him the name of the team leader.

Arnon hung up the phone and said, "Pack your vacation clothes, Teresa. The FBI is giving us an all expenses paid trip to cottage country."

***

Nils was an avid student of human nature. He was not surprised at how quickly the Harpt brothers lapsed into complacency once they thought they had a plan and that their own skins were not in danger. Andrieas Winter was easily handling any of the work that the brothers should have been doing.

Tony Harpt would have been a problem had Nils actually needed him to do anything. Nils thought of him as a beef cow. A bit of a nuisance to have around, but worth keeping close when the time to slaughter came. It was his understanding that Simon Harpt was a very different type of creature.

Spracker and Bosch had been resentful when Andrieas had appeared out of nowhere and became their boss. Nils let their anger fester until there were a couple of scenes of insubordination between the two older men and the younger Winter. He stepped in with the suggestion that Spracker and Bosch join his 'outside' team. Andrieas was quick to accept the offer to be rid of the two of them, and while the other two men didn't care for Nils, working with him seemed to be the lesser of two evils.

He took great pleasure in sending Spracker off with the Harpt boy to kill James Stuart.

***

Arnon and Teresa drove out to Bayfield the next morning. The FBI team leader met them in the lobby of the hotel. After talking with him for fifteen minutes, Arnon decided he would be good to work with. The FBI had rooms arranged for both of them.

Arnon and Teresa drove out to the cottage with the team leader. The overgrown end of the laneway had been considerably trimmed back and when they got closer to the cottage, Arnon understood why. The FBI had brought along a lot of their toys including a couple of mammoth portable labs. There were a lot of people milling around the area by the cottage.

Once they had been introduced, they were asked to stand by until the profiler was ready to speak with them. They were invited to visit the evidence tents but were told to touch nothing.

***

Spracker enjoyed the drive to the place where Stuart was working. Tony Harpt was inexperienced, naïve and frightened. Spracker was seldom in the company of someone of lesser intellect than he, so he was making the most of it. He regaled the young man with stories of the various killings he had taken part in.

Nils had assured Spracker that the minimal security Winter had arranged for Stuart had been paid and sent away. Spracker had been provided with a key to the rear door of the house. He was armed with a silenced, long barrelled Colt revolver. When they stepped into the small back entry of the house, music by AC/DC was blaring from a stereo somewhere. Young Tony Harpt thought the place was appalling.

Spracker could move surprisingly lithely for his size. He went from room to room, moving toward the front of the house. The music grew louder as they approached the door of a brightly lit room. Cigarette smoke hung in the air.

Tony was suddenly grabbed by Spracker who made a shush sign and then directed him to look into the brightly lit room. Tony saw a young man, perhaps twenty, sitting back on a sofa. He was naked from the waist down and his legs were wide apart. A fully clothed man was kneeling in front of him with his mouth on the younger man's crotch.

Spracker pulled Tony back and grinning widely gave him a thumbs-up sign. He braced himself against the doorjamb of the room and spent moments taking careful aim with his pistol. When he fired there was a slight popping sound and the beginning of a scream. Spracker fired again and the scream was cut off.

"Come and learn, young Tony," said Spracker.

"See here. The first round severed Stuart's spinal cord at the base of his skull. The Colt fires a heavy round so it also castrated the young man that Stuart had probably paid a great deal of money to blow. The second round blew most of the young man's brains into the cushion of the sofa. That's how it's done, young man."

Tony Harpt puked over the table holding computer equipment while Spracker poured gasoline in liberal amounts around the living room and then down the stairs to the basement of the house. There were many empty Perrier bottles in the kitchen. Spracker filled one with gasoline, stuffed the neck with some cloth from the discarded underwear of the young man and set it alight. He smashed a window from outside of the house into the main room.

"Stay here until you hear me start the car," said Spracker. "Then throw that into the house and run like hell."

The gasoline fumes had built up so the kid was covered in glass shards when he dove into the car. He had a lot of small cuts on his face and hands. Spracker told him that it would make him stronger.

They drove forty miles from Stuart's house and Spracker found a phone.

"The computer man is dead," said Spracker.

"Good. I wish I had something else for you, but we've not confirmed that Sterling is at his home. Call me again in twelve hours. Remain out of sight until then," said Nils.

Chapter Twenty-nine

Teresa was called in to talk with the profiler first. Arnon spent some time talking with one of the CSIs about the significance of a bit of dyed feather that had been found near the cottage. The CSI was convinced that it had come from an arrow.

Arnon spent an intensive hour with the profiler and looked for Teresa when his debriefing session was over. He found her outside of one of the evidence tents. Teresa told Nick that she had something to show him and led him to the tables where the techs were laying out the items from the two bedrooms of the cottage.

Arnon was bemused. There was a wide selection of dildos and other sex toys on the table surrounded by all manner of skimpy lingerie. Arnon counted four sets of padded handcuffs, several gags and blindfolds and a wooden bar with leather straps on it.

"What the hell is that?" he asked, pointing at the wooden bar.

"That's the very question that I posed to one of the techs. It is a leg spreader. It's used to ensure that one's sexual partner keeps everything available, all the time."

"Jesus Christ!"

"Notice the wide selection of lubricants and oils. I must say that I didn't know that there are so many flavours to be had."

"Now I understand why there was no TV in cottage."

"Yes, they obviously found ways to occupy themselves. "

Teresa pointed out a large bottle half full of clear liquid.

"This is a special warming personal lubricant. The label says it will set your lover on fire when applied to his or her genitals. Judging by the state of some of the bed sheets, it was applied generously to someone. There are two different sets of prints on the bottle."

Arnon stood staring at the table, trying to reconcile what he was seeing with what he knew about Jenna Van Velt.

"The profiler is going to have some thinking to do when he sees this stuff."

"At least it's going to be easy to find out where they've gone now," said Teresa.

"How so?"

"All the FBI has to do now is call every sex shop in a four state radius and find out which had a couple come in and drop three grand on toys and lube."

"I love it when you say toys and lube in the same sentence."

***

An orderly at the hospital where Winter was being treated was placing calls on a regular basis to Maarten, keeping him up to date on the man's condition. The orderly wasn't overly bright but he knew when doctors were worried. They were clearly worried about Karl Winter's postoperative infection.

Maarten was an intelligence professional and he knew that to be effective, he had to know as much about what his employers were doing as he did about what their enemies were involved in. Karl Winter would have been outraged if he knew how much of the money he provided to Maarten was spent on keeping tabs on the Cerebus Corporation. But Maarten was effective at monitoring the secretive Legacy Organization as well.

Franz Von Hesse was the LO member that Maarten devoted the most resources to. His very public life and playboy lifestyle made it easy to have people monitoring his activities. Among Maarten's retainers were a number of paparazzi.

It happened that one of them was dogging Franz Von Hesse as he arrived at a charity gala in Berlin. The photographer was very close to Von Hesse when what he described as a good looking older broad grabbed Von Hesse's arm and held on fast. The photographer said that Von Hesse looked like he had seen a ghost.

The photographer caught enough of the short conversation Von Hesse had with the woman to learn that she and a man named Walter had the formulas and that they must be used to stop the dreadful epidemic in Africa. Von Hesse had leaned close to her and said something that caused her to let go of his arm. The photographer had gotten several close and clear photos of the woman and had heard Von Hesse tell her to get back to Holland immediately.

Maarten had arranged to pay the photographer handsomely for his information and photos. And had ensured that the young man died of a heroin overdose two days later. He still enjoyed thinking about Winter's reaction, over two years ago, when he first showed him the photos of Gerta Ten Haan.

The scar on Winter's face that engorged and reddened when he was angry had instantly become livid when Maarten had walked into his study and one after another, laid the photos on his desk. By the time he had placed the sixth photo down, he was alarmed that the scar tissue would explode. Instead, Winter did.

"That whore. That filthy whore. I had so hoped that she would have died a painful death by now."

"We've spoken of this woman and her friend Erich Krohl. Which of them do you hate the most?"

"This bitch! Only because Krohl has to have died by now."

"I am sorry to give you more distressing news, Herr Winter, but you still have to prioritize whom you hate most. Krohl is still alive and I will soon know where both he and Ten Haan are hiding." It had taken no persuading on the part of Maarten to have Winter write him a very large check and in the subsequent months he had earned many more such checks. He was sad when he finally gave Winter Gerta Ten Haan's address in the Woods.

***

Ing's mother died at 2:21 a.m. Ing and her brothers were with her to the end. When a doctor had pronounced her gone, Ing had said she was going outside for a cigarette. Her brothers and their wives did not notice her pick up a large backpack that had been on the floor of her mother's room.

There was a post box near the elevators on each floor of the hospital. Ing dropped an envelope addressed to her oldest brother in the post box as she waited for the elevator and then rode down to the basement of the hospital. She took a corridor that led to the employees' entrance at the rear of the building. As she had expected, a couple of cabs were waiting outside for a fare.

As Ing rode away from the hospital, her 'close' watcher, a nurses' aide who was glad to pick up a little extra money from Claudio's man, was on the phone to his assistant informing her that Ing's mother had died. He told her to stay close to Ing and to call him the minute it looked like Stoller was going to leave the hospital. He tried to get in touch with Chuck Holt's people.

The aide had not noticed Ing's backpack and didn't panic when Ing was not in her mother's room. The aide thought it perfectly natural that Ing had gone outside for a smoke. She had noticed that the Stoller woman was becoming a more frequent smoker as her mother's condition worsened.

The aide's first moment of concern was when the two sons of the dead woman and their wives came out of the room and walked toward the elevators. Ing Stoller was not with them. The aide stepped up and expressed her condolences. She asked them if their sister was all right. One of the brothers said that she was outside smoking.

The aide rushed to a phone and called Holt's man.

"She is outside smoking. Her brothers are going downstairs now to leave."

Claudio's man used a CB radio to alert the snatch team.

"She's outside smoking. Take her now."

In less than ten minutes the leader of the team called Claudio's man to say that there was no sign of the Stoller woman outside the hospital. Claudio's guy rushed to the hospital and confronted the aide. She could tell him only that Stoller's brother had said she had gone out for a smoke after her mother died. The man waited until he was outside of the hospital to start cursing. By then, Ing was half way to the airport.

***

Jenna was nearly finished pulling articles that she had identified when Audrey found her.

"Did you know that Brazil fought alongside our armies during the Second World War?"

"Have you been sniffing white-out, Audrey?"

"The mysterious Brazilian who visited the camp with William Allen was an army Colonel who commanded some aircraft in Italy. He and Allen became good friends during the war. His name is Mendez and his family is one of the richest in South America. How are you making out?"

"I should be done here soon and then I can start photocopying stuff. That'll take an hour."

"I got everything I could from here and I told the staff to copy what I need. You can pay for that when you finish your copying. I'm going over to the university library. We'll meet back at the hotel and start organizing things. Have you found much on the German man?"

"The Von Hesse family came through the war with most of their wealth intact and they weren't close to Hitler's crowd, so they did very well post-war."

"That Von in the names tells me that the family is older than dirt and richer than most kings."

"Yep. They make their dough in pharmaceuticals and electronics manufacturing and give just enough of it away to seem like they care about the hoi polloi."

"I'll see you at the hotel. Get us some wine, Jenna. We're going to need it."

***

Sam was becoming tired. At most times the work of the Legacy organization had required a comparatively small amount of his energy. That had changed and the effort he was putting into the organization was taking a toll on him.

He was deeply troubled by the calls that he had been receiving on a regular basis from Claudio. The Legacy organization was learning the magnitude of the South African's covert bio and chemical warfare efforts. Claudio was also able to paint him an increasingly clear picture of the epidemic that was sweeping through South West Africa.

Most disturbing was the evidence that Claudio was finding concerning the work of Karl Winter and the suspicion that his companies had likely been bankrolling some of the work of the South African researchers. As Claudio had said at the last meeting, the South Africans had been indiscriminate about what documents they chose to hang on to. Claudio was bribing officials and stealing everything he could get his hands on that pertained to the bio warfare projects in the country.

Franz was not providing encouraging news from Europe either. Someone - Sam suspected the South Africans - had launched a wholesale assault on the families of the Collaborative. The hits they had taken in Europe coupled with what Chuck Holt had unleashed against them in the States must have the remaining members shaken to their core. Sam wondered what would happen if Karl Winter did not recover from his injury. He dearly wanted to hear from Joachim Maarten.

***

Ing bought the first flight she could for the 'new world'. It was to Cancun. She was nervous while waiting in the departures area for the call to board the flight. She needn't have been.

The leader of the people watching her still had a crew at her home. After two hours had passed with no sign of her there, he sent teams to the airport and the railway station. Ing's plane was taxiing by the time the people pursuing her entered the terminal.

He sent his cleaners into her office area and established that she was not at work. One of her co-workers there told one of the cleaners that she would likely be on bereavement leave for a few days. The leader of the watchers had to fight back nausea as he dialed the number for Chuck Holt.

***

Each day that slipped by with no news of the whereabouts of Jenna Van Velt increased Sam's anxiety level. He was questioning his decision to not have Holt's team grab her right after Gerta's murder. Sam was anxious to hear from Holt and Sterling. Holt called first.

"Sam. What's up?"

"There's a lot going everywhere. I need to know what's up with you, buddy. Do you still have a line on the Stoller witch?"

There was a pause.

"We've temporarily lost track of her, Sam. Her mother died and she took off."

"Of course she did, Chuck. She had probably been briefed by Van Velt's new boyfriend."

"You're pissed, aren't you?"

"You're fucking right I am, Chuck! The Stoller woman was our link to Van Velt."

"Sorry, Bud. I'll follow up on this Stoller thing big time."

Sam was gone from the line quickly. Chuck Holt felt like he needed to kick some serious butt and he knew he should start with his own.

Chapter Thirty

When Jenna and Audrey returned to their hotel after a fifth day of work in the libraries, Tom was waiting for them in the lobby. Jenna was glad she was wearing sunglasses because her eyes teared up when she saw him. Audrey spoke sharply to him.

"I've been watching the BBC news, Tom. I take it that you have been responsible for creating the latest havoc in Zimbabwe?"

"That's not a topic I'd talk about in the lobby of a crowded hotel."

Audrey made a sniffing sound and marched off to her room. "I'll pack and meet you two down here in thirty minutes," she said.

The first part of the trip home was silent. Once Tom got them clear of the city traffic, Audrey asked him question after question about what had transpired in Africa. Jenna was shocked at what Tom told them. Audrey, once she had established that the people who had died were some of the most vicious terrorists from the bush war, changed the topic and told Tom what they had learned about the men who had visited Namibia.

"So in conclusion, Mr. Robbins, these men are all from families that have been filthy rich for a long time. They all appear to have friends in extremely high places. And most telling of all is that none of our research has yielded even a hint of something called the Legacy Organization."

They dropped Audrey at her home and headed for their place. As soon as Tom turned off the road to the laneway, Jenna unbuttoned her shirt and took off her bra. She was completely naked by the time Tom parked the jeep in front of the house. Tom gave her a bemused look and then stripped off himself.

"I do remember Canadian winters, Tom. I think we should spend as much time as we can in this state."

She got no argument from Tom.

Tom had grabbed a beer for him and a glass of wine for her and had gone outside. She found him seated on the front porch, reading his mail.

"Anything interesting?" Jenna asked.

"Gary, my buddy who helped me out in Zimbabwe, has safely got to Australia. So far the Zimbabweans haven't placed him with Ed and me."

"Did you really kill over twenty men?"

"Actually, I didn't fire my rifle or sidearm at all. I lobbed one rocket into the truck that had a heavy machine gun on it. Gary tripped some claymore mines and Ed and Ben did most of the shooting."

"Does that make you believe your hands are clean in all this?"

"Interesting civilian-type question. You pose it as though I should be losing sleep about the deaths of those guys in Zimbabwe. To be clear, I wouldn't have gone back to take them out on my own get-go. But I didn't object strongly when I realized what old Ed had drawn me in to."

"That seems really fucked up to me, Tom."

"I'm sure it does. To put it into perspective, if you had twenty Aunt Gertas and every one of them died the same way that she did, at the hands of the same people, how would you feel about getting a little payback?"

"I don't know."

"And that is the only answer you could give. Because you haven't had the experience I just put to you."

"So, you're saying that war changes people."

"I'm saying that trauma changes people. War is definitely traumatizing. Hell, training for war is traumatizing!"

"I'm not sure I get that."

"I know a lot of cold warriors - Brits, Yanks, Canadians. They spent years training to go up against the Warsaw Pact. It never happened in the big conventional warfare way that was anticipated. But the very fact that they spent years training to tear each others' guts out in Europe totally altered the way thousands of guys who never heard a shot fired in anger think and see the world. I can only imagine how many people are going to come back from Desert Storm majorly fucked up."

"You're losing me. Back to Aunt Gerta, please."

"Did you find it traumatizing to learn that your Aunt had been brutally murdered in your back yard?"

"It didn't seem so at the time."

"Did you find it traumatizing to learn what your Aunt was doing in Namibia?"

"I found it surprising, icky, disturbing."

"How about the fact that a whole bunch of guys with guns came looking for you at the wrong cottage because of what they didn't get from your Aunt?"

"Well of course that was terrible. And before you ask; yes, I am scared all the time. When I get a moment to think about the mess we're in, it makes me feel panicky."

"So there you have the essence of trauma. Prolonged fear and the stress it causes changes you and it takes things from you. Things like innocence and a sense of security."

"Alright. I see that violent events are life altering."

"The effects of trauma are incremental. It's a case of one damned thing leads to another."

"So I can look forward to discovering incremental changes in my personality and my view of the world?"

"You must know that we're not out of the woods on this little caper. That would be why you're still coughing library dust out of your lungs."

Jenna didn't say anything for a long time.

"Alright Tom. I am in one of the most beautiful places I have ever been, having conversations with one of the most interesting people I have ever met, who is also the best fuck I've ever known. And it all seems to be capable of ending badly in a nanosecond. Any words of comfort you can offer me?"

"Trauma can make a person stronger, Jenna. You learn things. You get mentally tougher. You adapt."

"So that which does not kill us makes us stronger?"

"Hell yes! I've got that T-shirt somewhere in my gear." Tom sat quietly for a few moments. "I'll concede that trauma doesn't make everyone stronger. But it's worked that way for me and a lot of my buddies."

***

During the course of her mother's illness, Ing had felt drained and sick many times. She put it down to stress. Once she was in Mexico and far away from the trials of her mother dying, she was ready to be sick. She took a hotel room in Cancun and slept and sweated and blew snot into tissues for four days.

Throughout her days of sickness in the Mexican hotel, Ing had a lot of time in between bouts of fever to think. Her first priority would be to let her brothers know that she was all right and explain to them that she simply could not have borne to stay for her mother's funeral. Her second priority would be to let Jenna and Tom know that she was on her way to see them.

On the morning of her fifth day in the hotel she awoke feeling drained and shaky, but without a fever. She forced herself to eat some breakfast in the hotel restaurant and hurried back to her room expecting that the food would make her sick. Two hours after she had eaten she actually felt a bit better, so she went out into Cancun, looking for somewhere to make some calls from. She found an American Express office with a business centre.

Ing needed to hear a friendly voice so she called the number that Jenna had given her. It rang several times and Ing was about to end the call when Jenna came on the line and somewhat breathlessly said hello.

"Good God, Jenna. You sound out of breath. Did I interrupt some wild beach hut orgy?"

"Ing! Where are you, lady?"

"I take there is no need to use any of Tom's veiled speech during this call?"

"Not unless you're being held prisoner by the forces of darkness."

"I'm in Mexico. Cancun, to be exact."

"Oh, Ing. I'm so sorry. Obviously your mom has died."

"She has. And it was a bloody good thing that the poor lady is gone. That won't stop me from missing her terribly, but she was suffering so much."

"You need to get here as soon as you're ready. There are hugs and sunrises waiting for you."

"That sounds heavenly. I'll probably head out of here in two days. I got as sick as a dog as soon as I got off the plane here. I've barely been able to move for the last few days. You know how it is when you drive the body hard in a crisis and then suddenly you can relax a bit."

"Poor you. I know exactly what that is like. Are you on the mend now?"

"I'm feeling a lot better today. I'll give it a couple more days before I climb into another airplane. I should fly into Toronto, right?

"That's right. Let us know the time and flight number and we'll be there to pick you up. We're really excited that you're coming to stay with us."

They talked a bit longer and then Ing reluctantly ended the call. She left the business centre to buy a bottle of water and then went back and after some thought, dialed her eldest brother. She expected that he would immediately start in on her about not being present at her mother's funeral. Her sister-in-law answered the call and quickly got her brother on the line.

"Ing. Where are you? We've been worried sick about you."

"I thought you'd be pissed as blazes at me."

"You did all the hard stuff as mom was dying. Only fair that you left some of the funeral stuff to your brothers."

That choked Ing up a bit because it was so unexpected.

"So you got everything handled, big brother?"

"We managed, Ing. We didn't do things as well as you would have, but it was alright. How are you, sis?"

"Well, I've actually had a bug for a few days but I'm getting better now. It's probably the water here in Mexico."

There was silence for some time and she spoke her brother's name, wondering if the call had been disconnected. When he spoke next it was very softly.

"Ing. The health department and the Red Cross people have been coming around mom's house a lot."

"Well, they shouldn't be. All the nurses and home helpers were fully paid off."

"That's not what they're on about."

"Well, what the hell do they want, then?"

"They want to talk to you."

"What the hell for?"

There was another long silence. Then her brother asked her if she had been following the news in South Africa over the last few days. Ing said she hadn't.

"There's a bloody great scandal here with the blood supply. Some blood donations weren't properly tested, or screened, or whatever. The health department is running around like crazy to talk to people who had blood transfusions on certain days in certain hospitals since they may have gotten tainted blood."

This time it was Ing's turn to be silent. Finally she asked, "Tainted with what?"

"Now sis, the news is saying that there's only one chance in ten that the people in those hospitals on those days got the bad stuff."

"Tainted with what, Kenny?"

"This HIV thing. The thing they're calling 'slims'."

Ing felt her insides turn to ice.

"So sis, you've got to get back here and get tested. Chances are everything will be as right as rain."

"That's sweet of you to say, Kenny. I won't be coming back to South Africa. I'm getting my old job back in L.A."

Kenny stopped trying to persuade her to come back home when he realized the line was dead.

He was telling his wife about the call with Ing when the doorbell rang. It was yet another person from the department of health asking if he'd heard from his sister. Kenny was not in a good mood.

"Yes. I bloody well have. She's in Mexico on her way to her job in America and she isn't feeling well. I hope you people haven't killed her with your poison blood."

The person at the door felt there was no point in having a lengthy conversation with Kenny. And besides, the person had the information he had been looking for.

***

Nils was becoming bored. He had a quick talk with Ernst Harpt and learned that it would be another two days before his son Willem would be at the Chateau. He idly leafed through a magazine and he had an epiphany. He knew how Karl Winter was going to die.

He was eager to get on the road to carry out the next part of his plan, but Adolph Harpt would soon be returning from the hospital and Nils wanted an up-to-date report on Winter's condition. There was a new housemaid working in the Chateau and Nils amused himself by thinking about the changes that he and Hanna would put her through once the current work was done.

Adolph Harpt entered the chateau in an agitated state. Karl Winter, he reported, would undergo some further surgery early the next morning to remove a small area of necrotic tissue. The doctors said that the surgery was necessary to clear up the infection that was interfering with his recovery. They had assured him that the surgery was low risk but that Winter would be quite groggy for a couple of days from the general anaesthetic. Nils was overjoyed at the news and left the Chateau soon after speaking with Adolph.

He drove fast into the nearest large city and took a room in a good hotel. A good Moselle was delivered to his room and he permitted himself a glass before he called Hanna. She was a bit grumpy with him because, she explained, Angelique was tied to the bed begging her to only make her come once more.

"What is your dress size, Hanna?"

"Ten. Why?"

"And Angelique. What would her size be?"

"A seven. No, more likely an eight."

"Winter is having more surgery tomorrow. He'll have general anaesthetic and will be groggy for a couple of days. While he is in that weakened state you and Angelique are going to kill him."

"How?"

"I'll tell you the details later. Tomorrow I am picking up habits and wimples for you and Angelique. The two of you are going to become Grey Nuns for a few hours."

"This sounds delightfully evil, Nils. Godspeed on your shopping trip."

***

Ing spent the next two days on the phone in the business centre of the AMEX office in Cancun. It was a struggle to get numbers and to call places in Toronto, but eventually she had the information she needed. She booked a flight into Canada and then called Tom's number. Tom picked up.

"Tom, you mercenary bloody bastard. You just had to go back into Rhodesia and kill a few more, didn't you?"

"They had it coming, Ing. I'm sorry about your mother."

"I am too. Can I come for a visit tomorrow?"

"We've got the jeep gassed up for the run to Toronto. When do you get in?"

Ing gave him the flight number and arrival details and Tom gave her a rundown on the local summer weather conditions. There was a pause and then Ing told him that she had a request to make.

"Sure, Ing. What do you want?"

"Book us a couple of hotel rooms in Toronto. Somewhere near University Avenue and Dundas Street. We'll just need them for the night I arrive. There's something I want to do with Jenna before we head out into the countryside. I'll explain when I get there."

Tom hung up the phone with a lot of thoughts in his head. "What has that crazy lady got up her sleeve?" he wondered.

Jenna was outside planting a shrub that she assured Tom would look incredible in the spring. He told her that Ing wanted them to stay a night in Toronto and that she had something that she wanted to do with Jenna.

"She's clearly feeling better. But I feel my heart quiver a tad. You will intervene if the proposed activity seems too extreme, won't you, dear Tom?"

"Ing? Extreme?"

Jenna threw a handful of dirt at him.

***

When the woman who had posed as a worker from the department of health came back to the control station to report her conversation with Ing's brother, Chuck could have embraced her. He asked a few questions and then told an admin person to pay them all off. They were all given a sizeable bonus. One of them went immediately to a pay phone. She had lots of coins.

Chuck called Sam to tell him that Ing Stoller was in Mexico. Sam was only moderately interested. He asked Chuck if he had a precise location and when he learned that he didn't he was about to dismiss the call.

"She might have this HIV/AIDS thing," said Chuck.

"Talk to me," said Sam.

"There's big trouble here. Not only does this fucking virus spread through fucking, it spreads through blood. People who need transfusions are getting fucked up by it. Sam, a fucking plague is being created."

"Chuck. Go home for a week. I'll talk with you after you've been there for seven days."

"Are you fucking sidelining me?"

"I'm the head dog. It's my call."

"You're gonna fucking need me!"

"Go home and rest up. You've no idea what I've got in store for you."

***

Jim Curtiss sent Arnon five men to help comb Tom Robbins' neighbourhood for useful information. Arnon brought three of his own guys and they split into pairs and each took a two block area to knock on doors.

Arnon learned that Robbins was a regular patron of the local deli, and the manager of the Marienbad Restaurant said that Robbins dined there a couple of times a month, usually with a stunning young woman whose accent he couldn't identify. When asked about the last time Robbins had been in the restaurant, the manager thought it must have been early June. He mentioned that the last time Robbins was in he had two stunning women with him.

When Arnon and his partner got back to the rendezvous point, one of the FBI agents walked up to meet him.

"I think you'll want to talk to the barkeep just up the street at the Charles Dickens."

"Was Robbins a regular there?"

"Yes. And so was his girlfriend. What's really interesting is who else Robbins hung out with."

The bartender was bored and watching daytime TV when Arnon and the FBI agent went to talk with him. Arnon showed him his ID and the man said he would happy to answer questions about Tom Robbins and

Ing Stoller. He hadn't seen either of them in weeks and was worried about what might have happened to them.

"So how long has Robbins been coming to your bar?"

"Must be more than three years now."

"And his lady friend, Ing Stoller?" asked Arnon.

"Two years ago on New Year's Eve was when Ing made her entrance here."

"I take it that she made an impression on you?"

"Ing made an impression on everybody in the place. Our sales would be up by twenty or twenty-five percent when she spent an evening here."

"What's so special about her?"

"She's crazy. Crazy funny. Crazy beautiful. Crazy sexy. Totally full of life. When Ing was here it was like we had a floor show."

"And she and Robbins are a couple, right?"

"Sure. Not in a conventional way but they hung out together often."

"What does 'not in a conventional way' mean?"

"Well maybe Ing said it best. She said that they swapped bodily fluids on a regular basis but that she wouldn't be doing Tom's laundry for him or cooking him pot roast."

"So it's a friends with benefits kind of relationship?"

"More like very good friends with incredible benefits."

"What kind of incredible benefits?"

"You spend an hour here when Ing is in a dancing mood and you'd know what I mean. I'd gladly give up a month's worth of tips to have twenty minutes in the sack with her."

"Twenty minutes? Are your customers lousy tippers?" asked the FBI agent.

"I make a lot on tips, buddy. Twenty minutes would be all of Ing I could handle."

"Did Robbins have any other friends who came in here?"

"He was on good terms with all the regulars, but I wouldn't call them his friends. He had five or six guys that weren't regulars who would come and have a beer with him from time to time. Hard looking boys like our Tom."

"When did you last have these two characters in here?"

The bartender didn't have to think long to give them a rough date. Arnon wasn't surprised to learn that it was before the night of the gunfight.

The lead FBI agent who had accompanied Arnon to the bar offered to stay with the rest of people who had done the canvass and to write up a report that made Arnon like him a great deal. He went to his office and called Curtiss.

"Jim. We did a sweep of the neighbourhood. Tom Robbins was a regular in a pub called the Charles Dickens. It caters to Brits and other former citizens of the British Empire. Robbins is Rhodesian."

"Interesting. I wonder if he became a Zimbabwean when things changed over there?"

"Maybe. He obviously told the bar keep that he's Rhodesian. He was also in the Selous Scouts. Heard of them?"

"Oh yes I have, Nick. They were an elite counter-terrorist unit. A lot of them became mercenaries after the blacks pushed them out of Rhodesia."

"Robbins was often in the bar with a South African woman named Ing Stoller. The bartender lusts for her."

"I take it that would have been the other woman you saw at Van Velt's cottage when you went out there."

"That would be my guess. Damn, I wish we could have gotten closer to them. The barkeep says she is a knockout."

"Probably best for you, given that Teresa was along, that you didn't get too close."

"I hear you," said Arnon. "Your lead guy, a fine young man I must say, offered to write a report on what we found out today."

"Great! Catch you soon, Nick."

***

When Sam Allen's phone rang at seven in the evening he reached for it eagerly, hoping it would be Daniel Sterling on the line. The caller had a German accent.

"Am I speaking with Mr. Sam Allen?"

"Yes. Who is this?"

"It's Joachim Maarten. I think it must be ten years since we last spoke."

"Twelve. We talked about the South African Flash."

"I have tried to keep memories of those harrowing times at bay."

"We all try to do that. Without much success."

"I'm sure that you're aware that I am a consultant for the Cerberus Corporation."

"I would say that you're Cerberus' Chief of Intelligence, but if you prefer the term consultant I'll go with that."

"Mr. Allen, as you know, the Corporation is experiencing a great deal difficulty right now. I know that since the misguided attempt to abduct the niece of Gerta Ten Haan, your organization has been making great strides in dismantling their network of friends in America. To the best of my knowledge, though, your organization has not been on the offensive against them in Europe."

"That is correct."

"Someone is."

"We think that, too. What's your appraisal of who's coming at them?"

"It could be some splinter group of the South African Government or Army. It could be some multi-national group who wants some particular research they believe the corporation has, that they think can help them find a remedy for the plague in Africa that is spreading to the rest of the world. Right now I don't know. I have a theory."

"Would you be willing to share that theory?"

"I would. But only in a face-to-face meeting, Mr. Allen."

"A face-to-face meeting poses huge challenges."

"I agree that it does. But sometimes one must accept the risks to have a truly meaningful communication."

"What do you have in mind?"

***

Early in the morning Nils was awake and clear of his hotel. He sat in the parking lot of a theatrical costume place for a half hour waiting for it to open. His visit to the shop was quick he and reached the hotel where Hanna and Angelique were staying before noon. As he drove, he thought of what he would say to Angelique to persuade her to participate in his plan.

Both Hanna and Angelique were clearly glad to see him. Hanna was getting restless and would be up for anything. Angelique seemed to have picked up some of Hanna's sensuousness. Nils was aroused by the presence of the two women.

"I gather that you two have been getting along," said Nils.

"If the fact that Hanna knows about thirty different ways to make me come is an indicator of getting along, than I would say we're getting along well," said Angelique.

"That would be a good indicator," said Nils. "I hope you weren't put off by my rather unusual request that I asked Hanna to pose to you?"

"Not at all. Surprised, but not put off. We've done as you asked. Would you like to see?"

"I would, Angelique."

Angelique was wearing a short skirt. She approached the chair where Nils was sitting and stood in front of him with her feet planted quite far apart. When she lifted her skirt Nils could see that she had not a trace of pubic hair left.

"Superb. Completely superb, Angelique. Your blond curls were lovely, but there is something I hope you will help Hanna and me do and the lovely golden floss had to go for a while. I look forward to watching the curls come back."

That statement clearly struck a chord with her.

"Do you hate Karl Winter, Angelique?"

"I... I... Of course I do. The man is a disease."

"Would it surprise you to know that he tried to get me killed in America?"

"Oh my god! Nils, I had no idea. I thought he doted on you."

"Winter dotes on no one, Angelique. We're all on this earth to be used by him. As you were. As I was."

"He is hateful!"

"Hanna, will you please take off your bathrobe?"

As Nils had instructed, Hanna was wearing nothing under the robe. She let it fall from her shoulders onto the floor. Nils asked her to turn her back to them.

"See that scar that mars Hanna's back, Angelique?"

"Yes. I've wanted to ask Hanna about it. But I didn't."

"Who arranged for you to experience the pain that the scar is witness to, Hanna?" asked Nils.

"Karl Winter," was her answer.

"There is nothing I want to do more right now than to taste your lovely bare pussy, Angelique. I want to spread your lovely legs and explode inside you. Do you know why I have not taken you to the bed?"

Angelique shook her head.

"Because I want you to join Hanna and me as we kill Karl Winter."

"I'll join you to do whatever is necessary to end that horrible man's life. I am totally committed to you, Nils, and Hanna too. But why can't we go to bed? You and I or all of us?"

Nils outlined his plan for Winter's destruction. Angelique listened intently and actually giggled when her part in the plot was described. Nils felt grateful to Hanna for the tutelage she had provided to Angelique.

***

The five principles of the LO adhered to a very rigid schedule of contacts. This evening would be Daniel's regular check-in. Sam sent his wife and daughters out to dinner. And he waited by the phone. As always, Daniel's call was within a minute of the time allotted for contact.

"Hello, Sam."

"You've been to the house that we identified as the place of interest to Winter and his crew?"

"I have. Got there in time to see the fire crews rush up to try to save the pile of bricks. Fruitless. The lads who torched it used a lot of accelerant. Regular grade petrol would be my guess."

"Daniel, we have what you Brits would call a very dicey situation, I think."

"Be careful, Sam. Dicey is a word we Brits take very seriously."

"I had a call from Joachim Maarten last night Daniel. He wants to meet with me and Franz."

"That is dicey. Where?"

"That's the curious thing. He wants it to be somewhere in England."

"So he's afraid and on the run. Any idea what has happened to bring this momentous meeting about?"

"The members of Cerberus are dropping at a prodigious rate. Maarten says he is concerned about what is happening inside the Corporation. He wouldn't give me anything more unless we meet. I think Franz and I should meet him. Where do you propose that should take place?"

There was no hesitation on Sterling's part.

"The top of the keep at Dover Castle."

"Dover Castle? It's summer. The place will be crawling with tourists."

"Of course it will be. All those tourists milling about will let both you and our new friend Joachim have lots of security on site, dressed like Americans and Japanese on vacation."

"It might be a bit difficult to have a meaningful conversation in that environment."

"I could try to rent you and Maarten a nice office building that would be mutually agreeable, but I don't think we've got six months to set this little tête-à-tête up."

"He hasn't talked to us in twelve years. Think there would a problem in taking our time with this?"

"I'll repeat myself, Sam. He's afraid and on the run. The fact that he is asking to meet in England is an admission of that. I'm the only Brit in the LO. Maarten loathes me, and for good reason. I'm not proud that I took out a great many of his family members. But I had to. He's chosen England to make you and Franz feel more secure and because Germany has become too dangerous for him."

"Maarten is the man who might be able to tell us what motivated Winter to go after Gerta and Walter and to turn that misconceived little blond machine Witt loose in the States.

"Alright. I'll get into Heathrow the day after tomorrow. You tell Maarten one p.m. on the roof of the keep the next day. Franz has a shorter trip than me, so he should have no trouble with that schedule."

"A question for you, Sam. This niece of Gerta Ten Haan, do we know where she is?"

"Not at the moment."

"Does anyone else?"

"I don't think so. Chuck has a lead on a friend who may still be in touch with her, but the friend is using some pretty good trade craft."

"That's extraordinarily interesting. Did Gerta leave a manual of deception for this apparently vacuous young niece to embrace? Anyway, Sam, we'll have Dover castle keep in lovely shape for the meeting."

Chapter Thirty-one

Ing boarded her flight to Canada with a couple of hundred hungover Canadians. She was glad that her fellow passengers were mostly sleepy and silent as they flew back to their homes. She did not look forward to what she and Jenna had to do once she was in Canada.

When she cleared customs at Pearson International airport and had collected her bags, only Jenna was waiting for her in the arrivals area. Jenna gave her a big hug, grabbed her bag and led the way through the throngs of people. Once they were in a quieter part of the vast building Jenna explained that Tom had stayed with their vehicle to "make it easier to get clear of this batshit crazy place".

Jenna opened the back door of the jeep for Ing, tossed her bag in the back hatch and then slid into the front seat. Her door was still closing when Tom started rolling. "Welcome to Canada, Ing, and to the worst traffic in the whole country. You and Jenna talk. I have to focus to get away from these maniac drivers."

"How was your trip, Ing? You look great, girl. You are slim and trim."

Ing winced at the word slim.

"I'm so glad to see you two. And even more glad to be away from South Africa. When I left before I said that the only thing that would get me back there was my mom. That's no longer an issue."

"I'm so sorry you've lost her, Ing."

"I had her a lot longer than you had yours. Where are we staying?"

"The Delta Chelsea. It's a big hotel about five minutes walk to the intersection of University Avenue and Dundas Street as per your instructions, madam."

"That's great. Have you two had dinner?"

"Nope. We'll check into the hotel and then decide what we want to eat. Toronto has something for everyone."

"Just so long as we can eat without being spied upon. The warnings you gave were right on. Those fucking healthcare people were prying into every part of my existence."

"Do you think you were able to make a clean break?" asked Tom.

Ing gave them a rundown on the last night at the hospital and told them that she had called her brother from Mexico. Tom said, "Well done, lady."

The Chelsea was an older hotel that still had adjoining rooms that allowed the guests to visit one another without going into the public hallway. Once they had checked in, the three of them sat in Tom and Jenna's room sipping wine. Jenna found it fascinating to watch Ing's stress diminish. Tom raised the topic of dinner.

"Can we order something to the room?" asked Ing.

"Of course. But we're good to go if you would like to sample a bit of Toronto's night life."

"I'm sure that would be lovely," said Ing, "but let's order room service. There's something I need to talk to you two about."

Their chairs were grouped near sliding doors that opened onto a balcony. Tom picked up a pack of cigarettes and stepped outside the room. He told Ing that he could hear her perfectly and lit up.

"When I got caught up in that street riot and my foot was badly cut, I was taken to a hospital where they sewed me up and gave me a couple of units of blood. I'm sure you've heard about this thing called HIV/AIDS that is such a problem in South Africa. Turns out that South Africa also has a problem with its supply of blood."

"Are you okay, Ing?"

"We'll begin the process of finding out tomorrow. It took some doing, but I have arranged for a blood sample to be taken and tested to see if I have this particular plague, to be fast tracked. That's why I wanted us to stay here in Toronto."

"We'll come with you," said Jenna.

"Damn straight you will, girl! You offered to be a support to me when mum was dying and I couldn't take you up on that. I want you with me now. And I should mention, Tom, that this is going to cost you a few thousand."

"Hell, Ing. Wait till you see what the room service bill will be. I ordered wine for you two and scotch for me. I'll be coming along with you two tomorrow as well."

They had dinner and about eleven Ing and Jenna changed into their PJs. When Ing said she was tired, Tom and Jenna took her to her room to tuck her in. They all slept together in Ing's bed.

***

It was nearing the dinner hour when Nils arrived at the hospital. He observed that Winter was in a state of helplessness from the operation and the anaesthetic. The arm of the affected shoulder was completely immobilized. Winter's other arm was also affixed to a bed rail so that he could not, in his drug-addled state, reach to tear out the many tubes that the doctors had taken such care to place in his body.

Bosch was bored and his two minions had moved to a state beyond boredom. They brightened when they saw Nils because to them he represented some sort of action. Nils whispered to Bosch that perhaps they deserved a slightly longer dinnertime and perhaps an extra beer or two. Bosch was very happy to convey that news to his men.

Nils and Bosch talked for a moment and then Nils excused himself to make a phone call. Angelique and Hanna were waiting in a deep alcove hidden by shrubs. Hanna took Angelique by her shoulders and turned her to face away from Nils. The younger woman leaned forward and steadied herself against Hanna. Nils lifted her heavy skirt to expose her naked buttocks. He took her hard and quickly and Angelique felt the hot spurts of his ejaculation deep inside her. Nils dropped her skirt back into place and left them.

When he went back to Winter's room he proposed that, given the quiet of the place, they slip outside and have a couple of the excellent Cuban cigars that Nils had bought while he was in Holland. Bosch thought that to be a great idea.

The hospital was served by both black and grey nuns. Two of the grey nuns walked by as they stood smoking.

"Ever wondered what's under all those robes or habits or whatever they're wearing, Nils?"

"In some cases a lot of potential, I should think."

"You're damn straight on that, Nils. Those two weren't my cup of tea. But damn, I've always wanted to strip a nun bare and give her the best of my beast."

As the two nuns had walked by him and Bosch, Nils had marvelled at skill that Hanna displayed with makeup. With their hair covered by black wimples and their figures concealed by layers of heavy clothing, only their faces could be seen. Hanna had used makeup to alter the lines of both hers and Angelique's cheekbones and the shape of their eyes. And of course, neither of the women looked like they were wearing any makeup at all.

No one gave the two nuns a second glance as they made their way up to Winter's room. He was sleeping when Hanna quickly locked the door of the room from the inside and then went to Winter's bedside. He turned his head to look at her and mumbled "sister" as Hanna quickly pressed the reset button on the vital signs monitor, peeled the sensor off his arm and applied it to her own.

Despite the effects of the medication he was on, Winter's face displayed bewilderment when Angelique climbed on to the bed and hiked up her skirt. Hanna thrust her finger into Winter's mouth and confirmed to Angelique that his partial denture had been removed. Angelique positioned herself carefully and lowered herself so that her genitals were pressed tightly against Winter's mouth and nose.

Hanna made sure that Angelique's skirt did not cover Winter's eyes as he lay on the bed gasping for air. He struggled only weakly and Hanna was surprised by the short time it took for him to die. When

Angelique had first positioned herself on Winter's face, Hanna had leaned forward and whispered to Winter.

"Do you recognize this cunt that is about to smother you? I wonder how you will like the flavour of Angelique when she has just been fucking Nils?"

She saw horror in Winter's eyes.

When it was clear that the man was dead, she helped Angelique down from the bed and then went to the monitor panel, pressed the reset button and stuck the sensor back on Winter's arm. Angelique had the door unlocked and open so that the two of them were down the hall and around a corner before the thirty second cycle time for the monitor to reset had lapsed. As it turned out, one of the duty nurses was using the washroom and the other was in a patient's room so a full three minutes elapsed before the signal from Winter's monitor was noticed.

***

It was only a short walk from the hotel to the private medical lab where Ing had arranged an appointment. In less than half an hour a lot of vials of blood had been taken from her. It was extremely hot and humid as they walked back to the hotel. Ing said that the heat made her feel drained. Both Tom and Jenna groaned at her effort at humour.

Tom got them clear of Toronto as fast as he could and it was mid-afternoon when they arrived back at Port Burwell. Both Jenna and Ing were napping when Tom eased the SUV up the driveway and parked by the house. Ing stirred as soon as the vehicle was shut off and sat quietly looking at the house.

"Have you named it yet, Tom?"

"Canadians aren't big on naming their houses, Ing."

"Well this place must have a name. I'll provide you with advice on that once you and Jenna have given me the grand tour. Wake up your beautiful lady and let's 'carpe diem'."

Tom saw a pile of mail on the table inside the front door that Audrey must have picked up for him when she was in town. He left Jenna to show Ing around the house while he glanced at the postmarks on the envelopes. One was from a town in Georgia and it took an effort for Tom to resist opening it.

Instead, he put some wine and beer and plastic glasses in a cooler and went out to the Argo shed. The green monster fired up immediately and Tom drove it to the front of the house. He spread towels on the seats of the vehicle and was sitting at the tiller bars, naked, when Jenna and Ing finished their tour.

"The no clothes rule is Jenna's," said Tom.

"I bet it is," said Ing.

"Jenna. Step up here," said Tom.

Jenna mumbled something and began to disrobe. Ing started to laugh and said, "You are starting to kick apart the white picket fence, my friend." They climbed into the Argo and Tom took them on a meandering tour of the property. Ing was intrigued by the stone circle in the woods and there was much laughter as Tom and Jenna described the murals that had been painted over in the great room. Tom drove them down the hill toward the beach. Ing was astonished by her first glimpse of Lake Erie.

It was a hot windless day and the lake was very calm. Tom drove the Argo to the water's edge where tiny waves were lapping at the sand. Ing asked if the water was warm.

"It's a hell of lot warmer than the liquid ice that Jenna forced us to swim in at her cottage."

They waded into the tepid water of the lake and swam and soaked for half an hour. It was a weekday so there weren't many sunbathers on the beach. They sat soaking up the sun, sipping their drinks and talking for hours with periodic dips to cool down.

"When I was in Africa waiting for my mum to die, I realized something. It struck me that once she was gone, the only two people in the world that I really cared about would be you two. I kept sane some days by thinking about what it would be like to come to Canada and see you two again."

"Ever since Tom and I had to run away from the cottage, I've been lost. I feel better now that I'm here, but now that you're here I can almost believe life will go on in some coherent way. I'd say I see you as my sister except for the implications of incest that would rear their ugly heads."

"And because of the fucking tainted blood thing, we have to make this a sex-free zone until we get the tests results in ten days. I have to tell you that the thoughts that kept me sane in African did not involve the three of us sitting naked and non-jiggy by a warm lake."

"It will be five days," said Tom. "I gave the head guy of the place some additional motivation to fast track the lab work. You've jumped to near the head of the queue."

Jenna squeezed Tom's hand and Ing said, "Thanks, Daddy Warbucks."

"What are you two going to do about this mess that dear old Aunt Gerta has gotten you into?"

They told Ing about the research that Jenna and Audrey had done. Tom mentioned that he had a letter waiting in the house that might provide him with some more information about Sam Allen.

"So if you find this guy, what's the plan?"

"We don't have one yet. But three heads are better than two. For the next five days, we have nothing to do but eat, drink, sun, and swim. I'll have a look at what my contact has found out for me while you two make dinner and hopefully that information will be useful."

"In the meantime, Ing," said Jenna, "the plan is to lay low here in paradise. I'm glad that you're able to be with us."

They were getting hungry so Tom fired up the Argo and they drove back to the house.

***

Chuck Holt did not like being sidelined. He called Sam from his home for an update and was incensed when he learned that Sam would be meeting with Maarten in England and that Daniel Sterling was running the show. After a lot of arguing, Sam agreed that he could bring a three-man team to England to stand by if Maarten played something underhanded. That concession did little to mollify Holt.

Sam was about to leave for the airport to fly to Heathrow when Claudio called him. He was clearly excited.

"Sam. We've had a breakthrough here."

"What have you got, Claudio?"

"I'm in Capetown. One of the shadow companies that the South African Army set up to do bio research had an office here. It took some very large bribes, but I just spent four hours in their file room."

"Okay?"

"My guys brought out four boxes of research records on floppy disks."

Sam didn't know what the hell he was talking about.

"Records of what?"

"All of the research that Winter did after he was thrown out of Namibia. We have every bit of data that was collected as he tried to develop the same sort of virus that our team was working on."

"Talk to me, scientist."

"Sam, once I have a chance to look at this data with my team, it will be quite easy to determine if the work that Winter did is actually the AIDS virus."

"Winter and the South Africans will be demonized if we could prove that."

"True. But the exciting thing is that with Winter's data, we can see what he did wrong and likely modify the work that our team in Namibia did to quickly come up with some effective ways to respond to this virus."

"Have you any data from the team's project? My father always speculated that South African Intelligence managed to steal some of it."

"No, Sam. But we know who has it. Surely you've located the Van Velt woman by now?"

"We're making some progress, Claudio, but so far we don't have her."

"That's insane. How has she managed to elude both us and Cerberus?"

"It appears that she has some pretty good help," said Sam, briefly describing Van Velt's travelling companion. He also told Claudio about Maartens' request for a meeting.

"Be very careful, Sam. Tell Daniel to be exceptionally sharp."

"I'll let you tell him that, Claudio. Not something I'd say to an SAS officer."

"How will I reach you, Sam? I should have a lot of information in about two days."

"I plan to get back to Virginia as soon as I've met with Maarten. I should be home in two days."

"Godspeed, Sam."

***

Nils and Bosch finished their cigars.

"Are you coming back up to see the old man again?" asked Bosch.

"No. I need to call Joachim Maarten to see what's happening in the broader world. We've been making too many long distance calls from the chateau so I'll go to a business centre in one of the hotels and call from there. Will you be checking in with Andrieas soon?"

"Yes. I have to call the pompous little prick at seven."

"Tell him that I've gone to make some phone calls. I should be back at the chateau in a couple of hours."

Nils drove off and Bosch went back into the hospital. He was appalled to learn that Winter had been dead for at least twenty minutes.

Nils went to the Hilton and called Joachim Maarten. Maarten had put people on the ground to learn that the house where Stuart was working had been totally destroyed by the fire. He reported that Holt was at his home in Texas, Allen was in Virginia and Von Hesse was attending a charity event in Frankfurt.

Nils was telling Maarten about his most recent visit to Winter when Maarten excused himself from the call for a moment. When he came back on the line he sounded shocked.

"Nils. They have called from the chateau. Herr Winter is dead."

"That's ridiculous. I saw him just an hour ago. He was very groggy from the anaesthetic, but the doctors said the surgery had gone well."

"Bosch is reporting that Winter has been murdered, Nils."

"Where is Bosch now?"

"At the hospital. It's swarming with police."

"Tell Andrieas that I will be at the chateau in twenty minutes. And find that motherfucker Sterling!"

***

The chateau, as Nils had expected, was in a state of chaos when he got there. The elder Harpt brothers were beside themselves with anxiety. Andrieas Winter was nearly paralyzed at the news of the death of his uncle. To complicate things just a bit more, Willem Harpt had just arrived from Australia. It took a five minute conversation with him for Nils to realize that he was not as smart as his brother.

There was little news coming from the hospital. Bosch was being held by the police and grilled about his relationship to Winter. Hospital staff had told police about the security arrangements that Bosch had put in place for Winter, and that had grabbed their interest. Nils reasoned that Bosch would be a reluctant guest of the police for a good forty-eight hours.

"Andrieas is the closest relative to Herr Winter. For that reason, it is he who must reach out to the police and the staff at the hospital to learn all he can about the death of Karl."

"I agree," said Ernst Harpt.

"And the sooner the better," said his brother.

"The police will want to know why there were people guarding your uncle."

"What do I say to that?" asked Andrieas.

"By now, the doctors will have told the police that Winter entered the hospital with what looked very much like a stab wound. You will tell them a bit of truth."

"What bit of truth?" asked Adolph Harpt.

"I think it best that you tell them that Winter had a visitor from Britain named Daniel Sterling. A business associate that none of the staff had seen before. Tell them the man had some connection to Winter's business associate, Sam Allen. Tell them that Allen was at the chateau hours before the man from Britain arrived."

"Alright. I will do that," said Andrieas.

"Be very clear that you were called to the chateau, as were the others, after your uncle was attacked."

"Certainly."

"I think it best to say that Karl and the British visitor had gone for a walk on the grounds and that one of the staff found him lying on the ground near the carriage house. There was, of course, no sign of the visitor."

"There were staff in the house that day. Surely the police will talk with them when they hear Andrieas' story," said Ernst Harpt.

"There was only one maid present that day. All the others who were here were Bosch's men. It is likely the maid heard a gunshot, but she knew no details of what became of Winter's attacker. She is here today and I shall ensure that she is sent away immediately."

"But she will know that Karl was not found outside the house," said Harpt.

"True. What's most important is that she had very little information to gossip to the other staff about."

"But she will give the lie to Andrieas' story about Winter being found outside."

"No, she will not," said Nils.

"How can you be sure?" asked Adolph.

"Because young Willem will soon undertake his first assignment as a member of the Collaborative. Willem and I will ensure that the young housemaid never meets with the police. Pack a bag for several nights, young Willem. We have places to go."

***

Daniel Sterling had everything in order for Allen's meeting with Joachim Maarten. He had six two-person teams who would enter and exit the meeting area during the time that Allen and Maarten were talking. At least one team - they were all male/female combinations posing as tourists - would be on the roof at all times.

Sterling could only just tolerate Chuck Holt in meetings of the LO. He was appalled to learn from Sam that the man would actually be in Dover with a team of his own men during the meeting with Maarten. The most charitable term Sterling would apply to describe Holt was 'gunslinger'.

He was somewhat mollified when Sam assured him that Holt would be nowhere near the castle and was only there to standby if Maarten violated the terms of the meeting. Sterling told himself to forget about Holt and to concentrate on ensuring that the day unfolded as it should. His first priority was making certain that the house where Allen and Von Hesse would meet and wait in before the meeting was secure.

***

Willem Harpt was not pleased that he would have some sort of assignment. For all the twenty-one years of his life, he had had no demands placed upon him. He was a blond bronzed giant with reasonably good skills as a surfer. Being from a wealthy family suited him well.

He had heard about Winter and Nils and their constant work to ensure that the money continued to be available. Those talks had bored him. Now that he had met Nils, he was not impressed. The man was seemingly fit, but his stature and presence was foreboding rather than imposing. Willem was used to hanging out with movie star types. He grudgingly packed a bag with his father at his shoulder, telling him that he must learn a lot from Nils. Willem thought that would be a waste of time.

Nils made it his business to know as much as he could about each of the staff of the chateau. Steffie, the red-haired maid who had been present the day Winter was stabbed, had a liking for cocaine and aspirations to be a rock-and-roll diva. Nils had gone to a local bar one night when her band was performing, and she did have an impressive set of pipes. No range, but she could belt out a song.

He found her in the anteroom, dusting, and asked her to join him for a walk outside.

"Steffie, how would you like to go to America?"

"To do what?"

"The new fellow that has just arrived here. The tall blond one. Would you be willing to be his travelling companion to L.A.?"

"L.A.! Would I have to fuck him?"

"Not in the biblical sense, Steffie. As I understand it, you have studied English all your life because you would like to get far away from your family and make a new start."

"You understand things pretty fucking well."

"You were here when Herr Winter was attacked and Bosch and his boys took out the man who did that. You are very smart. You know you have a valuable piece of information."

"I know that."

"I think you should take that valuable information with you to America. Once you have it safely there, I would feel better if it never came back to Europe."

"And what about my travelling companion?"

"I would be deeply grateful to you if he never came back to Europe either."

"How grateful?"

"How about two hundred thousand dollars U.S. grateful? If he is found dead in a low-end motel room, naked, the victim of an overdose."

"Would that be in cash?"

"Half now. Half when it is clear that he is dead."

"I talk to the other young staff. You've fucked all of them. But you've never tried to fuck me. Why?"

"You gingers scare me." Nils did not share with her that heavy drug users could never be trusted.

"And rightly so. Do you have the money with you?"

Nils drove Steffie and Willem to the airport himself. She was lewd on the drive, talking about showing off her 'candy floss pubis' on the nude beaches. Willem was clearly intrigued.

Chapter Thirty-two

Sam, Joachim and Franz got to the right place at the right time. They were blessed by the thin sunshine that the British called a stellar day. All of them seemed to be tired.

"Thank you for meeting with me," began Maarten.

"There has sure as hell been a lot of carnage, both in my world and yours."

"I am sorry I tried against your convoy in Namibia in the seventies. I want no war."

"Nor do we," said Sam. "But what fucking light can you shed on the latest bullshit? Gerta Ten Haan was tortured and then raped to death with a fucking baseball bat. What the fuck is that about?"

"If you will permit me, I would like to talk about motivation."

"Motivation. What about motivation?" said Franz.

"I'll start with my own. The major goal in my life has been to kill Erich Krohl."

"What the fuck," said Sam.

"Krohl was the cause of the death of my father's eldest brother. Since I was twelve, my father made me study pictures of Krohl. He made it clear to me that he would regard me as a failure if I did not hunt Krohl down and give him a very hard death."

"I know a good deal about your family, Joachim. Your father and your uncles were all in the SS."

"Yes, they were. And my eldest uncle was an Oberst who was entrusted with catching Krohl when he deserted his post."

"I knew that Hitler ordered the execution of your uncle. I've always thought he was somehow caught up in the Von Stauffenburg plot. The assassination attempt."

"No, Franz. He was killed because of Erich Krohl's treachery."

"So you're telling us that you have allied yourself with Karl Winter and the rest of Cerberus for the sole purpose of getting your hands on Krohl?"

"Karl Winter's father and mine were firm friends. I'm sure you know that. I got to know Karl when he first came back from Africa. Once he trusted me, he told me a great deal about what you were trying to do in Namibia. I showed him photos of Erich Krohl without telling him who he was. He confirmed that the photos were of a scientist named Walter Danzig."

"That is how I learned that your Legacy Organization had retained the services of that horrid man in the 1960s. From then on, your LO was my enemy. I wanted him more than I wanted wealth. And then he showed up dead outside of Cologne cathedral."

"Yes, he did," said Franz.

"If it was Krohl you were after, why did your people murder Gerta Ten Haan?" asked Sam.

"Motivation," said Maarten. "This time, the motivation of Karl Winter."

"Winter wanted Gerta Ten Haan dead?"

"Karl Winter wanted three things in this order: the scientific data that Krohl and Ten Haan had snuck out of Africa; the death of Walter Danzig; and the death of Gerta Ten Haan. Underlying Winter's desire to kill Danzig and Ten Haan, I think, was an intense wish to humiliate Gerta sexually. But none of that matters now."

"How did you know that the two of them had the formulas?"

"Do you remember the night that Ten Haan accosted you outside of a large public event?"

"Of course I do", said Franz.

"I have arrangements with a number of paparazzi. One of them was standing not three feet away from you when you had to shake Gerta Ten Haan off your arm. He showed me the photos of the two of you that he got that night and he told me what he had overheard of your conversation with her. And very importantly, he heard you tell Ten Haan to go back to Holland."

"Holland is a small place, isn't it," said Sam.

"A very small place," said Joachim. "It didn't take the people working for me very long to find her."

"Why didn't you move in then?" asked Sam.

"The Corporation had a strong network in America. We tapped Krohl's phone. We knew where they were going. It seemed that it would be easier to deal with them once they were in California."

"How did you miss getting Danzig or Krohl when you took out Ten Haan?"

"Krohl wasn't missed. California was Winter's operation. He went after the data and Ten Haan. He forbade his nephew to lay a hand on Erich Krohl."

"Because?"

"He wanted to show Krohl what had been done to Ten Haan. I agreed because it would have been torturous for the old bastard."

"You're telling us, Joachim, that you had no part in what happened in California?"

"I told Winter where the Ten Haan woman could be found and I told him that I would be part of the next phase of the operation, which was to ensure that Krohl had as unpleasant a demise as possible. That is all."

"How did they manage to lose track of Krohl the day of Ten Haan's murder?"

"The people on the ground there were sloppy. They missed the fact that he had a second apartment. I was about to unleash a search operation of a massive magnitude when one of my friends on the Cologne police service called me to say that an old Nazi had been taken to the morgue."

"You must have been angry, Joachim."

"I was very disappointed. I was filled with disgust. A man such as Krohl should never have been permitted to die of natural causes, a free man, in the city of his birth."

"You must be pretty pissed with us, the LO, for having protected Krohl all these years."

"That anger was gone the moment I learned that Krohl was dead. And I understand why your organization protected him. He was a useful tool to you."

"A useful tool doing a nasty job. You know what we were doing in Namibia."

"Yes. And I know why. I know the exact words your father used when he addressed your people at that camp in the bush."

"Go on," said Sam.

"He told them that he had visited Nagasaki and Hiroshima. He said that there would always be wars and that the team had to find new weapons "because the atomic bomb must never, ever be used again.""

"My father was a Major General when the Japanese sued for peace. He was among the first Americans to see the effects of the bombs. It changed him."

"It would have had to. Perhaps a man like Krohl could have viewed those cities without being changed. But most men could not. Your father was correct when he spoke to the people in Namibia. We cannot use nuclear weapons."

"Did you know that Karl Winter died a day ago, Joachim?"

"Yes. Murdered, it seems."

"The question is, by whom?" said Von Hesse.

"I disagree," said Joachim. "It is more important to know who arranged for Karl's death. And I am quite certain that person was Nils Witt."

"You began this meeting talking about motivation. Why would Witt want a member of his own organization dead?"

"At first I thought that Nils had snapped and was on a blood rampage. I've known him since he was a murderous adolescent. But what is happening now is something different. I believe he is bent upon dynastic change."

"You mean he wants to take over Cerberus?"

"Mr. Allen, Nils, I believe plans to be the Cerberus Corporation."

"That would explain a great deal, Sam," said Franz.

"We've been sitting about as long as we can without attracting attention to ourselves" said Sam. "It's time to talk about what happens next."

"Agreed," said Joachim. "I plan to stay out of Germany for the foreseeable future. There are numerous things that I must attend to from a business perspective. If you wish, our next meeting could be in America."

"We have very safe areas there," said Sam.

"Blessedly safe. Which is why I wish to ask a very large favour of you, Mr. Allen."

"Alright," said Sam.

"My assistant and very good friend is a woman named Trudi Kastner. Would there be some place in one of your safe areas in America that she might be able to come and stay for a time? Perhaps for a few weeks until these problems in Europe are resolved."

Sam didn't have to think about it.

"Have her fly to Washington as soon as she can. Let me know when she's coming and we'll arrange for everything as soon as she lands. I'll be back in the States the day after tomorrow. Here's a number where I can always be reached." He handed Maarten a very plain business card.

"I am in your debt."

"Do you think Nils Witt is coming after you, Joachim?" asked Franz.

"He said during a recent phone call that Winter had once mentioned that my assistant Trudi was enchanting. He probably will concentrate on liquidating the Collaborative members, but he is a man of immense energy. He will come for me sooner or later. I have a good intelligence network. Hopefully it will be of use to all of us as we deal with this menace."

"Alright," said Sam. "When do you think you'll be able to come to the States?"

"In a week or ten days. May I share two more things with you?"

"Certainly."

"I know that the LO is turning over stones on two continents in an effort to find Ten Haan's niece. When we next meet, I would like to know why. Do you wish to get the data she likely has to find a cure for this epidemic that is unfolding? Or do you wish to erase the last trace of what your organization was doing in Africa?"

Neither Allen nor Von Hesse responded.

"That is a question for next time. What I can tell you, today, is that Nils Witt and the Corporation aren't showing the slightest interest in that young woman. The obsession with finding that data seems to have died with Karl Winter."

"That is very interesting news."

"I can also tell you that Ten Haan's niece is likely near a place called Port Burwell in Canada. I give you this because I want you to understand that my intel network is still functional. Who is going to depart this venerable castle first?"

Sam went first, followed in due course by Franz Von Hesse. Franz glanced back at where Maarten sat as he descended the ancient staircase from the top of the keep. Maarten looked deeply tired and troubled. He wondered if he would ever see the man again.

***

The letter that Tom had received from his friend in Georgia contained some useful information. It gave Tom a pretty good idea of the scope of the estate that Sam Allen lived on in Virginia and of how much money it would take to live that kind of life. His friend described the Allen family as 'American nobility'.

Audrey had come out to dinner the night that Ing arrived. Ing and Audrey seemed to connect immediately and the wine flowed freely. There had been much talk about the previous owners and their Wiccan beliefs. Audrey decided the three of them would become a coven. Ing insisted that everyone fill their glasses.

"I have a truly portentuous announcement to make," Ing announced.

"Speak to me, oh far-seeing one," Audrey had said.

"I see a great rock near the road with words cut deeply into it."

"And what are the words, wisest Ing?"

"Tulgey Wood," said Ing.

Tom simply stared at her. Jenna asked if she'd been drinking the sketchy brandy that they'd bought by mistake. Audrey smiled broadly and said, "You clever girl. That's the perfect name for this place."

Tom had one by one put each of them to bed. Ing went down first, which wasn't surprising considering her alcohol intake. Jenna was next, asleep as soon as her head hit the pillow. Audrey stayed up for a while.

"You have the place you've always wanted, Tom. You've got, or have the potential to get, more money than God when you sell off the rest of your ill-gotten gains that are stored at my place. Are you happy?"

"Ask me that in two days, Audrey."

"Not the answer I was expecting. But upon reflection, I rarely get the answer I expect from you. Care to elaborate?"

"Nope. But please keep your eyes peeled and your ear to the wall. There are a couple of things in my life that need to be resolved. I'm hoping they don't come here, but you never know."

***

When they left the castle, Sam and Franz went back to the secure location that Sterling had set up. Daniel let them sit there for thirty minutes before he joined them to say that nothing was amiss. Sam went to his luggage and returned with a serious looking bottle of brandy.

"Are you in radio contact with Chuck, Daniel?"

"Yes."

"Tell him to get his ass over here. Eighty percent of the LO is going to have a meeting."

Holt joined them in twenty minutes.

Sam was feeling drained. He asked Franz to summarize what they had heard from Joachim Maarten. It was hard to tell whether Holt or Sterling was the more fascinated.

It was interesting to see how Holt and Sterling reacted to the information they received. Chuck was like a hunting dog that had just been told that pheasant season had begun. Sterling seemed to coil up like a rattler in preparation for striking.

"I'd be happy to entertain your thoughts, gentlemen," said Sam when Franz finished speaking.

Chuck was in first.

"I want to take my guys to see what Witt is up to. All of them speak great German. If Maarten was telling the truth, we need to know everything that bastard is doing."

"Does anyone object to this?" asked Sam.

No one did, but Sterling cringed at the thought of Holt and his men moving about semi rural Alsace-Lorraine.

"When I get back to the States, I'll follow up on this lead about the place in Canada that Maarten gave us," said Sam. He tossed it out to show that his intelligence capability is still intact, so he must be pretty sure of his information."

"If we find the Van Velt woman, what will our approach be?" asked Holt.

"As Teddy Kennedy once said, we'll cross that bridge when we come to it," answered Sam.

"That is bloody funny," said Sterling.

***

Maarten went to a secure place and called Trudi. She wasn't concerned about the instructions he gave her. He had never caused her a moment's grief in the time they had known each other. She looked forward to a trip to North America.

***

Chuck Holt was anxious to get back to his team. Contrary to what he had told Sam, he actually had brought six men with him. He had them join him in his room at a hotel in Folkestone.

"There is a huge shit-storm going down here, guys. The asshole that created the shoot-out in California is close by and he is wreaking havoc. If we stop him, the world gets more stable. We're going to take this sonofabitch."

"Is this guy in England, boss?"

"No. Right now he's in Alsace Lorraine. I know that you three speak German," said Holt, pointing at some of his men, "So you'll come with me to Germany. You three will stay here in England where folks speak English so you can get some work done."

"What's our job here in pub and castle land, boss?"

"Your first job is to stay out of the pubs. At least most of the time. I want you guys to do two things. You stay in tiptop condition because it's very likely that you'll be coming to Germany to do some shooting. The second thing you'll be doing is to research the hell out of some buttfuck place in Canada called Port Burwell."

"We'll be ready and we'll have you everything you need to know."

"Spare no expense, guys. There is some place in London, England that can give you 1 over 25.000 maps of everywhere in the world. Get those maps of this place in Canada. We're gonna need 'em."

***

Arnon's captain called him and Crane into his office and asked for an update on the Ten Haan case.

"The FBI tore apart Jenna Van Velt's cottage. She and her friends had been doing a lot of drinking, wine for the ladies, scotch for the gentleman, and they had a lot of sex toys. It would appear the guy was armed with something that fires a 7.62 mm round. He may also use a bow. Other than that, they got nothing."

"You told me this guy is some sort of mercenary?"

"Yeah. He was in Rhodesia and then South Africa. He had a security consulting company here in LA until he bagged off."

"What do the Feds say comes next?"

"They're not saying anything."

"Have they clammed up to cut us out of the case?"

"Maybe. I think it's more likely that they don't have anything to say."

"You both have a lot of vacation time on the books. Both of you take a week off. Starting now."

***

Holt didn't like Germany. His grandfather had been with a Marine division that saw some hard fighting in 1918. Chuck had heard his stories. Germans were not Chuck Holt's favourite people.

Chuck had been through the morass of the Vietnam War, and he constantly looked for something that was ideologically cleaner to focus his anger on. He had settled on the Nazis as his arch-enemies. It pleased him greatly to be hunting the Winters, the Witts and the Harpts.

Once on the ground, Chuck and his men quickly concluded that it would be impossible to keep Winter's chateau under covert surveillance. The estate was located nearly a mile up a private road. Holt had two of his men rent motorcycles and he and his other guy set up shop in a building they rented that sat right where the road to the Winter estate joined the public road.

Each time a vehicle left the estate, Holt would radio to one of his motorcycle riders to follow it. The two riders had been shown photographs of Nils Witt. Near the second full day of surveillance one of the riders followed a Mercedes with heavily tinted glass to a hotel in a nearby town and hit paydirt. He radioed Holt to tell him that a man answering the description of Nils Witt, only with dark hair, had just entered the Black Swan hotel in Krefeld.

Holt left his guy in the rented building and joined the motorcyclist who had tailed Nils. Not long after he arrived, Holt observed Witt and two women leaving the hotel. He recognized Hanna Spader immediately. Witt drove off with the two women and Holt's rider went after them. Holt got to a phone and called his team members in England.

"How's the research going, Tommy?"

"Just fine, Mr. Holt. We found the map place and spent a good piece of your money. Got the 1/25000 sheets for the whole area in around this Port Burwell place. Two sets of sheets. It's in the province of Ontario."

"Good work. Any idea how far is it from Toronto? That's where the main airport is."

"We've got a good road map of the south part of the province. Port Burwell is on Lake Erie, about a hundred miles west of Toronto."

"That will be an easy drive. Are you guys fit?"

"We did a fast six miles through this Hyde Park here in London this morning. There were a lot of runners out on the trails but none of them were going as hard at it as we were."

"No doubt. Grab your pen and paper, Tommy. I need you guys to pack up and get to Germany tomorrow as soon as you can get a flight. Bring all your stuff because we'll likely go straight to Canada from here."

Holt gave him several tasks to deal with and the name of the hotel that he wanted the three men to be at by eight o'clock the next evening.

***

Jenna had noticed that Ing mostly pushed food around on her plate during meals. Jenna thought that she had lost more weight in the short time since she had joined them in Canada.

All three of them were becoming very brown. Audrey had gone to Tillsonburg for something and had come by to drop off Tom's mail. They had all been asleep on deck chairs and had awakened when Audrey loudly observed that they were looking like red Indians. She wasn't the least bit shocked that all of them were butt naked.

On the morning of the fourth day of their wait for the results of the tests, Ing smacked them all back to reality during breakfast. She said that they would each pour a large coffee and go out to the patio to decide what to do with Gerta's "demon seed fucking computer thingies".

"In less than forty-eight hours I am going to find out if I'm going to die horribly from this fucking HIV thing. I can tell you that people die horribly from it because I saw several of the poor wretches in Africa. They become walking skeletons. Then they just drown in their own snot."

"You've gotta stay positive, Ing. You don't have it. And you can always do one more thing," said Tom.

"Don't hand me your Selous Scout fucking mottos, Tom."

"Actually the Scouts motto was 'Forward Together', I got the one more thing idea from a Special Air Service guy."

"Well, great. Fuck off with that line of thought for a moment and tell me what you know about this rich American bastard whose father was fucking Jenna's Aunt and creating pestilence in Namibia."

"His name is Sam Allen. His main home is in Virginia. My buddy tells me that presidents dine there and that it would take more money than God has to maintain the place."

"Do you have a phone number for this scion of American society?"

"I do."

"Then here's what I'm thinking. Once we hear from the medicos in Toronto, I think you should find an honest lawyer and a media type with a lot of integrity. You take Gerta's diaries to the lawyer and leave them there with a description of how they came about. You tell the lawyer that if anything goes bad, if the slightest thing goes south with Jenna or you, the journalist gets called and the diaries go public."

"How the hell did you come up with that, Ing?"

"It was a special skillset I developed when I was an anti-Apartheid protestor. Sometimes the only way to stay out of jail was to make it too painful for the government to come and take us away."

"I've definitely been thinking we need to get all of Gerta's stuff away from here," said Jenna.

"You're fucking right you do! In less than two days I'm going to know what life is going to be or not be like. Once we hear about that, I have a plan to put all this shit that your Aunt has caused to rest."

"You're gonna be okay, Ing," said Tom.

"Yes I am," said Ing. "I will always be okay and I have tremendous decision making capabilities. I developed them when I was nine. Perhaps I'll tell you how I attained them some day. We have less than two days to go. Think we could get Audrey out here for dinner so that we could play some Euchre this evening?"

"I don't feel like playing cards. All I can think about is what we're going to hear tomorrow," said Jenna.

Audrey and Ing dominated Jenna and Tom at cards. During a break in the game when Tom went outside for a smoke, Audrey joined him.

"I've spoken to all of my friends here in town, Tom. If they see anybody around that doesn't seem to be a camper, a cottager or a fisherman, they'll let me know."

"I appreciate that, Audrey."

"Anything you'd like to share about this, Tom? Is it connected to something from your days in Africa?"

"Believe it or not Audrey, this time it has nothing at all to do with me."

"I knew from my first talk with Jenna that you had decided to play the white knight. You've picked the right damsels to rescue, Tom. I like them both."

Tom left Audrey and Ing talking quietly and led Jenna to their bedroom. "I've got a big chest, Jenna," he said, and he held her until she had cried herself to sleep.

Chapter Thirty-three

Holt was working with limited resources and he didn't know a fuck of a lot about Germany. The Corporation's people picked up on the motorcycle riders on the second day. Nils was a keen observer of the security staff at the chateau and had identified a young man who was his height and very similar to him in stature.

Nils had himself photographed, measured the young security man's head, and dispatched one of the other security people to a wig shop in a city about sixty miles away. While the man was on his task, Nils had the young security guard summoned to his room. Nils explained that one of the female staff was going to shave his head and that the young man would then select an outfit from Nils' wardrobe.

A landscaping company was called and asked to send a van full of pesticides to the chateau the next day. When all was in place, the young security man left driving a BMW with the heavily tinted windows. The landscaping van went twenty minutes later, driven by a man with Nils' Glock pressed to the back of his head. Six of the Corporation's best marksmen were crouched in the van with assault rifles. A second delivery van with more men followed along in a few minutes.

Holt was in radio contact with the motorcyclist tailing the BMW. It was parked in front of the hotel where Spader was staying and she and the other woman emerged from the hotel to greet the man driving the Mercedes. Holt had his three men who had came in from England waiting in a car in the area of the parking lot farthest from the entrance to the hotel.

Holt himself was sitting in a car in a small parking lot across the street from the hotel. He was so intent on watching Spader and the others that he did not notice that another vehicle had parked just down from him. Holt raised his radio and gave his team the command to drive forward and take out the three people by the car.

Both Nils and his driver saw Holt using the radio. One of the men in the second Corporation van warned Nils that a car was moving down the parking lot. Holt and Nils had never met, but both had spent considerable time looking at photos of each other. Holt recognized Nils first and hammered his car into reverse, then he rocketed out of the parking lot with smoking tires.

Nils was tempted to follow him, but the scene that was unfolding across the street claimed his attention. The car approaching Spader and the others was about fifty yards from them when Nils' men pulled up beside it. The driver of the car immediately reacted to the threat by veering into the bigger vehicle. Nils' man who had targeted the driver for Holt's team was initially off balance from the impact of the sideswipe from the smaller vehicle. His first burst of fire missed the driver of the car.

It was happenstance that two of Nils' men had targeted the man aiming at Angelique. He died without firing a shot and Angelique had a split second to get to safety. She nearly made it.

At the first sound of gunfire, Hanna had reached into her purse for her automatic. Six rounds hit her abdomen before her fingers touched the pistol. She was hurled back over a shale rock planter, bleeding profusely onto the rough hewn rock.

The security man dressed as Nils died a short moment before the last of the Holt's men were killed. His body was riddled more than Hanna's. Nils ran to the scene and started issuing orders.

The car that his lookalike had driven was shot up but no tires were flat and it looked like it would run. He detailed a man to get it going and then crouched by Angelique. She had a bullet through her calf and was bleeding profusely.

"You," said Nils indicating one of his men who he knew was trained in first aid. "Get her in the car and stop the bleeding. Go to the safe house. Keep her alive and wait for instructions. Go!"

"The rest of you! Load those dead into that vehicle and get the fuck out of here. Go to a cheap hotel and call the Chateau."

"It's hot. There's blood all over. They'll start to stink in a few hours."

"I think in minutes, not hours, you idiot. Go now. I'll join you in less than an hour. Search that fucking vehicle."

When they had left, Nils lifted Hanna's body and carried it to the back of the landscape van. He'd garotted the original van driver as they'd pulled into the parking lot and he left his body there to fuck up the police. He and two of his men drove off with Hanna's body .The entire episode had taken less than seven minutes.

Nils and one of his men stayed in the landscaping van while the other one rented a non-descript cargo van. Once they had transferred Hanna's body to the new vehicle and abandoned the landscaper's vehicle in a deserted warehousing area, Nils found a phone and called Andrieas Winter.

"We've just had a gun battle outside of the hotel in Krefeld. The security guard who was dressed to look like me was killed. The rest of our men are fine and we killed three of the attackers. One of my friends was killed and another wounded."

"My God," said Andrieas. "Who did this?"

"It was men from the Legacy Organization. Led by Holt, one of their principals. He unfortunately was able to get away from us."

"What should be done now?"

"Has Bosch returned from his visit with the police?"

"Yes."

"Put him on the line, Andrieas."

Nils spoke quickly to Bosch and then asked to speak with Andrieas again.

"I have given Bosch instructions of where to take you and the Harpts. You must move immediately. The police will be swarming the chateau within an hour. Take lots of money and your passports. Tell the staff that you're rushing off to be with a family member in Hamburg who is very ill."

"Where are we going?"

"Bosch will have time to tell you that. I don't. Be driving in fifteen minutes or plan to spend a lot of time with policemen. Has anyone called you with the name of a hotel?"

"Yes. The Brandenburger."

"Forget that you ever took that call."

Nils climbed into the van and told the driver their destination. Half an hour later, he was sitting in a seedy hotel room going through the contents of Holt's men's luggage. His men sat near him quietly sipping beer and easing their jangling nerves. The only thing of interest that Nils found in the pile of stuff taken from the car used by Holt's men was two complete sets of detailed maps and pages of notes about a place in Canada. He packaged those up and told his men to disappear for a few weeks.

**

Holt was not the best of drivers and he knew it. For the first few blocks after he fled the parking lot he expected to be overtaken at any moment. Eventually he realized that he was not being pursued.

When he first tried to raise his men by radio, only the motorcyclist who had followed the car from the chateau to the hotel was within range. And the signal was very weak. Holt got his bearings and told the man to ride northwest. Eventually they had a strong enough signal to talk.

"Did you see what happened at the hotel after I left?" asked Holt.

"All of our guys are dead. This Witt guy that was driving the black BMW is dead and so is the tall woman. The younger woman took one in the leg. The bastards who did the shooting cleaned up and got out of there fast. They took the bodies of our guys."

"That's because they wanted to search them. What a fuck-up!"

"We lost three guys, boss, but at least we got this Witt asshole."

Holt was about to tell him otherwise but stopped himself.

"Go get our guys. Get to Britain and stay at the hotel by the airport that we stayed at when we first came over here. I'll meet you there in two days. Ditch all weapons and ammo."

"Right, boss. Where to next?"

"Canada. Just as soon as we can fucking get there."

***

Joachim Maarten's intelligence sources were indeed intact. He heard about the shooting in Krefeld an hour after the first police arrived on the scene. He waited two hours as some of his most well-placed people gathered further information about the incident in Krefeld and then he called Sam Allen.

"Hello, Sam. It's Joachim Maarten calling."

"Hello, Joachim. The young lady you sent our way is enchanting. She is enjoying her stay here in the States."

"I'm very glad and thankful. Sam. Have you heard about the nastiness in Germany?"

"No."

"There were two groups of people outside of a hotel in Krefeld that started killing one another about three hours ago. Citizens report many dead, but when the police arrived there was the body of one man resembling Nils Witt, until his wig was removed, and the body of another man who worked for a local landscaping company at the scene. There are numerous blood pools in the vicinity. There are a great many police being assigned to this. I am very glad to have had no part in it."

"I haven't ordered any action, Joachim."

"I thought not, Sam. But someone did."

"Thank you for this," said Sam.

***

It was the day that the lab had promised to call, and for the first time in weeks rain threatened. Ing, Jenna and Tom stayed indoors and because the temperature was cool, wore clothes. Ing remarked on the coming injustice of the Canadian winter. They had agreed that Ing would answer all calls that day. The phone rang at 11:11.

"Hello."

The caller rang off.

"Wanker!" said Ing. "Probably someone you owe money to, Tom."

At around noon the phone rang again. Ing answered and it was Audrey wanting to speak with Tom.

"I've just made you a bunch of money, Tom. All of the Thomas Jefferson documents that you had now belong to a Brazilian who had a lot of disposable income."

"That's great, Audrey. I'll drop around to see you next time I'm in town."

"Make it sooner rather than later, Tom. I hate having a few hundred thousand dollars in cash tucked away in my freezer."

The third time the phone rang, Ing picked up.

"This is Ing Stoller."

"Ms. Stoller, we have completed the analysis of your tests and we regret to inform you that you have the HIV/AIDS virus."

"Of course I fucking do! I was given a blood transfusion in South Africa when the idiots thought only blacks could get it."

"We'd like to review your options for treatment, Ms. Stoller."

"Thank you. I've already figured that out. I am grateful for your information."

Ing ended the call and sat silently for minute. "It would seem that the South African government have finally succeeded in killing me."

Tom and Jenna were both in shock. They both went to where Ing was sitting and Jenna sat beside her and pulled her close. Tom sat on the floor with his hand resting on her knee. First Jenna, and then Ing began to sob.

***

Holt assembled his team in London and they booked a flight out of Heathrow to Pearson airport in Canada. It was very easy to obtain black market firearms and ammunition in Canada. Holt was feeling more in control. He and his three men rented two jeeps and headed off to Port Burwell. Nils was a hundred miles ahead of them.

***

Ing let Jenna hold her for perhaps five minutes. Then she sat forward on the sofa.

"Get your hand off my knee, you fucking pervert," she said to Tom. "It's afternoon and no one has had the decency to offer me a mimosa. Could you please see to that, you lazy Rhodesian bastard?"

Ing stood up and looked outside. The rain had ended and the yard was filled with sunlight. She peeled off her pyjamas and said, "Back to Jenna's rules," and went out onto the patio. By the time Tom took them drinks, they were sitting naked, soaking up the sun.

"As the person with the shortest life expectancy in this company, I propose that I get to call the shots around here for the next few weeks."

"That seems fair to me," said Tom.

"Great. First thing I want to do is contact this Allen asshole and get rid of Auntie Gerta's computer disks. The next thing is to go to that nursery in that little place back up the road. The place I call the litter box."

"Stilton," said Jenna.

"Right. The place that smells like a thousand cats have all taken a gigantic piss at the same time. We'll go there and I'll pick out the perfect rock to put at the end of the laneway. You are going to accept my idea of naming this place Tulgey Wood. Right?"

"Of course. Although it would mean a lot to me to know what the hell a Tulgey Wood is, Ing."

"Up lift yourself, Robbins. Lewis Caroll. The poem the Jabberwock. Tulgey Wood is where all that crazy Jabberwock shit went down. A magical but twisted place. That's why it's the perfect name for this den of inequity that you and Jenna have here."

"I have been educated," said Tom.

"It's a start," said Ing. "Is there a tombstone carver guy around here?"

"Probably. I've noticed cemeteries in the area."

"Smartass. We'll need one of those guys to come and carve the name on the rock. I'll print it out for him so he doesn't fuck it up."

"Okay. I should probably get someone out here to pour a concrete pad to sit the rock on so that it doesn't sink out of sight."

"No worries there, me bucko. You're going to be buying a very fucking big rock."

"What else have you got in mind, Ing?" asked Jenna.

"Plenty of sex. I plan to watch the two of you have plenty of sex. I've done a lot of research and if latex condoms and gloves are worn so that my bodily fluids aren't passed on to you, you won't get AIDS."

"Let's both do her before dinner," said Jenna.

"Let's both do her now," said Tom.

"No glove, no love, Tom. Get your ass to the pharmacy."

"I'll do that. I'll get you two fresh drinks and head into town for supplies. I have to see Audrey anyway."

"See if she's up for a rubberized foursome, Tom."

"I'm sure she'll find that enticing. A guy may drop by to give me a price on roofing the Argo shed. Maybe put some pants on while he's here. He's new order Mennonite."

"Maybe he'll be Wiccan by the time he leaves here," said Ing.

"Did you see that, Ing? I just shuddered."

"Off to the town to do your errands, silly fellow. When you come back, we can talk about our upcoming trips to London, Ontario and beautiful Muskoka."

Audrey was visibly relieved to get Tom's money out of her house and Tom was visibly embarrassed when he bought condoms, a tube of personal lubricant and a box of latex gloves from a teenager working in the tiny drug store in the village.

***

When Nils got to the town of Tillsonburg, he stopped and found a telephone booth with a more or less intact directory. After some reading of the Yellow Pages business listings, he found a business that interested him with an address in Port Burwell. He jotted down the phone number and address and then started feeding change into the phone. After what seemed to be an endless wait, he got Joachim Maarten on the line.

"Joachim, it's Nils. Are you aware of what took place in Krefeld?"

"Yes. One of your men at the safe house called me. Are you sure it was Charles Holt of the LO in charge?"

"I'm sure. I was about fifteen feet from him briefly. He recognized me first and dashed off. We couldn't follow because Holt's men were about to attack some of our friends."

"Yes, I understand that they succeeded in killing your decoy and the Spader woman. The other young woman is going to be fine, by the way. We brought in one of our tame doctors and she is being well looked after."

"That is good to hear. The Harpts and young Winter?"

"Bosch checked in. They stayed in Lille last night. So far the trip has been uneventful."

"That is how we want to keep it. I suppose that Winter's chateau is in a state of occupation by the police?"

"Old Hans says it's like Berlin in '45 with the Russians."

"Let's hope they don't rape the female staff and steal the flatware."

"Where are you, Nils?"

"Somewhere far away from Krefeld. And I'm likely to be far away for a while. I'll check in every day or so. I need you to send me some things. Anything else?"

"Perhaps. Young Willem Harpt. Have you heard from him?"

"I don't expect to for a few more days. He was to escort the staff member, Steffi is her name, to California and stay out of sight for awhile."

"Your network in America is very sparse, thanks to the LO and their tips to the fucking FBI, but there is a report of a German national dead of an overdose in a hotel in L.A. My source on the ground thinks it might be Willem."

"Shit. Does he have a history of drug abuse?"

"Nothing he's ever been arrested for. But possibly."

"These young surfer kids! I'll call soon, Joachim."

***

Tom had expected to find Ing and Jenna well into their cups when he returned to his Alice in Wonderland Estate, as he had begun to think of it. Instead, they were both immersed in deep conversation. The carry bag that contained the computer disks that Gerta had left in Jenna's attic rested on the patio table.

"You two look like you're plotting," said Tom.

"Bring us drink and we'll let you in on the plot," said Ing.

Tom took his parcels inside and went down to the lower level where he had a metal fireproof safe. He put the money he had gotten from Audrey away, and on impulse he reached into a cupboard and removed a nine mm Browning pistol that he had placed there. He checked the action and ensured that it had a full magazine. Jenna and Ing were still talking intently when he went outside.

"You already know that Ing is mad as a hatter, Tom, so what she is about to say isn't going to surprise you at all."

"Let me guess. She wants us to buy a bunch of black horned animals and turn this place into a petting zoo for Wiccan families?"

"That's a cool fucking idea, Tom, but it's not what I have in mind."

She pointed at the bag of disks.

"Those things are evil, Tom. Evil people want them. I say we give them to them."

"Jenna and I had talked about that. The question is how do we do that and remain alive?"

"You know that people with the sort of power and money that this Sam Allen has will eventually find you two."

"I agree with that," said Jenna.

"So I say we do two things. Stash the diaries the way I suggested, and we go to London and have Jenna call this Allen guy."

"Why London? Why have Jenna call?"

"London is a good-sized city with an airport. And we can drive there in a little over an hour. Allen will know the call came from there, but for all he knows, Jenna could be hopping a plane to anywhere."

"And where would we propose to meet this lovely man?"

"You said he has a cottage here in Canada. Why don't we tell him to give us directions to it and I'll meet him there to hand over the disks. And we want Jenna to make the call because her Aunt left her a letter with those code words about 'killing a lion'. There is supposed to be a chunk of money from these guys as Jenna's legacy."

"Why do you think you should deliver the disks?"

"They don't know me from shit. As we all know, I have the least to lose. And I want to talk with the guy who arranged for Jenna's Aunt and her friends to kill me."

Tom sat thinking for a long time. "I'll get us more drinks." When he came back outside, he looked serious.

"First, I agree that we will eventually be found. We have to keep in mind that there are two groups of people trying to get their hands on these things. Which is why the Brown's cottage got turned into a battlefield. Getting these disks to one of the two might, just might, get them off our backs. The next step would be for the other group to learn who has the damn things. In which case they might get off our back too."

"I guess I had blocked out that there are two groups of people looking for us," said Jenna quietly.

"I agree with getting a room in London and making the call from there. Chances are we'll have to get him to call us back because I'm sure he's a busy man, so we might as well be comfortable while we wait."

"Excellent idea, Tom. An evening of Latex sex in a hotel room is just what I need. And as a bonus, it will be up to the hotel staff to try to get the sheets clean. Go get us a room. The sooner we get this phone call over with, the better."

"I thought you wanted to buy a rock today?"

"Trust me, Tom. The rock I have in mind isn't gonna go anywhere."

***

Joachim Maarten's intelligence network did not fail him. A French Foreign Legionnaire stationed in Lille that was on his payroll called him.

"Herr Maarten, your man Bosch was here in Lille last night. He and his companions are having a late breakfast at the Café de Fleurs Rouge right now. It's on Catherine Street."

"Thank you for this."

Maarten rang off quickly and called another man in Lille who worked for him. When the group left Lille they would be discreetly followed.

***

Tom made reservations at the Delta Armouries hotel in London and called Audrey to tell her that they would be gone for perhaps a few days. Audrey asked if it had anything to do with the outstanding barriers to happiness that she had talked with Tom about.

"It does," said Tom. "But I think we have come up with a way to resolve this crap. We should be gone no more than four days."

"I'll get your mail, and as you know I have spies everywhere."

"I'm counting on you, Mata Hari," said Tom.

It took them a little over an hour to drive to the hotel in London. When they got in their room, Ing was all business. The cooler was opened. Tom placed a sheet of paper with the number in Virginia where Allen could be reached and wine was poured. Jenna dialed.

A woman answered with an accent that made Jenna think of "Gone With the Wind."

"Hello. I hope you're having a fine day."

"May I speak with Mr. Sam Allen?"

"Mister Allen is not available right now."

"It's important that I speak with him as soon as possible. May I leave a message?"

"Surely you can. I have my paper right here."

"Please tell him that it is Jenna Van Velt, the niece of Gerta Ten Haan, calling. Please tell him that I need to speak with him as soon as possible. I will give you a telephone number."

"I got down Van Velt but you're gonna have to spell the other name for me, honey."

Jenna did and verified that the woman had taken the number down correctly.

"Mr. Allen will be calling to a hotel. Please let him know that the room is in the name of Tom Robbins."

"I will. I will. You have a lovely accent, Miss. Is that Canadian?"

"It was a while ago. When do you expect Mr. Allen to be available?"

"He's out riding one of his horses with his daughter. Dinner is always served at seven, so he'll be back before that. I'll make sure he gets this as soon as he's out of the saddle."

"Thank you so much."

Jenna hung up the phone and told Ing and Tom what had been said on the other end of the line.

"So now we wait," said Tom.

Chapter Thirty-four

Ing and Jenna talked a bit, speculating that a man like Allen wouldn't call until he had enjoyed his dinner. Tom knew that men as successful as Allen took care of business first. Their phone rang at 6:15 p.m. Jenna answered.

"Am I speaking with Miss Van Velt?"

"Yes. Is this Mister Sam Allen?"

"It is. Thank you for your call."

"Mister Allen. I am Gerta Ten Haan's niece and I expect you know that she was brutally murdered."

"I learned that with deep regret and I am sorry that it happened. And sorry for your loss."

"My Aunt and I were not close. I would have liked to have spent time with her to get to know her better. Instead, I have gotten to know her by reading her diaries from the time that she was in Namibia."

"To be completely honest, I am surprised they still exist."

"My Aunt was apparently a clever woman, Mr. Allen. She talked a South African army officer into taking them out of the camp and then took them to Europe and on to California. They are very detailed and accompanied by a wealth of photos. Including a bunch of nudes of my Aunt that I think your father possessed a set of."

"He did, Miss Van Velt. I destroyed them recently."

"I have the diaries and the photos in a safe place. I have a clever lawyer who is connected closely with some investigative journalists who are not afraid of anything. Should anything negative come into the life of my friends and me, some Canadian journalists will be breaking some big stories."

"Understood, Miss Van Velt. My people have no intention of harming you."

"Well, someone sure as fuck does. You are aware of the shoot-out in cottage country north of L.A.?"

"Yes. My people were the ones who intervened."

"I also have a large carry bag full of computer disks. I have not had them looked at, but my Aunt left me a note saying they contain the product of what the group did in Namibia."

"I would like to have those disks, Miss Van Velt."

"We are in total agreement on that point. I would like you to have them. Do you have something to say to me?"

"I beg your pardon?"

"My Aunt left me a note that said I should give the disks to someone who would say a certain phrase to me."

"I'm so sorry. Yes, of course. I was there when Johanna killed a lion."

"Congratulations, Mister Allen. You have just won a big bag of computer disks. I propose that my friend brings them to the dock of your cottage in Canada."

"You've done your homework. I agree to that. I can be there in two days. Will a Mr. Tom Robbins be the man making the delivery?"

"Actually, no. It will be an attractive young woman in a string bikini so that you will have no need to worry about concealed weapons or anything of that nature. I hope it will be a warm day."

"I hope so, too. I ask for two days because this is a quid pro quo. You are entitled to your Aunt's legacy and it shall be given to you."

"Thank you. My last question is to ask whether there is a way to convey to your adversary organization that you have the disks and that there is no good reason for them to pursue me and my friends?"

"I can do that. Let me tell you how to find my place in Canada."

***

Chuck Holt quickly realized he had made a tactical blunder when both of the jeeps rolled into Port Burwell. They drove down the main drag to the beach, and he immediately ordered the other two men to go back to Tillsonburg and take a room in a motel. The tactical situation he faced was not to his taste.

"This place is smaller than my home farm. How the fuck are we supposed to move around here without being made?"

"It's a small berg," agreed his driver.

"I counted three eating places on the street on the way down here. A bottle store, a variety store and some benches full of old gaffers watching every fucking vehicle that drives by."

"I grew up in a little place like this, boss. Everybody knows everything everybody else is doing."

"Christ! Get us back to that last place that we were in that had three story buildings."

The driver set off for Tillsonburg. Audrey got a call from her seventy-year-old friend that ran the florist shop telling her that ominous black jeeps had gone down to the beach and then had disappeared to the north.

When Jenna got off the phone, Tom assured her that it would be an easy drive to Muskoka. Ing sipped only a small amount of wine and indicated that she was tired. She and Jenna undressed and climbed into bed. Tom went down to his vehicle and retrieved a map of central Ontario. He took the directions that Jenna had noted during her call with Allen and figured out the route they would take to get to Muskoka.

Jenna and Ing were both asleep with their arms wrapped around one another. Tom slid quietly into bed beside Ing. Neither of them stirred as he rested his arm lightly on both of them

***

Sam Allen was relieved when he was able to reach Daniel Sterling. Sam started to tell him about his phone call from Van Velt, but Sterling cut him off abruptly.

"Did I miss a critical vote of the LO, Sam?"

"No. What makes you think that?"

"It was my understanding that if we are to engage in murder we need at least two of us to agree to the necessity of the action."

"That's the rule, Daniel."

"Chuck Holt launched an attack in Krefeld against Hanna Spader, another woman, and a man who resembled Nils Witt so closely that he had to be his security body double."

"What the fuck! Joachim Maarten told me about the shooting but he didn't tell me that Holt was there."

"What the fuck is right. Actually, the attack was a total fuck-up. The man resembling Witt was killed. His body and that of a seemingly innocent bystander were found at the scene. There is enough blood evidence at the scene to attest to the fact that Spader and the other woman were hit."

"Jesus Christ!"

"I've saved the best for last, Sam. Three men were found in a car in a warehouse area not far from where the shooting had taken place. Someone had thoughtfully placed their American passports on each of their bodies."

There was a long silence.

"Do you know the names of the guys that Chuck usually works with?"

"I have the list. Hold on just a minute. Alright, who are the dead guys in Germany?"

Sterling read off three names.

"Shit. Those are all Chuck's guys. But they're not the guys he had with him in Dover."

"It would appear that he had a whole entourage with him, Sam."

"I was clear as to how many he could bring to Europe."

"I think we were clear when we met in Dover that he was only supposed look in Germany. Not to take offensive action against anyone of the Corporation."

"Yes, Daniel. I think we were clear."

"He's becoming a serious liability, Sam."

"Agreed, Daniel. When I have my next contact with him I'll order him to go home invoking you as a vote in favour of that, if you don't mind."

"I hope he contacts you soon, Sam. Before he creates another debacle like the one that just occurred here. What do you have for me?"

Sam told him about the call from Van Velt and the arrangements that had been made. Daniel agreed to get to Muskoka as soon as possible. Sam told him that he already spoken to Franz and that he would be in Toronto in time to share a seaplane ride the next day.

"Do you anticipate any trouble from the woman who is bringing you the disks, Sam?"

"No. I get the sense that Van Velt and her friends have really thought this through. I've no doubt that they've done what they've said they have with the diaries."

"I hope to be there in time to watch the exchange, Sam. Do you have the money yet?"

"Yep. Half the amount in American cash, half in bearer bonds. She agreed to that."

"Does she know the amount?"

There was a pause. "Now that you ask, Daniel, the amount never came up."

"That's a good thing. An heir should never ask the executor of an estate what is it they're going to be given. Bad form. See you as soon as possible, Sam. Do speak sharply to Holt should you get the chance."

***

Nils went to a small town that was a half hour drive from Port Burwell. He took a room in a motel near a used car dealership and presented the Canadian ID he was using when he bought a well-worn pickup truck from the tired looking car salesman. He visited a nearby store and bought a pole, some fishing tackle and a tackle box. His last stop before going back to his room was a thrift store where he found all the clothing that he would need for the next few days.

***

For the first few hours of the drive they all were quiet. Jenna would have loved to be heading back to the beach. They stopped for a break in a town called Gravenhurst.

Tom struck up a conversation with an older couple, asking about the area. He mentioned where they were heading and the couple straightened in their chairs and looked more closely at him and Ing and Jenna.

"Are you TV people?" asked the woman.

"I watch it sometimes," said Tom.

"Don't be funny with me," said the old lady. "You're going to millionaires' row. Goldie Hawn has her place there. Why are you asking directions? The people who go there get picked up by limousines."

The awkward situations that Tom was used to had always been resolved by fists or sudden gunfire. Jenna arose from her chair and approached the old couple's table.

"We're going to a surprise party for Sam Allen. They told us that a bunch of extra limos and such in the area would tip him off so we drove up to this lovely place from the airport in Toronto. Could you tell us where we might be able to rent a boat?"

The couple was happy to give Jenna a wealth of information.

***

Holt and his three men bought a couple of cases of beer and met in Chuck's hotel room.

"How the fuck are we going to be able to do anything in that little shithole?"

"Andy did a bunch of research while we were in England, boss. This Robbins guy recently bought a place outside of Port Burwell in the country."

"And Nils fucking Witt has all of Andy's research and is likely already there," said Holt. "How did Andy find out that Robbins bought a place there?"

"There's a registry office in a place called St. Thomas that tracks all property purchases and such. He had to send them money for faxes, but they gave him everything he needed."

"Alright. It's clear that we can't go back into Buttfuck Ontario and not be made. Here's what I want you guys to do."

Holt gave them a lot of instructions, told them how to access the money they needed, and sent them on their way.

***

Jenna handled the negotiations for the boats. She rented them a twenty-four foot pontoon boat and a fourteen foot aluminum runabout for two days. The owner warned them twice that they would be liable for all gas. They would pick up the boats at the dock at noon the next day.

They talked about dinner and decided upon cheese and sausage and crackers in their room. Tom stayed with the vehicle while Jenna and Ing picked up food. Ing was carrying a huge parcel when she returned to the jeep. The two of them were talking animatedly about butter tarts.

"What the hell is so exciting about a butter tart?" asked Tom.

"Wait till you see these whopping great sugar pies," said Ing.

"I saw two great sugar pies last night," said Tom.

"God, your boyfriend is a crude bugger, Jenna," said Ing. "I'm glad I brought my lovely security blanket."

"Say what?" said Tom.

"Ing likes Hudson Bay blankets, Tom," said Jenna.

***

Sterling, by driving through the night to an airport, managed to arrive in Toronto before Sam and Franz. The three of them shared a pontoon plane ride to Muskoka. They said nothing to one another during the flight.

They carried their bags up to the house and staff took them away. A table had been laid with heavy crystal glasses, an ice bowl, and a decanter of deep amber liquid.

"Sam," said Daniel. "Could I have one of your Canadian beers? An Alexander Keiths, perhaps?"

"I'm with Daniel. Life is heavy. Give me something light."

They were all to bed early and up at dawn. Sam had been in contact with Claudio who had assembled his team in Tunbridge Wells in England. Sam was surprised at that until Claudio started talking gibberish about connectivity to a web thing. Sam asked him if they had adequate protection. Claudio said that he'd been in touch with Daniel and that everything was in order. It left Sam thinking that he needed to spend more time talking with Daniel.

"When I spoke with Claudio, he told me that you've set him up with a place in Tunbridge Wells. I take it that it's secure?"

"It's secure, Sam. Military Intelligence used it to develop some of their special gadgets during the war. I have in place pretty what they had by way of security."

There was time to kill before their guest was expected. The three of them were deeply good friends. Franz began the conversation.

"Your families embraced mine because we thought alike. We'd fought one another in two great wars for all the wrong reasons, and when the second war was over we realized we had a mutual enemy."

"I think our fathers realized that there was the potential of many mutual enemies," said Sam. "We wanted to preserve some sort of order that made sense to our race and our idea of how the world should be."

"Our fathers did. I think we've just followed along," said Sterling.

"And they thought that way because they knew that the Cold War was starting and that no one, ever, should unleash another atomic or nuclear weapon."

"But it got so out of control. Namibia is a case in point. Our fathers and their supporters were so terrified of nuclear war that they went down the road of developing bio weapons to inflict genocide on specific racial groups. Is there anything that could be more immoral than that?"

"I asked my father that question when he briefed me as I stepped into duties with the LO. He steadfastly maintained that future wars would be fought using weapons of mass destruction and that such weapons could not be nukes."

"What our families set into motion was wrong. I realize that we tried to stop it. We're damn lucky that the young woman who is coming here today will give us another chance to atone for the work in Namibia," said Sterling. "It's time we found a remedy. Our fathers created a very subtle sort of genocide."

The three men were sitting in the coolness of a shaded porch. Lake Muskoka glistened in the bright sunshine about a hundred feet from where they were sitting. It was a hot and humid day without a breath of wind.

Sam had been glancing at his watch repeatedly. A small aluminum boat had rounded the headland of the island to the east of Sam's place. There was a single figure in the boat. It was too far away for Sam to tell if a man or a woman piloted it, but the timing was right. He muttered "Show time", picked up a large carry-all and walked down to the dock. Franz and Daniel sat in the shadows of the porch, watching intently.

***

When they took charge of the boats, Ing had shown herself to be adept at handling the small runabout.

"I used to fish with my uncle all the time when I was kid," she shouted over the sound of the motor. "His boat was pretty much the same as this one."

Once they had the two boats moving across the lake, Ing had removed the cover-up that she had worn at the urging of Tom and Jenna while they were in the marina. Both of them had told her that her string bikini would likely cause all manner of marine disasters within the crowded confines of the slips. Jenna marvelled at Ing's attitude about her body.

"With this rig on, Jenna, your American friend won't have to worry about any concealed weapons. And I want him to pay attention when I have a few words with him."

"You'll have his attention, Ing. He likely won't hear a word you say, but you'll sure as hell have his attention."

They drove their two boats to a small island near Allen's place and then split up so that Ing would head for Allen's dock from one end of the island and Tom and Jenna would enter the picture from the other end of the island.

"Remember what I told you about the bag he gives you, Ing," shouted Tom as they pulled away from one another.

The Allen dock was one of the larger ones on the lake. She could see a single man standing alone near a tie-up spot with a ladder. Tom and Jenna had just rounded their end of the island when Ing cut the throttle of the runabout and glided to Allen's dock. As she eased the boat close in she called out "Line" and Sam Allen caught the thrown rope and tied the runabout to the dock.

Ing grabbed the carry-all and climbed up the ladder to the dock quickly. Allen had stepped back a few feet to stand beside a large duffle bag that he had placed on the ground. Unlike Ing, he wasn't wearing sunglasses. He was clearly surprised at Ing's choice of clothing.

"I take it you are Mr. Allen?"

"Yes. And you would be?"

"Ing Stoller. I'm a good friend of Jenna Van Velt."

"You must be an extremely good friend of Ms. Van Velt. Most people would do everything they could to avoid a meeting like this."

"Actually Jenna is doing me a favour by letting me deliver this bag."

That statement set Sam's pulse racing. He involuntarily glanced at the carry-all she had set at her feet. Ing was watching him closely.

"I have nothing in my bag but computer disks, Mr. Allen. I don't want to harm you. But I sure as fuck want to talk to you."

"I'm listening."

"I have heard every word that Jenna's Aunt wrote about the work the group was doing in Namibia. I know all about what they were trying to do."

"I hope that you and your friends are going to keep that information to yourselves," he replied.

"That information will only see the light of day if you or your organization comes after us. It will be just as Jenna said when she spoke with you on the phone."

"We will not take any action against you and yours."

"Mr. Allen, I presume that the information on these disks could go a long way to making a cure for HIV/AIDS. I'm guessing here but I don't think you've met anyone who is dying of AIDS."

"You're right. I haven't."

"Well, now you have. I have the disease. I'm in the early stages of it, so I look and feel pretty good right now. Most people don't know they have it until they get really sick. I was diagnosed early because I was given a transfusion of tainted blood in South Africa."

"I am sorry, Ms. Stoller."

"Right now I look pretty good, don't I?"

"Yes, you do."

"Four months from now, maybe sooner, by Christmas perhaps, I'll look a lot different. I'll have thirty to forty pounds gone. My hip bones and ribs will be trying to poke through my skin. My boobs will be empty hanging pouches of skin. I may be covered with lesions and my hair will likely be falling out in clumps. Did you know that in Africa they call AIDS 'slims'?"

"No. I didn't know that."

"As I said, Mr. Allen, I'm remarkable because I know I have the disease early in its progression. Despite the fact that I am the early stages, my life is changed already. Would you like to know how it has changed?"

"Yes, I would."

"Eating is no longer a pleasure. It is difficult to convince myself to take in any food. Meals that I once loved are becoming repulsive. I've lost six pounds in the last week."

"Are there supplements that you can get? My organization would be happy to assist with the cost of such things if that is an issue."

"That offer just pissed me off. No. Supplements aren't an option. The other pleasure that I've lost is sex. I used to joke to my boyfriend that I could kill him with my pussy. Now I truly can. I'm twenty-nine years old, Mr. Allen, and the only sex I can have - when I can find someone who is brave enough to get it on with me - has to include a lot of latex protection."

"Again, Ms. Stoller, I am sorry."

Ing leaned down, unzipped her bag and showed its contents to Allen.

"You and your buddies created this plague, Mr. Allen. I sure as fuck hope you're going to use this information to end it."

Allen said nothing. He picked up the bag he had brought and made to hand it to Ing. She motioned him to set it down.

"Open it and move things around in there so I can see what's in it."

Allen did as he was told and Ing watched closely. There was nothing in it that looked like the bomb or the remote tracking devices that Tom had warned her about.

Ing picked up the bag and handed the one containing the disks to Allen.

"If you'll be kind enough to cast me off, I'll be on my way."

"Ms. Stoller. Would you please give my thanks to Ms. Van Velt and tell her that we will be notifying the other interested group that we are now in possession of this information."

"I'll tell her that."

"There is a card in the bag with a phone number that will get through to me at any time. Please tell Ms. Van Velt to use it should the other people become troublesome. We have some influence with them."

"I'll tell her that, too. Line, please."

Allen tossed her the rope and she pulled the outboard into life. Tom and Jenna were moving slowly down the channel. Ing cut the angle and was close to the pontoon boat as it turned to go behind the island again. Once they were out of sight of Allen's cottage, Ing came alongside and they towed the runabout back to the marina.

***

Once the young woman had gone out of sight, Sam picked up the bag she had given him and walked slowly back to the house. He took a seat without saying anything to Franz or Daniel.

"You had quite a conversation with that scantily clad young woman," said Franz.

"She's beautiful woman. Superb body."

"What did she have to say, Sam?" asked Sterling.

"She had a lot to say about HIV/AIDS. She has been privy to everything in Gerta Ten Haan's diaries. She knows exactly what went on in Namibia."

"That makes her a dangerous woman to us, Sam. It makes them all dangerous to us," said Daniel.

"I don't think so. I believe that if we leave her and the other two alone they will keep their mouths shut."

"Why do you believe that? And why did this woman deliver the bag? Why not Van Velt or this man Robbins?"

"She made the delivery because she wanted to talk to me. And because she has nothing to lose."

"How so?" said Franz.

"She's South African. She needed a transfusion and got tainted blood. She has AIDS."

"What did she say, Sam?"

"She said she wanted to the meet one of the people responsible for her death and told me what would be happening to her body during the coming months."

"God, Sam. Such a beautiful young woman."

"What do you want us to do now?"

"Franz. I'd like you to get these disks to Claudio in England. Tell him to get his team on them and see if there's anything useful on them."

"To find a cure for this AIDS virus?"

"Yes."

"And if Claudio finds one, Sam, what do we do with it?"

"We can figure out what to do with a cure once we have one. For now let's just fucking find out if there is a way to stop this fucking plague."

Chapter Thirty-five

The boat rental guy was extremely surprised to see Tom, Jenna and Ing back at his dock within hours of the commencement of their two-day rental. He helped them tie up and was a bit agitated as he demanded to know if there was something wrong with one of the boats. He was flabbergasted when Tom handed him fifty dollars for gasoline used and told him that they were happy to pay for two days, but that they were finished with the watercraft. They left him standing on the dock trying to think of something to say.

"I think your cavalier manner with money has left the poor man speechless," said Ing.

"I think he lost the power of speech when he watched you scramble into the runabout to get your cover-up," said Jenna.

"I think we should haul ass for Burwell, or what is it, Ing, Tulgey Wood?"

"We get to go home?" asked Jenna.

They drove with only one stop. While Jenna and Ing visited the facilities of a service centre, Tom transferred the contents of the bag that Allen had given them to another carry-all. He found a fuel tanker and wedged Allen's bag into the supports of its tank. If there were any sort of transponder concealed in the bag it would not be helpful to the Legacy Organization.

They climbed back into the vehicle and got back to Tom's place at last light. Ing had fallen asleep two hours into the trip and was dazed when Jenna woke her as they parked outside the house. She went straight to bed.

"She seems to tire quickly," said Tom.

***

Holt's men had identified the property that Tom Robbins owned west of Port Burwell. His guys were doing twelve-hour stretches in some scrub brush near the laneway to observe traffic. For twenty-four hours there was none. Then a vehicle with two people pulled into the driveway at last light. Holt's guy had a radio that wasn't working well. He had to wait until his routine pickup to tell Holt that people were on the property.

***

Joachim Maarten called Sam Allen. Sam had been back in Virginia for less than forty minutes.

"Sam. The Harpt brothers and the young Winter are in a private house in Courselles sur Mer."

"I know the name but can't place it," said Sam.

"It's where the Canadians landed on D-Day. Arguably the worst defeat the Nazis took that day. Not the sort of spot that the elder Harpts would visit to take a trip down memory lane."

"Why the hell would they go there?"

"As always, you pose the right question. I've confirmed that young Willem Harpt will eventually be identified by the Los Angeles police as the dead body in a hotel room, victim of an overdose. The police are, not surprisingly, having difficulty contacting the boy's next of kin."

"So, aside from Nils Witt, the last members of the Cerebus Corporation barring Tony Harpt's son, are all in Normandy?"

"That is so," said Hugo.

"I'd be grateful to hear your take of this, Joachim."

"Let me have my people dig a bit more, Sam. I will call you again soon."

***

Once Ing was in bed, Jenna and Tom took glasses to the third floor. Lake Erie was only in a playful mood. The waves were barely audible. They sat outside on the narrow deck. It had been a hot day in Muskoka but on Lake Erie, the evening air was cool. Tom fetched a blanket for Jenna to wrap up in.

"Are we done with all this, Tom?" asked Jenna.

"We're never done with this. Even if we never hear from this thing that Sam Allen runs or the thing the other guys run, we're never done with it because our friend is dying. I've had a lot of friends die. That stays with you forever."

"I know. I feel I have to stay alive, because as long as I do my father is sort of still alive as well. As long as there is one person who remembers you, thinks of you, you have a foot in this world. I feel the same way about Ing."

"Agreed. Ed Cromwell will be here until I and all of his daughters and all of his friends are dead. And then, maybe it doesn't matter because we'll all be together having a turkey dinner with lots of good brandy somewhere. I wonder what Ing said to Sam Allen today. Have you looked at your legacy in the bag?"

"Tomorrow. Let's sleep and wake up to give Ing the day she wants."

"If you're willing, I think that the two of us should give Ing several days that she wants. I think we should give whatever she wants until her last day."

***

Nils took a circuitous route to Port Burwell in the morning, swinging west and approaching the town from the direction of a little hamlet called Copenhagen. He drove slowly, checking the fire numbers displayed on blue signs at every laneway. He wasn't surprised to discover that Tom Robbins' laneway was heavily treed on both sides and there was no view of his house from the road.

During his drive the previous day he had identified a spot by the river which would afford him a good position to observe traffic on the main street and on the bridge which was used by people west of the village and those accessing the large provincial park. He dropped his line in the muddy water of the creek and settled down to wait. It was 11 a.m. when he made the first man of Holt's team.

The man did a run down the main street to the beach turnaround and drove slowly back through town. He then crossed the bridge and headed west on the road where Tom Robbins lived. He crossed the bridge again in about twenty minutes and headed off north toward Tillsonburg. Nils packed up his fishing gear and went to another restaurant, one with a small patio, to have a light lunch. During his meal, he observed a different vehicle cruising the main street, driven by a clean-cut hard-looking man. One of the locals at a table near him pointed at the vehicle and said something to his friend that Nils didn't hear.

Nils went back to the creek-side for a three more hours and concluded from the number of times the two vehicles he was watching drove west out of the village, that some sort of action against Tom Robbins' place was imminent. He drove west out of the village and was surprised to see a large flatbed truck and front-end loader parked on the road across Robbins' laneway. There was a gigantic rock sitting on the flatbed. Nils drove on past Robbins' place, looking for a place where he could stash his truck later.

***

Tom was sitting outside sipping a coffee when Jenna stepped onto the patio, tying the sash of her bathrobe.

"It's a bit cool with the breeze off the lake. Is Ing still sleeping?"

"I think so. She's been down for ten hours."

"I wish I knew more about this AIDS disease. I'd like to know what to expect so that we can help her."

"The public health unit in Tillsonburg will likely have some information on it. I'll go in to see what's available next time we need groceries. I had a look in the bag that Allen gave Ing. There's a fuck of a lot of money in here, Tom. I'm not going to count it now but I think we're in a position to buy all the bread and milk we need. Do you have a safe?"

"I do. I'll deal with that once we've sat and had a coffee together."

Ing slept in, but when she got up she was full of energy. She came downstairs naked, carrying some clothes.

"I'll play along with nudie thing during breakfast but then you two lewd gawkers will have to stop ogling my lady flower and get some clothes on. We're going rock collecting today."

"How did you sleep, Ing?"

"The best I have in weeks. I think somewhere deep in my head I'm relieved that your Aunt's demon disks have left the building. Drink up your coffee. We have a mission today."

They got to the nursery just after it opened. Ing was wearing shorts and a white tee shirt with no bra. The owner of the nursery was happy to help them, but his wife sent him off on an errand and served them herself. Tom thought that she gave him a special price on the rock Ing chose just to get them away from her husband. The nursery had a standing agreement with a trucking company, so they were able to immediately arrange for the rock to be transported.

Their next stop was at a monument maker outside of Tillsonburg. The stone carver was a very fit looking man in his thirties who was clearly delighted to be visited by two good looking young women. He was a bit taken aback when he learned a four ton rock would be rolling into his parking lot within an hour. Ing handed him a slip of paper with the words Tulgey Wood written on it and told him she would supervise the carving.

When the rock arrived, Ing climbed on top of it and sat in a lotus position while the carver did his work. Tom, Jenna and the flatbed driver sat in the shade and watched Ing flirt shamelessly with the carver. It took him two hours to do the job. He probably would have finished sooner but Ing kept leaning forward to check his work and her breasts were clearly a great distraction to the man. He readily accepted Ing's invitation to come out to the farm and see his work placed into its setting.

The flatbed driver phoned his shop and told the front-end loader operator to get moving and they formed a mini convoy with Tom and Jenna leading followed by the flatbed. Ing insisted on riding with the stone carver so that he wouldn't get lost. When they arrived at Tom's place, the loader hadn't arrived yet. Ing told Tom and Jenna that she was going to show the carver the view of the lake. Tom gave her the keys to the house.

The carver parked his truck near the house and Ing said she had to get something. When she came outside she was naked.

"We usually don't wear clothes around here. Are you okay with me being naked?"

The carver grinned and nodded.

"Do you know much about this thing they call AIDS?"

"Nope. I've heard tell of it."

"It's a sexually transmitted disease that you get from swapping body fluids. Do you want to fuck me?"

"I sure as hell do!"

"Well, here's the deal. You can't kiss me and you can't eat me. If you want me to suck your cock, you'll have to wrap it up first. You can put on these gloves and diddle my ass and finger fuck me, and as long as you've wrapped up your cock, you can have my pussy and my ass as much as you want. You will use lube if you're putting your fingers or your cock in me, and if you go into my ass you don't get into my pussy until you've put on a fresh safe. Any questions?"

"No."

"Are you getting a hard-on?"

"Yes."

"Good boy. Come with me."

***

Holt's guys were delighted to see the activity at the end of Tom's laneway. It took the crew an hour and a half to get the ground prepared and the rock in place. Two of Holt's men made several passes as the work took place and were able to report to Holt that a man and women who had to be Jenna Van Velt and Tom Robbins were at the site the whole time.

"Alright, guys," said Holt when all of them were back in his room in Tillsonburg. "We're going in tonight. I would have liked to have a done better recon but as you know, it's difficult."

"What's our mission?"

"You guys are my backup. Your job is to neutralize this boyfriend of Van Velt's by whatever means necessary. Don't be cocky with this guy. He was a fucking Selous Scout."

"There are three of us, boss. We can handle it."

"I will go in to the Van Velt woman. If she is willing to hand over what I want quickly, we'll be out of there quickly. If not, it may be necessary to bring her with us for some further discussion."

"Not back here, boss?"

"Hell, no. I've found a deserted building that we can take her to for the few hours I might need with her."

"If you think we might need to transport her, I guess we'd better take the jeeps. More space."

"Absolutely we take the jeeps. You said you've picked out a spot to park them?"

"Yes. About half a mile from this guy's house. If we need to transport the woman, it won't take us long to bring a jeep up to the laneway."

"Good. Fuel up your vehicles, check your gear, and have something to eat. It gets dark just after nine. I want us to be moving toward the house by ten."

***

Nils drove back to the motel and was relieved to have a parcel waiting from him at the front desk. The markings on the package indicated that it had come from a bookstore in Toronto. Nils took it to his room and thirty minutes later he was armed with a Glock nine millimeter in a shoulder holster. The ratty jacket that he had bought in the thrift store concealed the gun nicely. Nils called Joachim Maarten.

"Thank you for the arrangements you made. The parcel arrived today and I'm happy with it. Please give your man in Toronto a nice bonus."

"He's been well paid."

"What's what?"

"Bosch says the Harpts and young Winter are safely in the house by the seaside. They are on edge."

"As well they should be. What's happening in Germany?"

"The Krefeld police have brought INTERPOL into the mix since three of the dead men were Americans. There is a great hue and cry. There are still daily visits of police to the chateau. Doktor Kepp is still there, earning his salary. The police are mollified when they talk to a Doktor."

"That's to be expected. Anything else?"

"Two things. Spracker has been in contact with Bosch. He wants to know what he should do with young Adolph Harpt."

"Tell him to take the kid on a slow drive to Normandy and leave him with the others. I take it that Spracker has shown him the kind of time in Paris that he won't want to share with his father."

"You can rest assured of that."

"You said you had two things."

"A bit of news. Hanna Spader's body was pulled from a river yesterday."

"Can you anonymously get a note and cash to the appropriate authorities saying she should be cremated and her ashes held for pickup."

"I'll see to it."

***

The positioning of the rock by the laneway became a major production. The front-end loader operator made a nice level spot to set it, but he balked at trying to lift the rock off the truck. He said it was simply too heavy for his machine. Jenna went to the house for a much needed bathroom break and called the trucking company. They said their mobile crane would be on the way in minutes. There was no sign of Ing and her new friend.

When the crane arrived, it was necessary to block traffic on the road for several minutes. Tom and the flatbed driver acted as traffic controllers. The stone was finally set in place at about three in the afternoon. Tom paid the equipment operators and the truck driver in cash.

"Thanks very much for all of your trouble. This became quite a job. We even had to turn you into a traffic cop for a while," he said as he paid off the truck driver.

"There was a stupid amount of traffic for this road today," said the truck driver. "I can't figure out why there are so many people around who don't belong here. Tourist season is over."

The men left and Tom and Jenna admired the stone for a minute or two.

"Do you like it, Tom?"

"I suppose it will grow on me. Let's go to the house. I've got to call Audrey."

When they got to the house, the carver was just starting his truck. Ing was standing on the patio, naked. She blew the carver a kiss as he pulled away.

"Did you and your new friend have a good time, Ing?"

"What he lacked in technique he made up for in enthusiasm. I'll give you the details after I shower. I am covered in lube."

***

Nils bought some energy bars and bottled water at a variety store and at five o'clock he parked his truck in field laneway down the road from Tom's house. A stream ran through a culvert just two hundred yards from Tom's laneway. Nils followed it onto Tom's property, found a thicket at the edge of a deep spot in the stream and put his line in the water.

He napped on and off until the light started to fade. There were rocks strewn all along the side of the stream. Nils chose one the size of a tennis ball and slipped it into the foot and twelve inches of leg that he had cut from a pair of leotards that he had bought at the thrift store.

He moved several hundred yards closer to the house to a treed rise of ground that he had identified from the topographical map that he had taken from Holt's man in Germany. From his vantage point, he could see the front of the house well. He put on the night vision goggles that had been shipped with the Glock from Toronto, and waited.

***

Tom's call to Audrey was short and informative.

"I'm glad to hear from you, Tom. Where have you been these last few days?"

"London. Muskoka. Rock collecting. You name it."

"Rock collecting? I think you must have rocks in your head."

"That may be. Anything unusual going on around here?"

"There certainly is. We've had strangers, young men who look a lot like you did when came back from Africa the first time, constantly driving through town and up and down your road. Everyone I've talked to in town has remarked about them."

"Have they been talking to anybody?"

"No. But four of them had lunch at the Lighthouse a couple of days ago and they certainly sounded to be Americans."

"What do their license plates say?"

"All the vehicles they've been driving have Ontario plates."

"Thanks for this, Audrey. If you hear any other good tidbits, please give us a call."

"You may be certain that I will."

When Tom got off the call he found Jenna and Ing sunning themselves on the patio.

"Did you go see your rock, Ing?"

"No, dear Tom. I know it is perfect there and will go see it tomorrow. Right now I have to rest my greedy and deeply bruised orifices. That country boy proved that he can carve more than rocks."

"You've probably spoiled him for all other women," said Jenna. "Will you see him again?"

"No. But activities of this afternoon have helped me make a decision that I will share with you some other time." She held her empty glass out to Tom.

Tom fetched them each a glass of wine, got himself a beer and sat down on the patio.

"We're likely to have visitors tonight. Audrey tells me there have been four guys scoping out the town and driving up and down our road. They'll know we're here now after all the action out at the lane today."

"What are we going to do?" asked Jenna.

"Come with me, please."

Tom led them into the study and flipped the latch on the panel to let them downstairs to the hot tub area. He showed them where the handgun was and Ing remarked that it was a good thing that Tom had taken her to a firing range a few times when they were in California. They went back outside.

"Audrey says that there have been four guys around. They are likely planning to leave a couple outside while two of them come in to talk with us about Gerta's computer disks. We'll turn off all the lights in the great room and you two will take the cordless phone and the pistol and lock yourselves in the hot tub room."

"Where will you be?"

"Outside. I'll have my bow and my Browning with me. I figure that I'll use the night vision glasses and will likely be able to tag a couple of them quietly. Once the herd is thinned out, the others will likely decide to leave."

"If that's the way you think it will be, Tom, why don't Jenna and I just sit in the great room reading magazines?"

"Do you have a better plan, Ing?"

"You know I don't. Someone needed to remind you that Rambo was fiction."

"Why don't we just leave?" asked Jenna.

"Whoever these people are, Allen hasn't convinced them that they should back off. I'd rather deal with them in a place I know. I'm gonna go put on my bush outfit. Maybe you two should think about what you want to have down in the tub room with you."

After Tom left to make his preparations, Jenna turned to Ing.

"He's going to get killed, isn't he, Ing.'

"No. Not here. Not with the hometown advantage. But we can help him out."

***

Sam was disturbed by the call he took from Chuck Holt's wife. She hadn't heard from her husband in days and had been worried by the visit she had had from FBI agents. Sam did his best to reassure her. Sterling was not happy to learn of the gist of the call when he and Sam next spoke.

A staff member handed him a note indicating that he should call Joachim Maarten as soon as possible. Sterling glanced at the number that Maarten had left while Sam was on his call with Holt's wife. He said it was an area code from the south of England.

"Joachim, it's Sam Allen. Are you well?"

"Well enough, given all that is going on in Germany. INTERPOL is now involved in the Krefeld shootings. You should know that Chuck Holt has been listed as a person of interest in that case."

"That is bad news. Have there been any further incidents?"

"No. But the body of Hanna Spader has been removed from a river not far from Krefeld. I think we can be certain that she was one of the people that Chuck Holt's team targeted."

"Any news of the Corporation members?"

"They are sitting quietly in their seaside villa in France. I am quite certain that Nils Witt is in Ontario, Canada."

Allen was appalled to hear that bit of news.

"Do you have his exact location?"

"He had me arrange to send him a sidearm and a night vision device to a motel near a town called Aylmer. He's confirmed delivery of the package. I haven't looked at a map to see where this Alymer place is."

"Can you get in touch with him?"

"No. He calls me."

"Joachim. This is important. When you next speak with Nils Witt, tell him that the information that the Corporation is looking for is no longer with Ten Haan's niece. Jenna Van Velt has given that information to me. Tell Witt there is no reason to make contact with her."

"As I told you in Dover. I don't think he gives a damn about that information, Sam."

***

Jenna and Ing's anxiety levels were not lessened when Tom came into the great room dressed in a ghillie suit, carrying his bow case. He had smeared green camouflage cream on his face and hands.

"It's time to go downstairs, ladies."

He led them through the study and had Jenna open the panel because of the camo cream on his hands. Tom watched her carefully as she latched and locked the panel of the study wall. They descended the stairs, Ing picked up the handgun and ammo bandolier and Tom ensured that the door into the tub area was locked behind them.

"No matter what you hear, do not open this door. This glass area is totally hidden by shrubs outside. And unless somebody knows about the hidden door in the study, they will never find it from inside the house. It's highly unlikely anyone will come down here. I will rap on the door deliberately three times if I want you to let me in; otherwise, you leave it locked and don't make a sound. If someone forces the door, kill them as soon as they enter."

"How long will we be down here?"

"No way to tell. If I'm not back by sun-up, call Audrey and have her get the police out here."

"Why not get the police out here now?" asked Jenna.

"Because they would just scare these guys off and they'd come back, more carefully, another time. Right now, they don't know that we're onto them."

Tom climbed out of the access door of the glazed area of the room with some difficulty due to the bulk of the ghillie suit. He slipped into the bushes and was out of sight in seconds. Jenna locked down the access door.

"I am scared," she said. Ing gave Tom a few minutes to get away from the area and then handed Jenna the phone and told her to follow her. They went back up the stairs and Ing took a position inside the darkened study where she could see the front door of the house. Jenna heard her cock the gun that Tom had given her.

***

Nils was hyper alert and was constantly scanning a wide arc in front of his position. He was reminded of boyhood walks in the Black Forest. At one point he thought he saw some movement north of the house but he wasn't sure. He did not expect to see anyone approach from that direction. He glanced at his watch and saw that it was 9:50. The moon had risen and shadows formed everywhere.

The first of Holt's men walked passed him on the right at a distance of ten yards. He took up a fire position about thirty yards in directly in front of Nils. A second man took a spot twenty yards to the right of the first man. Nils assumed that there would be another man in position even further to the right.

A fourth man closed up behind the middle rifleman and they knelt and talked quietly for a moment. The fourth man started to move off and instantly Nils heard a strange hissing sound. The rifleman in front of him collapsed sideways. Nils froze, hardly breathing.

He knew there was movement on his left but it took him a moment to realize that it was a man wearing heavy camouflage. The man knelt only a few feet in front of Nils and raised his bow. Nils was fascinated when the camouflaged bowman killed the second rifleman with an arrow that embedded deep into his skull.

After that shot, the bowman moved toward the house and was obviously trying to spot the man who had gone forward. He knelt at the end of the tree line and scanned for a time and apparently spotted the man in cover near the front door of the house. Nils assessed the situation and began to move.

Tom was faced with a hard decision. He needed to engage the man who was about to enter the house but the range was far too long for his bow or his pistol. To get closer would mean exposing himself to the third rifleman who he assumed was down in the bush to his right. The Scouts had taught their men to make decisions quickly. Tom peeled off the ghillie suit, dropped his bow and quiver, and broke cover at a full run, jinking from side to side to throw off the last marksman.

The rifleman saw him immediately and swung up his weapon so that he could watch Tom through his night vision scope. He expected one of the other shooters to fire at any second. As the runner kept moving, he concluded that his teammates had somehow been taken out.

Tom was fifty yards from the house when the rifleman placed the laser dot on the base of Tom's neck. The shooter let out all of his breath and was squeezing the trigger when the side of his head imploded. Nils grabbed the shooter's rifle as he fell to prevent an accidental discharge. When he looked up, he saw the bowman approaching the front door of the house that had been kicked in by the fourth man.

When he got near the door of the house Tom, crouched behind a pillar, was catching his breath. He knew that he would be silhouetted by moonlight as he passed through the door, so he bunched his muscles and dove into the room. The man inside was waiting for him and fired a single shot. Tom felt that he had been hit in the side by a red hot steel bar. He was lying on his side when the man who had shot him quietly said, "I expect there is no point in asking you where Jenna Van Velt would be in this monstrosity of house, so I will simply kill you."

Tom was straining to see where the man was when there was a single pistol shot. Tom heard a body fall to the floor and lay there trying to figure out why he was still alive. A different voice spoke.

"Given that I've just killed your assailant, can I assume you have no interest in killing me?"

"Reasonable assumption," grunted Tom. "Who are you?"

"Let me get some lights on."

"There's almost certainly another shooter out there," said Tom.

"His shooting days are over, my Canadian friend."

Lights were turned on around the room and he heard the man walk over to examine the person he had shot. He came and knelt by Tom. The man was very fit and Tom thought he was about forty years old.

"Where are you hit?"

"Right side."

The man helped him sit up on the floor, leaning back against a sofa. He pulled up Tom's shirt and looked at his wound closely.

"You are a lucky man, Mr. Robbins. The shot went in and out and I don't think it clipped any vital pipes. We need to get some pressure on it, though."

"We'll take care of him," said Ing, stepping into the room. Nils Witt examined the two women who had entered the room with great interest.

Jenna grabbed a long sleeved blouse that Ing had left hanging on a chair and she fetched a tea towel from the kitchen. She folded up the towel and used the shirt to hold it in place as she put pressure on the wound.

"You're not losing a lot of blood, but you're going to need some stitches and antibiotics, Tom."

"I told you two to stay out of sight."

"My bad Tom. You shouldn't have taught me how to shoot. I had a sight on this dead asshole, but our new best friend here killed him first. Who the hell are you?"

"My name is Witt. The man over there on the floor was Chuck Holt."

"You knew each other?"

"We'd never met, but I've known about him and his colleagues for a long time. He's a member of a group called the Legacy Organization."

"I take it that you're not part of that organization?"

"Correct. I am part of a different organization that doesn't get along particularly well with the late Mr. Holt's people."

"Why are you here tonight?"

"I had some unfinished business with Mr. Holt. He has been the cause of the death of two of my good friends recently."

"So you came here to kill him? A lucky break for me," said Tom.

"I also wanted to get a message to Jenna Van Velt. I assume one of you two ladies is Ms. Van Velt?"

"That would be me," said Jenna.

"Ms. Van Velt. I deeply regret that my organization misguidedly murdered your Aunt. You may rest assured that we have no intention of having any further impact on your life."

"Jenna has given me a pretty good idea of what was done to her Aunt. Your group seemed pretty serious about wanting something from her not so long ago," said Tom.

"As I said, we were misguided in our efforts back in May."

"What changed?"

"Change is a process, Mr. Robbins. The leadership of my group is going through a period of rapid evolution. In fact, I need to get back to France as soon as possible to carry on the process. Do you know a man named Sam Allen?"

"Yes I do."

"A great truism is that it is easy to kill someone but harder than hell to get rid of the body. You have quite a mess here. Mr. Holt is soiling your carpet over there and there are three more bodies out in the woods. I'm impressed by your archery skill, by the way. If you ever would like some well paid work I could certainly employ you."

"I'm semi-retired. But thank you."

"I must be on my way. Both gunshots were inside the house and the lake is quite noisy tonight so I doubt that anyone heard them. I suggest that you get on the line to Mr. Sam Allen and tell him that his man Holt has been a nuisance and that you expect the Legacy Organization to get up here and make this situation right."

"I'll do that."

"Alright, Mr. Robbins. Don't move around too much until you've had some medical attention."

Nils left the house quickly and Tom asked Jenna to bring him the phone. He called Audrey.

"What the devil is going on out there, Tom? I called to tell you that there are two jeeps parked in the laneway of Gordon Masson's cornfield and there was no answer."

"I have a couple of huge favours to ask. First, will you take a look out of your front window and see if the OPP cruiser is still parked outside the office?"

"You're a strange man, Tom Robbins. What else do you want me to do?"

"Do you still have access to your discreet friend who was a doctor?"

"I do."

"Can you get him out here with his kit just as quick as you can?"

Audrey hurriedly let him know that the one police cruiser assigned to the village wasn't moving. She said she would have her doctor friend to the house momentarily. Without being asked, Jenna brought a bottle of brandy to Tom.

"Jenna. Get that number that Sam Allen gave Ing. We need to call him right now."

***

Nils walked along to the road to where he had parked his pickup truck. He had left his gun and holster on the patio of the house, pleased that its disposal would be one more thing for Sam Allen to deal with. He drove the truck back to the Inn where he had left his rental car. It was nearing one a.m., but Nils felt full of energy. No one was stirring in the parking lot of the Inn, so he changed clothes by his car and set off for the airport at Toronto. By ten a.m. he was on a Heathrow bound flight.

Chapter Thirty-six

It was a wet, cold day when Tom and Jenna drove to the airport to fly to L.A. They had spent the previous two weeks getting Tulgey Wood ready for winter. Jenna enjoyed the fall nesting feeling, but was looking very forward to some California sunshine. Ing had arranged for them to stay in the hotel near the airport where she was living for the time that she would be in the city. Tom and Jenna had their arguments prepared as to why Ing should come back to Canada with them.

They caught a shuttle to the hotel and called Ing from their room. She rapped on their door within minutes and the hugging started. Jenna reckoned that Ing had lost five pounds since she had seen her last.

"So, you two. Welcome to a place where the weather is civilized all year round. Did you have to take a dog team to get to the airport to fly down here?"

"It's not quite that bad yet. But it's great to see the sunshine. What have you been up to?"

"I've spent some time at my office, helping them get up to speed with the portfolios I handled. I reconnected with some friends briefly. Nothing at all exciting. How are things in Tulgey Wood?"

They talked for a long time about the place in Canada, went out for a Mexican dinner, and sat in their hotel room sipping wine until nearly midnight. Jenna started to turn the conversation to Ing's future plans, but Ing shut that down quickly. She went back to her room to sleep, reminding them that one of the group was gainfully employed.

While Ing was at work the next day, Tom and Jenna visited the storage locker that Tom had arranged for their furniture. There was little that either of wanted, but Jenna did arrange for the mirror she had bought when she first set up her apartment and her photography equipment to be shipped to Canada. The operator of the storage area was delighted when Tom told him to distribute the stuff in the locker to charities.

"You know he's going to sell it, don't you?"

"Of course he is."

"You're okay with that?"

"He'll be ready and willing if I ever need a favour from somebody in L.A."

"Tom the planner."

When they met Ing that evening she said she was tired and glad it was Friday. They ordered room service and Ing left them to go to bed at ten. Jenna and Tom talked about her until midnight.

The next morning Ing was on a mission. She insisted that she and Jenna go off together and gave Tom directions to a garage about six blocks from the hotel. She told him that they would be going on an outing the next day and her friend Pietro would show Tom how to use the equipment they would need.

Tom was surprised at what Ing's friend had waiting for him. It was gasoline powered railway maintenance 'scooter'. The thing had small railroad steel wheels so that it could carry three or four people along the tracks. Pietro explained that they were used to get crews out to do minor maintenance. It was loaded on a small flatbed truck. Pietro showed Tom how to load and unload the thing, which must have weighed five hundred pounds. The operation of it was simple.

Ing had made the arrangements for dinner Saturday night and said that she had someone joining them. The man was an AIDS activist who had a lot to say about the disease and the government's disinterest in funding research to bring the epidemic to an end. It was not a cheery meal. When the man was preparing to leave, he slipped Ing a small package and asked her if she was still certain that she wanted to proceed. She assured him she was.

"What was that all about?" asked Tom.

"Back to the room. I'll tell you there."

The walk back to the hotel was quiet. Jenna was certain that she would not want to hear what Ing had to say.

Once in the hotel room, Ing told them they were now subject to the Jenna Rule, and undressed. Tom followed suit, so Jenna stripped.

Ing fetched wine and beer and glasses and when they had drinks she took a seat on a pillow on the floor in a lotus position.

"So my friends, I need to you listen to me, try to understand why I'm saying what I'm saying, and then support me."

"I don't like this, Ing," said Jenna.

"Since I found out I'm HIV positive, I have had sex once with the stone carver guy. I won't be having sex anymore."

"Why, Ing?"

"Because I don't like this rubberized version of sex. I like to smell my pussy on a guy as he kisses and fucks me after he's been down on me. I like to taste a cock in my mouth, not a plastic wrapped rod. I like sex to be wet and squidgy and scented with my juices and the juices of whomever I've been fucking."

"I also like food. Or I did. Now practically everything I think about eating makes me want to hurl. I'm drinking disgusting nutrition shakes to keep my weight up. I will not be drinking any more of them."

"My skin is changing. I'm using a bottle of very expensive lotion every week just to keep from drying out and blowing away. I look pretty good, don't you think?"

"You look real good, Ing," said Tom.

"Thank you, kind sir. The point is, I am getting sicker and soon the shakes and the lotion won't be doing the trick. I'll be a walking skeleton with nasty patchy skin. And please don't tell me that there are new drugs coming onto the market every day. I've researched them and they may help ward off some aspects of the virus. But they have horrible side effects."

"I want you to remember the crazy good times we've had and to think about quality of life. Tom. If that asshole who shot you had put his bullet a couple of inches to the left and severed your spinal cord, would you have wanted to live out your days in a wheelchair, shitting and pissing into plastic bags?"

"Truthfully, no."

"I don't blame you. I know who you are and you would find that horrible. You both know who I am. I don't want to lose any more of my quality of life."

Jenna was silently crying.

"I can't help you commit suicide, Ing."

"Of course you can't. I just want the two of you to take me on a little drive tomorrow and I need Tom to rig up a tarpaulin for me."

"I don't get it, Ing."

"I apologize for saddling you with our dinner companion tonight. He is part of a group that makes available the drug cocktail that will let a person exit life without pain. The group won't give the cocktail to anyone unless they can show they have supporters around them."

"So you duped us?" said Tom.

"No. I just reversed the order of things and decided to talk the two of you into going on a ride tomorrow after I had gotten my hands on what I needed. I'm going to do this. It would mean so much to me if my two best friends would be with me tomorrow."

Jenna had seated herself on the floor beside Ing and was hugging her and crying. Ing put her hand on Jenna's head and stared at Tom.

"What's your plan, Ing?" asked Tom.

"There's a railroad siding not too far north of where Jenna used to live. My friend with the rail scooter that you picked up today used to take me out to the line on Sundays. The siding is never used on a Sunday. No one goes out there and it is so peaceful. Nothing but brush and birds."

"So now I know what were using Pietro's toy for."

"I've got a tarp and rope and my blanket from Canada. I want to fuck the cops' heads up. You know I don't like cops."

"I've heard you say that, Ing."

"Tomorrow we'll ride Pietro's rail rocket out the line. I'll pick a spot away from the rails, spread out my blanket and get naked. You'll rig a tarp above my blanket so that no random wanker flying over low will notice anything. I'll take my little bit of medicine and drift off to sleep in about ten minutes. You and Jenna will take my clothes and my water bottle and vamoosh."

"Are you sure about this, Ing?"

"Dead certain. Hey! I just made a pun."

It was silent for a while.

"Listen, you two. This is what I want. Given my circumstances, I hope you'd understand."

"But why naked out in the middle of nowhere?"

"It's peaceful out there, Jenna. It is very likely no one will find me for a very long time. If they do, I want to be the beautiful naked mystery woman with nothing around her to identify her. Now that we have a plan, let's drink wine."

Sometime late, the three of them crawled into bed for a few moments of fitful sleep.

The next morning Ing showered, did her hair and make-up and told Tom and Jenna that they could get their morning coffee from a drive-through. She gave Tom directions to a level crossing north of the Woods and expertly helped Tom get the scooter onto the rails. She called out all aboard as Tom started the engine of the scooter.

They drove down the tracks at a brisk pace until Ing told Tom to slow down. They were creeping along when suddenly they could hear water running. Ing told Tom to stop and she got off the scooter and walked into the bush. "Bring the stuff over here," she called out.

Tom tied the tarp to some trees while Jenna helped Ing lay out her blanket. Ing handed Jenna her clothes and quickly swallowed the six pills that she had gotten from the activist. She laid down on her back on the blanket carefully arranging her hair.

"I love you two so much. You never know what is going to happen, but I hope you two have amazing times together. He really is a good man, Jenna. And you are the sweetest person I've ever met. I am so glad you two met."

Ing lay silently for a time then she yawned and said "I love you," and her eyes closed.

Jenna and Tom stood watching her, then Tom leaned over Ing and felt for a pulse. He put his arm around Jenna's shoulders and led her back to the scooter. Both of them were crying.

Tom wanted to drop Jenna off at the hotel before he returned the scooter to Pietro, but Jenna insisted on staying with him. They rushed to their room and Tom lay on the bed with Jenna a long time while she sobbed. Finally he got up and went to the telephone.

"I've got us a flight to Toronto that leaves in four hours, Jenna. Let's go home."

***

It was a slow Monday in homicide. Arnon was glad because it had been a busy weekend with Teresa. His phone rang at 8:45. It was his captain.

"Nick. We've got a report of a naked, dead female in the brush alongside a railway track north of the Woods."

"A rape/murder?"

"I don't know, Nick. That's why I'm sending two detectives out there to detect if it is a rape/murder."

The captain's marriage was on the rocks and his sarcastic side was coming out.

"I'll take Crane."

The captain gave him directions to a rail yard where he was to meet up with people who could transport him to the scene. Arnon found Crane.

"Come with me, Tony. We've got a report of dead female just north of the woods."

"What do we know?"

"Nothing yet."

"Well, at least we know this woman has nothing to do with Gerta Ten Haan or Jenna Van Velt."

Arnon grunted a qualified assent.

Made in the USA
Charleston, SC
02 June 2015